MERCY

Book One

ASHLEY MATTHEWS

For those who have helped me become the woman I am today.

ISBN: 978-1068888601 (eBook)
ISBN 978-1-0688886-1-8 (Print)

Copy edited by Nicole Fegan
Proofread by Kimberly Seymour
All photographs by Colleen Issa
Cover design by Antonya Radu

All biblical quotes are sourced from the King James Version

Send permission requests to **requests@ashley-matthews.com**
www.ashley-matthews.com

1

A cavernous silence greeted Brooklyn as she attempted to enter the church. It was like an invisible wall, warning her to stay out. She stood with the door open and looked back at her friend, Page, who was egging her on from the sidewalk.

Page crossed her arms. "You're not gonna do it. You're too scared." Her blue eyes gleamed with excitement while her raised eyebrows dared Brooklyn to prove her wrong.

They had driven by the small church, nestled in the oldest part of the Glebe, and Page had the bright idea to send Brooklyn in on a bet.

Brooklyn bit her lip. *It's just a building.*

Deep down, however, she knew that wasn't true and she wasn't prepared to convince herself otherwise. It was a temple of lies filled with self-righteous patrons. All churches were.

"Come on, let's go. I know you can't do it. Let's grab some breakfast or something," said Page, rolling her eyes.

Brooklyn looked down at her party dress with its sequins catching the weak morning light and marveled at her and her friends' ability to stay out all night.

"I'm gonna do it!" Her words slurred from the tail end effects of whatever pills she had taken, courtesy of Page's boyfriend who currently stood off to the side, uninterested in the unfolding events. Brooklyn turned to enter the church and the smell of balsam almost crippled her. Nausea clawed at her gut and for a moment, she feared she would throw up all over the church's ornate door.

"Come on, Brooklyn. This isn't fun anymore and I'm hungry," Page said, her face a picture-perfect mask of boredom. She was a waif, tall and skinny with never-ending limbs. Hair that was naturally the kind of platinum blonde that women spent hundreds of dollars to get framed her elfish face with a severe bob cut. Whatever life had to offer had been hand-delivered at her feet, thanks to her looks and parents' money. So, Page was always bored, always looking for the next thrill.

And today that thrill was up to Brooklyn. She eyed the purse hanging off her friend's shoulder and imagined the crisp hundred-dollar bills folded neatly in half to fit in the impractically small bag. One of them could be hers. That meant she could make rent the following month without sacrificing half her meals. She turned back to the entrance with renewed determination. The booth, with its insides hidden by a partially closed, deep red curtain, wasn't too far from the door.

I just have to go in, confess something, then I'm out. In that moment, she stopped overthinking it and made a beeline for the box, closing its curtain quickly as if it could protect her from the demons of her past.

She sat in silence with her eyes shut tight and took deep breaths, doing her best to keep from gasping. Her fear squeezed like a vise around her chest and made it hard for her to inhale, so her breaths ended up shallow, almost non-existent.

The priest cleared his throat, making her jump.

One song for the righteous. Two songs for the honest. Three songs for the wicked. And no songs for the choir. She repeated the mantra in her head. It had been taught to her by her one and only childhood friend.

"Shall we begin? In the name of the Father, the Son..." he prompted in a measured tone when she still said nothing. His smooth and low voice was almost soothing, but not soothing enough to steady Brooklyn's racing heart.

Her head shot up. Looking straight ahead, she tried to remember why she thought any amount of money would be worth this kind of trouble. The air weighed down heavily on her, pressing in from each corner of the small space. The walls quickly followed, and she pressed her hands against the sides of the confessional to keep it from caving in.

"Is this your first time in confession?"

This time, his oddly calming voice made an impact and the walls stopped moving. Her ragged breaths slowed, and for a moment, Brooklyn almost forgot that she was in a church.

"If so, I can lead you through it."

"Um, yes. Kind of," she managed to say.

"Kind of?"

"It's a long story." Brooklyn's tone was clipped; it was a story she didn't want to share. She pulled her hands away from the walls and tried to let them rest in her lap, but she pressed her thumbnail into the palm of her hand instead—the pain gave her something else to focus on.

"Take a deep breath and tell me what you've come to say. There's no right or wrong way to do this. The point is you've come for absolution, and I can help you with that."

"Absolution. Ha." Brooklyn laughed, or at least she tried to. The sound came out disjointed. "I don't need absolution. I'm here because of a bet." She laughed again, shaking her head at herself. "I'm actually not a fan of churches, and my friends thought this would be funny." But it wasn't funny at all. Old wounds that she had desperately tried to patch up were threatening to burst open.

The priest was silent for a moment. "Are you under the influence, child?"

Brooklyn giggled. "Maybe. I guess I could confess that if you want me to confess to *something.*" Despite her best efforts, her candid giggle soon turned into a barely stifled sob.

"Child, if you could compose yourself for a moment and listen carefully. I'm sorry you feel unease in the house of God, but despite the... unusual circumstances that brought you here, you *are* here for a reason."

Brooklyn looked up at the grate dividing them for the first time, and her breath hitched. Instead of the repulsion she would normally feel at the sight of a priest, she was overcome with intrigue. She couldn't quite make out his eyes but she could feel their piercing gaze through the grate and it lit a fire in her cheeks that spread to her chest and belly. From what she could see, he was older, as was expected, with fine but strong features and a buzz cut, not the usual parted comb-over most priests seemed to wear. However, that's not what drew Brooklyn in; it was his energy. He emanated the same sense of calm his voice inspired—and safety.

Like most people did when faced with someone they found attractive, Brooklyn absentmindedly ran her hands over her hair and sat up a little straighter. And was it her imagination, or was he returning the same look of interest?

"And what reason is that?" she asked, hating that she was curious about what this captivating priest had to say.

"Just speak whatever comes to mind and we can figure that out." His even tone lulled her, and her erratic breathing slowed even more.

Brooklyn bit her lip. "I don't... know."

"What keeps you up at night?" the priest asked suddenly.

The question took Brooklyn by surprise. "A lot of things. I guess."

"Tell me about them."

Brooklyn went to speak but stopped. "You know what? This was just a joke. I didn't actually come in here to bare my soul to you. I sat in the box and talked to you. That should win me the bet. So, goodbye. And sorry. I guess. For wasting your time." She got up as she spoke and tugged at her dress. Her forgotten fear returned without mercy, as if whoever had hit pause had just decided to hit play. The air found its weight and the walls began to close in again.

"Wait, please, just try," the priest implored.

In her haste to escape, Brooklyn's heel snagged in the curtain and she fell to the floor. She tried to shake her foot free from it. With her imagination fueled by fear in the cruelest of ways, she panicked, convinced the church was doing its best to hold on to her and drown her in its indignation.

Flashing images from her past of cold, dark rooms, rosary beads, and judgment assaulted her every time she blinked. They made it harder for her to untangle her stiletto from the folds of the confessional's curtains that seemed to have taken on a life of their own. She tried to dash the images away by pressing the heels of her palms into her eyes while kicking at the material. Her shallow breaths returned and came out in barely audible spurts.

She was being swallowed.

Only it wasn't by the church, as she had imagined, but by her own crippling yet justified fear.

"Please, child, let me help you." The priest had come out from his side and extended a hand towards her.

"Leave me alone!" Brooklyn continued to desperately kick at the curtain until her foot finally came free. She stood on unsteady legs and reached for a nearby pew. A tear splashed onto the back of her hand. "I have to get out of here! *What* was I thinking?" she cried out to no one in particular, looking around like a caged animal.

A loud buzz filled her ears, and she couldn't make out what the priest was saying anymore. Brooklyn's limbs felt heavy. It took great effort to force them to move forward. Each step was a challenge, with her lungs struggling to take in air, the front doors stretching further away. Then, like an elastic snapping, everything came into focus, just long enough for her to make an escape.

Brooklyn half stumbled, half ran to the doors and looked back to find the priest looking on helplessly. When she burst from the church, she gave Page the show she had wanted. Tears. Hyperventilation. A full-blown panic attack. And instead of helping, Brooklyn's friend reached into her purse with a laugh and pulled out one of the coveted hundred-dollar bills. She held it between her second and third finger.

"Worth. Every. Dollar. You *never* disappoint, Brookie," Page said with a cool giggle that came from deep within her throat. She flicked the bill towards Brooklyn, who watched it float to the ground.

Shame filled Brooklyn as she bent over to pick up her prize money, still hiccupping from her fear. Instead of feeling like she had won a bet, she felt like she had been paid to be the clown. Part of her wanted to rip up the bill and throw it in Page's face, but her financial situation didn't leave much room for things like pride. Or dignity.

Page and her boyfriend were already walking towards his car. She turned. "Are you coming or what? I'm still hungry."

"Um, I think... I think I'm... just... gonna go home," mumbled Brooklyn. She unfolded the bill and smoothed out the single crease down the middle, keeping her eyes on it. If she looked up, Page would only see anger, and Brooklyn didn't want her to know just how deeply affected she was.

"Well, Sam can drive you home. *After* breakfast. 'Kay?" she said, referring to her boyfriend.

"I'll walk home. It's fine." Brooklyn's bottom lip quivered as she turned to see what street she was on.

"Honestly, Brook, get in the car. I don't understand why you insist on ruining a perfectly good time."

"I just want to go home. Besides, that's where we were going."

"Yeah. But now I'm hungry," said Page, speaking pointedly as if addressing a small child. "And I'm sure you are too after"—she paused before letting out a chuckle—"all of this." Page gestured towards Brooklyn with her hands.

"I'm not. I'm just tired."

"Get. In. The car."

Brooklyn wanted to turn and walk away, but something kept her feet rooted to the ground.

Page sighed. "Don't try to make me feel bad because you got a little upset over a bet *you* chose to take." When Brooklyn didn't respond, Page continued to Sam's car. "Let's go, Brookie," she sang over her shoulder.

And Brooklyn went. She spared a glance at the church and saw the priest standing at the door she had crashed through just moments ago. She didn't know why, but she felt deep shame at the realization that he'd just witnessed what had happened and rushed to Sam's car with her head down.

They went for breakfast, and Brooklyn spent the entire time analyzing her scrambled eggs while trying to pretend that everything was alright. But it wasn't alright. She hated Page for her ability to make her feel like garbage. She hated her even more for eating so slowly when all she wanted to do was curl up in bed, cry, and sleep off the previous night's revelries.

"Can I please go home now?" she whispered when they were done eating.

"Actually, I was thinking you could come over to save having to go back to your place."

"I want to go home." Brooklyn's stomach churned at the thought of facing her apathetic friend for longer than she needed to.

Page pressed her lips together. "Fine."

When Page and Sam finally dropped her off at the designated pick-up and drop-off point, which was a couple blocks away from her home, Brooklyn let go of the breath that she had been holding for what felt like the entire drive. She walked to the rooming house she called home—a row of old, three-story, red-bricked houses that had been repurposed for the needy and the down and out folk. It stood on the corner of intersecting streets with its front doors sealed shut. This forced the residents to go in through the back doors so that the rooming house could maintain the inconspicuousness its historical structure afforded. However, the back of the building wasn't any more private than the front, so Brooklyn figured it was a reminder that yes, they might live in a posh area, but they were still classes apart from their neighbors.

Brooklyn trudged up to her third-floor room, closing the door with a sigh as she leaned against it. The small room was her only personal space, as she shared the house with two women and four men. Despite having lived there for over a year, she still hadn't bothered to learn any of their names. She avoided the common areas as much as she could so that she was as invisible as possible. For a kitchen, Brooklyn had set up a microwave atop a small table with a mini fridge next to it. The rest of the room was furnished with an old sofa that served as her bed (with which she had taken a chance and picked up off a street corner), a scuffed-up coffee table (another street corner find that doubled as her dining room table, countertop, bar, and medicine cabinet), and milk crates stacked on their sides to serve as makeshift shelves for her everyday clothes. The dresses and accessories for nights like last night were stored in plastic bins that were stacked in a corner.

Stripping down to her underwear, she went to hide under the duvet (a strings-attached gift from Page), but sleep eluded her despite the fact she had been awake for over 24 hours. Brooklyn tossed and turned with the early morning's events on repeat in her head. Replaying each moment, she tried to find the point of no return. That's what she called it—that one moment she could have made a small, different choice that would have avoided the subsequent events. She finally gave up and sat up with a grunt. Maybe she could have suggested a different detour home when they came up on a closed section of Bank Street. Or, if she went back far enough, she could have kept her secrets and fears to herself. Clearly, Page didn't know how to be gentle with the fragments of Brooklyn's past that had been shared in confidence.

What is a phobia of churches even called? Brooklyn reached for her phone and searched her question.

"Ecclesiophobia." She said the word out loud, doubtful of its pronunciation. With a sigh, she put her phone down and stared up at the ceiling. In one corner, the "old" water damage, as the landlord liked to describe it, had grown some more. The brown stain bloomed from the crown molding and Brooklyn wondered how long it would take before it reached the ceiling directly above her sofa.

An almost empty bottle of cheap vodka was within arm's reach. She considered finishing it to help her sleep, but Brooklyn's stomach turned at the thought of drinking anything else. She got up instead and brushed her teeth, attempted to run a comb through her long, thick, chestnut hair, and threw on yoga pants, a t-shirt with a pink "IDGAF" graphic across the front, and a black sweater.

At twenty-two, Brooklyn looked rougher than she should, thanks to her lifestyle of endless nights of partying, drinking, and doing drugs. Her once tanned, glowing skin now had a sickly pallor. Her large, round, gray eyes were still beautiful, but they had sunken and lost their sparkle long ago. And with her diet of booze, potato chips, and instant noodles, her body was nothing but an echo of the soft curves it used to boast.

After she was done changing, she felt decent enough to walk among other humans and left to wander through her neighborhood, vaguely remembering the street the church had been on. She walked north, towards the way they had come after their nightlong partying. *It must have been on First Avenue,* she decided. Then there it was: a small, old, Roman Catholic church that announced its age through weathered stone and simple architecture. There were no frills besides the two stained-glass windows that flagged the front entrance and its doors that had been carefully carved with the standard church-like designs from its time. The building almost looked like a protest amongst the large modern houses that had most likely replaced older, humbler homes.

Attached to the church was a tiny bungalow, and a low, wrought iron fence lined the entire property, as if to keep out the encroaching houses it was protesting. The garden further reflected the church's modesty with a spattering of lilies and asters under each window.

Brooklyn stood across the street. The priest's expression when she had seen him standing at the doors haunted her, and it compelled her to explain that she wasn't as pathetic as she must have looked. She crossed the street and walked up to the doors. She couldn't ignore the building's ode to conservative ideals and its obvious condemnation; she could feel it.

Her heart pounded heavily against her chest. "It's just a building," she whispered as she pressed a hand against one of the doors.

2

Just as Brooklyn went to grab the door's handle, her phone rang. She let go and backed away as she took out her phone with trembling hands. Page's picture graced the screen.

Clearing her throat, Brooklyn answered and tried to keep her voice as steady as possible. "Hello?"

"Hey, Brookie. Let me pick you up for lunch."

Brooklyn took a few more steps away from the church and stared at the closed doors.

"Brook?"

"I'm sorry. Sure, okay," she said absentmindedly.

"'Kay, I'll be there in half an hour."

Brooklyn shoved her phone into her sweater's pocket and continued to stare at the doors, horrified that she had ever considered going back in. Seeing Page was the last thing she wanted to do, but she was grateful for her friend's unwitting intervention.

Brooklyn dragged her gaze away from the church and down to her attire. Knowing Page, it would be a good idea to change into something a bit more presentable, but the idea of jeans or anything fitted was unappealing. She walked back home as slowly as she could to kill time and opted to risk Page's trademark nose-scrunching and not change. Multicolored leaves peppered the sidewalk, and she kept her eyes trained on them the entire way as she berated herself. What was wrong with her that she had been willing to go back? Or that she needed to explain herself to a stranger? Worst of all, to a priest!

When she reached her building, she continued walking towards the pick-up spot, a small park where she could wait for Page. They did this to avoid revealing Brooklyn's connection to someone with wealth to the people with whom she shared the house. Most of her housemates were the type who walked a fine line that barely kept them on the right side of the law. Along with her generally antisocial disposition, that was the main reason why she kept to herself. But if there was one thing she had learned about them, it was that it wasn't completely due to any fault of their own. Like her, circumstance

11

and society had chewed them up and left them in the fringe. The only thing that separated Brooklyn from them was that she happened to have a rich friend.

Hugging herself, Brooklyn sat on a park bench facing the street and waited. Page pulled up and rolled down the passenger window with a smile. On top of nose-scrunching, Brooklyn had anticipated a scalding critique of her outfit, but as she approached the car, Page said nothing about it. In fact, she was even uncharacteristically dressed down in a pair of jeans and a plain, long-sleeved t-shirt. Brooklyn envied how her friend still looked runway ready in the simplest of clothes.

"How was the rest of your morning?" Page asked as Brooklyn got into the car.

Brooklyn immediately thought of the church and how Page's call had most likely saved her from another panic attack. "It was okay."

"Cool." Silence. "Look, about this morning, I hope you're not still upset about it."

I am. "I'm fine."

"Sooo, you were upset?"

Brooklyn looked out the window so Page couldn't see her face. "No, I meant I wasn't actually upset."

"But you seemed pretty bothered to me. Like, you were sulking all through breakfast and made me feel super guilty."

Brooklyn pressed her thumbnail into her palm in panic. She knew Page wouldn't buy her lies, but she also knew she couldn't tell her just how angry she had been. "I'm sorry, that wasn't my intention."

Page stayed quiet. It wasn't enough.

"Okay, I was a little upset, but I was just being sensitive," said Brooklyn, clasping her hands together in anticipation. She hoped that would be enough and they could move on, because navigating these kinds of conversations with Page was like walking through an obstacle course.

Page sighed with relief. "'Kay! Good! You know I love you, Brookie, and I would *never* mean to make you feel bad or anything. Right?"

Brooklyn nodded. "Where are we going for lunch?" she asked, wanting to change the topic.

Page smiled. "Finnegan's."

Brooklyn looked at her friend in surprise. "But you hate that place."

"Maybe. But for some reason, you love it."

Only then did it dawn on Brooklyn that Page was trying to apologize. "We don't have to go there."

"No, no, I want to. I'll even eat a few french fries."

Brooklyn chuckled and relaxed into the plush leather of the car's seat. "I'll believe it when I see it."

Finnegan's Diner was a far cry from the places Page usually frequented. The booths were held together with duct tape, decades' worth of spilled coffee stained the tables, and grease was the main ingredient in all their dishes. Brooklyn would even argue that their salad wasn't spared from unnecessary amounts of fat and calories. But what they served was the epitome of comfort food.

The remaining resentment her heart had clung onto from earlier that morning immediately melted away when she saw Page gingerly sit on the duct tape patchwork booth. Her friend tried to hide the grimace and barely managed it.

"Thanks for this, Page."

"It's nothing, really. Get whatever you want. I promise I won't bother you about the damage it'll do to your figure."

Page ordered a salad and, true to her word, stole some fries from Brooklyn's plate between easy small talk. *Why can't she be like this all the time?* wondered Brooklyn.

"Well, I should get you back home. My father wants to talk to me about the credit card bill." She rolled her eyes.

Brooklyn smiled and wished that could be her sole financial burden, and for Page to know that it could be so much worse. But she kept the thought to herself. She had learned early on that her friend would never understand what it was like to be without, and she wasn't going to ruin a perfectly good afternoon over it.

Sleep finally came to Brooklyn after Page dropped her off at home, but it wasn't peaceful. The priest's face with his pitying eyes haunted her dreams, and every time she opened her mouth to try to explain that she wasn't as pathetic as she must have seemed, no sound came out. When Brooklyn woke up, her skin prickled with a clammy chill. The sun had set, and she checked her phone for the time. It was 3:00 in the morning; she had slept for over twelve hours. The unexpected lengthy sleep disoriented her and put her in a sour mood. She reached for that almost forgotten bottle of vodka and took a few swigs. The liquid burned on the way down, a feeling Brooklyn welcomed with a quiet hum. She finished off the bottle and lay back down, staring at the ceiling and trying to make out the water stain in the dark.

She waited for the sweet dulling of her senses and sank into the feeling as it plucked away every unwanted thought and wrapped them in translucent plastic. They were still there, but harder to make out and focus on. She forgot about her shame. Forgot about what exactly caused her pain. All that remained and all that mattered was how peculiar her face felt when she breathed.

The sun's first rays eventually peeked through her makeshift curtains made out of discarded tablecloths and woke her from the half sleep state she had managed to fall into. In the sweet space between consciousness and rousing sleep, it felt like nothing was wrong. Then she saw the water stain and felt the sofa's errant coils against her back, and the entirety of her existence crashed down on her. With a sigh, she got up, dressed, and headed out into the crisp, fall morning. Unsettling dreams had to be dealt with. As irrational as the need was, she needed the priest to know she had dignity. So, she began walking back to the church.

Brooklyn rounded the corner of the block the church was on and came to an abrupt stop. How unsuspecting the tiny building looked with its quaint facade. In fact, it was its size that had initially caught Page's attention yesterday. She had squealed, exclaimed how cute it was, and then arrived at the bright idea that it's unassuming appearance would be easy for Brooklyn to conquer. Clearly that hadn't been the case.

Brooklyn's next steps were slow, each one taken with care as if testing the ground before fully trusting it. Her stomach protested the closer she got, her throat tightening. Brooklyn's entire body rang its alarm bells. It screamed for her to turn back. Pushing away the incessant, flashing images from her past, she pulled the door open.

Brooklyn reminded herself that she had already gone in and nothing bad had happened. Sure, she had panicked a little—or maybe a lot—but the priest hadn't judged her. Or threatened her. And she had been the image of sin. If anything, he had been empathetic—an attribute Brooklyn had thought priests could not possess. Just thinking of what would have happened to her back home had she been caught like that made this church feel a little bit safer.

It took a few seconds for her eyes to adjust to the church's darkness. Due to its tiny windows and towering neighbors, the sunlight struggled to illuminate the church's interior. She found the priest sitting in a pew towards the front, deep in thought. The nave was much smaller than her fear had remembered it. From where she stood, the altar couldn't have been more than fifty feet away.

"It's okay," she said to herself when her heart jumped up to her throat. Brooklyn remembered how her fear had vanished while speaking to the priest, so she kept her eyes focused on him. She walked quickly but quietly, afraid to disturb the stillness that always seemed to be common in Catholic churches.

"Excuse me," she whispered. Her voice wavered. Brooklyn stole a glance up at the giant crucifix that hung behind the altar, then chose to look at her hands instead. Her palms were littered with red, crescent-shaped indents from digging her thumbnails into them.

The priest broke out of his reverie and looked up at her. There was no recognition. Of course, Brooklyn looked nothing like she did the day before.

"I was here yesterday morning. The girl..."

"Yes, yes. I remember. You've come back," he commented with surprise.

Brooklyn shoved her hands deep into the pockets of her sweater to keep from fidgeting. "Can we... talk? Outside?"

The priest noticed her discomfort and nodded. He stood up and towered over Brooklyn with broad shoulders that tested the seams of his shirt. Without the grate between them, Brooklyn was able to study his face better.

She wanted to find evidence of the cruelty she knew priests to be capable of; the security she felt around him made no sense. She found none.

The priest had a well-balanced face, meeting society's standards of symmetry, but nondescript features, other than eyes that were a startling shade of glacier blue. His firm lips were thin in their pressed-together state, and she wondered what they would look like when he was relaxed. Brooklyn could only define him as striking—not because of his features, but because of how he carried himself. It was that same demeanor that slowed her pounding heart and made her feel as if all the answers were within reach.

He led the way out and they sat on the front step. "What would you like to talk about?"

Brooklyn didn't answer him right away. She had barely managed a proper breath while inside and was now taking huge ones to make up for it.

"What you saw yesterday," she started, once her breathing was somewhat back to normal, "with my friend..." Brooklyn stopped. Why was she even explaining herself to him? Why did she care?

"She's not a very kind friend, is she?" the priest commented.

Brooklyn looked at him as she considered his observation. "Page is... okay," she eventually said. "She's just..." Brooklyn shook her head. "I honestly don't even know what I'm doing here."

"I can help you, child."

"Help me with what?" Brooklyn tensed, expecting judgment followed by a promise that he could make it all better... *but* only if she stripped away everything that made her... her.

"Direction. Guidance. Healing."

"I don't believe in God," blurted Brooklyn. Her cheeks burned. Never had she been brave enough to voice those words, and now she had said them to a priest himself.

"That's alright. That doesn't mean you can't benefit from his unconditional love. I choose to believe that you came into my church yesterday, and then came back, for a reason."

"Right. Well, I don't know if you noticed, but I can't stand churches."

"Yet you came back. Why is that?"

"Because... because of the way you looked at me." Brooklyn looked up at the large trees across the street. They boasted the classic red maple leaves, holding onto their branches before they too would drop like the temperature. "You pitied me, and I don't need pity," she added. Only then did she understand what truly bothered her. She didn't want pity from a priest. Brooklyn needed him, and any other man of God, to see her as strong. Capable.

"I wasn't looking at you with pity."

"Then what was it?"

"Empathy, child."

"Oh." Brooklyn sat quietly, weighing her next words. "I don't know if I..."

"What do you have to lose to give it a try?"

"You have no idea." Brooklyn looked down and focused on pushing away the memories from her earlier encounters with the church.

"Maybe not, but I do know that whatever it is you fear, it doesn't exist here at St. Anthony's."

"How could you say that when you don't even know what 'it' is?"

The priest smiled sadly. "I am devoted to my faith and religion, but that doesn't make me blind to the darkness misguided folk can make of it."

His frankness further surprised Brooklyn and the initial intrigue she had felt grew. She had always regarded priests as one-dimensional heralds of torture in the name of God. They could supposedly do no wrong and excuse anything. But this priest seemed, by this one slight admission, more... human.

"If I say yes, you won't try to 'save' me?" Brooklyn asked after a long pause.

He chuckled. "Child, you need guidance, not salvation."

That's new. Brooklyn bit her bottom lip. "Okay," she said slowly. "I'll come back. I guess." *Bad idea! Bad idea!* But she couldn't resist the opportunity to see him again, and to see just how different he was from the typical "man of God."

"Come on Monday. At around eight a.m."

Brooklyn nodded.

They stood. "By the way, I'm Father Mathias." He smiled and held out his hand. She took it. It was warm and that warmth crept up her arm and to her cheeks.

"I'm—I'm Brooklyn."

"Pleasure to meet you. And I look forward to seeing you on Monday, Brooklyn." The way her name sounded on his lips caught her completely off guard. Her cheeks prickled as they went from warm to scalding. She quickly pulled her hand away and spun on her heel.

"You too," she said mid-turn before briskly walking away.

War waged inside Brooklyn after she left. Torn between her fears and intrigue, she couldn't decide whether or not she was testing her tolerance a bit too much. The church triggered an all-encompassing darkness that wasted no time in swallowing her whole. So far, its threats to resurface had been momentary and deferred by her curiosity about the priest. But her fear was like an allergic reaction; yesterday, today, or even tomorrow, it could be mild, until one day, it could be lethal. Then she would find herself searching for that point of no return that she had missed while trying to pull herself together again.

Yet it still wasn't enough to dissuade her completely. Something in her gut told her to go back, and it spoke loud enough that she knew she would regret it if she didn't. The question was: Which would be worse? Regret, or an unraveling?

"I have until Monday," she whispered to herself. "I'll decide then."

3

Monday came and despite the internal back and forth that continued even as she walked to the church, Brooklyn's decision was no surprise. Father Mathias was already sitting on the steps when she turned onto the street. He smiled when he saw her.

For a priest, he really is pretty hot, Brooklyn thought as she approached him. She shook the thought away with horror, reminding herself that he was the last person she should look at in that way for multiple reasons.

"Good morning, Brooklyn."

The way he said her name made her blush. It took a moment for her to compose herself enough to reply. "Good morning. I'm sorry I'm late."

"That's quite alright. I would like for you to try to come inside today."

"Can't we just stay out here?" Brooklyn's eyes briefly drifted to the doors that made her think of a yawning beast's mouth—seemingly asleep and uninterested, but ready to devour you if you got too bold and too close.

"We could, but I'm afraid we'd end up quite wet." He looked up to the sky to make his point.

Brooklyn followed his gaze and saw that the clouds were dark and heavy. Even the air was thick with humidity and promised rain. She twisted the cuff of her sweater as she weighed her options.

"I assure you; you will be safe. Nothing bad will happen." The priest spoke slowly, his voice filled with such palpable conviction and concern for her welfare that Brooklyn couldn't help but believe him.

She nodded slowly and followed Father Mathias inside. It was a little easier than the last time. Still, the smell made her stomach clench, and the giant crucifix that hung behind the altar was disconcerting. It had no place in such a tiny church and made the space feel smaller and bigger all at the same time. Brooklyn looked away from it and stayed close to the priest to draw on the comfort she found in his presence.

"We'll go to my office. I think you'll feel most comfortable there." And he was right. Aside from the pictures of various saints hanging on the walls and the smell that seemed to accompany most houses of worship, one could pretend they weren't inside a church. The room was plain, and the two small windows oddly lacked the expected rounded or pointed tops. It was enough to ease her anxiety to a manageable level.

Father Mathias went to sit behind his desk and she sat across from him, her hands clasped together tightly as if they could keep her from coming apart.

"How are you doing?"

"I'm okay. I think."

Father Mathias was silent, and Brooklyn knew he was giving her time to relax. His obvious patience eliminated any notion of pressure, and she was grateful for the time and space to settle. Brooklyn took a final deep breath and met his gaze, signaling she was ready.

"Are you able to tell me where your dislike for the church came from?" he asked gently.

Brooklyn sat back. She looked away and out one of the windows, afraid he'd see her story in her eyes. "I had a strict mother." Her tone was final.

Father Mathias got the hint and didn't pry any further. "I understand. How about we focus on the present. Are you happy with where you are at the moment?"

"No." The word slipped so effortlessly through Brooklyn's lips. One word and it meant so much. She wasn't happy. Her pain held her captive; she wasted her days drunk or high, and she lived in a dump. At twenty-two, she still had no clue how to even begin to move forward in a meaningful way.

"If there was one thing you could change right now, what would it be?"

Erase my past. But saying that would mean bringing up exactly what she wanted to avoid. *My drinking.* But she didn't really want to change that. Not drinking meant she had to feel. "I don't know."

Father Mathias tapped the desk with his finger in thought. "You don't know? Or you don't want to say because it's linked to your past? Which you don't want to talk about."

Brooklyn's mouth crept open in surprise. *How did he know?* She wondered if she had spoken her thoughts out loud without realizing it.

"Well?" he prompted.

"I don't want to talk about it," Brooklyn forced out, crossing her arms.

"I know." He held up his hands to placate the threatening uprising of Brooklyn's emotions.

"This is a waste of time, isn't it?"

"Far from it, child. You need to feel safe and to trust me before opening up about such matters... a difficult task for anyone, let alone with someone who by default poses a threat to you."

Brooklyn's face reddened and she immediately felt bad that he had sensed her apprehension towards him.

"I take no offense, I just recognize the barriers and am letting you know that I'm willing to work with them and hopefully, at some point, around them."

"Why?" It was all Brooklyn could say. His kindness, understanding, his validation... everything seemed so out of place for someone in his position, at least from her experience.

"Because I believe that helping those who are hurting is my purpose." He spoke plainly, as if stating a widely accepted fact, and Brooklyn could find no signs of deceit.

She sat back and relaxed her hands. "But if I can't talk about my problems, how will this work?"

"As I said, we'll focus on the present. I just need to ask the right questions." He paused briefly. "What's something you enjoy doing?"

Drinking. Fuck! Was she so simple that she had reduced herself to substance abuse and running from her past? Brooklyn's breaths quickened as she struggled to find something. At this point, she didn't want to answer for the sake of trying to work with the priest, but rather to save face.

"Um, horseback riding," she blurted. Her eyes widened because it wasn't something she did anymore. It was yet another thing from her past.

"Do you get to do it often?"

She shook her head.

"Ah, from the past, got it. What's something you've done in the last week that you've enjoyed?"

"Party," she answered quietly.

"With your friend?"

"She's really not that bad, you know," she said defensively, having picked up on his disapproving tone. "Like that day, she took me out for lunch and apologized."

"What did she say exactly?"

Brooklyn didn't like the look on his face, as if he saw something she had missed. "That she didn't mean to hurt me and assured me she would never do anything to intentionally hurt me."

There was another look. "Did she use the words 'I'm sorry?'"

"Well... no. But that's because she has a hard time apologizing. She does it with actions. And to me, that's worth more than words."

"Give me an example."

Brooklyn was getting irritated now. "When she took me out to lunch, she took me to my favorite spot, which she hates. She was... I don't know... softer? Page can be pretty blunt usually."

"So, she treated you the way a good friend should treat you regardless?"

"You don't understand." Brooklyn returned to pressing her thumbnail into her palms.

"Are you alright with me asking one more question about Page?"

"Sure. Whatever."

"What are Page's top five attributes?"

Brooklyn's hands relaxed again, and she smiled as she thought of her friend, picturing how she moved through space and how self-assured she was—everything Brooklyn wished to be. "She's confident. No one can make her question herself and she claims whatever space she walks into. Um, she knows what she wants. Always. But I guess that falls under confidence. She takes charge and is organized. Once, she made a caterer sort out an impossible mix-up for a party her parents were throwing. She's honest. You never have to second guess where you stand with her or what she expects of you. And in a weird way, she's intuitive. If you don't know what to do or what you want, she somehow knows just what you need and helps you get it or do it."

As she spoke, Brooklyn had looked off to the bookshelf behind Father Mathias, and when she looked back at him, he had yet another look on his face. This one she couldn't quite decipher, but he was studying her with such intensity that it made her uncomfortable.

"What?" she eventually asked when he said nothing.

Father Mathias pressed his lips together and touched a fingertip to the space just above his upper lip—his cupid's bow. She recognized the frantic deliberation that was much like her own before deciding to meet him.

"Nothing," he finally said. "Would you be willing to come back tomorrow?"

"Why?" She knew it—she was beyond help. And it seemed now the priest believed it too.

"I need to think about how to best proceed..."

"I'm that difficult."

"I never said that."

"Then what? You were looking at me funny and then you want to end this meeting like what, ten minutes into it? Just be honest. You think you can't help me and are too egotistical to admit it because I told you from the beginning that you couldn't."

"On the contrary, I believe I can," he said quickly. Probably too quickly because he winced as if pained by the words he'd said. "But it's irrelevant because I'm limited by my position."

Brooklyn laughed. "Limited? Let me guess, you realize I need a much bigger intervention than you had anticipated. Who do we need to call in? The Bishop?"

"Please, do not twist my words."

"I swear to God. All of you are the same with the same superiority complex where you need everyone else to think they're not good enough. Because if they did, that would make you irrelevant. Right?" Brooklyn did her best to remain calm, but her eyes burned with threatened tears.

Father Mathias didn't react to her unflattering analysis of priests. A tear made its way down Brooklyn's cheek and his continued silence created a tight knot in her chest. She balled her fists and stood up.

"You know what," she whispered to keep her voice from cracking, "fuck this. I don't need any of this."

"You seem intent on misconstruing not only my words but my silence as well." He paused to take a calming breath, but Brooklyn didn't miss his clenched jaw. "I'm empathetic to your need to satisfy whatever beliefs you came in here with, but it's not constructive. Is it? I showed up with the intention to help you. Why did you come here today?"

Brooklyn's cheeks reddened. She couldn't admit it was because he himself had caught her interest. Despite her initial intent, it only took ten or so minutes for her to somehow slip back into seeking validation. From a priest. This made that knot in her chest grow a little tighter.

"Why can't you help me?" She hated herself for asking the question, but she needed to know if Father Mathias had come to the same conclusions as people from her past had. Because if he did, maybe she really was the problem; this was her greatest fear.

"It's not that I can't. Or won't, for that matter," he said carefully.

"Then?"

"As I had said, my position limits me and my first thoughts on how I could help you aren't possible. So I need time to collect my thoughts."

"What are your first thoughts?"

"I can't say. I'm sorry. Please, come tomorrow and we can figure out how to best approach your troubles." His eyebrows furrowed the slightest bit.

Brooklyn shook her head with a resigned sigh. "No. I'm not coming back. This was a terrible idea anyway." She turned to leave and stopped at the door. "And you're right," she said, without turning to look at him, "I didn't come with the right intentions. I'm sorry for wasting your time." She went to open the door.

"Wait," the priest called out suddenly. "If I tell you what I was thinking, will you consider coming back?" he said hesitantly.

Brooklyn knew she should leave. Their brief meeting proved she was incapable of tolerating the situation. But curiosity already had her in its grasp once again. "Okay?" Brooklyn said, returning to her seat, waiting expectantly.

"I don't know how to start," he began. He kept his eyes on his desk, his lips thinned more than usual as he pressed them together in thought. "Your troubles aside, I have a sense for recognizing a certain type of person." He paused, though Brooklyn wasn't sure why. "From experience, I have found that this specific type of person responds well to a certain type of guidance that may not..." Father Mathias's eyes shifted to the door and suddenly, his solid self-assurance that had already begun to waver came completely undone. This piqued an intense curiosity in Brooklyn and she leaned forward in her seat.

He sighed, as if resigning himself to a decision he had just made but was unsure of. "Child," he started, his voice so low Brooklyn had to lean in closer to hear him. "God creates all his children equally. And we are all equally special. However, there are some of us that He created to be... particularly special, in ways most cannot understand. I had suspicions before, but after your description of your friend and her traits that you obviously value, I'm convinced *you* are one of these special creations—a creation that requires a skilled approach to helping you find yourself."

Brooklyn sat back. "I don't understand," she laughed, both at him and at herself for having thought anything of interest would come out of his mouth. "According to you people, I have a one-way ticket to hell waiting for me. So how am *I* a 'special creation of God?'"

Father Mathias leaned forward and folded his hands on top of his desk. "I understand your skepticism, child. You are so completely lost, which is common for people like us who haven't discovered the meaning of our nature."

"Our... nature?"

"If I may be frank..."

"Please," said Brooklyn.

"You are a natural born submissive."

Brooklyn could feel his intense gaze; she knew he was weighing her reaction. "Submissive?"

The priest nodded.

"And what does that have to do with anything?"

"Well, someone like you, depending on upbringing and such, is vulnerable to toxic personalities." He paused. "Like your friend and, I can safely assume, like the prominent figures in your childhood."

"And you think you can help me with that?"

"As I said, I can't, due to my position."

"But if you weren't in your position, you believe you could help?"

"Well, I believe I could have helped you understand who and what you are and taught you how to express that part of you without exposing yourself to cruel people who take advantage of your divine nature."

"People like Page?"

"Exactly."

"I still don't get how that would help me."

"If you're unwilling to face your past, this could give you a starting point from which you could build a more solid foundation that would, in turn, give you the strength to face your past and heal from it. It can also provide a healthy example of how to experience an interaction with someone who would lead you to your growth, rather than to your detriment, as I believe was your experience in the past."

"I'm sorry. Wait one second? You're saying you're into that stuff? Like when you say 'submissive' and 'offering guidance,' are you literally talking about domination and submission? Like, whips and chains?" Brooklyn was in so much disbelief that she was prepared to pinch herself to make sure she wasn't dreaming. Maybe she hadn't managed to make it out of her room and was suffering a horrible leftover trip from drugs she forgot she had taken.

"I understand you must find it shocking—"

Brooklyn smiled. "Oh no, not shocking. *Satisfying.* You church people always like to look down on everyone with your puritan eyes and judge and condemn. *But,*" she said with a laugh, "you're just as depraved as the rest of us." This was way better than anything Brooklyn could have dreamed up. Just moments ago, she had been seeking validation from this man, as if he could finally convince her that she was good; convince her that she was worthy of kindness and an actual chance at life. Instead, he had granted her a real-life peek at evidence that "they" were not above human faults.

The priest looked at his door nervously. "I will admit that my beliefs don't line up with the general consensus of my peers, which is why I said these thoughts weren't worth mentioning."

Brooklyn paused for a moment. Something wasn't fully lining up. "And how would I trust that you're not one of these toxic personalities?"

"That's irrelevant, because as I said, I can't help you in that way. I only mentioned it so you would understand that my needing to regroup had nothing to do with you or your potential for healing."

"I know. But, hypothetically, how would I know?"

He looked at her curiously. "By slowly building that trust," he said. "I would never expect for you to just take my word for it."

Brooklyn crossed her arms. "And what if I told you I've *never* done well with authority? Especially your kind."

"Ah, now you're trying to disprove my observation."

Brooklyn shrugged with indifference. She didn't like his apparent ability to read her. It meant she was more exposed than she cared to be.

He stood up and went to stand in front of Brooklyn and leaned against his desk. "Without a way to properly channel that precious gift within you, it's no surprise you have issues with authority. Imagine having an innate urge to do something or to be a certain way, but it always gets you hurt, and you don't understand why that urge persists in spite of it. When the wrong people recognize what you can be or do for them, they exploit you. Much like your friend. Whereas the right people suffer your contempt."

That struck a chord. Brooklyn sat back as her mind raced to refute what he had said, even though it made absolute sense. Suddenly, her focus shifted from needing to prove him wrong to her very real struggles. Father Mathias had answered this big question she hadn't even known she was asking. Still, Brooklyn disliked the idea that she was meant to serve someone. *Isn't that what I've done my entire life? First with my mom? And now with Page?* Brooklyn's bravado deflated so quickly it left her feeling disoriented with no other emotion to take its place.

"I hope I didn't offend you. And I do hope you'll consider coming back tomorrow. I'm sure we can find a way to work around your past."

"How do you know I won't say anything?"

Father Mathias paused before saying in an even tone, "I took a chance by being honest with you with the intention to earn enough trust for you to come back. What you do with that is your prerogative."

Brave. "Hm, I guess no one would believe me over you anyway." As nonjudgmental as Father Mathias seemed, her words rang true, and his expression confirmed it.

"I need to go." Brooklyn jumped up and left. She dashed through the church and managed to get out without a panic attack.

Serve? I was born to serve? thought Brooklyn. She kicked at a small rock and shoved her hands in her pockets. She looked back at the church, wondering if his impression of her was true. *It doesn't matter,* she decided. She promised she wouldn't go back, and she'd do her best to forget the priest and everything that had happened.

4

"Brooklyn!" Page shouted through the phone.

"Hey, what's up?" Brooklyn held her phone up to check the time, squinting from the glare of the screen. It was 1:00 in the afternoon.

"I tried calling you. Twice!"

"I was sleeping, Page."

Page made a sound of disgust. "There's a grand opening party this Saturday at that new lounge, Verona. I got us in. So, we need to go shopping. We need to look our best. And before you start crying about how poor you are, don't worry, it's on me. Like always." She sang the last part, as if it could make up for the sting of her words.

Brooklyn chewed the inside of her cheek and took a deep, calming breath. She could just picture Page's eyes rolling as she said, "I don't know if I'm up for partying this weekend."

"Why? Are you still upset?"

"No, I'm just..."

"Cool! Meet me at the mall in a couple hours. 'Kay?" Page hung up, not giving Brooklyn a chance to object. Brooklyn was now painfully aware of her responses to Page after what Father Mathias had pointed out. Normally, she would meet Page without a second thought, but she didn't want to live up to the priest's impression of her. Then the worry of angering Page took over. Brooklyn could picture her friend waiting, expecting for her to show up without a shadow of a doubt. Because Brooklyn would show up—every time, without fail.

"Not today," she muttered and hid under her duvet... that Page had bought for her.

It didn't take long for the guilt to settle in. Brooklyn groaned and got up to get ready. She took the bus downtown, arriving at the mall a few seconds before receiving a text from Page, instructing her to meet at her favorite clothing store. When Brooklyn got there, Page was already looking through the racks, her face contorted with displeasure.

"Find anything?" asked Brooklyn.

"There you are!" greeted Page with annoyance. "I already started our dressing room. Let's go." She hung up the dress she had been looking at and led Brooklyn to the dressing rooms where the largest one was filled with countless choices. Brooklyn hated sharing a room. She felt uncomfortable changing in front of Page's watchful eye when Page was, in pretty much every way, perfect.

"Do I have to try on all of these?" groaned Brooklyn. Without needing to ask, she knew which side held her things to try and which side held Page's. Her friend had very a distinct taste for herself, and a different one for Brooklyn.

"Of course."

Brooklyn stripped out of her yoga pants and t-shirt with a sigh.

"Wow. I'm offering to buy you, like, a seven-hundred-dollar dress and you're acting like I'm forcing you to pull off your manicure without soaking it first or something." Page gasped and grabbed Brooklyn's hand. "Which reminds me. Your nails. How are they?" She inspected Brooklyn's nails and scrunched her nose. "We're gonna have to deal with these too. And your hair. And your face. When was the last time you exfoliated?"

"The last time you dragged me into a spa."

Page shook her head. "Come on, we have lots to do today. I swear, if it wasn't for me, you'd probably look like..." Page stopped herself. "Never mind, just try on the clothes. 'Kay?"

Brooklyn suppressed another sigh and tried on the dozen-plus dresses that Page had picked out for her. She didn't even bother looking in the mirror; she just waited for Page's verdict. Finally, her selective friend was satisfied with a shimmering emerald green dress that was reminiscent of the sixties which coaxed out her natural glow from beneath the pallor that plagued her.

"This dress is going to be a dream to accessorize! What do you think of this one?" She held her arms out like a princess and turned slowly. She modeled a rose gold babydoll dress with layer upon layer of chiffon and a low-cut V-neck that plunged beyond the dress's high waistline. The material had been woven with gold and silver threading, giving the garment an ethereal look.

"I think... you look stunning."

Page clapped her hands in excitement and smiled. "I do, don't I?" She really did look beautiful when she wasn't frowning or looking down her pointed nose.

The rest of the day was a whirlwind of shopping for shoes and accessories and Page yelling at the receptionist of her favorite salon to squeeze her and Brooklyn into their fully booked schedule. By the time Brooklyn got home, she was completely drained and grateful Page didn't insist on dinner. However, her stomach grumbled in protest. It would have appreciated a proper meal after such a hectic day. *Well, we'll have to settle for instant noodles.* Brooklyn opened a pack of noodles and put them in a bowl with water before putting it in the microwave.

Her hunger grew when her room filled with the smell of simulated chicken flavor, and she all but burned herself when she ate it without letting it cool first. Her stomach grumbled as she set the bowl down; the bowl of soup wasn't enough.

Sleep.

Sleep was a good salve for hunger, so she stripped down to her underwear and settled in for bed, wishing she hadn't already finished the vodka from the other day. The faithful water stain captured her attention as she desperately called upon sleep to take her to where hunger couldn't be felt. It was still early, but she hoped she would manage to sleep through the night.

Vibrations from an incoming call woke Brooklyn up. She answered it, disgruntled; the hunger pangs wasted no time to greet her.

"Hi, I need you to come in ASAP, Melanie didn't show up again," said Sandra, her boss.

Brooklyn held the phone away to check the time. It was 6:30 in the morning, a half hour past the start of the morning shift. "Okay, I'll be there."

"What's your ETA?"

"I'll be there before the rush," she said, referring to the onslaught of government employees and bankers they served every morning. Brooklyn worked in a trendy coffee shop in the business precinct. It was the only job she had been able to hold on to for more than a few months, mostly because she wasn't working full-time. Or even part-time. She worked on-call and it suited her just fine. They called her in enough that she could make rent and have some money left over for her generic brand potato chips, but not so much that she resented having to go in. She loved how it was always busy and time flew by. Making the complicated coffee orders was mind-numbing, as close to effective meditation as she could get.

She hung up and closed her eyes with a sigh, mustering the will to get up and get ready. The only downside to working on-call was the inability to mentally prepare herself for a day of smiling and speaking to strangers. Still, she tried her best to do so while she brushed her teeth and pulled on black jeans and a black t-shirt. She tied up her hair into a messy bun, threw on an over-worn fall jacket, and left to catch the bus. On days she didn't have to rush in, she would usually do the thirty-five-minute walk into work, the length of which helped with the needed mental preparation. On days like this, thirty-five minutes shrunk to half the time on the bus. Brooklyn guessed she should be grateful for the short commute. In this city, it could be a lot worse.

As promised, she arrived in time for the rush and dove right into filling orders. By now, her coworkers knew how to read her, knowing when to test her social waters and when to steer clear of her. Today, they knew it was best to do the latter and Brooklyn manned the espresso machine and steamers in silence with her head down until the flurry of coffee addicts subsided. She wiped down the counters then went on her break, opting to walk the streets instead of spending it in the break room where someone would most likely try to talk to her to avoid awkward silences, which only made things that much more awkward, in Brooklyn's opinion.

She came up to a gallery that had just opened and seemed so out of place between the nondescript facades of the buildings that graced most of the street. The windows showcased beautiful, vibrant artwork—a burst of color among all the gray. The artist had mixed different medias, plastering clippings of black and white photographs over oil and watercolor paints. It looked chaotic but made perfect sense at the same time.

"It's beautiful, isn't it?"

Brooklyn turned to the man who spoke to her and nodded in a way to discourage further conversation.

"So is the artist," he continued.

This piqued Brooklyn's interest. "You know the artist?" She couldn't quite understand why, but she felt kinship with the creator of the work.

He nodded. His nod seemed so morose and full of regret. Brooklyn noticed then that his fists were clenched and his shoulders hunched.

"You should tell her," Brooklyn said.

"Tell her what?"

"That you think she's beautiful. I know I'd like for someone to tell me that. And mean it. But like, *really* mean it. You know?" Brooklyn stunned herself with her involuntary admission. But she could see her words had made an impact.

The man looked at her and she felt he could see her darkness. It had her feeling uncomfortably exposed, much like when she was with the priest. He smiled sadly. "If it weren't for her," he said, nodding towards the art display, "I would have given you my card. I'm a life coach, but I'm currently taking a break from my business. I can tell you're suffering, and I hope you can find peace." He stopped again and let out a choking sob so small, Brooklyn thought she may have imagined it. "Your kind and simple words have given me mine. I will tell her. Thank you." He turned and melted into the ebbing mass of people on the sidewalk.

The stranger's sudden exit had Brooklyn wondering if the exchange had even happened, but it left her thinking of the priest and his determination to help her. The man had wished her peace, but she wasn't sure if she knew what that even felt like, or what it was. She knew fear. Heartache. Shame and guilt. Turmoil. But not peace. How could she find it without help? The man had called himself a life coach. Those cost money. Money she didn't have.

Brooklyn shrugged away the subsequent thought that the priest might be a viable option to explore and walked back to work.

5

The rest of the week passed without event until Saturday arrived. Brooklyn took the bus to Page's to get ready—or, rather, for Page to get her ready.

"Good, your skin still looks radiant!" said Page when she answered the door.

"Thanks."

Page's face was covered with a clay mask and her hair was wrapped up in a towel. A silk robe graced her shoulders and Brooklyn again envied her friend's ability to look stunning, this time with a bunch of gunk on her face.

"Come on, we're running late!" Page said, panicked. It was five in the evening and doors didn't open until nine. Knowing Page, she wouldn't dare consider showing up before eleven, so that gave them just under six hours to get ready.

Page ushered Brooklyn to the vanity and did a quick cleansing routine before applying makeup. Then she worked on Brooklyn's hair. These were the moments Brooklyn felt her friend was more than just an entitled pseudo-socialite. Page's passion for hair and makeup ran deep, and it was sad that she would never consider making a career of it, simply because she didn't need to. When Page was done, Brooklyn looked like she belonged at her friend's side. Page had swept and pinned Brooklyn's hair so that the perfectly sculpted curls cascaded over a shoulder. Brooklyn had learned enough from her friend to know that this was a tactical choice. Brooklyn's face didn't quite suit up-dos, but her dress and necklace needed her thick hair to be contained. This type of hair style was a compromise. Page had given her smokey eyes with hints of purple to tease out the hidden specks of lavender in Brooklyn's gray eyes, and her lips weren't far from nude, with just a faint tint of pink.

"Perfect," sighed Page. And Brooklyn believed her.

Brooklyn pulled on the green dress and slipped on her new shoes. After putting on her jewelry, Brooklyn noted that she was wearing at least four thousand dollars' worth of clothes and accessories. It made her sick. That was a little under half a year's worth of rent. But this feeling wasn't new to her. Page regularly spent her parents' money carelessly, and all for the sake of partying, status, and appearances. Since Brooklyn was by her side,

Brooklyn was part of her appearance... and an extra cost, which Page had no reservations about making her painfully aware of.

Brooklyn sat and waited, careful to not tousle her hair. Two and a half hours later, Page emerged looking like she had stepped out of a modern fairy tale. Now, part of getting ready involved photos, pre-drinking, and letting the outfit "set," as Page called it. But Brooklyn privately wondered if maybe even her socially adept friend needed to prepare herself for the night, the same way Brooklyn needed to mentally prepare herself for work. And part of her ritual was to do just that.

Sam arrived to pick them up and they made their way to the new lounge. Page turned and handed Brooklyn a baggie with a pill in it.

"I'm not doing anything tonight, Page." Brooklyn's stomach was turning at the thought of taking anything.

"But you're no fun sober." She feigned a pout and implored Brooklyn with her eyes.

"Fine." Brooklyn took the baggie and decided to pretend to take it when it was time.

When they arrived, the lineup took over the street relegated to pedestrian use, spanning a couple blocks.

Page giggled. "Half these people won't get a chance to see the inside." With her head held high, she led the way to the VIP line and then went to the front of it. The bouncer didn't bat an eye and motioned them through. Brooklyn always felt guilty as they passed disgruntled party-goers who looked on at them with envy.

The entrance was dimly lit and split off into two corridors. The one on the left had another bouncer standing at its entrance. Again, there were no questions and he stepped aside to let them through. The subsequent corridor was long and got darker just before the lights from the lounge lit up the rest of the way.

Verona proved to be a stunning venue. The city's nightlife was lacking, something that Page complained about all the time, and failed to provide a variety of attractive options. Most places that claimed to be a lounge ended up being another over-hyped club with terrible music, or a venue that was truly a restaurant that simply played music at a slightly higher decibel. But Verona was truly a lounge hidden in the underbelly of a Sparks Street building. Luxurious black leather sofas and glass tables filled the entire space. Modern chandeliers hung from the ceiling, casting a candle-like glow. With all the glass and soft lighting, Brooklyn couldn't help but feel like she was in a dream. Even the music was carefully mellow—loud but somewhat muted, almost as if the speakers had been set to their maximum volume but then swathed in cotton balls. Now Brooklyn understood Page's choice of dress, which seemed to glow just the right way under the lighting, making it seem as if the place had been designed after her and not the other way around. What Brooklyn also failed to notice was how Page had done Brooklyn's appearance great justice, while simultaneously making sure that she would look as out of place as Page looked like she belonged.

"Isn't this place great?" asked Page as they sat at a reserved table that overlooked the rest of the lounge below where the seating wasn't as plush and the service slightly less attentive. Down there, people had to fend for their own drinks at the bar if they weren't ordering by the bottle. Brooklyn nodded. It was always at that moment that Brooklyn would allow herself the vapid fantasy that she belonged and was better than the people below. She gave herself permission to do so because she was hyper-aware of the truth: She was garbage dressed in couture.

Page beamed and pulled out her choice drug for the night after ordering bottles of vodka and tequila they would never be able to finish. More money wasted.

"Is anyone else coming?" Brooklyn asked.

Page shook her head. That meant none of her other friends had managed to get in, at least not into VIP. To ensure her status over them, Page opted for her entourage of two rather than inviting her friends to a table that clearly had space for more. "The more, the merrier" didn't exist in Page's dictionary. Sam poured the shots when the bottles arrived, and Page motioned for Brooklyn to take out the pill she had given her earlier.

"I'm gonna take mine in a bit," said Brooklyn. She looked back at the people below. From here, she could pick anyone she wanted. Any guy would flirt with her, thinking she came from money and wanting to share the bottles that would go wasted either way. She never did take advantage of the borrowed status. If she did, then all of *this* suddenly wouldn't be solely for

Page's benefit. Somewhere deep inside, there was a wise voice that knew the moment she did that, Page would own her.

"You should take it now, it takes a while for it to kick in," said Sam, referring to the pill. Both he and Page watched her expectantly.

Brooklyn pulled out the little baggie and put the pill in her mouth, planning to spit it out when she had the chance. She kept it under her tongue, but it dissolved too quickly.

"So, like anything, stay hydrated and don't drink *too* much," said Sam, leaning back and putting his arm around Page.

Brooklyn smiled and nodded.

Page lifted her glass in the air. "To an *unforgettable* night!"

The sunlight woke Brooklyn. The rays that peeked through the curtains hit her head like hot spikes and she covered her face to stop the resulting searing pain.

"What the hell?" she mumbled as she sat up. Her head spun and felt heavy as she reached out for her aspirin. But there was no coffee table, just more bed. And a person? She gasped and drew her hand back, confused. Brooklyn squinted to make out her surroundings, terrified she had acted on the desire to use her VIP status to get whomever she wanted. Of course, reality was worse than what her drug-bogged mind could come up with. She was in Page's gigantic bed with Page on one side and Sam on the other. "Page! What the fuck am I doing here?"

"Shut up and go back to sleep," mumbled Page, her voice muffled by a pillow. She reached out to pull Brooklyn to lie down but Brooklyn swatted her half-asleep friend's hand away.

Crawling to the foot of the bed, she tumbled to the floor. Her legs trembled as she tried to stand. "I can't keep doing this," she cried to herself. She was naked, and as she looked around for her clothes, she tried not to think about what might have happened last night. Which proved to be difficult because her vision was still hazy, and each movement came with a serious threat to throw up. Somehow, she managed to get herself dressed and stumbled out of Page's condo and to the elevator. It could have been her imagination spurred by self-consciousness, but the doorman all but shook his head as she staggered out the automatic sliding door and onto the sidewalk.

She didn't know what she was doing when she stepped off the bus and walked to the church. Brooklyn didn't allow herself to stop and think as she went inside. Maybe it was because she was still heavily intoxicated, but the usual unease she felt in churches was almost absent. Father Mathias was sitting in a pew, turned slightly to face the middle-aged woman he was speaking to. Brooklyn watched as the woman listened intently and nodded.

It took her a moment to notice the church's slightly increased activity compared to previous visits. Of course it would be busier; it was later in the day. Brooklyn checked her phone. Almost 2:00 in the afternoon... a Sunday.

"Can I help you?"

Brooklyn jumped. It was another priest. She pulled her coat closed to hide her attire and pointed at Father Mathias. "I'm here to see him."

He eyed Brooklyn's appearance, and although one could pretend that her clothes were modest, she failed to consider her makeup-smudged face and unkempt hair.

"Is there any way I can be of assistance? As you can see, Father Mathias is busy."

"I-I can wait."

"Very well then. Please, have a seat." The priest left and Brooklyn sat in the very last pew to wait.

She watched as Father Mathias took the woman's hands in his and they bowed their heads in prayer. Her soft sobs drifted across the nave and Brooklyn felt awkward, feeling as if she was intruding on a personal moment. They stood up, and Father Mathias bid her goodbye before his eyes landed on Brooklyn. He motioned for her to go to him.

As she carefully made her way down the aisle, doing her best to walk straight, Brooklyn couldn't help but feel shame about how she had spoken to him before, given that he still looked upon her with kindness.

"You've returned, yet again."

"Please don't be smug."

He smiled. "I'm not smug. Just pleasantly surprised?"

Brooklyn bristled at his response and the doubt that came and went so easily returned.

"So?" he prompted.

She looked down at her hands and bit her lip in thought, then looked back up at Father Mathias. "I think you were right," she grudgingly admitted with a sigh, "about me. After I saw you, Page called me and convinced me to go out with her this weekend. And I did, even though I didn't want to. And then this morning... This morning I woke up and I have no idea what happened last night and I'm just really, *really* tired. I don't know what I'm doing anymore. I just know that I don't want to do... I don't want to do this"—she pointed at herself—"anymore."

"I see. And what are you hoping for now, coming here today?"

She bit her lip and thought of her strange exchange with the man in front of the gallery. "I want peace." Brooklyn looked up at him beseechingly. Her voice cracked as she said the word. It didn't even feel right for her to say it, as if some unseen judge questioned her audacity to even think she had any right to wish it, let alone speak it.

Father Mathias's face softened. "I know, child."

"I need help." She choked on the words, not wanting to admit such a thing to a priest.

"You do know, for this to work, you need to let go of your prejudice... or at least not cling to it so tightly."

Brooklyn nodded. "I do want your help. I need it." She stopped to quell the trembling in her voice. She refused to cry. "After last night... I just feel lost and right now you make the most sense." She looked up at him, desperate for the anchor he had promised that would keep her from continuing in her state of constant drifting.

"There is no need to convince me. If you want my help, you have it. I just want you to show up in a way that will aid your success."

Brooklyn shook her head in an attempt to clear away some of the fog. He wasn't understanding her. "No. I mean, *you* make sense. Your first thoughts," she said, speaking in code she hoped he would interpret.

Father Mathias's eyes widened; he took a few steps back. "I'm not sure that's the best idea."

"You said it yourself, right? Well, I want to try it that way. Otherwise, what else is there? You're gonna make me read the Bible?" Brooklyn's words began to slur more noticeably, and she had to reach out to steady herself on a pew.

Father Mathias looked around to see who else was in the nave. "I should have never mentioned such nonsense. I think you need to go home and rest." Panic laced his whisper.

"Please." Brooklyn's voice was so incredibly small.

"What if we give the conventional approach a chance first?"

"I think you already know that won't work."

Father Mathias's eyebrows furrowed. He closed his eyes and took slow, intentional breaths. The silence stretched between them, weighed down by his uncertainty and her desperation.

"It wouldn't be..."

"I know it's a big ask, but I promise I won't cause you any trouble. Even if things don't work out, I won't say anything. I promise."

"Brooklyn, it's not a matter of causing trouble, but ethics." He looked around again, his discomfort growing.

"Fuck ethics," Brooklyn hissed a little too loudly.

"Hush, please!" he whispered desperately.

"No!" Brooklyn proclaimed, but in a lower voice. "Do you know how unethical you people can be? How is this any different? It's the only way I'm willing to come to you for help. I want to..."

"Alright!" He held up a hand to silence her.

Brooklyn wasn't too hungover to know she should be surprised. "You will?"

"Yes." The word was barely audible. "But I have one condition." Father Mathias searched her eyes. "First, I'm going to ask you to go home and think about it. I don't think you're..." He paused, trying to find the right words. "Clear-headed. You've come to me out of desperation, and you seem to be slightly intoxicated. If, tomorrow morning, when you're sober *and* calm, you still feel as you do now, come to me at five in the morning. And we can start immediately."

"No! I'm super clear-headed. Clearer than ever." Her body betrayed her with a precarious sway.

"If that's the case, then you should have no issue taking the time to confirm it with some thought, and I will see you tomorrow at five."

"Can't we start now?"

"No, child. Tomorrow," he said, lowering his voice and making a point of looking around. They weren't alone and people had begun to stare.

"Okay." Brooklyn didn't move, not wanting to leave the reach of his grounding presence.

"Is there anything else?"

Brooklyn shook her head. "No. Guess not. Bye." Her steps were quick; as soon as she left his side, the church's malice towards her came rushing in, and she had sobered up just enough to feel it.

6

The alarm startled Brooklyn even though she was already wide awake. She had slept through most of the day and through the night, yet her head still ached. The aftereffects of Saturday night weren't the only thing that contributed to her current rough state. The hazy memory of her begging the priest to employ his "first thoughts" had morphed into a very uncomfortable dream loop. In the loop, unlike reality—although she wasn't sure her memory was accurate—the priest had rejected her plea, claiming it had been a test and she had proven, beyond doubt, that she was made of nothing but sin.

The dream had shaken her enough to question pursuing such a relationship with Father Mathias, and now she sat frozen, unsure of whether she should go. Gingerly, she got up and turned on the lights. The four walls held what had become her story. Discarded empty liquor bottles that she was saving up to return for their deposit, a trash bin overflowing with food wrappers, and furniture that others had retired to street corners, much like her. She was a throw-away, with no home and no place in the world.

Brooklyn wasn't aware of her decision to go through with meeting the priest until she stood on the sidewalk in front of the church. She checked the time. It was seven minutes after five, meaning she was late. She walked up the path and hesitated at the door, then tested it, expecting it to be locked; a part of her still couldn't believe he had agreed to meet her under her conditions. But the door opened, the only resistance being its own weight and Brooklyn's uncertainty.

To her dismay, Father Mathias wasn't in the nave. She paused, gripping the door's handle, then took a tentative step into the church and scanned the space more closely, including the confessional, for any signs of movement. Shadows shrouded the far corners. The day had barely begun, and with fall mornings growing darker by the day, there was little natural light to illuminate the church that seemed to still be asleep.

"Hello?" Despite her effort to call out, her voice was barely above a whisper. She took another step inside. *Maybe I did misremember. Or maybe he changed his mind.* Brooklyn wasn't sure what to do. The door creaked shut

43

behind her, making her flinch, and the nave became even darker. With a shake of her head, she turned to leave, deciding she was being foolish. But something between curiosity and desperation kept her put. There was one other place she could check: his office. Much like the day she had met him, she gathered her courage by choosing to not overthink and rushed towards the back of the church to where his office was. She knocked quietly, doing her best to stave off the oncoming panic.

"Come in."

Brooklyn sighed with relief. She opened the door and stepped in, her trepidation quickly dissipating. The priest proved to be akin to a safe haven on church grounds. The shadows that hid in the building's corners and the strife embedded in the walls couldn't penetrate the invisible force field that surrounded him.

"Good morning, child."

"Why weren't you in the front?" she asked.

"When someone truly wants something, they're willing to overcome any obstacle, which you have. I needed to be sure that you were certain about your choice. The empty nave would have turned you away had you been unsure. Wouldn't you agree?"

Brooklyn didn't like his answer, but he was right. She would have given up and gone home. "I almost did," she admitted.

Father Mathias smiled sadly. "I'll be honest and say I'm relieved you didn't. But for both our sakes, part of me wishes you had."

"Why?"

"I would think the reason is obvious."

Brooklyn fidgeted as she stood in the doorway and took the opportunity to really look at his office. Now that she had given in to her captivation with the priest, she wanted to glean as much information about him from his surroundings as she could.

The rectangular room lacked personality, its modesty echoing the rest of the church. From where she stood, his desk was to her left, facing the wall to her right. In the far-right corner was a coat rack and mirror. Bookshelves lined the wall behind Father Mathias's desk and Brooklyn guessed they all must be religious texts. She wondered if he read anything else for pleasure or if he devoted all his reading time to studying the word of God. Besides the images of saints that hung between the windows, the office lacked décor, meaning it gave nothing away about the priest. There was nothing personal; no photos, no knickknacks, and even his desk calendar seemed standard issue and with nothing written on it.

"What are you thinking?" asked Father Mathias, startling her.

"Whether or not you read fiction."

He smiled. "That... I did not expect. What would me reading fiction mean to you?"

Brooklyn paused to think about it. "That you're more than just a priest," she said with a shrug.

Father Mathias chuckled. "Why don't you come in?"

Brooklyn was still too jittery to sit, so she wandered over to one of the windows to look out of it. Any view it may have had had been choked out by the siding and fabricated stone of the neighboring house. "I wonder what this street will look like in ten years." The Glebe still retained its unique charm, despite the pockets of geometric atrocities that threatened it.

"Whatever it will look like, it won't be as beautiful. I'm not one for cities."

Brooklyn turned to him, wanting to grab hold of the new tidbit of information. "Yet here you are." She chuckled softly. "Although it's not quite a city, but definitely not a town."

Father Mathias nodded. "Not so much by choice, but I'm sure I'll learn to love it with time."

"Hm, I'm sure you will." Brooklyn had felt the same way when she had first arrived. As much as she despised where she came from, the noise, people, lights, and smells had been overwhelming and she had longed for the quiet of the countryside. But eventually the municipality had grown on her. "So, you haven't been here for long?" This was good; small talk she could do. Slowly, the tension left her shoulders until only her fingers showed subtle signs of distress.

"A few months."

"What brought you here?" Brooklyn felt a bit bolder and went to inspect the bookcase. As expected, it was filled with religious books. No fiction in sight. Although, she mused, the factual nature of the books was questionable.

"Father Isaac is retiring and I'm replacing him."

She looked at him. "Oh. And you couldn't say no? I mean, if you preferred where you were before."

"I never said I preferred it." The priest cleared his throat, signaling the end of their small talk. "Are you ready to begin?"

Brooklyn wanted to talk more about him and learn about what he preferred over the city. The coast? Mountains? Open fields? "I guess," she said quietly.

"Have a seat."

Brooklyn sat on the edge of the chair. Yes, she had managed to overcome the obstacle Father Mathias had set for her, but she was still unsure. In fact, she didn't fully understand what she had asked for. Like most people who were plugged into the internet, she had vague knowledge of the BDSM lifestyle, but she wasn't informed enough to know whether mainstream media's anecdotes were complete or even accurate.

"I'm thinking we can meet weekday mornings at this time. Does that work for you?"

"Sure. I work at a cafe, and I get called in on short notice sometimes."

"If you're not here by five after five, I'll assume you're at work then. Now, I understand your apprehension towards the church, but for this to work, you'll need to do your best to let some of that go. Do you think you could extend me the benefit of the doubt and the preliminary trust that comes with that?"

"I guess. I mean, I'll try," she amended when she saw his dissatisfaction with her response.

"Brooklyn." There it was again, her name on his lips. "Trust goes both ways. I need to trust that you're serious about this."

Brooklyn nodded. "I am."

"What do you know of D/s dynamics?"

"I don't really know what those letters mean."

Father Mathias thinned his lips. "Are you sure you understand what you're asking for, child?"

"No. But..." she said quickly when doubt colored the priest's face. "I understand in here." Brooklyn pressed her hand against her chest and then her belly. "And here. Even though I don't fully understand and I'm still a little unsure, something is telling me I need to be here."

He sighed. "Alright, then." He pulled out a small notepad and wrote something down quickly before ripping out the page and handing it to Brooklyn. It was a short list of books. "I suggest reading any one of these or, better yet, all of them. We will proceed with today, but I do feel it's imperative you educate yourself."

Brooklyn took the piece of paper and folded it carefully, taking her time so she could draw out the task of tucking it away in her pocket.

"D/s stands for domination and submission. This is what my 'first thoughts' were referring to. I need to be sure that you understand what you're consenting to."

Brooklyn nodded.

"I will assume the dominant role, and you the submissive. We will speak more on what that will look like. But for today, I feel action would be worth more than words. Is that alright?"

"Yes."

Father Mathias searched her face then continued, "I want you to know that I will not touch you or ask anything of you that does not serve an ultimate purpose. You have the free will to say no without any consequence. Do you understand?"

Brooklyn nodded.

"Good. I want you to go and stand against the far wall, facing me."

"What?"

He looked at her pointedly, and Brooklyn went to do as he had instructed.

"Now get down on your knees."

Brooklyn didn't move right away, taking a moment to give him another questioning look before falling to her knees. Father Mathias went to her to nudge them apart so that her legs were slightly spread.

"Now put your hands behind your head."

"Why?"

"I told you that you could say no without consequence; I didn't say you could question me."

It would have been easy for her to stand up, give Father Mathias the finger, and leave. Every part of her wanted to do just that, so badly, but a small, persistent part kept her rooted in her position. Thinning her lips in displeasure, Brooklyn did as he said, and he returned to his desk to work. This confused Brooklyn further, but she didn't move and waited for whatever would come next. And she waited for longer than she cared to. Occasionally, Father Mathias would glance up at her, sometimes with a vacant expression, other times with a faint smile. It was the intermittent smiles that quelled Brooklyn's bubbling need to lash out on some vague principle that, really, was just her aching pride.

Brooklyn's knees began to hurt. She did her best to ignore the pain until she couldn't help but to sit back and rest on her heels. The movement caught Father Mathias's attention. He dropped his pen and bore his eyes into her. She knew she had done something wrong.

"Why did you move?"

"Because my knees are hurting. Why do I have to do this?" She let her hands drop as well in defiance.

"Because you chose to be here, and I want you to. Now get your bum off your heels, put your hands back behind your head, and stay that way until I tell you that you may rest." Before returning to his work, he gave her a look that communicated he was confident she would obey. And she did.

Reapplying pressure to her already tender knees was worse than the pain that had made her sit back on her heels in the first place. The dull ache was white hot, and small muscles that she didn't know existed cramped up in protest. Brooklyn looked at him, silently imploring him to give her a break. Not only were her knees hurting, but her core failed her, making her lower back tense up as well. Brooklyn searched for a place in her mind to hide from the discomfort. She reminded herself that she could end this at any moment, and a part of her pounded imaginary fists against imaginary walls, angry at whatever it was that spurred on her compliance. *I'm curious to see where this will go,* she thought to herself. Of course, that could be the only practical explanation for her subjecting herself to something that appeared to be so nonsensical.

"You may rest," he said after some time, finally allowing her sore limbs to relax.

She sat but kept her hands in place.

"You may place your hands on your thighs, child." He stood back up and approached her. "Do you have any questions?"

"Yeah. How is this supposed to help me?" Despite the challenge in her tone, she remained seated, even though it meant having to look up at him.

Father Mathias crouched so that he was eye level with her. He smiled the way one would smile before letting someone in on a big secret. "If only you knew just how divine you are." He held out his hand to her. "Come sit."

His offered hand proved to be necessary as she straightened resistant knees and stood on unsteady legs. She held onto him as he led her towards the chair at his desk.

"I wanted to show you what our arrangement involves," he answered once he was seated. "It's one thing to know or have an idea of it; it's another to feel it. So, how did it make you feel?"

"I don't know."

"I think you do know, you just don't want to be honest about it."

"I didn't like it. I hated not having any other choice but to listen."

"But you *did* have a choice."

Brooklyn shook her head. "That's what I mean. I knew I had a choice, but something kept me from moving and I hated it."

The priest's silence hinted that her words had impacted him profoundly, but he didn't let on as to why.

"I still don't understand how this will work. How will me serving you do me any favors?"

He chuckled. "You should ask yourself that. *You* are the one who came to me in a time of need, asking specifically for this kind of intervention."

That made Brooklyn think. "Only because you said it could help me."

"Words I spoke not as a suggestion, but to earn your trust that I wasn't passing judgment. This was not my intended path, child."

"So why did you agree, then?"

Father Mathias's eyes shifted, and he took a long pause before speaking again. "Because I wanted it as well. I am not infallible, child. But I do think it could help, and I know from experience. I'm never more at peace than when I'm graced with the blessing to hold dominion over someone such as yourself. And you said yourself that peace is what you're hoping for."

Peace. That word hung in the air, and she thought of that man outside the gallery who had wished her peace. She couldn't ruminate on it for long because Father Mathias continued.

"I only have two speeds with these matters and I need to know... Are you still absolutely sure this is what you want?"

Brooklyn grew frustrated. What more did she have to do to prove that she wanted this? Even in her uncertainty about whether it was right, she had proven that she was sure enough to face her fears for it. But she didn't say all that. She just said, "Yes."

Just like that, a switch had been flipped and she got the sense there would be no more checking and double-checking on his part. Father Mathias relaxed, and his face resembled that of a new king who had finally accepted and sat on his throne—eager for the responsibility and sobered by its weight. This sent a small shiver of excitement up Brooklyn's spine.

"I want to also point out, to eliminate any doubt you may have about yourself and your capacity for servitude, that despite your claim to have never done well with authority," he said, referring to their previous conversation, "you followed my commands even when you, by your own admission, didn't want to. Even when you had absolutely no reason to. If you wanted, you could have refused. I had promised that there would be no consequence. You could have gotten up and left."

Brooklyn's cheeks reddened and she looked down, playing with the cuffs of her sleeves. He was right, and she didn't like it. "Maybe I was just curious to see where things would go," she said, voicing her earlier thought halfheartedly. She looked back up at him when he didn't respond.

Father Mathias stood and walked around his desk slowly, his eyes never leaving Brooklyn's. As he got closer, she looked down again, unable to bear the intensity of his gaze. When he was in front of her, he prodded her to look back up with a gentle touch under her chin.

"You may think it's easier to fight your will to obey, but you will only make this harder on yourself. We are now committed to the process. Unless you are having second thoughts?"

There it was, the triple-check, and the king readied to vacate the throne.

"If you change your mind, I promise you, child, that I am committed to helping you, and no matter what you decide, my help will always be an option."

Brooklyn's breaths quickened from the contact and the tone of his voice further warmed her cheeks. "I want this," she whispered.

Father Mathias cleared his throat and withdrew his hand quickly. "Before you leave, I want you to light a candle. I want you to do this after each time we meet. You will light that candle and pray for strength, humility, and an open heart. You'll need all three to be successful in your training. Do you understand?"

"But I don't believe in..."

He held up his finger. "Hush, child. Do as I say."

"Fine," she said, biting her tongue.

"That's all for today."

"That's it?" Brooklyn didn't want to leave. It wasn't until that moment that she realized she had briefly tasted peace and she wanted more. As much as she had suffered as she kneeled at the end of the room, her mind had been quieted. Few things had existed in those moments. It had just been the priest, her, and the act of experiencing the moment.

"It's almost six and the day is starting soon for the church, child."

Brooklyn blinked, stunned at how time had escaped her.

"Until tomorrow, child."

She was in such a daze when she left that she forgot to light a candle and pray as Father Mathias had asked.

7

Brooklyn didn't really know what to make of her time with the priest. She sat in her room and stared at the wall as she tried to replay each moment, but her memory of Father Mathias's touch under her chin distracted her from any worthwhile introspection. Every time she tried to think, her mind would jump to that instance and her breath would hitch.

She took breaks from her daydreaming to snack and sleep, but even with her preoccupation, the hours of the day dragged by. On days like this, she wished she would get called into work or for Page to pull her out for some frivolous excursion. Checking her bank account, Brooklyn decided to treat herself to an actual meal. Her shamefully earned money from Page had given her enough wiggle room to justify the splurge. She headed to Bank Street and walked towards Lansdowne since that stretch held the most options. She weighed her options as she passed them, searching for that balance of value and food crave-ability. She settled on a mom-and-pop burger joint and ordered their cheapest meal to go to avoid the pressure of paying a tip.

With food in hand, she walked to Lansdowne Park to take advantage of the unseasonably warm day. Brooklyn sat on a bench that was one of many in a row lined with young trees. It was a popular pit stop for teens and young adults on dates, and Brooklyn watched people sit close to their partners while they shared a gelato or pretzel. They seemed so carefree, and she envied their ability to enjoy simple moments. She also envied their ability to spend seven dollars on a small cup of overrated ice cream.

Brooklyn turned to her food and ate slowly, enjoying the fats from the meat that were almost too rich for her pallet which was accustomed to cheaper, more processed foods. The toppings were fresh, and the bun was like a cloud. Brooklyn sighed. She was tired of being poor, constantly scrapping for her existence without reprieve. When she ate the last french fry, she wrapped up her garbage sadly and went to throw it away.

Her fingertips brushed against paper when she shoved her hands into her pockets. Brooklyn had forgotten about the prescribed reading material and pulled out the list. She scanned the titles and wondered if the public library offered books on such taboo subjects. Father Mathias was right; it would be good to educate herself on what she was getting involved in. So, Brooklyn pulled out her phone and searched the public library's website. None of the suggested books were carried but a general search for BDSM returned some results. Some non-fiction and a couple fiction.

With limited resources, Brooklyn settled on what the library offered and was thankful that the one closest to her had a copy. The walk wasn't far, and she made her way up the perpetually busy street. Once at the library, Brooklyn took a while finding the book. One of the librarians probably could have found it more quickly, but she was too embarrassed to ask for help, considering the subject matter.

She used her library card for the first time to check out a book. Up until then, it had only been used for the free internet and cheap printing. The book's cover boasted all the appropriate dark hues, with a black and white photo of a woman in a blindfold and a crop held across her face. Its synopsis promised education on everything that BDSM encompassed and how to explore it safely. Brooklyn appreciated the self-checkout stations and tucked the book under her sweater as she walked home.

Wasting no time, she pulled it out immediately once she was in her tiny room and skimmed over the introduction. One chapter was dedicated to power dynamics and the different forms they could take. She learned that there were varying degrees of submission and different ways to express it. Some dynamics had people completely handing over power, while others were carefully negotiated as to what could and couldn't be controlled. Father Mathias hadn't specified what kind of dynamic he was offering other than what he called "D/s." Brooklyn read on, only putting the book down to go to the bathroom, and continued to read until her eyes grew heavy. The words blurred together and when she couldn't bring them back into focus, she checked the time. It was 1:00 in the morning.

With a sigh, she closed the book and burrowed under her duvet. She had only a couple chapters left, but she was positive she had read enough to know what questions to ask and to recognize if he was taking advantage of her. There had been a chapter on red flags, and so far, she couldn't identify any other than the already existing power imbalance due to his position. But she felt that maybe in their case, that put the power in her hands. Father Mathias was vulnerable and was opening himself up to a world of potential scandal.

Somehow, Brooklyn felt that this would ensure he would do right by her, so as not to spite her and trigger retaliation.

The alarm went off and Brooklyn silenced her phone with a groan. The library book rested on her chest, face down and open on the last page she had read. She had some time before she had to leave, so she continued reading, being sure to check the time periodically. She put down the book to get ready when it was time to go, pulling out her typical outfit that consisted of yoga pants and a sweater. Once dressed, however, she second guessed her go-to attire.

Brooklyn bit her lip and returned to the milk crates to dig out a black flared skirt with a faded flower print and a fitted black t-shirt. It wasn't great, but the effort could be seen. She found thick tights, prayed they were hole-free, and was relieved to find as she pulled them on that the only run was in the left heel. Time was running out, so she tied her hair up into a quick ponytail then rushed to walk to church.

Again, Father Mathias didn't wait outside for her, and this irked Brooklyn. How many tests would he subject her to until he believed she wanted this? Her annoyance bolstered her, and she went inside with borrowed confidence and marched to the back of the church. As she approached the office door, that borrowed confidence dissipated and nervous excitement took its place. She knocked.

"Come in." His voice had Brooklyn closing her eyes so that she could savor its sound, a sound she was looking forward to hearing more and more. She found him leaning against the end of his desk so that he was facing the door. His arms were crossed and there was a calm about him that hadn't been there during their last couple encounters.

"Good morning," greeted Brooklyn.

"Good morning, child. I appreciate your punctuality. Come in and have a seat."

Brooklyn went to her chair and he took his. They sat in silence. Brooklyn waited patiently, doing her best not to squirm under his observant look.

"I've been doing a lot of thinking," he started.

Brooklyn's heart immediately sank. He was going to back out.

"I was hesitant about continuing down this path we've started. But as I've asked you to fully commit, I must do the same, and I felt it would be important for me to share with you that there is thought and decisiveness behind my choice to show up today and will be in the days that follow."

Brooklyn sighed with relief and nodded. "Thank you. I'm committed too. I took out a book on BDSM from the library. I read most of it yesterday. It's not one of the ones on your list. It was all the library had, and I can't really spend money on books right now." She spoke quickly with the intent to further convince him and possibly further convince herself. Brooklyn was running on instinct and her logical mind was still playing catch-up.

"I'm pleased with your initiative and relieved that you've taken interest in educating yourself."

"I do have questions." Brooklyn laughed self-consciously. "The book answered a lot of them, but it also had me asking way more."

"That's wonderful. What would you like to know?"

"So, I read that D/s dynamics can look different from dynamic to dynamic. What exactly does D/s mean for you?"

Father Mathias smiled, pleased. "That is a great question. I cannot clearly define what our dynamic will look like because it varies depending on the individual one engages with. But typically, my dominance is task-based when it comes to the non-physical. Physically, I have an appetite for pain, specifically inflicting it."

Brooklyn blushed. She hadn't expected such a blunt answer from the priest after all the euphemisms and code-speak. "I also read that we should be negotiating before we get into anything."

"Absolutely."

"So, how do we start?"

"I'd like to set some ground rules. If you object to any, please speak up. See this as... a preliminary negotiation."

Brooklyn nodded.

"They're simple: You must always be honest, I expect you to communicate the good and the bad feelings, and, to instill respect and position, you must be certain to always refer to me as Father. I want to honor the dynamic that was already there while we transition to the dynamic I hope to achieve with you." He raised his eyebrows when she didn't respond.

"Okay."

"I beg your pardon?"

"I mean, yes... Father." Had Father Mathias not been, well, a priest, Brooklyn would have found it an extremely odd title to address someone in this situation.

He smiled. "Very good. And how would you feel about a physical element being included?" It was like he was doing everything but giving her a conspiratorial wink. Father Mathias stood up as he spoke and walked around his desk to lean against it directly in front of her, like he had done before. There was no doubt it afforded him a more assertive position than the seated one behind his desk. Now, he was above Brooklyn, once again forcing her to look up.

There was something deliciously macabre about lying in bed with the beast of her past. She nodded vigorously. Maybe this would be akin to seeing your tormentor in a more human light. A cassock-less, collarless Father Mathias might give her a glimpse of what was underneath the holy armor.

"Good. For future reference, all your responses must be verbal... unless..." he said, his lips tilting devilishly, "for some reason you cannot speak. Understood?"

"Yes, Father," she said, her voice heavy with growing obedience and assertion of his position over her.

He closed his eyes. "Everyone refers to me by that title, but it's been a while since someone has addressed me with such a tone." He leaned over her so that he could look her in the eyes as he spoke. "I can't wait to show you your potential. Especially when you allow me small glimpses of it without even realizing it."

Brooklyn blushed fiercely and licked her suddenly dry lips.

"I will say, I have as much or maybe even more to gain from this than you do. Because soon, as a consequence of the process, the only thing that will concern you is pleasing me. I'm very much looking forward to that." His face betrayed his even tone. They were entering the rabbit hole and that was a scary place to be. Brooklyn could imagine the war waging within him—torn between staying true to his desire to help her and taking all he could from the situation. He was a priest, but he was also human. At least that's what Brooklyn was hoping to confirm.

She needed to look away, but Brooklyn was trapped in his gaze, seduced by his promise of her complete submission and in awe of his confidence that remained even in the face of his evident ethical turmoil. So instead, she whispered, "Yes, Father." Each time she uttered those words, she felt like she was sinking further and further into his promised world.

Father Mathias groaned and grabbed her face with one hand. He searched her eyes. "You stir up a painful appetite within me, child. But it shall wait until a more appropriate time." He let her go and she fell forward; how eager she was that she was leaning into his almost too tight grip.

He cleared his throat. "Whenever you are within the walls of this church, you must obey every instruction I give without question. However, if at any time something doesn't feel right, I do expect you to tell me. No matter what it may be. Of course, it will all be within the parameters of what we agree on." He paused, waiting for her agreement.

"Yes, Father."

"Good. Go and pray, child. I'll see you tomorrow morning at five." And with that, he left his office, cutting their meeting short.

She felt almost... high. And it was better than any drug she had taken. So much so that it trumped any disappointment she felt over the short meeting. Brooklyn left in a daze, forgetting to light a candle and pray once again. As she walked home, she touched her cheek where she could still feel the priest's hand and recalled the delicious discomfort of his tight grasp. A sudden heat came over her and Brooklyn felt silly about getting so worked up over him just grabbing her by the face.

Her phone buzzed and Page's caller ID popped up on the screen. Just seeing her face drained Brooklyn, and she was suddenly reminded of what may have happened on Sunday. She hesitated before answering her friend's call.

"Hey, isn't it too early for you to be up?" Brooklyn said. Page's sleep schedule was closer to that of a vampire than a human.

"Well, I wanted to see what you were up to today because I *was* supposed to go the spa with Sofia. You remember her, right? You know, the one who thinks she's better than everyone because she owns her own clothing line?

A hideous one, if you ask me. Anyway, she totally blew me off which is no surprise because she's a flaky bitch. So, I figured..."

"Page?"

"What?"

"Not today. I'm tired." And she was. Going from the high that Father Mathias had given her to this sudden low when Page called left her feeling out of sorts.

"Okay. Wow. Well before you cut me off, I was going to say fuck Sofia, I should go with my BFF. But now you're just blowing me off. Just like her. Nice."

Brooklyn took a deep breath and blew the air out through pursed lips.

"I'm sorry?" Page said, clearly irritated. "Did you just sigh, like you're annoyed? I didn't realize I was such a burden. And here I am thinking I'm doing something nice for my friend."

Guilt. Lots of it. Brooklyn closed her eyes and ground her teeth. "Page, I really am tired. It has nothing to do with you. I'm just not in the mood to go anywhere right now."

"Ha! I can tell you're not at home. Why are you lying?"

"Oh my God! I'm on my way home! That's why I'm tired. I had an early morning."

Page was silent for a moment. "It's not like I'm asking you to go dancing or something. The spa is relaxing. If you don't want to hang out with me, just say so."

"That's not it." Brooklyn held the phone away from her face so Page couldn't hear her sighing again. "You know what, I'm sorry. Thank you for thinking of me, I'd love to go to the spa with you."

"Awesome! Meet me at my place in an hour." And she hung up.

Brooklyn didn't need to ask where they were going. Page, as erratic as she could be, was habitual when it came to things like where she pampered herself and where she shopped. It explained the early morning call; the spa was a bit of a drive to get to. There was still ample time, so Brooklyn skipped taking the bus that would connect her with the one that would take her to Page's place and walked instead.

Sam was waiting at the curb when she reached Page's condo building like the ever-attached puppy dog.

"I didn't realize you were coming." Brooklyn felt uncomfortable seeing him when she was still suspicious about what had happened the other night.

"I'm just the ride. You know Page hates driving long distances."

Brooklyn nodded curtly then looked up at the building, willing Page to hurry up so that she wasn't alone with Sam for longer than she needed to be. She finally came and, in the end, Brooklyn was grateful for Sam's presence because Page spoke to him the entire drive.

The spa catered to all classes of people with their multi-tiered packages and services, but Brooklyn always managed to feel out of place when she went there. Still, there was no denying how happy she was once she was on a massage table or in the sauna. Even in Page's presence.

When they arrived, Page rushed Brooklyn into the changing rooms that boasted dark wood lockers and an attendant that looked as if she had eaten something sour. Page was already swathed in an over-sized robe with her hair pinned up and face scrubbed clean of any makeup when Brooklyn emerged from the changing stall. Page looked a little less divine and more human, but still so beautiful that Brooklyn found it unfair.

"So, what's going on with you?" asked Page once they were stretched out on massage tables.

"What do you mean?"

"I dunno, you just seem... different."

"Different how?"

"Ugh, like how you were talking to me on the phone."

"Can we just relax, Page?" Brooklyn really didn't like the idea of having this conversation in front of the aestheticians that had begun exfoliating their arms and backs.

Page didn't respond but Brooklyn could feel that she wanted to say something. "Are you being weird about the other night?" she blurted after a lengthy silence.

Brooklyn tensed up. "Please, let's not talk about it."

"Fine. I just don't want things to be weird, you know? Like, you're my only real friend. And I don't want to lose that."

Brooklyn desperately wanted to ask about what had happened to confirm her suspicions. Not knowing was torture, but she wasn't sure that knowing would feel any better. With everything Page said, those suspicions seemed more and more likely. An awkward silence hung heavily in the air and Brooklyn wished she could sink into the table and through the floor.

"I booked mani-pedis too. I know we just got our nails done, but there's nothing wrong with switching things up. I was thinking of something different, like orange, but burnt orange. Perfect for fall, don't you think?"

This is unbearable, thought Brooklyn. Whenever Page reduced the conversation to something like what color she wanted to paint her nails, Brooklyn knew she was feeling guilty about something. Page hated small talk.

"Did you actually plan to come here with Sofia?" asked Brooklyn. This spa visit was starting to feel more like yet another attempted apology.

"What are you talking about?"

"You heard me." Brooklyn sat up and faced her friend.

"Why does it matter? You're here, enjoying a spa day you couldn't afford without me. Why do you always have to throw my gifts back in my face?"

"You know what, I need to go. I forgot I got called in for a shift," Brooklyn lied. She climbed off the massage table then turned to Page before leaving. "And maybe it's because *you* always throw your gifts in my face," she whispered as she hastily threw on her robe. She fled, not ready to face the possibility—no, fact—that she had slept with both Page and her boyfriend. Her eyes stung as she made her way to the showers. As she stood under the impossibly decadent stream of water, Brooklyn tried to summon the feeling she had when she left the church. That grounding, yet simultaneously floating feeling.

She closed her eyes and thought of her time with the priest, in disbelief over just how much he made her blood run hotter than she could stand, when he spoke to her in *that* tone. The increasing longing for him left her body so sensitive and receptive to her fantasy that even the water felt sensual on her skin. She pictured Father Mathias's hands running up and down her body while whispering his forbidden promises. She imagined them wiping away everyone else's touch and replacing them with his own. Her hands mimicked her fantasy and worked their way up to her face where she squeezed. The feeling instantly brought her back to that moment when the priest had grabbed her, and she let out an involuntary soft whisper of a moan.

"Brooklyn!" came Page's shrill voice.

Brooklyn's eyes snapped open; she stood still and waited.

"I know you're in here."

"What do you want, Page?"

"To talk."

"Not now. Please, I'm begging you, for once, let me be when I ask for it. I shouldn't have come." Brooklyn held her breath as she waited.

"Fine," came Page's mumble after a few seconds of silence.

Letting out a sigh of relief, Brooklyn rushed to wash away the rest of the body scrub, then peeked out into the change room to make sure Page had, in fact, left. The coast was clear, and she left in such a haste that she didn't realize she had put her shirt on inside out. She knew Page wouldn't give up a day at the spa, so Brooklyn called Sam and all but begged him to drive her home.

"Is everything okay?" he asked when she got into the car.

He must know what all of this is about. "Mhmm."

He pulled away and the most awkward silence fell between them. Brooklyn even pretended to fall asleep so as not to feel obligated to talk.

"Brook?" Sam shook her with a gentle touch on her shoulder.

In her pretending, Brooklyn had managed to actually fall asleep. She woke up with a start and pulled away from him.

"Sorry, I didn't mean to scare you."

"No, it's fine." She looked around to gather her bearings and found that they had arrived at the park up the street from her place. "Thank you for driving me. I'm sorry for making you do an extra trip."

"Don't worry about it. Oh! Before you go." Sam reached out to stop Brooklyn as she was getting out of the car.

"Don't touch me, okay!"

He quickly withdrew his hand. "What the fuck is wrong with you?"

Was he not there or had he been as fucked up as I was?

Sam shook his head, annoyed. "Look, I was just gonna say to go easy on Page. She's been real cut up about whatever's going on between the two of you."

Brooklyn didn't know what to say to that, so she left without saying anything.

8

When Brooklyn arrived at St. Anthony's the next day, she found Father Mathias standing at the lectern. She slowly walked down the aisle. Her eyes darted from his body to his eyes, to anywhere but him, then back to him. She stopped when she reached the end and waited with her hands clasped in front of her. He closed what looked like a notebook.

"You're early," he noted, pleased.

Brooklyn blushed, assuming he must know the reason behind her punctuality: She had been eager to see him and for the opportunity to feel the heat of his touch again.

"I only live a few blocks away."

Her attempt to downplay her eagerness didn't escape the priest's notice. An uncomfortable silence ensued, and Brooklyn found herself struggling to find a place to land her eyes on once again. She eventually settled on the lectern and waited. Somewhere, a clock ticked, and her heartbeat grew louder in her ears. She fidgeted and wondered if she should say something or if he expected her to wait.

"What is your greatest fear, child?"

Brooklyn peered up at Father Mathias, stunned by the sudden sound of his voice breaking the church's pious silence. "That I have no place in this world, Father," she answered quickly, speaking the first thing that came to mind. Her own words surprised her. Had she stopped to think about it, she would have said her mother, but in her uncensored state, she admitted something deeper than the fear of her childhood tyrant. And that was what her mother had incessantly reiterated throughout Brooklyn's youth—that she was all sorts of wrong and had no business existing.

Father Mathias tilted his head to the side. A mixture of emotion danced across his face. There was sadness, surprise, and... hurt? "If only you knew how wrong you are." He stepped down from the lectern and went to Brooklyn. Reaching out with both hands, he cupped her face between them with a sad smile. "It pains me that a creature as perfect as you could think such a thing."

"I'm not perfect." Brooklyn thought of everything she had done and of everything she would most likely continue to do.

"I'm hoping our time together will show you otherwise." He cleared his throat and let his hands drop away from her face. "Let's go to my office."

Brooklyn followed Father Mathias down the short hallway that never seemed to be lit, then into his office. He gently closed the door behind her.

"We need to talk about your limits," he said once they were seated.

"My limits?" Brooklyn knew what he was referring to; there had been a chapter in the book about that too. She just wanted to make sure that his idea matched her learned definition of the word.

"Yes, things that you enjoy, things that you are willing to try or have tried and disliked, things that you aren't willing to try, and so on."

"I was wondering about that. I did read about limits and negotiations in the book and I understand the importance of making sure no lines are crossed. But isn't the point of this—me doing what you tell me to do—no questions asked?"

"Far from it, child. This is about so much more than that. Yes, I aim to get you to a place where you'll want nothing more than to please me, but your well-being and growth is more important than that, and furthermore, that's the actual point. Or have you forgotten? Even so, it is the foundation of your ability to serve me well. And forcing you to do things that make you miserable would be counterproductive."

"Oh."

Father Mathias pulled out sheets of paper that were stapled together and slid them across to her. "I want you to look over that tonight. It's a list of potential activities that may or may not interest you."

Brooklyn skimmed the first page and blushed when she read some of the acts.

"A lot of those things aren't quite relevant, but I still think it prudent to find out exactly where we stand."

"Yes, Father."

"Now, I wanted to speak to you about yesterday. You chose to disobey me and didn't pray before leaving."

Brooklyn opened her mouth to say something but changed course. "I didn't. Father," she eventually said, opting to forgo excuses. Instinct told her that they wouldn't be appreciated.

"Why didn't you?"

"I was... distracted." Her cheeks reddened at the memory of his hand grabbing her face.

"By?"

She looked away. "You," she whispered.

When he said nothing, she looked back and his eyebrows raised slowly with curiosity. "What exactly about me had you so distracted?"

Brooklyn didn't want to explain how affected she was by such a seemingly small act. It was embarrassing. But Father Mathias wasn't going to let it go.

"Well?"

"When you grabbed my face," she finally admitted. Speaking it pulled her right back into that moment and another one of those small, almost imperceptible whispered moans escaped her lips. Her eyes closed involuntarily as her mind gave in to the flashback, wanting to sink into the moment and relive it as vividly as possible. It lasted only for a few seconds, and when Brooklyn opened her eyes and met his, the festering need in her belly roared. Her skin felt tight, aching for his touch, and she wondered when he would satisfy her hunger next and if it would be enough.

"Come with me." Father Mathias's voice was low and held some sort of promise. Of what, Brooklyn couldn't be sure. He led her back to the nave and upstairs to the small balcony where the choir sang. It was wide enough for two rows and wrapped around towards the front of the nave. The undisturbed dust on the floor suggested that no choir had sung there in decades.

"When rules are broken or a task is failed, there will be punishment." The priest's voice was heavy with his own need.

"What do you mean?" Fear crawled up Brooklyn's back and she began to tremble.

"Shh, you are safe." Father Mathias pressed a palm against her chest and looked into her eyes. "You're safe, child," he repeated.

"I won't be left alone?" She could feel Father Mathias's pause.

"What did they do?"

Brooklyn pulled away. "I said I don't want to talk about the past."

The priest pulled her back to him gently by the waist. "Then we will focus on the present."

Brooklyn nodded.

"And I will not leave you alone."

There was such a deep commitment in his voice that it made Brooklyn want to cry. A single sob made it through.

"Will you accept your punishment?"

"Yes, Father."

"Good." He turned her to face the front of the nave and bent her over the railing. "Look straight forward, and do not look back."

"Yes, Father." She concentrated on the immense crucifix. From that vantage point, she could make out details she hadn't noticed before. Like how Jesus's eyes stared straight forward and not upwards, like in most depictions of him on the cross. It was as if he was looking directly at her.

She squirmed with both anticipation and nervousness when she felt the priest lifting her skirt. He gathered the material neatly around her waist and pulled her tights down to her knees, but not once did his hand make contact with her skin.

"Do not move."

She stood still. Her stillness in the silence were like a breath being held.

The spank echoed through the church and she cried out in surprise, expelling that imaginary breath. He hit her again before she could say anything. Brooklyn tried to move but the hand on her waist held her firmly in place. She wanted to look back and object, but he had asked her if she would accept her punishment and she had said yes.

"Will you do as I say from now on?"

Brooklyn felt humiliated and Jesus's suffering eyes caught her attention again. She cried out louder when the hits grew harder and faster.

"Answer me!"

"Please!" she begged.

He stopped and forced her to look at him by pulling on her hair. "Do you want me to stop?"

To her surprise, she shook her head. "No, Father," she whispered. Her face was flushed as she panted, her eyes wide and bright with confused excitement.

"Do you understand what you must do from now on?"

"Yes, Father!" she gasped when he gave her hair another tug.

"Look forward, then. And try to be silent," he growled.

Brooklyn pressed her lips together as tightly as she could to keep from crying out. Of course, with her upbringing, she had been spanked before, but not like this. This was different and she couldn't identify what about it made it so. The prickling sensation grew with each hit until it became uncomfortable and hot. When she was certain she could take no more and was about to beg him to stop, he stopped and pulled up her tights and rearranged her skirt.

"Stand up."

She stood and turned to face him.

"I did not say to turn."

Brooklyn turned back around and waited for his next words. He removed her hair tie that was now holding onto mere strands and brushed her hair back with his fingers. Gently, he re-tied her hair into a low ponytail.

"You may turn now."

Brooklyn turned slowly and kept her eyes downcast.

"I will walk you downstairs and stay nearby as you pray." The priest kept his promise to not leave her alone and guided her back to the stairs, towards rows of candles waiting to be lit by St. Anthony's faithful parishioners.

Brooklyn felt self-conscious as he watched her strike a match and light a candle. "I'll be okay," she said to the priest.

Father Mathias nodded and went to give her a quick kiss on the forehead. "Well done today, child."

Brooklyn waited for him to leave before awkwardly dropping to her knees and bowing her head in prayer. She clasped her hands tightly and tried to concentrate, certain that the priest would know if she faked her prayer, but flashbacks from her past assaulted her.

"This isn't the same," she whispered over and over again. But she could hear her child-self reciting Hail Mary for the hundredth time while kneeling on rice; she could feel her mother's foreboding presence looming over her.

One song for the righteous. Two songs for the honest. Three songs for the wicked. And no songs for the choir. Brooklyn fell back onto her mantra but there was no use. The church still closed in on her. She couldn't bear it and decided punishment would be worth her escaping the horrible feeling, so she fled.

Once outside, she pressed her hands against her chest and gasped for air as she looked back at the door. It slowly swung shut with a creek. Brooklyn couldn't help but feel the door was purposefully nonchalant, as if it was alive and mocking her fear of something clearly harmless. *It's just a building!* She scolded herself for personifying the church and tried to push away the images of creeping shadows inching towards her while trapped in a church's basement. That was in the past and St. Anthony's was different, at least with Father Mathias around.

The thought of not going back crossed her mind again, but as much as she hated and feared the church, she needed to see Father Mathias again. So, she made her way home, determined to shake off the negative feelings lurking from her past. Thankfully, it didn't take much effort and they evaporated with ease. As she walked, the sensation of her uncomfortably warm bottom had her focusing on her visit with the priest. Brooklyn marveled at the image they must have made: a stern priest punishing a degenerate young woman on the balcony of a small historical church. She smirked and her cheeks grew warm, mimicking her bottom. If she was honest, it excited her in more ways than she cared to admit.

His voice echoed in her mind, and she imagined what it would have been like had he touched her intimately, even if it had just been tracing a finger across her skin. Brooklyn wondered why he hadn't touched her. From his well-crafted words, she had understood that there would potentially be some kind of intimacy. Maybe she had misunderstood.

When she got home, she stripped and went straight to her sofa and got under the covers. Brooklyn touched herself the way she wished Father Mathias would have, running her fingertips lightly across her breasts. She closed her eyes and pictured his lips thinned in concentration and his eyebrows furrowed in thought. Slowly she moved her hand down and let her fingers trail along her stomach, over her navel, and past her pelvis until they reached the opening folds of her vulva. Keeping her touch light, she pressed two fingers between her labia and found she was already wet. This surprised her. Sure, Brooklyn was aware of her attraction to the priest and didn't even bother pretending to deny it, but her body's response attested to the depth of that attraction. It was more than just a preoccupation with the taboo and the satisfaction of witnessing a priest doing unholy things; Brooklyn truly wanted him.

Just as she was about to press her fingers deeper into the folds of her labia, her phone rang. With a sigh, she reached for it and saw it was work calling. Brooklyn was tempted to ignore the call, but she couldn't afford to miss a potential shift, so she answered. Her boss needed her for another last-minute shift, meaning she had to abandon her fantasy and get ready.

There was very little enthusiasm as Brooklyn filled the orders for the morning rush. All she could think about was Father Mathias and her sore bottom. She wondered if anyone could tell what had happened by the expression on her face and that only managed to fluster her further.

"Medium, non-fat caramel latte with two and a half pumps of sugar-free hazelnut and a pinch of salt," called out her colleague in a tone that suggested she was repeating herself.

"Sorry. Got it," mumbled Brooklyn. "Non-fat caramel latte for Margot!" she called out once she was done making the ridiculous drink. *Yup, you look just like your order—high maintenance and self-important.* Brooklyn judged, but she wondered what it would be like to have the ability to put so much thought into your morning coffee, or to know what you wanted and exactly how you wanted it.

The next order was simpler. "Medium americano for Stephen!" A tall, unbelievably well put together man approached the counter. *Oh my God, it's that Stephen!*

Stephen. Everyone's *favorite* customer. Considering everyone at the coffee shop was female or gay—save one or two exceptions—it made sense. Stephen was young for someone so successful who seemed to have it all figured out. Such as which haircut suited him best or that he looked better without a beard or mustache despite the facial hair trend that had come back with a vengeance and with strange staying power.

Brooklyn's hand shook as she handed him his order. Like always, he didn't spare her a second glance, but he did leave a tip.

"Oh-ho-ho, you choked," laughed Gregory, the only coworker Brooklyn liked.

"I bet you'd like to choke on him," Brooklyn shot back.

"As if there was any question about it." They high-fived with a giggle and continued on with the frenzy.

The buzz between the baristas shifted now that Stephen was in the cafe and got his drink to stay. Usually, he would take it to go, but there were days when he chose to sit at one of the small, round, piazza-inspired tables. During his uncommon and brief stays, things were dropped more often, orders would get mixed up, and whispered conversations annoyed the other customers. Brooklyn didn't have to interact much with her colleagues to know about their rich-man/poor-girl aspirations. She gagged at the idea of hoping he would one day take notice of one of them and pluck them out of the fray, like some kind of Prince Charming that could see beyond the coffee grinds. But she sure loved looking at him.

Brooklyn wiped down the counter where they put completed orders and tried her best not to stare. This proved incredibly difficult. Stephen's thick black hair begged to be admired and touched.

"Psst, Gregory, how much do you think he spent on that haircut?" asked Brooklyn.

Gregory openly stared at Stephen while deliberating.

"Oh my God, you weirdo, stop staring like that."

"Seventy... six bucks. I only say that because I spend a good fifty on mine. Can you tell?" he said, wagging his eyebrows.

Brooklyn smiled and shook her head. "So weird."

Stephen left, and normalcy resumed in the cafe. Without the eye candy to distract her, Brooklyn's mind returned to its drifting thoughts of her morning with Father Mathias. Her bum prickled from the echoing sting of his hand and the reminder made her blush.

By the time she got home, she was painfully aroused again and dove under her duvet. She reached down to touch herself but was too worked up for anything slow, so she rubbed herself quickly until she came. Having rushed it, the orgasm was unsatisfying, and she regretted her lack of patience.

The rest of the day yawned before her. "Idle hands are the devil's workshop," she said out loud, reiterating the saying her mother would tell her anytime she wasn't occupied with something she deemed productive, like praying. Brooklyn sat up and looked at her room and considered cleaning it, but other than the coffee table, it was spotless.

The sudden light on her phone indicated unseen notifications so she decided to sit back and scroll through social media. This was more mind-numbing than cleaning. She scrolled past a post from Page. Usually, her friend would have called her by now, and Page's silence only gave her fears more reason to toil. Brooklyn clicked on Page's handle and scrolled through her latest posts. When Page wasn't partying, she was at the spa with her other friends, a group of girls just like her, benefiting from their parents' money without a care in the world. Page despised them. Brooklyn was convinced they all hated each other and only tolerated each other's presence for the sake of showing off "Daddy's latest gifts." That was another hint that Page's foiled spa day was a ruse to get Brooklyn out; she couldn't imagine any of those vapid, plastic Barbies giving up a chance to upstage one another.

Brooklyn sighed and clicked off her phone. How was she ever going to face her friend after last weekend? Hugging her phone, she stared at the ceiling while going over potential awkward conversations with Page. Would it be best to face it head-on or agree to pretend that it had never happened?

A knock on the door roused Brooklyn from her thoughts.

With a groan, she got up and went to the door. "Yes?" she said, speaking through it.

"Can I come in?" From the voice, Brooklyn could tell that it was the woman from the room next to hers.

"No."

"Um, okay. I just wanted to ask if you had any extra vodka."

Brooklyn ground her teeth. "I don't."

"But I see you buy it a lot. You must have some. I'll buy it off ya."

Brooklyn wanted to tell her to get lost and to never bother her again, but her housemates had proven they could hold grudges, so being civil was required for peace. "I'm sorry, I'm all out at the moment."

"You sure?"

No, I'm not sure about what I have and don't have in my seven-by-ten piece of paradise. Brooklyn rolled her eyes. "I'm sure."

"What about a couple bucks?"

Brooklyn sighed and opened the door just enough to peek her head through it. "Listen..."

"Barb," the woman supplied her name.

Brooklyn forced a smile. "Barb. I'm just as poor as you. I live off chips and Mr. Noodles..."

"And vodka. I saw you get a lot of vodka."

"You got me!" Brooklyn's voice dripped with sarcasm, and she had to remind herself to reign it in. "And vodka. If I had money right now, I'd spend it on vodka. But I have none. So, no vodka means no money and no money means no vodka." Brooklyn managed another smile in an attempt to lessen the sting in her words.

"Okay. Sorry to be a bother," said Barb, before stumbling back into her room.

Brooklyn took a moment to marvel at how the woman felt safe enough to leave her door ajar the way she did, then she closed her own door and deadbolted it. When she turned to face her apartment, the limits list caught her attention. *Maybe I should get started on that.*

The list was in alphabetical order and started with a myriad of anal-related activities. When she got to the bottom of the first page, Brooklyn felt it would be a good idea to fill it out as she read because the list was extensive. To the right of the activities were bubbles she could color in that corresponded with answers related to her experience and enjoyment of those activities. The nape of her neck prickled with embarrassment over reading some of the acts and over her clear lack of experience. Some things she could have never dreamed up on her own and she wondered about the people who came up with these ideas and tried them for the first time.

When she was done, Brooklyn felt emotionally exhausted from needing to constantly push past her clearly delicate senses. But she was proud and couldn't wait to hand the list back to Father Mathias. Shameful or not, she had been honest and found that she was pretty open-minded, and her emotional exhaustion wasn't just from her shyness, but from her constant state of arousal over imagining doing the things on this list with Father

Mathias. She hoped he would be just as interested in some of the activities as she was.

9

Brooklyn knocked on Father Mathias's office door. Entering the church had gotten progressively easier, but after yesterday's attempt at prayer, she was back to trembling.

"Come in, child," called out Father Mathias.

Once in the priest's office, her unease dissipated. Brooklyn felt a level of calm that she only experienced with Father Mathias. Even in her distressed state the first day she had met him, she had felt it.

"Please, have a seat."

Brooklyn sat and waited expectantly for his next words.

"I see you have the list with you." He nodded towards the papers that she held with a tight grasp.

Brooklyn tried to relax her hands and the papers stuck to her sweaty palms. She handed them over to him and watched his face closely as he looked over the first page, hoping to find signs of mutual interest rather than judgment. She had reminded herself when she was filling them out that he couldn't judge her responses because he himself had given her that list which, in her opinion, was somewhat of an admission on his part.

His expression gave nothing away. But there was something amiss. "Is there something wrong, Father?"

"I should have waited until we finished negotiating before spanking you yesterday. I apologize."

"I was... I *am* okay with what happened yesterday," she said quietly, embarrassed to admit such a thing.

"It wasn't a fair assumption of me to make, but I had assumed." They looked at each other silently, the priest in obvious deliberation. "Bend over across my desk." His command was quiet and Brooklyn instinctively knew it was because he felt he had lost some level of entitlement in his role over her. This only strengthened her trust in him.

Brooklyn moved quickly to exaggerate her eagerness in hopes of reassuring him that she was alright and still wanted to be there. She looked at him with anticipation. Her face was so close to his chest that she could tell he was doing his best to control his rapid breathing from excitement. Father Mathias stood and walked around his desk to stand behind her.

"May I see your bottom?"

"Yes, Father," she answered right away. Brooklyn wore pants this time, and he pulled them and her panties down to her knees in one swift motion.

"How did the spanking make you feel?"

"I don't know. Humiliated, I guess," she mumbled.

He pinched her still tender flesh.

"Father!" she added.

"Yet you say that you're okay with what happened?"

"It wasn't in a bad way. I don't know how or why..." Her voice trailed off when she heard his stifled groan.

"How else did it make you feel?"

"Turned on," she whispered, "Father."

"Hmm. Have you looked at yourself?"

Brooklyn shook her head, but she had rubbed the sore spots throughout the day.

He gently squeezed her bum. "Does it still hurt?"

"A little, Father."

"Whenever you felt the tenderness of your bottom, how did it make you feel?"

Her cheeks turned red when she remembered her day yesterday—having to work in a constant state of arousal.

"Answer quickly."

"It reminded me of you and made me very wet." She hid her face between her forearms, pressing her forehead against the cool wood of his desk. It struck her then, the irony of her ability to admit anything related to her sexuality to him. A priest.

"Mmm, very good. You have a delightful response to pain, child. As I'd suspected."

What exactly, Brooklyn wondered, were the tells of how someone would respond to pain? She thought back to the moment he had landed the first spank. It hadn't been a welcome sensation. So why had she been alright with it happening and with the prospect of it happening again?

"Are you going to spank me again today, Father?" she whispered.

"Is that what you want?"

"I said I was okay with it, Father," she said meekly.

"Is that... what... you want?" he repeated.

Brooklyn pressed her lips together. She wasn't sure what she wanted.

"Answer the question, child. Do not make me ask you again."

Brooklyn's cheeks burned so hot she could barely feel them. "Yes, Father," she whispered.

"Speak up, child."

"I want you to hurt me!" she blurted. "Please, Father." Her own words surprised her. They had left her lips before she could really deliberate if and why that was what she wanted. However, she was grateful for her impulsive answer because it saved her from the torture of having to truly own up to her decision. Accountability she could willingly deal with later when she was alone, whereas shame always found her one way or another anyway.

Father Mathias pressed his palm against one cheek, then the other, before landing two sharp and quick slaps on each one. They drew out a small whimper from her. He leaned over her, his weight pressing her hips into the edge of the desk, and made her turn her head to the side as he pulled her hair away from her face. With his thumb, he traced her hairline down to her ear before leaning in closer so that she could hear his whispered words.

"Close your eyes, child. What you felt yesterday was but a taste of what you will endure."

She did as she was told but was filled with trepidation. She could hear him move to one end of the room and then felt him near her again. Soft material was pulled over her head, covering it and her face, and something cold and hard was being rubbed against her bottom.

"Are you ready, child?"

"Yes, Father." She wasn't sure if he could hear her whisper, but suddenly the first impact came, and it rang through her body. It wasn't terrible, but it felt different from his bare hand. She received a dozen or so impacts—some light, some a bit heavier. But then he began hitting her with intent and Brooklyn had to bite her lips to keep from crying out too loudly.

He stopped for a moment. "Now, child, if it ever becomes too much for you to bear, you must call out, "Mercy." I will not listen to anything else. You may cry, you may beg... but I will not stop unless you say that word. However, it is not one to be used lightly. Do you understand?"

"Yes, Father," she said between ragged breaths. She knew this was their safe-word; she had read about it in the library book and understood the gravity of it.

The onslaught began again. The implement bit at her skin and he barely gave her time to recover between impacts. All Brooklyn could focus on was bearing the pain. It stung but carried weight, until the sharp feeling dissipated and was replaced by a dull ache that burrowed deep into the muscle. Closing her eyes, she tested her will with each hit, daring herself to take one more. She sagged against the desk, surrendering to the sensations and giving in to her need to cry out. Now that she knew her cries wouldn't stop him, they came more freely. And when she thought that he was tiring, the impacts only grew harder. She tried to move away, but then the hits came from the direction she was moving in, forcing her back to her original spot on the desk.

Her brain buzzed with sensory overload and her will to hold on slipped away at an exponential speed. That was when Father Mathias stopped, as if he could read her mind. Brooklyn flinched when his hand met her screaming skin, and it took a moment for her to realize the touch was gentle.

"Spread your legs," he commanded.

She did. And waited. An almost nonexistent draft revealed to her what he must be seeing: her wetness coating her labia and upper, inner thighs. Heart racing, she went to close her legs, but a sharp command instructed her to stay still. *I'm sorry,* she wanted to say out loud, but she kept her lips firmly pressed together. She couldn't imagine him, a man of God, approving of such a carnal response. Shame burned her so fiercely she thought she might throw up.

Silence ensued and Brooklyn wanted to beg him to let her pull up her pants. Instead of a plea, a deep guttural moan came out when she felt a single finger run between her lips. *Finally,* she thought as she pressed into his touch to show her willingness for the contact, but the pleasure was short lived.

"Stand up and turn around."

She wanted to protest—beg him to touch her again—but she silently obeyed. He pulled off the hood and the light blinded her momentarily. He held up his finger. When her vision adjusted to the office's soft lighting, she saw it was glistening with her wetness.

"Each day you surprise me, child. This"—he brought his finger to her lips and coated them with her own juices—"pleases me more than you could imagine."

She tasted herself and another small moan escaped from her lips. Time slowed and she basked in his affirmation and the feel of his finger, slick with her wetness, against her mouth.

Father Mathias pulled his hand away and went to sit behind his desk. "Pull up your pants and come sit with me."

It took Brooklyn a few seconds to process what he had said. Once his command sank in, she pulled up her pants and scurried over to him, eagerly sitting on his lap. The material from her jeans felt rough against her tender skin, but she ignored it, choosing to focus on the feeling of having his arms around her. Even though everything about it was wrong, nothing could have felt more right to Brooklyn.

Father Mathias pulled her closer and made her rest her head on his shoulder. She quickly became drunk off his scent, one that, not long ago, triggered horrible anxiety attacks.

"'So, husbands ought also to love their own wives as their own bodies. He who loves his own wife loves himself; for no one ever hated his own flesh, but nourishes and cherishes it, just as Christ also does the church.' Ephesians chapter five, verses twenty-eight and twenty-nine," he said as he played with her hair and massaged her shoulder. "Although it speaks of husbands and wives, it is very much applicable to masters and their servants. In all that we do, in all that I do to you, never forget that I cherish you. I am at the mercy of your perfection, my child."

"Yes, Father."

They sat that way for a short while as he played with her hair, lulling her into a deep state of bliss.

"How are you feeling?"

"Really good." Brooklyn all but hummed her response.

"You did so well, child."

"Thank you, Father."

Father Mathias made her sit up and Brooklyn reluctantly opened her eyes.

"Thank you for today and I will be sure to review your responses to the list. May I assign you a task?"

Brooklyn nodded. "Yes, Father."

"I want you to buy a journal, and for your first entry, write about one thing you'd like to change in your life. Although I'd prefer if you do, you won't have to share what you write. I'd also like for you to journal about today's experience. This I will need you to share as it will help me learn what works for you and what doesn't."

Before Brooklyn could protest the required purchase, Father Mathias reached into his desk's drawer and pulled out an envelope. He nodded for her to open it after handing it to her.

"I want you to buy a journal you'll enjoy writing in."

The envelope held five twenty-dollar bills.

"You have until the end of the week to complete your task. Now go and pray, and I look forward to seeing you tomorrow."

"Father?"

"Yes, child?"

"I didn't pray properly yesterday, and I don't think I can do it. It brings back too many... *memories*." Brooklyn whispered the last word.

Father Mathias checked the time.

"Maybe it's time you tell me about what haunts you?"

Brooklyn buried her face in his neck and shook her head. "Please don't make me. I can't."

Father Mathias held her away from him so that he could look her in her eyes. "You do not have to speak of it until you're ready. I will leave that up to you to decide when that is. Until then, you do not have to pray if it causes you too much distress. I realize now it may have been too much to ask of you. For that, I apologize. It was insensitive of me."

"Really?"

"Child, as I had said, I am not here to demand only what I want. I'm here to help you blossom into the woman you were meant to be."

Brooklyn thought for a moment, still unable accept his words. She tried to search for an angle, struggling to imagine him being so selfless, so unentitled, when he had asserted himself as her superior. But there was no angle, at least not one that she could see. "Thank you, Father."

He nodded. "And it's a perfect example of a limit," he said with a smile, tapping the small stack of papers. "I'll see you tomorrow. No prayers necessary."

Brooklyn stood on unsteady legs with a shy smile. She left slowly, reluctant to leave. He had been so gentle with how he held her. It surprised Brooklyn. She didn't think him capable of such tenderness, or of her ability to feel enough comfort to relax into his embrace the way she had. She walked through the church slowly, too high on endorphins to care about where she was. Then a strange feeling bubbled up inside her.

Strength.

Having endured what she just had, Brooklyn felt special. *Invincible.*

Stepping out of the building, sunlight pulled her out of her subdued state. *No,* she thought. *Peace.* That's what it was. She had found peace both in those moments bent over his desk and when being held in his arms. She had found peace in the pain. Maybe Father Mathias knew what he was talking about and wasn't simply waxing poetic for the sake of manipulating her.

The ritual she had become accustomed to of half-hearted contemplation over whether she should go back didn't happen. She already knew that not returning was no longer an option; that she would go back whether her pride wanted her to or not. That game of *should I or shouldn't I?* was long over. If Brooklyn was honest with herself, it had never even started in the first place.

Unlike yesterday, she was interested in seeing what the priest's impacts had done to her skin. She rushed home and wasted no time in pulling down her pants and inspecting her backside in the warped mirror that hung on the door to her room. The sight startled her. Angry, wide, red welts littered her skin and looked grotesque to her inexperienced eyes. It was shocking to think she had endured something that did *that* to her flesh. Brooklyn ran her fingers over the hard welts. They felt warm to the touch. Her skin tingled and then quickly grew itchy, but scratching wasn't an option. Not with such tender skin. She rubbed her bottom and winced—even *that* hurt. The itch eventually subsided, replaced by an ache.

Pulling up her pants, Brooklyn's newfound confidence about this situation was replaced with a familiar uncertainty. How could something

good look like that? The unsure thoughts drifted from the marks to Father
Mathias. Was he actually good?

Brooklyn was less enthusiastic about her new task, but she made her way
to a bookstore in the afternoon and went to the stationary section where
a wall-to-wall display boasted beautifully bound journals. The options were
overwhelming. Usually, the only factor in her purchase making was price,
but now she had an envelope with one-hundred dollars dedicated to this
one item purchase. A journal with a lavender cover caught her eye. "Joy.
Happiness. Peace." had been embossed into the leather-like material in silver
foil.

She ran her fingertips across the words before picking it up. It was heavy
with its pages of luxurious stock paper. Flipping it over, she found it was
forty-five dollars. She bit her lip. Father Mathias hadn't said what she should
do with the change. The section also had pretty office materials and she
found a beautiful pen in the same lavender color as the journal. A store
promotion meant Brooklyn still walked out with just under twenty dollars
in change. She decided to keep it in the envelope and return it to the priest.

Mild fall days would be gone soon, so she opted to go to a park to finish
her journaling task. She sat against a tree and rested the journal on her knees.
Brooklyn took a moment to enjoy the beauty of the book and the fact that
it was hers. She also took the time to enjoy the weight of her new pen after
pulling it out of its plastic pouch. Unlike the things that Page purchased for
her, Brooklyn was able to take ownership of these new items because she
knew they wouldn't be held against her, and she was grateful for it.

When she opened the journal, the first page waited expectantly for her
thoughts. Brooklyn bit her lip as she weighed Father Mathias's prompt:
What was one thing she wanted to change in her life? She had to consciously
remind herself that this didn't have to be shared. But as she deliberated that
one thing to change, she realized the truth was hard to write even if it was for
her eyes only. She wrote "Dear," then stopped, unsure who to address it to.
"Dear Diary" seemed juvenile. Brooklyn settled on "Dear Father Mathias."

Dear Father Mathias,

I want to change my sadness. I'm always sad. Even when I smile, on the inside I feel so much pain. Constant pain. And I'm scared I'll always feel it and will never be able to escape it.

Brooklyn choked on an unexpected sob. Seeing the thought in black ink on cream paper and out in the real world was too much reality to face.

I'm afraid there's no hope for me because of my past.

Closing the journal, she decided that was enough. Brooklyn took a moment to push away the unwanted feelings by closing her eyes and taking slow, even breaths. This was when she would normally reach for her vodka, but she still had the rest of her task to finish. She reopened the book and flipped a couple pages past the one she had written in an attempt to put some kind of distance between herself and her truth.

Dear Father Mathias,

I enjoyed our time together. It was nice to be able to focus on the pain outside and not the one on the inside. I felt safe.

Brooklyn bit her lip and contemplated writing the next thought that came to mind. This was meant to be honest.

I wish you would have touched me more.

She wrote it vaguely. Touch in their situation could mean many things.

I'm eager to continue exploring with you and am open to trying more. My only negative feeling towards what happened is about the marks. I was shocked when I saw myself and have a hard time thinking something like that can be good.

She felt she should write more but she didn't know what to say. Brooklyn wasn't the best with words or feelings. It would have to be enough, she decided.

10

The following morning, Brooklyn found Father Mathias sitting in the middle of his office with a small basin of water by his feet. She hesitated at the door.

"Good morning, child," he greeted. His warm, welcoming tone made her feel guilty about her growing doubts about him and what they were doing.

"Good morning, Father."

"How is your bottom feeling?"

"It hurts, Father," she replied, trying to keep her voice even. She wasn't ready to let on that she was questioning what they were doing. At least, not yet.

"Come here and kneel by my feet."

Brooklyn tucked a strand of hair behind her ear and shyly went to him.

He took her small backpack and placed it on the floor next to his chair. "Take off my shoes and socks."

Brooklyn hit a mental block. She wanted to wait to talk to him about yesterday, but obeying him wasn't coming so easily today, and instead of her eagerness, she felt reluctance.

"Child?"

Brooklyn couldn't bring herself to admit this to him, so she complied. Her hands trembled and she fumbled with the laces of his polished shoes. When she was done, she placed them neatly off to the side and waited with her hands folded in her lap and her eyes downcast, unwittingly presenting the perfect image of submission.

Silence ensued. Brooklyn wanted to peek up at Father Mathias but couldn't bring herself to. She could only picture him looking down at her with that *look* on his face as he contemplated his next words. He still didn't speak, or move, and Brooklyn began to pick at her nails, wishing he would say something.

"One of the most commending works of Jesus was the washing of feet," he started, speaking as if giving a lecture. "He'd wash the feet of the outcasts—those shunned by their community for their sins and shortcomings. The feet are special because they are the lowest part of the body and considered the most dirty." He leaned down and cupped Brooklyn's chin, making her look up at him. "But the lesson Jesus taught us was that even as the Son of God, he was still humble enough to perform this act of service for even the lowest human. I've told you: You are a divine creation of God. You are absolute perfection. You are a gift to this depraved world. Now, I want you to wash my feet." His grip tightened slightly with each word.

"Yes, Father."

He released her and sat back, watching her intently and making her feel even more self-conscious than she already had been. Brooklyn pulled the basin closer so he could put his feet in. Her hands shook more than ever, and it took extra effort to concentrate on her task.

"What is it?" he asked when he saw her hesitate.

"Your pants will get wet, can I roll them up, Father?"

"You may." The smile in his voice helped her relax a little, and she continued her task with steadier hands.

She washed his feet with care. Despite the seed of reluctance fueled by uncertainty taking root, the switch had already been flipped inside her days ago. She quickly gave into her involuntary will to serve him, slipping into that place where the only thing that mattered was showing up to the moment the best way she could. It wasn't long until the faint smell of soap and the soft swishing sound of water further lulled her into that subdued state she had found the previous day. When she finished, she removed the basin of water and dried his feet, then rolled his pant legs back down and put his socks and shoes on.

"Stand up, child." The priest stood up as well and helped her to her feet. "Now sit in my place."

Confused, Brooklyn sat in his place and watched with wonder as he took her vacated position.

"Now listen to me carefully, child. I've told you of your divinity and perfection. But the affirmation of your status comes from serving those of us worthy to receive the gifts God has bestowed upon you. I am below you because *you* are perfection. But I am above you because *I* allow that perfection to come to fruition. Do you understand what I'm telling you?"

She thought for a moment. "We need each other?"

He nodded. "You are child because I am Father. I am Father because you are child. Those titles hold no meaning without the other. So now, my child, I will wash *your* feet."

His touch was tender and made Brooklyn wonder if there was more to this than just the roles they played. He removed her once-white canvass shoes and her ankle socks, then pulled the legs of her jeans up to her calves before bringing back the basin of water. She watched his face, filled with reverence and adoration. She felt it in every touch.

He spoke as he worked. "'For who is greater, the one who reclines at the table or the one who serves? Is it not the one who reclines at the table? But I am among you as the one who serves.' Luke chapter twenty-two, verse twenty-seven. So, you see, my child, you have come to us to serve, just as the Son of God had. You are divine. You are divine."

Tears streamed down Brooklyn's cheeks before she realized she was even crying. What Father Mathias described was beautiful and she desperately wanted to be a part of it. To experience the surefire trust of being fulfilled by fulfilling. Something like that could never leave you feeling empty or drained. Brooklyn wanted it so much, her chest tightened.

He dried her feet, fixed the legs of her jeans, and put her socks and shoes back on.

She looked up at him through hazy eyes as he stood. "Thank you, Father."

"You are more than welcome, my child. Now go bend over my desk."

Brooklyn's eyes widened with fear. She couldn't imagine receiving even the lightest spanks on her sore bum. Just kneeling had been painful.

Father Mathias's laugh surprised her. "Do not look so frightened. I will not spank or paddle you until you've healed."

"Yes, Father," she said with relief. She went to bend over his desk and waited, instinctively knowing she should look straight and not look back without him telling her to.

He approached her and pulled down her pants and panties with care. Brooklyn held her breath. Would he feel the same way she did about the marks? Would he find them ugly? The indescribable sound that came from him when he saw her bottom lit a fire in her belly and was void of disgust. In fact, it was the exact opposite.

"Have you looked at yourself this time?"

"Yes, Father."

"And? What do you think?"

"I think..." She stopped herself. How could she say that she found what he'd done to her ugly? Or that it had tainted her sentiment towards him in those moments when she saw what he had done?

"Speak, child."

"I... I didn't like the way it looked, Father," she said slowly, her head hung low.

"Why do you speak with such shame?"

"Because of the way it made me feel about you."

Father Mathias was quiet, and she knew he wanted her to elaborate.

"I was disturbed by it." She felt the warmth of his palm against her skin.

"But you enjoyed the pain?"

"I did, Father."

"Well, we can explore other methods that won't leave marks."

"What do you think of them?" Brooklyn asked. She wanted to understand the appeal of seeing her ravaged skin.

"Come."

They walked over to the corner of his office, her pants still around her knees, where he had a mirror.

He turned her around and motioned for her to look. Her backside's appearance didn't shock her as much this time since it wasn't a completely new sight. It also helped that the marks had faded quite a bit. The welts were completely gone and had left soft hues of magenta in their wake.

"I imagine yesterday they were a bit brighter. I didn't hit you hard enough for anything to be too lasting."

She ran her fingers across her bottom and her skin tingled in response. The memory of the darkness of the hood and the feeling of wood rubbing against her bottom flooded her mind. As did the pride from when he had told her she had done well.

"What are you thinking, child?"

"They're reminders of what happened."

"And?"

"They're good memories. Just now, I was brought back to those moments and the memory felt so real. And the soreness makes it that much more real." As she spoke, she could see his expression change.

Father Mathias pressed his lips together with a deep hum and grabbed her by the hair. Her heart pounded when he brought his face close to hers. He was going to kiss her, finally. But instead, he buried his face in her neck. Still, she was not disappointed. He squeezed her bottom, and the pain mixed with the tickle and warmth of his breath on her neck made her dizzy with desire.

"You learn so quickly and so beautifully." He took a deep breath and let her go with a grunt. "Pull the chair up to my desk and sit, child."

The frustration came on suddenly and it took blinding willpower for Brooklyn to keep from complaining. She needed his intimate touch so much she felt she'd lose her mind without it.

"I said to go and sit."

Brooklyn did as she was told, bringing her backpack with her. She sat, clasping it so tightly her knuckles turned white. Father Mathias took his seat.

"Did you complete your task?"

Brooklyn silently pulled out her journal and the envelope with the change. Father Mathias took the items and inspected her choice.

"It's beautiful. May I read both entries?"

"Yes, Father."

Without a word, he handed her the envelope back and opened to the first page. Brooklyn wanted to watch his expressions, but she couldn't. Instead, she looked down at her hands and waited.

"I know I didn't write a lot. I found it difficult," she said when she felt he'd had plenty of time to read her few written sentences.

"What you wrote was enough, child. Do you feel the only way to be happy is by dealing with the past?"

Brooklyn nodded.

"What if I told you that the past doesn't have to define you? That it can be painful without determining how you choose to show up in the present?"

"I'd say that's easier said than done, Father."

He smiled sadly. "You're absolutely right, child. Easier said than done, but not impossible."

Brooklyn looked up at him then. *Not impossible.*

"You will find your peace." His conviction almost had Brooklyn believing it would undoubtedly happen. "Did you write the second entry?"

"Yes, it's a few pages over, Father."

Father Mathias skimmed what she had written and smiled. "Is it safe to say we addressed what you wrote here already?"

Brooklyn nodded sheepishly.

"I'm happy with how promptly and how well you completed your task. I have also had the chance to look over the list you filled out. I will respect what you have slated as hard limits and we will discuss any soft ones before we do them. Did you have any questions about anything listed?"

"No, Father. I searched whatever I didn't know."

"Good. I must say, I'm both surprised and pleased at your willingness to try new things. And I look forward to exploring some of those things with you."

"What are *your* interests, Father?" Brooklyn all but whispered the question, embarrassed to ask it.

"That's irrelevant, child." He paused before continuing, "As far as our tasks go, if anything requires a purchase, I will fund it. And again, if anything doesn't feel right, I expect you to tell me."

"Yes, Father."

He tapped the envelope. "And you can keep whatever is left over," he said, referring to the change from her purchase.

Brooklyn looked at the envelope and hesitated.

"Is there something wrong?"

Brooklyn didn't know how to voice whatever it was that made it difficult to take back the money. What she had spent was for him. This... this was a handout.

"See it as a reward for being efficient with your spending," he said, surprising Brooklyn, yet again, with his ability to read her. Sometimes, it felt he could tell what was going on in her mind before she could acknowledge it herself.

Father Mathias pushed the envelope towards Brooklyn. She took it and put it in her backpack. "Thank you, Father."

"That is all for today."

11

Brooklyn was grateful for Page's distance since the spa, but it was the weekend and that annoying itch to go out and get forget-my-name-drunk returned.

"Oh wow, you decided to call *me* for once," Page offered as a greeting.

"What do you mean?"

"Oh, nothing. Just that lately I always seem to be the one reaching out to you. I was starting to wonder whether you still wanted to be my friend."

"You know that's not true." Or was it?

"Okay, good. So, I was literally just about to call you to tell you to come over to my place. You can just borrow something. We're going out to The Rooftop tonight. I'll see you at eight, sharp. Byyyye." Page was like a hurricane; she was in and out before you had any idea what hit you.

Brooklyn held her phone away to look at it in awe over how Page could pelt out commands then hang up with full confidence that they would be obeyed. This only made her cringe because she was about to prove Father Mathias right, again.

Brooklyn chewed on her bottom lip as she rode the bus to her friend's, wondering how to go about asking Page about last Saturday night and what might have happened. Things were decidedly more awkward after Brooklyn freaked out at the spa. There was also the option of just forgetting about it and pretending that she hadn't woken up naked between Page and Sam, or the fact that Page spoke of that night as if something really had happened.

Brooklyn arrived at Page's condo at eight and was immediately pulled to her walk-in closet without even a hello. Page's closet looked like it belonged in a doll's dream house with its rows of dazzling couture and shelves boasting designer shoes. White drawers with dainty gold handles hid accessories, and cabinets with lights displayed shoes, purses, and wallets.

"Try this. It'll totally show off your awesome cleavage," said Page, shoving a garment into Brooklyn's hands.

Before, Brooklyn wouldn't have read much into the comment, or even noticed it. Now, she wondered if there was more behind the things Page said.

She hesitated, gripping the hanger that had been thrust at her. Brooklyn put the dress on a foot stool. "Page?"

"And these shoes. Oh my God, yes! These will look great."

"Page?"

"Aaaaand, hmmm, what about this necklace. The pendant will hang right between..."

"Page!"

"What?!"

"What happened last Saturday?"

"Ugh, talking about things that already happened? How boring."

"Seriously. What. Happened?"

Page's face lit up. "I know what you need. You need something to make you less... uptight. And I might have just the thing." She opened a drawer and clawed at the back of it.

"Please, stop."

Her friend sighed and turned, abandoning her hunt. "We all got really fucked up and horny and had a threesome. 'Kay?"

"Did I..."

"Fuck my boyfriend? Yes. You did." Page went to Brooklyn and coyly reached for her hand with a smile that would rival the Cheshire Cat's. "And it was hot. You were hot. Now, can you get over it?"

Brooklyn felt like she was going to throw up and pulled away from her friend. "How can you be so..."

"Chill about it? Oh my God, how could you be so dramatic? We all had fun. I think you had the most fun." Page sidled up to Brooklyn and pressed herself up against the length of her body. "It was nice getting to know you in more... intimate ways. I knew you'd be the bestest friend I ever had. You never disappoint."

"Page, stop!"

Brooklyn's tone made her friend draw back. "I knew you regretted it," she said with a pout. Her eyes filled with tears and her bottom lip quivered. "I was so happy about it and then when you left in the morning without saying anything... I just knew." Page turned away and hugged herself with her head hung low.

She's actually going to cry? thought Brooklyn in disbelief. Page never cried. Not one tear managed to drop, but it was enough to soften Brooklyn's resolve.

"I don't know what to think, Page. I don't remember anything. That's what bothers me the most."

Page looked at her over her shoulder with hope. "So, it's not that you regret sleeping with me?"

Brooklyn didn't know what to think. She was positive she'd never seen Page this... dare she say *vulnerable* before. "No," she whispered. Her answer was for her friend's sake, and she managed to justify it with the fact that one couldn't regret something they couldn't remember. Of course, had she remembered, she was almost certain she would be drowning in so much regret that she wouldn't have been able to muster the lie to save Page's feelings.

"Great!" Gone were the almost tears. "Here." Page went back to the drawer in which she had been rummaging and pulled something out.

Brooklyn had just made out that it was a small bag with pills when one was shoved into her mouth; she had no time to protest.

"Maybe we'll have a repeat tonight. Now go get dressed."

"Page, I don't want a repeat." Brooklyn spit out the pill into her palm.

"But, I thought, you said..."

"Can't we go out without this?" She held up the partially dissolved pill. "And, I don't know, stick to tequila or something?"

Page took Brooklyn's hand and brought the fingers holding the pill to her lips. "So, a repeat, but without the drugs?" Page's tongue snaked out and she licked at the pill, taking it into her mouth.

Brooklyn felt trapped. She knew about Page's fragile ego when it came to rejection, and never in a million years had she thought she'd be in this situation. "Page..." Her voice trailed off. How was she going to say no without consequence?

Before she could react, Page pulled her closer and kissed her. Brooklyn could feel the grainy texture of the dissolved pill on Page's tongue on her own.

"You'll thank me later. You really are no fun sober," Page said, pulling away. "Go get dressed, Brookie."

Brooklyn had a bad feeling and regretted her choice to call Page, but she picked up the dress and went to the ensuite bathroom to shower and get ready. She pressed her cheek against the glass of the shower stall and tears stung her eyes. "What am I even doing here?"

Whatever Page had given her worked quickly. It didn't hit her as hard as most of the things she'd taken; instead, it left her feeling mellow and relaxed, but not sleepy. It became impossible to feel worried about anything, and Brooklyn gave in to the drug's effects. It was a lot easier than dealing with her shame. She pictured the water washing away the tension as if it was something that coated her skin and continued to sink into the soft euphoric wave.

"There's my BFF!" shouted Page when Brooklyn came out with a smile. "Let's go party!"

Brooklyn twirled, showing off the navy blue Marilyn Monroe-inspired dress.

"Brooklyn? What the fuck happened to your ass?"

"What?"

"Your ass. It looks like..."

"It's nothing! Let's go have fun! I fell," said Brooklyn when her friend made a face.

"Seriously? A fall did *that*? Let me see."

"Now who's being a drag?" That was enough to convince Page to drop it. "Can I have another?"

Page smiled mischievously and pulled out another pill. "We did share the last one."

Brooklyn's reservations were gone at this point, so she didn't argue when Page opted for the same method of administering the drug via a kiss.

"Figured we'd share that one too. It's nice, isn't it? Sam said it's a new cocktail and we're the first to try it."

"It is nice." Brooklyn nodded with a serene grin.

Page pressed her forehead to Brooklyn's and looked at her through her lashes. "You see, I'm good to you, right? I'd hate it if you thought I wasn't when I try my best to give you everything." Page ran the backs of her hands up and down Brooklyn's arms.

"You are a good friend," Brooklyn said with a nod.

"I am, aren't I?"

Brooklyn tried to focus on Page's face, but it was too close for her to manage it. Page went in for another kiss when they were both startled by Sam.

"Well, well, well, what do we have here?" he asked.

Page giggled. "None of your business."

"Shit, are you two already lit?"

"Just a teensy-weensy bit." Brooklyn couldn't feel her lips moving, but the sound of her voice confirmed that she had spoken.

"Well, let's get a move on!" said Sam, ushering them to the front door. "Hopefully this will be another one for the books."

It was like déjà vu. Brooklyn woke up, not knowing where she was, only to find herself in Page's bed between her and her boyfriend.

"No, no, no, no." Brooklyn stumbled out of bed and looked for her phone. She rushed out and went to her place to shower and change, then began walking to church. It was Sunday, but she had to see Father Mathias.

Second Mass was just letting out when she arrived, and she waited across the street until most of the crowd, if it could even be called that, had dispersed. Her early mornings never allowed her to see the church in full swing, and she felt more out of place than ever. St. Anthony's parishioners consisted mostly of elderly couples who had probably grown up in the Glebe and then raised a family of their own in it.

In her haste, Brooklyn hadn't made an effort with her appearance, and she hugged her hoodie tightly around her body as she walked into the church. Father Mathias stood up at the front, speaking to one of the elderly couples, so Brooklyn sat in the last pew and waited. He hadn't even noticed her. When he finally entered the confessional booth, Brooklyn rushed to it before anyone else could.

"I'm so sorry for coming unannounced," she said right away.

"You wear your reckless night out on your face so clearly I can see it through the grate," he said in a cutting tone. And as easily as he claimed to see her recklessness through the grate, she was able to see his disdain with his furrowed eyebrows and thinned lips.

Brooklyn was shocked to feel her eyes stinging with tears. "I'm so sorry, Father."

He sighed deeply. "Go to my office and wait for me there until I'm done here."

"I have to tell you something first. And I need to do it in here."

There was a long pause before he said, "Go on."

"I think... I think I may have done something wrong." Her voice shook with shame. They hadn't spoken about what their arrangement meant for her and seeing other people, but she still felt as if she may have betrayed him.

Father Mathias was silent. "How so?"

"This morning..." She stopped and tried to collect her thoughts. "Remember when I came to you the other morning in a panic? Well... today I woke up in my friend's bed between her and her boyfriend. Again." She stopped to choke back a sob. "I don't remember anything. But I did find out that we did have sex the last time and, and... it may have happened again. Last night. I'm really sorry," sobbed Brooklyn.

"Go to my office."

"Are you upset with me?"

"I said go to my office."

Brooklyn needed to know then and there if everything was going to be alright between them, and that need kept her from moving.

"Is there something else?"

She was silent. She couldn't speak. She couldn't move. The idea of having ruined everything overwhelmed her and she could feel the beginnings of a panic attack.

"Child, go wait for me in my office."

Brooklyn nodded with defeat. "Okay. Yes, Father," she whispered, then left with her head hanging low. As she walked to his office, she took calming breaths between panic-induced hiccups. The last thing she needed was a meltdown. Instead, she figured staying calm and taking responsibility for her mistake was the best thing to do in this situation.

Once in his office, she looked at the chair she usually sat in, but it was always with an invitation. Brooklyn was unsure whether she should sit without one, so she stood in the middle of the room and waited. She thought of her choices that had brought her to that moment and tried to find the point of no return. It was easy: She shouldn't have called Page in the first place. Or maybe she could have been firmer about not taking anything. Or she could have been honest instead of trying to spare Page's ego.

Brooklyn's heart pounded when she finally heard his footsteps in the hall. She had been waiting with her hands clasped in front of her, her body unbearably tense with anxiety.

Father Mathias entered, walking quickly to his desk. He didn't say anything to Brooklyn, or even look at her as he sat.

"Father?" she whispered.

"You drank last night?"

"Yes, Father," she answered with shame.

"And you took drugs?"

"Yes, Father," her voice was reduced to a whisper again.

"I'm sure you know I am far from pleased with this kind of behavior. And it would most certainly earn you a punishment. But... it is a rule I haven't set yet. I will now. No more alcohol. And no more drugs."

"Yes, Father," Brooklyn said eagerly. New rules meant things weren't over and she was ready to agree to any terms to ensure it.

"I'm not done. I won't forbid you from seeing that girl you call a friend, but I am giving you the task to try and make new friends. Healthier ones."

Brooklyn shook her head. "I can't..."

"You can, and you will. The path you are on, child, is a reckless one. And dangerous. I would not be keeping my promise to you if I didn't address this issue."

"Yes, Father." Though his tone was colored with anger, his worry for her well-being was unmistakable. That realization almost brought Brooklyn to a fresh set of tears. She couldn't understand why someone like him would ever care for someone like her.

"As for your... unconfirmed activities." He sighed. "We never spoke about what you can and cannot do outside of... this." He twirled his finger in reference to the two of them and then was quiet for moment. His eyebrows drew in together in thought. "You don't remember anything at all?"

Brooklyn shook her head and a few tears slid down her cheeks. "I feel so gross about it," she said, hugging herself.

"Child, even if there had been an agreement, I cannot be upset with you for something you did not consent to. What your friend and her boyfriend did was wrong. Your friends violated your consent and that is not alright."

Brooklyn looked up at the priest. "But it's Page..."

Father Mathias took a deep breath and closed his eyes. "The more I think of it, the more I feel I should forbid you from seeing her. But that is a boundary I do not like to cross."

"She's my only friend, Father," Brooklyn said desperately. As terrible as Page could be, she was the only link to the outside world. Without her, Brooklyn faced the possibility of being alone with the monsters of her past. There was no question that they could cause more harm than Page.

"And I have given you the task to make new ones." Father Mathias stopped talking but Brooklyn stayed silent, noting that he was deep in thought. "I won't tell you who you can and can't see, but I will challenge you to create some distance for at least a couple of weeks. No texts. No phone calls. And most definitely no going out. And I hope that within those two weeks, you can see the benefit of your friend's absence from your life, enough where you can make the decision to end the friendship on your own."

Brooklyn knew he was right that Page was toxic. She knew because she had already reduced her contact with Page without meaning to and had felt better. "Yes, Father."

But the priest still looked troubled. "You understand why I'm asking this of you?"

"Yes, Father."

"Do you object to it at all?"

"No, Father. I know you're right."

His face relaxed. "Very good. Now, if you ever feel you cannot resist the urge to indulge in drugs and alcohol, come here first. I may not be readily available, but I want you to wait until I am." He got up and went to a filing cabinet in the corner. He pulled out a few printouts and a pamphlet. "There is some very good information here about substance abuse and addiction, and the pamphlet is for a support group the church runs at a nearby community center. There are other resources to help you if things get difficult."

Brooklyn took them and dashed away her tears with her other hand.

Father Mathias crouched in front of her. "Do not cry, child. You will see how, in time, things will get so much better for you. I see in you a light so bright it's blinding." He smiled sadly. "You are so beautiful in your tragedy; I can only imagine how stunning you'll be in your glory."

Brooklyn threw her arms around him and hugged him tightly. The priest hesitated before pulling her into his arms until she was off the chair and on her knees in front of him.

"Thank you," she said, her voice muffled by his cassock.

"Thank you for trusting me."

Brooklyn pulled away to look up at him. "It's easy to trust you. I felt that I could from the first time I met you. I just had a hard time with..." She looked down.

"I understand you haven't had the best experience with the church and I'm a part of it."

Brooklyn nodded. "I'm sorry."

The priest smiled sadly. "There is absolutely no need to apologize. I am grateful you found the strength to push past your fears and have granted me the opportunity to help." Father Mathias pulled her back to him. "Before you go, I have some bad news. This week will be a busy one. There are a lot of changes happening and it will take a lot of my time and energy, so I won't be able to meet with you in the mornings like I have. This week, concentrate on the tasks I have given you, then come back to me next Sunday at seven a.m."

"But..."

"There will be no discussion about this. I cannot make more hours in a day."

"Yes, Father."

"When I see you next, I hope to hear of your new friend."

12

Trepidation overtook Brooklyn the following morning. The thought of ignoring Page made her sick. A few days would have been difficult, but doable. Sometimes—though it was rare—Page would go three or four days without calling or texting her. Even then, that usually coincided with a trip or a luxury retreat. But two weeks? There was no way she could keep the distance without risking Page's wrath.

The phone rang and Brooklyn jumped. It was work. She had never been so happy to get called in, and she got ready quickly, showing up a half hour before she was due to start.

Gregory was behind the counter taking orders. *He would make a good friend.* When her shift started, she gave Gregory a bigger smile than usual.

"Someone is in a good mood," he commented.

Brooklyn shrugged. "I guess I am." *Not really.*

As always, the cafe was insanely busy, and Brooklyn wondered how she ever managed to keep track of the never-ending orders. When it was time for her break, she collapsed in a chair in the closet they called a staff room and put her feet up on the desk that served as table. Gregory came in shortly after to grab his things.

"Done for the day?" asked Brooklyn.

"Yes, thank God!"

Brooklyn picked at her nails, making it obvious she wanted to say something. Gregory noticed.

"Is everything okay?"

"Um, yeah. I was just, wondering, if, maybe, you wanted to hang out sometime?" Brooklyn decided to just go for it and tried to pretend that her face wasn't turning red.

"You do know I don't date women, right?"

Brooklyn laughed. "I know you don't. As friends, you weirdo."

"Okay then, sure. Why not?" he said with a smile. "I'm free tomorrow."

She looked up at him, surprised he was being proactive about finding time to hang out. "Oh! Okay. Cool! I'm always free. Unless they call me in."

"Don't sound so surprised," Gregory said with a chuckle. "I'm the one who should be surprised." They exchanged numbers and Brooklyn couldn't wait to tell Father Mathias the good news.

The rest of the shift went by too quickly and it wasn't long until Brooklyn was back at home. Alone. Fighting that all-too-familiar itch, which was worse now that she knew she couldn't scratch it. The longer she sat there, the more she realized her cravings weren't for the drugs and alcohol.

They were for Page.

Page made her feel bad, but she also satisfied something else. Brooklyn sat back heavily on her sofa—Father Mathias was right. It was moments like these, when she felt aimless, that Page helped her. Her friend gave her things to do and constantly awarded her with praise when she had done well, such as looking good in a dress or impressing her snobby friends. It was sad, and a little pathetic, Brooklyn thought, how much she needed Page. And the realization hit her in the gut.

"I need to stay busy," she said to herself. She looked around her tiny room. No wonder how Page managed to puppet her so easily. As horrible as she was, she rescued Brooklyn from her stagnant life. Brooklyn had no hobbies. Life was just a series of leaps from one rock to another in a rushing river, doing her best not to fall in and be washed away.

Her eyes landed on a pair of running shoes. "I'll go running?" She nodded, agreeing with the idea. Brooklyn put on the running shoes and her usual leggings and t-shirt. Once outside, though, she doubted her choice, feeling like an imposter. Running was for people who had their shit together and she was the poster-child for anything but that. She looked up and down the street and walked towards Bank Street hesitantly. The canal was beautiful to run by, so she did a light jog towards it, promising to earnestly run once on the path that followed the man-made waterway.

She kept her promise to herself and picked up the pace. Her lungs burned, but it didn't deter her. The pain, the rhythmic thwacking of soles against pavement, and her labored breaths took her mind off everything. Nothing else existed other than the difficult commitment to the next step. Once the burn reached her throat, Brooklyn slowed and went to rest on a bench. The sun was beginning to set somewhere behind her and the colors in the sky darkened. Shadows cast by the low-rise buildings made the air around her cooler and Brooklyn shivered. It was time to go back home. Starting again after stopping was difficult, and her motivation had run out, so she opted to walk. Checking the time, she saw she had managed to run for a good twenty minutes and thought that wasn't bad at all for her first time.

Brooklyn decided she would treat herself to two packs of instant noodles instead of one and watch something when she got home. While she waited for the soup, the collection of empty liquor bottles by her door caught her attention. There was a recently purchased, half-empty bottle under her coffee table. She took it to the bathroom and was about to pour the remaining contents down the drain when she thought of Barb. With a sigh, she went and knocked on Barb's door that was still left partly open.

There was a shuffling of feet and then Barb appeared at the door. Her eyes immediately went to the bottle and lit up.

"Listen, I'm not drinking anymore, so don't bother asking me for anything after this," said Brooklyn, thrusting the bottle towards the woman. She wondered if her kind act was really kind at all since she was enabling a bad habit.

Barb nodded and took the bottle as if Brooklyn had given her the most precious thing on Earth. "Thank you."

Returning to her room, Brooklyn put all the empty bottles in grocery bags and carried them down to the apartment building's garbage bin. Usually, she would take them to get refunded, but she wanted to get rid of them then and there. As she dumped the empties, she added up how much money she was throwing away. Five dollars. She bit her lip as she second-guessed her decision to not return them. Shaking her head, she decided it was worth it to avoid walking into a beer store. She arranged the bottles neatly in front of the large dumpster. One of her neighbors could take them.

Brooklyn's soup was cold by the time she got to it, so she showered before reheating it and put on a rom-com on her phone. The movie finished around eight in the evening. Brooklyn was proud of herself for intentionally going a day Page, drugs, and alcohol-free. It was liberating. Of course, the thought of doing it again was daunting. But that was a worry for tomorrow.

Page didn't call until the next morning. Brooklyn stared at the caller ID, tempted to answer. She wanted to pick up and all the reasons for why she should flew through her mind: Page gave her a lot. Page's anger was hard to deal with. Page didn't forgive easily. What if there was something wrong with Page? But most of all, the imposed distance had only managed to make Brooklyn earnestly miss her that much more.

She had to close her eyes when she hit the ignore button. Every ounce of willpower she'd mustered to do so dissipated when Page called right back. Again, Brooklyn hesitated before hitting ignore once more. But Page was relentless and called over and over again. Then her calls were followed by angry texts and more calls. There was no turning back. Now, Brooklyn avoided the calls to avoid Page's anger.

Between Page's incessant texts and calls, a text came through from Gregory asking her what time she wanted to get together. Brooklyn eagerly texted him back with a time. Once plans were made, she put her phone on silent and sat on her sofa to wait until it was time to go and meet up with Gregory. She stared at the wall. Usually, Brooklyn would use social media to kill time, but using her phone wasn't an option. She couldn't trust that she wouldn't give in and answer Page's calls or texts. Time moved at a snail's pace and Brooklyn grew antsy, so she got ready and went for a walk instead.

She met Gregory at a small movie theater that featured independent foreign films, then afterward hung out at a park that overlooked the canal's locks and afforded back-end views of the city's historical government buildings that were perpetually shrouded in scaffolding. Gregory was prepared with snacks and bottled water, which they enjoyed as they sat by a tree, surrounded by university students and government workers. Someone played a guitar in the distance and a game of soccer was taking up the large clearing in the center of the park.

"So, why'd you ask to hang out? Not that I'm complaining. You're pretty awesome. It's just... you kind of give off this 'leave me alone' vibe."

"I'm trying to turn my life around, I guess. I have only one friend and she really isn't that nice to me. So, someone had suggested I meet new people. And, I don't know, you just seemed like someone nice who I'd click with. And you're pretty much the only person at work I don't want to bash over the head with a steel cup."

Gregory smiled. "Well, I'm flattered. And thank you for not hitting me with a steel cup. My pretty face appreciates it."

Brooklyn nudged him playfully. "You should be, and you're welcome."

"Wanna tell me about your horrible friend?"

She wanted to decline the invitation because accepting it meant letting him in a little more than she was prepared to. But friends were supposed to open up to each other. Maybe that was one of the perks with Page. She didn't care to hear anyone talk about anything but her, so Brooklyn had never had to open up.

"She's apparently toxic," started Brooklyn. "No, not apparently. She *is*. She is toxic." Saying it out loud helped Brooklyn believe it a little more. "She likes to party and drink a lot and I get caught up in her whirlwind of a life, I guess."

"I totally get that. Before I met Kevin, I was a mess. I had friends that wanted to rave every weekend during festival season. It was all drugs and sex. Eventually, the emptiness was overwhelming."

"Wow," Brooklyn said, not knowing what else to say. It was hard to picture Gregory, someone who always seemed so well put together and levelheaded, as someone not so levelheaded.

Gregory smiled. "Hey, look at that, we have something in common," he said with a wink.

Brooklyn smiled and it felt good. It was genuine and relaxed, feelings that were foreign to her. Foreign but more welcome than she had expected. "Thanks for today. You really are easy to be around. It's nice to see that..." Brooklyn stopped, then shook her head. "I don't know. It's nice to see that I can feel comfortable with someone."

"It was a pleasure," he said with mock grandeur.

Brooklyn laughed. "Such a weirdo," she said, shaking her head.

"What? It was! Seriously. It was cool getting to see that you're more than a stuck-up, woe-is-me, stone-hearted..."

"I get the point!"

Gregory's descriptions turned to laughter. "Let's go, I'll drive you home."

Again, it was another early night. Brooklyn bit her lip while she figured out what she could do to keep busy. The room could use a tidy-up, so she settled on that. There was no rush as she refolded her clothes and stacked them neatly in their milk crates. Then she swept and wiped down the coffee table before calling it a night.

The rest of the week passed by slowly, and Brooklyn eagerly waited for Sunday. She ended up blocking Page's number and it eased a lot of her anxiety. Father Mathias had been right—not even a week and Brooklyn felt much better. Her room had never looked better after the borderline obsessive attention she had given it. It almost made her want to decorate it to make it more her own. Maybe buy a proper dresser or shelf.

Sunday morning finally came, and she woke up excited to see the priest. But when she got to the church, she found it quite busy and it overwhelmed her. Nearly every other time she had been here, it had been eerily empty and silent. A priest stood behind the lectern speaking to an altar server.

"Hello!" he greeted her jovially. "Are you the young lady Father Mathias said volunteered to help me pack?"

"Ummm..." Brooklyn was completely blindsided.

"I don't believe we've met. I'm Father Isaac. I really do appreciate your generosity. I don't know what I would have done! I got so caught up in my melancholy over leaving that things just crept up on me." He sighed and looked around the church. "I will miss this place very much."

"Oh, that's right. And Father Mathias is replacing you." She recognized him as the priest from the other day who had asked her if she needed help. Brooklyn was glad he didn't recognize her.

"Yes, and I'm sure he'll prove to be a good fit for St. Anthony's."

"I'm sure he will be." Brooklyn desperately tried to contain her cheeky grin. "So, what are your plans after this?"

"Italy." Brooklyn knew right away that "melancholy" was not the right word for this man; he exuded such childlike excitement that Brooklyn was in awe a man of his age could still manage it.

Brooklyn waited for him to elaborate, but he didn't. "Oh, that sounds great!"

"Thank you, thank you. Now, do you know how to get to the rectory from the inside?"

"Uhhh..."

"Go to the very back and turn right. There's a door at the end of the hall. Boxes have already been marked as to what goes where. Again, I appreciate your help."

Brooklyn turned to leave.

"Oh! I almost forgot. Father Mathias left this for you." He handed her a small, sealed envelope.

"Thank you." Brooklyn waited until she was towards the back of the church to open it.

My child,

Serve Father Isaac well. Speak very little and be stoic in your silence. I look forward to seeing you during Mass.

Your Priest

My Priest? My Priest! she thought, hugging the note to her chest. Brooklyn paused long enough to gag at her reaction, then decided to embrace her excitement. She couldn't remember the last time she had felt this centered and grounded. Brooklyn tucked the note away in her bag and went deeper into the back of the church, but once she passed Father Mathias's office, the familiar sense of unease came over her. The hallway stretched before her like a yawning mouth, threatening to swallow her up.

Brooklyn stumbled backwards and had to brace herself against the wall. Closing her eyes, she took deep breaths and did her best to calm herself down. Her Priest had given her a task, and she had to complete it. She took one last deep breath and stared down the hallway. *I can do this.* Her first step was hesitant, but each one after that became easier. She found the door and it opened to a small foot bridge, about five feet long, that connected the church to a tiny bungalow. It was a sign that either the rectory or church had been there first, and the other an afterthought.

The small house was quaint and dwarfed by the newer house towering over it from the other side. The rectory was just large enough to be comfortable yet small enough to avoid risking excess, silently shaming the neighbors for theirs. Brooklyn was all too familiar with the position the church took when it came to worldly possessions. St. Anthony's Church seemed to be a rare case where the ones who preached did as they preached. Then again, who knew, maybe the departing priest had wealth stashed somewhere.

As promised, boxes were already marked, and Brooklyn was able to sort the priest's belongings as he wished with little instruction. She took care to stack his notes and books so that the corners lined up perfectly, and she wrapped fragile items with diligence. She may be serving another, but her goal was to please her Priest, even if he most likely wouldn't see the work she had done.

Brooklyn checked the rest of the bungalow to see if anything else needed to be packed. The kitchen was uncomfortably small but fully equipped. A box sat on the countertop, but the drawers and cupboards still held basic kitchen dishes and cutlery, so she assumed those were to be left behind. The bathroom wasn't as small as the kitchen, but still small enough, and she found the medicine cabinet empty, as well as the drawers and the cupboard under the sink. The bedroom had also been packed already, with boxes waiting to be taken in the middle of the room.

Expecting a second bedroom, she opened the last door. It was too small to be a bedroom but too large to be a closet. The room confused her, but she shrugged and went to leave when she saw that it too had been packed. It seemed only the living room had been left for her, which meant she was done. She was about to close the door to the oddly sized room when she noticed that the packing boxes were from a different company. Upon closer inspection, she discovered they were labeled with Father Mathias's name. She ran her fingers over the packing labels.

"Mathias Duncan," she read quietly. *Duncan.* It only hit her then that she hadn't even known his last name. Brooklyn felt silly having shared the experiences she had shared so far without knowing such basic information.

Brooklyn bit her lip. Snooping was wrong, but she desperately wanted to know something more about him. She looked over her shoulder before turning on the light and opening one of the boxes. It held nothing but books and documents. The top box of another pile held more books and documents. *This is wrong. I shouldn't be doing this.* But she couldn't stop herself and she entered another box, and another. Everything proved to be impersonal. Nothing gave away the tiniest hint of what Father Mathias may be outside of his priesthood and his secret knack for domination.

Discouraged, she quickly closed the boxes and returned to the living room to finish the odds and ends of her task, making sure the boxes were taped and noted if fragile. Some time had passed, and Father Isaac came to find her.

He looked around. "My dear, I'm so grateful for your help. I can't believe how much you've managed to get done!"

"Thank you."

"Mass is about to start, and I wouldn't dream of keeping you from it. Thank you, again, and God bless you."

His blessing made Brooklyn feel uncomfortable and she worried if her reaction would give away her dislike for the church. So, she smiled and hurried to make it for Mass to avoid any opportunity for him to notice.

Brooklyn's excitement to see *him*, her Priest, overshadowed any discomfort she would normally have felt from sitting in church... during service... with other people around her joining in on the worship.

Brooklyn all but melted in the pew when Father Mathias approached the altar, dressed in a green vestment trimmed with gold. She sat on the edge of her seat and listened to every word he said. Thanks to her time with him, she could make out the double meaning in his teachings. If one listened carefully, they could hear his absolute faith in order and hierarchy, and his faith in one's calling to serve and one's calling to guide and receive. This was his first solo Sunday Mass at St. Anthony's, she learned, since Father Isaac's retirement, and it was in line with him introducing himself. Brooklyn couldn't help but feel that the sermon was directed towards her as she noted the strong parallels between his practice in faith and his practice behind closed doors. She felt smug, the way one gets when they are the only one privy to a secret, but also confused.

Father Mathias spoke of his calling to serve God. She couldn't understand how he could master her while serving another. Just the thought made her uncomfortable. But as Father Mathias continued, she began to see how his devotion to serving God displayed immense amounts of strength.

Strength needed to master her.

The Mass's ending caught her by surprise. Father Mathias never failed to lull her into that sweet, peaceful state she had begun to covet more and more. She stood with the rest of the parishioners and watched as they surrounded him to congratulate and welcome him as a permanent addition to the community. But before the crowd could disperse enough for her to talk to him, he was gone. Brooklyn was gutted by not being able to see him alone. Still, she waited until she was certain she really wasn't going to see him before deciding to leave.

The next morning, Brooklyn went to church at the usual time of five in the morning instead of seven, only to find the doors locked. Confused, she went to look at the hours and saw the church didn't actually open until six. That explained its emptiness during her meetings with Father Mathias and why he insisted on such early mornings. She sat on the steps and waited until an older woman arrived and went to open the doors.

"Can I help you with something?" she asked.

Not having expected someone other than Father Mathias, Brooklyn froze. "Um, I came for confession."

"Oh, I'm sorry, Father Isaac..." She smiled and shook her head. "I mean Father Mathias doesn't take confessions at this time during the week, only during the weekends."

"I didn't know, I'm sorry."

"No need to apologize, it's what I'm here for. I'm Janice, the church's administrator. I haven't seen you around before."

Brooklyn pulled at her sleeves. "I just started coming here."

Janice smiled and unlocked the doors. "Well, come on in. I find just sitting in the nave is enough to unburden one's heart in the meantime."

"Thank you," said Brooklyn, following the woman through the doors.

"Go ahead, I'll be turning on the lights. If you need anything, I'll just be in my office," she said, pointing to the left. A couple yards away from the main doors was a door with Janice's name and title.

Brooklyn nodded and walked tentatively to the front of the church. She looked over her shoulder to see if Janice was still in the nave so that she could go to Father Mathias's office. Although the woman had gone into her office, Brooklyn was too afraid to take the chance and chose to sit in a pew to wait. Father Mathias would have to show up eventually, so she waited until it was time for her to leave for work.

The following day, she showed up again, and again the doors were locked. Brooklyn figured it would raise suspicion if Janice came and found her waiting there again, so she left and returned shortly after the church was open. She waited in a pew for an hour, then left. Brooklyn did this for the rest of the week. Saturday morning came and she went, hoping to find Father Mathias in the confessional, but he wasn't there. However, the light in Janice's office was off. Who had opened the church?

As if in answer to her question, an alter server came from the back of the church. "Hello," he greeted with a smile.

"Hi," said Brooklyn. "Aren't these the hours for confession?"

The boy looked at her apologetically. "They are, but unfortunately Father Mathias isn't taking any confessions until possibly Wednesday evening. He's had other obligations with the transition."

"Oh, I see." Brooklyn felt lost. She desperately wanted to see her Priest, to tell him of her accomplishments. It was coming up on two weeks of being Page-free and she wanted to talk to him about how she should move forward.

The altar boy went to replace candles that had finished and returned to the back of the church. Brooklyn looked at the fresh candles and considered lighting one. She had done everything Father Mathias had set out for her to do, but she still hadn't prayed. Biting her lip, she lit a candle and tried to pray for the things he had instructed her to at the beginning. Brooklyn had to push away the flashbacks and did her best to picture Father Mathias's face and focus on it.

For the first time since she was a teenager, she prayed. Sort of. She doubted God would approve of her motive for the silent pleas and her inner voice stuttered as she tried to mentally articulate her words. It was unlike her to applaud herself, but she did. Maybe it hadn't been the prettiest prayer, but it was one—one that she had managed to finish.

This went on for the rest of the following week and she quickly grew depressed. Brooklyn wondered if she had displeased him in some way. Maybe she hadn't done a good enough job packing. Maybe he really wasn't okay with the fact that she'd had a threesome with Page and Sam.

Twice.

Or maybe he noticed that someone had rummaged through his things and knew it was her. The thought that he might be upset with her caused her so much distress that she turned down shifts and hid in bed whenever she wasn't at church praying. This distance gave new meaning to the marks he had given her. In his absence, the physical reminders of the moments they had shared together would have been comforting, and she regretted ever disliking them.

13

A bit of hot milk spilled on Brooklyn's hand while she contemplated whether she should go to Mass tomorrow. It wasn't expected of her, but it would be a guaranteed chance to see Father Mathias, one she had been too afraid to take the previous Sunday.

"Are you okay?" asked Gregory when she yelped.

She nodded. "I'm fine."

"That's what you get for not taking any shifts for a week," he teased. "Here, let me finish making this, you go and put some cold water on that."

Brooklyn handed him the cup and went to the sink. When the pain subsided, she returned to her post just in time to see Gregory fawning over Stephen as he handed him his drink. It was another rare day where Stephen had his drink to stay and sat at a table in the corner by the windows. He had a folder with him, which he opened and examined its contents with a slightly furrowed brow.

"I have a plan," whispered Gregory, loud enough to be heard over the coffee machines. "I'm going to tell Raph that I want to empty the trash bins today."

"Why would you want to do that?" asked Brooklyn. She remembered being the "new guy" who was always made to do it, and there was nothing inviting about the task.

Gregory rolled his eyes. "Well, because then I get to wipe down the tables *and* get a closer look at Mr. Hotshot. Can you just imagine me, him, and no counter between us?" He sighed dreamily, looking up at nothing with a wistful smile on his face. When he decided to come back down to Earth, Brooklyn was already talking to Raph. "I hate you!" shouted Gregory with a laugh.

Brooklyn kept her head down when she emptied the garbage and averted her gaze when wiping down the tables. When she got to the table next to his, she stole a peek at his perfect profile just as he looked up from his phone. They made eye contact and he smiled, flashing perfect teeth. Everything about him seemed perfect. His dark hair defied wind and gravity; his face would make any Greek God weep with envy with its strong nose and a jawline that hovered between masculine and almost too feminine for a man. Thick eyebrows showcased his serious but kind brown eyes.

He cleared his throat.

"Um, are you done with that?" was all Brooklyn could manage to say, pointing at his almost empty coffee mug.

"I am, thank you."

Oh my God! His voice! His voice! Without the hissing steamers and roaring coffee machines getting in the way, Brooklyn could hear just how deep and smooth it was. She willed her hand to be steady when she took his mug and prayed she wouldn't trip or fall or do anything remotely embarrassing as she made her way back to safety behind the counter.

Gregory was giggling. "You were walking like you had a stick up your ass!"

"Shut up!" Brooklyn threw the rag at Gregory and looked to see if Stephen had heard anything, but thankfully he was gone.

"Oh jeez, that was better than if I'd have gone out there. 'Are you done with that?'" he said, mimicking her.

Brooklyn fought her giggle, not wanting to indulge her almost-friend's teasing, but soon she was joining Gregory and the rest of the staff looked at them in confusion, wondering what was so funny.

"Thank God, I think that's the first smile you've cracked since walking in."

Brooklyn shrugged. "It's been a couple of shitty weeks."

"Wanna talk about it?"

"No, I'm sure everything will be okay by tomorrow." At least she hoped. Still, the reminder of her sour mood shadowed the brief moment of happiness.

Opting for a skirt, Brooklyn got dressed with trembling hands. She brushed her hair and tied it up in a ponytail, doing her best to tame the baby hairs that refused to cooperate. After one last inspection in the mirror, she set off for church. Brooklyn made sure to sit at the front when she got there. During Mass, her eyes remained glued to Father Mathias in hopes that he would make eye contact, but not once did their eyes meet. She was ready to throw a tantrum, pull out her hair, go on a hunger strike—anything to express her despair.

Mass ended, and like the Sunday before last, he was gone after the flurry of parishioners eased. Brooklyn lit a candle and prayed, staying there until the church's activity died down, her hands clasped together and her eyes closed. She prayed for his forgiveness if he was angry, for patience if he was busy, and for a chance to be alone with him soon. Brooklyn wasn't sure who she was praying to, but just putting the thoughts out into the universe offered her some solace.

"Do not open your eyes, my child."

His voice sent violent shock waves through her body. Her craving for him was immense and it took all her will to obey him.

"I am so pleased you have found the strength to pray."

"Was this a test, Father?"

"No, child. I don't play silly games. I have truly been busy and I'm afraid it will be like this until I've settled into my new role here at the church."

"For how long?" she hated the desperation in her voice.

"I'm not sure, but be patient." He paused. "I will have a bit of time tomorrow at nine in the evening. Come to me then."

Then she felt him leave her side. Tomorrow evening couldn't come fast enough.

Brooklyn didn't want to go home. She had been diligent about keeping herself busy, but it was exhausting. Out of habit, she went to call Page and stopped herself just before hitting send. The prescribed two weeks—and some—had gone by and Brooklyn only truly felt her friend's absence then. She asked herself what Page could offer her in that moment. *Trouble. Nothing but trouble.* She considered calling Gregory but felt she would be imposing even though she had only hung out with him that one time.

Brooklyn sighed. *I really need to get a hobby. Or a job with more hours.*

The church appeared impossibly still from the outside. The light within was faint and barely penetrated the stained-glass windows. Brooklyn tried the door, half expecting it to be locked like all those mornings, but it gave way. She headed straight for his office and found it locked. Thinking he may have moved to the larger one, she tried its door as well.

"Good evening, my child," Father Mathias greeted from the shadows.

Brooklyn jumped. "Oh! Hello, Father."

"Forgive me, I didn't mean to startle you. Come, we will spend our time in the rectory you packed up so well the other week." The mention of her packing job had Brooklyn blushing with guilt. She wondered again if he knew she had gone through his things.

Brooklyn followed him through the unlit hallway and to the door that led to the small foot bridge. The little bungalow featured the same furniture but different belongings. You could tell someone new now lived there, but the décor still did not give away any ideas as to who the person was. He motioned for her to sit and offered her a cup of tea before sitting on the sofa across from her.

"I thought you were upset with me, Father," she blurted.

"I'm sorry to have caused you any distress, but I must be discreet as a lot of eyes are on me right now during this time of transition."

Brooklyn nodded. "It was just hard, not seeing you every day like we had, and worse because I didn't know when I would see you next." She paused. "And there's something else, Father."

"Oh?"

"I looked through your things. That's why I thought you might've been angry."

"I see." The disappointment on his face gutted Brooklyn, so she looked away and down at the mug in her hands.

"I'm so sorry. I just wanted to know you better. You don't talk much about yourself and... I don't know, I just thought that..." She stopped and shook her head at herself. "I don't know what I was thinking, Father. And I'm really sorry."

"I can tell you've punished yourself enough with worry, so let's not speak of it again. And child?"

"Yes, Father?"

"Look at me." He waited for her to drag her gaze up to meet his before continuing. "You are not prohibited from asking me questions. If you want to know more about me, you just need to ask."

"Yes, Father."

"Now, as for continuing our meetings, from now on, when I see you, I will tell you when to come next. Mornings no longer work because Janice, the church's administrator, is back from vacation and I can't take any risks. But as the church settles into its new routine, I am starting to get a better idea of when it will be empty."

"Yes, Father. And I did meet Janice."

Father Mathias nodded. "She's a nice woman, but a gossip and quite intrusive. But enough of that. Now"—he sat forward—"when you arrive for our meetings, I want you to come straight here. Do not knock. Just enter and close the door behind you." He stood up and walked to where there was a small window with a little table under it. On it was a Bible and an unlit candle. "Since you have found the strength to pray, I expect you to do it when you arrive. And you will wait here until I come in."

"Yes, Father." Brooklyn leaned forward, hanging on to each and every word. His commanding tone stirred a smoldering heat in her belly that grew hotter as he spoke.

"Good. Now, tonight, my child, I have an appetite that may not suit you." He approached her and caressed her cheek, and she greedily nuzzled his palm.

He smelled of soap and balsam and she found comfort in the scent. It was his, and he was safe. The fear and pain-tinged memories were replaced by images of him and she was grateful for it.

"But before that, I'd like to hear about your last few weeks."

Brooklyn beamed at him, proud that she had accomplished her tasks, even though the excitement she had felt after the first week had waned with time. "I haven't spoken to Page, and I don't plan to, Father. I do want to talk to you about it, but you did say it was a decision you wanted me to make on my own."

"How do you feel now that you've put distance between the two of you?"

"Happier. Like this dark cloud that's been hanging over me is gone." It was a silly, anecdotal sentiment, but one that was accurate.

Father Mathias nodded with approval. "I'm glad."

"And I haven't touched a drop of alcohol or taken anything. The drugs I can't afford anyways. I always got those from Page. There were a few times where I was craving something, but it was always when I was bored." She paused, weighing the decision to tell him that alcohol was something she had previously used to help her sleep. Brooklyn decided against it. "So I've been keeping myself busy."

Father Mathias's eyebrows shot up in pleasant surprise. "And how have you been keeping busy?"

"I run sometimes. But mostly I just watch TV."

"That is such a huge improvement, and I am amazed and proud. But most important, are you proud of yourself?"

Brooklyn nodded reluctantly. It was a foreign feeling to her and acknowledging it felt strange.

"I'd like to challenge you to do even better. Running is fantastic—try to do it more often. And I want you to volunteer at a soup kitchen that the church runs out of a converted community center. Go as often as you'd like, but at least once a week."

"Yes, Father."

"Have you made any new friends?"

Brooklyn nodded with a radiant smile that seemed to catch the priest by surprise yet again. "One. His name is Gregory. We work together at the cafe. I'm still too shy to reach out to him, but we went to the movies then hung out at the park once. He's really nice."

Father Mathias smiled. "I am beyond pleased, child. And I'm curious, how did you find it in you to pray?"

Brooklyn shrugged. "I don't know. I just did."

"Are you ready to talk about what made it difficult for you to do so in the first place?"

She bit her lip and shook her head, her panic evident.

"Do not fret, my child. Only when you're ready."

"Thank you, Father."

Father Mathias moved to sit next to her and ran his fingers across her cheekbones, sighing. "You are stunning. Glowing. And I am in disbelief at how quickly you're blossoming." He smiled with a chuckle.

"What?"

"I'm thinking of how when you first sat in my office, you thought I believed you to be beyond help. Yet here you are, exceeding all expectations."

Brooklyn's cheeks reddened at the memory. The humor wasn't lost on her, but she couldn't help but to feel ashamed for how she had spoken to him. "I'm sorry, Father."

"Hush, child, there's nothing to be sorry for." He cleared his throat. "Now," he began with a smile, "get undressed and go lie face down on my bed."

Brooklyn froze. She had dreamed of Father Mathias taking her many times by now, but being naked in front of him terrified her. "Here, Father?"

He nodded.

"Everything?"

"Everything," he said evenly.

Timid, she put down her untouched cup of tea and stripped off her clothes. She felt clumsy when she stepped out of her panties and almost fell. Hugging herself to regain some sort of cover, she nudged her discarded clothes away from her with her foot. Her eyes remained fixed on the floor.

"The bedroom is the first door on the right."

She took halting steps, and he followed close behind. Brooklyn couldn't look at him as she climbed up onto the four-poster bed that was dressed in linens embroidered with gold, red, and cream-colored thread. At one end, various implements were laid out. Even though he probably wouldn't touch her in the ways she had hoped for, she was excited to get marked. Now with the reality of fewer meetings, his marks would offer some sort of consolation in his absence.

"Lay flat and put your hands behind your head."

Brooklyn did as he said, and her breaths quickly grew shallow with fearful anticipation. She waited, but nothing happened. Although she wanted to look up at him to see what he was doing, she kept her nose pressed to the bed and waited. The seconds passed and she grew more anxious. *What is he doing?* Before she could finish the thought, she heard him take in a sharp breath and let it out with a hum.

Then he started, lightly at first, with soft bare-handed spanks, massaging her bottom between hits. Brooklyn breathed deeply, doing her best to sink into the moment and into the feelings. But she couldn't stop anticipating—hoping for—an intimate touch. There was no denying that the pain he administered, especially when he prepared her skin for more, was an intimacy in and of itself. But Brooklyn wanted sex. She wanted the parts of her that throbbed and buzzed to be touched. And she wanted to touch him. What would it feel like to press her hands against his bare chest?

The impacts increased in intensity, pulling her out of her thoughts. Brooklyn's bottom was warm now and she shivered from the tingling that rippled across her skin. Then came the first implement. She recognized the sting of it from the other day and knew it was the paddle. She was proud that she didn't move or cry too loudly now that the pain wasn't as foreign to her.

The priest switched between various implements, working her until her cries were no longer controlled. This is where she found peace. Enduring the pain took every ounce of her conscious effort. There was no space for hopes, shame, or regret. Just pain—feeling it until it left her body, only to be replaced with another wave from another hit. Brooklyn could almost taste his hunger to mark her. On and on he continued until there was a pause and Brooklyn dared to peek at him. She found him wielding a long, narrow paddle with small holes cut among the intricate designs that had been carved into the wood. It resembled a gladiator-like sword. He wound up, his chest heaving for air and ready to strike her. Brooklyn closed her eyes, certain it would hurt more than the rest—but the blow never came.

"Turn over, child." He put the implement down and climbed up next to her to find her cheeks stained with tears. His fingers buried themselves in her hair as if on their own accord.

"You will be my undoing," he said, before he kissed her with abandon.

He pillaged her lips and kissed her with such hunger that it surprised Brooklyn. She had never been sure whether he just didn't crave her as much as she craved him, or if he had excellent self-control. With his kiss, she decided it was the latter. Brooklyn moaned and returned his kiss with equally violent fervor. She clung to him, desperate for the moment to continue and to get as close as possible.

He pulled her hair, forcing their lips apart. "That is all for tonight, child," he said breathlessly.

"No! Please, Father!" She tried to pull him back to her, but he was already standing.

"Control yourself," he said quietly.

"Why won't you touch me?" Insecurities came rushing back. Sure, he was deviant, but maybe not so deviant as to be sexually intimate with someone like her. Brooklyn wondered if she had misread him. Maybe this was strictly to help her, with no extra perks for himself.

"Sit up."

Brooklyn sat and winced from the pain.

"Do you pleasure yourself often?"

Brooklyn's eyes widened with surprise. "Yes, Father."

"When was the last time?"

"Last night." Her voice was small.

"From now on, you cannot engage in those types of activities without my permission. Do you understand?"

It was as if the air had been knocked out of her lungs. "Am I being punished?" She couldn't understand any other reason for him asking her to abstain.

"Not at all. You are being trained. Self-indulgence should be tempered. With that comes strength and much improved will. Suffering due to abstaining builds character," he said, the strain in his voice barely perceptible, but present enough for Brooklyn to wonder if he was telling himself the same thing.

Maybe if she pushed a little harder, Father Mathias's will would break. None of it seemed fair to Brooklyn. But she kept quiet and accepted the new rule. "I understand, Father."

"Wait here." He left and returned with a bowl of fresh fruit. "You should eat before you leave. I'll go get your clothes." Brooklyn stared down at the strawberries, cubed melon, and orange wedges. Their faint aroma connected her back to her body and it was only then that she noticed the chill under her skin. With a trembling hand, she ate the fruit. Father Mathias returned with her clothes and a bath robe which he wrapped around her. He sat quietly as she ate and rubbed her back, bringing her back down to Earth; she hadn't been aware enough to recognize she had been gone until she came back.

"Come back to me on Thursday. Same time." He left and Brooklyn got dressed. Father Mathias was nowhere to be found when Brooklyn let herself out. She wondered why he had been so quick to vanish.

14

Eager to start on her new task, Brooklyn went to the soup kitchen the next morning. It skirted the edge of a part of downtown that was best to be avoided, even during the day. People sat on the building's front steps and watched her with curiosity as she went up to the front door. The smell that seemed to plague most cafeterias—canned meat and boiled freezer-burned produce—hit her as soon as she walked in.

"Excuse me," she said, stopping an older man in an oversized jacket that had seen better days. "Who can I talk to about volunteering here?"

The man shrugged and walked past her.

Brooklyn bit her lip and looked around, trying to find someone who could direct her.

"Hello there!" said a bright and bubbly voice from behind her.

She turned and was facing a woman who wore a badge. "Hi, I'm looking to volunteer."

"Lovely! I'm Elizabeth. Welcome to St. Anthony's Hope Initiative!"

"Thanks, I'm Brooklyn."

Elizabeth smiled. "Well, isn't that an interesting name."

Brooklyn wasn't sure if that was a compliment or an insult, but she shrugged it off and followed the chipper woman to the back of the building and to an office. Everything in the room seemed to be secondhand and scuffed to a point where you couldn't even call it charming. Papers and folders were stacked haphazardly on the desk, shelves, and any other flat surface in the cluttered space.

"Have a seat." Once the two women were seated, Elizabeth handed Brooklyn a form and pen. "Go ahead and fill that out, then we'll have a quick chat."

Brooklyn filled out her contact info and paused at the question at the bottom of the form.

Why do you want to volunteer?

She couldn't very well say her Priest had tasked her to. Or could she? Brooklyn decided to write the truth, or as close to it as she could.

I have been trying to better myself with the help of St. Anthony's Church. Father Mathias recommended I volunteer to fill my time with positive things instead of resorting to old bad habits.

Brooklyn handed the form back to Elizabeth who skimmed over it. She watched the woman's face when her eyes neared the bottom of the form to see her reaction.

Elizabeth pressed her lips together and looked towards the open door. She went to close it, then returned to her seat.

Brooklyn immediately recognized the look of pity—the drawn eyebrows and slightly pinched lips—and hated it.

"Is there something wrong?"

Elizabeth measured her next words. "Can I ask you for a favor?"

"Sure." Brooklyn did her best to keep the bite out of her tone.

"Once you start, I'd like for you to take a meal for yourself."

Brooklyn laughed nervously. "Why?"

"It'll be like a thank you for your time."

"Do you thank all the volunteers with a meal?"

Elizabeth's mouth opened and closed a few times before she could find her words. "Well, no dear, but..."

"Then why are you doing that with me?" Brooklyn hated that her situation was apparently obvious, but she didn't want to assume the woman's motives. Still, she had an unreasonable need to find out what they were immediately so she knew how to feel.

"I recognized your address, but I didn't want to make you feel any type of way about it. It's just... I've dedicated my life to helping people and..."

"Thanks, but I'm fine. I don't need handouts."

"Understood. But, if..."

"I said, I'm fine." Brooklyn winced when her voice came out harsher than she had intended. Elizabeth only wanted to help. "I'm sorry. I appreciate your concern, but I promise, I'm fine."

Elizabeth nodded. "Alright, dear. Well, we'll need to do a police check. And do you have any food safety experience?"

Brooklyn nodded. The service industry had been her landing ground when she first left home. The cafe was just the latest in a string of employment stints.

Elizabeth continued to discuss the kitchen's mission and Brooklyn noted Elizabeth's genuine passion to not only help the needy, but to ensure they were respected by all the volunteer staff.

"I always say that even if you're not the one sitting at our tables to eat, it's important to prepare the food as if you were. Even small things, like being thorough with taking out the eyes from potatoes, are important. Some of our guests suffer from mental illnesses, so inconsistency in something like mashed potatoes could worry someone who suffers from paranoia. It's not just about respect, but empathy and compassion."

Brooklyn nodded. "I get it," she said with a smile. Soup kitchens weren't unfamiliar to her. There was a time when she first arrived in the city when she had relied on them for a few of her meals. One woman, a less bubbly version of Elizabeth, had helped her through a rough adjustment and period of recovery. Brooklyn felt guilty for not thinking of giving back to those who had helped her on her own.

"I'm certain you understand. Come with me. I'll introduce you to Caroline. She's the one who really runs the kitchen."

Elizabeth's approach to helping the needy earned immediate trust from Brooklyn. "Elizabeth?"

"Yes?"

"I'd like to accept your offer. For a meal, but only if I really need it."

Elizabeth's smile was unbelievably warm. "I'm happy to hear that." And she said nothing more of it, which Brooklyn appreciated.

As they approached the doors of the kitchen, the sounds of cooking and laughter could be heard. An unexpected wave of anxiety came over Brooklyn at the thought of walking into a room filled with people she would be introduced to. How many of them were regular volunteers? Was she going to be the "new girl" breaching an already tight-knit group?

Elizabeth noticed. "Don't worry, everyone here is lovely. Trust me, I'm a good judge of character," she said warmly.

Brooklyn smiled but was still nervous as Elizabeth swung open the kitchen doors.

"Caroline, we have a new volunteer," announced Elizabeth.

Some people looked up from their duties long enough to see who it was, but nobody stared. Caroline came up to them and welcomed Brooklyn with an unexpected hug.

"It warms my heart when we get a young person," said Caroline. "What made you decide to volunteer?"

The question caught her off guard and Brooklyn froze, failing to remember what she had filled out on her form. Had she gone with a veiled truth or a lie? Either way, concocting an answer was easy. One only needed to say that they wanted to give back or to be useful, but because her true reason was a scandalous secret, her brain stuttered with panic. "I don't know," she finally said.

Caroline laughed. "Well, whatever the reason, we're grateful. Come with me, I'll show you around."

Introductions were made and Brooklyn's suspicion that these people were regulars proved to be true. Most of them were retired and frequented St. Anthony's Church. So not only did they volunteer together, but they also prayed together, and this made Brooklyn uneasy. How many would see through her? How many have already seen her at the church? Brooklyn questioned Father Mathias's judgment with this task and felt it would have been smarter to have her volunteer at another kitchen that wasn't so closely tied to his church.

Caroline went on to show Brooklyn the building which served as more than just a soup kitchen. They had a recreational space in the basement that offered beaten up board games, arts and crafts materials, and a TV. The main floor was the kitchen and dining area, and the second floor held a few other offices and what looked like a conference room.

"We hold workshops and support groups in here," explained Caroline. "Now, I know there's still paperwork to be done, but we are short today and in desperate need of an extra pair of hands. Would you mind staying?"

"That was my plan. I had no idea there was paperwork involved." Brooklyn laughed nervously.

"Wonderful! Come with me." Caroline led them back to the kitchen and pulled Brooklyn to a round table piled high with vegetables.

"Today we're serving a hearty vegetable soup with ham sandwiches. You can help peel the veggies."

Two women sat at the table, already elbow deep in carrots and potatoes, and moved over to make space for Brooklyn. They were warm and welcoming, and it wasn't long before Brooklyn felt at ease and joined in on their light conversation.

By the time the food was being served, Brooklyn was glowing, happy to be a part of something that seemed to make a difference. She got to sit and talk with some of the kitchen's guests and even made a few new friends.

"I like you," said one man who she had learned was called Marius and used to be a chauffeur.

"Why's that?" asked Brooklyn.

"You're one of us."

"That's sweet," she said, not reading much into the comment.

"No, I mean it. I can tell. You're one of us. Lost, broken. But I can tell you're on your way up and I'm glad."

His words caught Brooklyn off guard and her smile faltered. Of course, Marius meant what he'd said as a compliment, but all Brooklyn could hear was how apparent her harsh life was.

"I'm sorry, I didn't mean to upset you."

Brooklyn forced a smile. "There's nothing to say sorry for. I hope you enjoy your meal, Marius." She got up and went back to the kitchen to hide from everyone else as she suddenly felt painfully cracked open with her insides on display for all to see. She wondered if Caroline could tell and if Elizabeth's concern was influenced by more than just her address.

"Hi! How was it?" asked Caroline.

"Great, you guys are doing great work here. I'm glad I was able to be part of it." *But I can't wait to get out of here.*

"Thank you! Will we be seeing you again? I heard you were a marvelous help today."

"Yes, I plan on coming at least once a week."

"Lovely! I'm happy to hear it! We could use all the help we can get."

Despite being shaken by Marius's innocent comment, Brooklyn was floating when she left and reflected on the changes her Priest had inspired. Not too long ago, she had been aimless and self-destructive. Now, she felt as if she could change the world. Or at least her life. Everything seemed brighter; her senses felt alive and so in tune with the world around her that she noticed how the breeze felt on her cheeks, how the sun felt on her skin, and how her heart beat in her chest.

It was the night before her next meeting with Father Mathias. Her hand wandered as she lay on her sofa, wide awake. She let it rest on top of her panties. Her fingers twitched, but she made sure not to rub herself. Brooklyn truly wanted to please him, no matter how difficult it would be. After all, he was helping her reclaim her life, and abstaining from self-pleasure wasn't much for him to ask of her. With a groan, she got up, deciding it was safer off the sofa. *I guess I'm going for a run.* The ache between her legs was impossible to ignore as she got dressed and went for a light jog. The new rule only seemed to exacerbate what she believed to be a normal sex drive and Brooklyn couldn't understand how this would temper it. Jogging offered little distraction or relief. Even with the expended energy, the ache continued, and Brooklyn went to bed in a sour mood.

The following morning, Brooklyn woke up before her alarm with the same dull ache, so she went for another run. Despite her misery, she felt good about being up so early, jogging with others who had their life together. Maybe one day, she'd be like them: focused, following a routine, and with places to be. Brooklyn smiled and picked up her pace. The cool morning air felt good on her face and reddened her cheeks. Fall was in full swing, she noted. By the time she finished her increasingly larger loop, the ache had finally subsided to a bearable pulse. Checking the time, she realized she was going to be late for work and rushed to get ready.

The day dragged as the rush of orders failed to numb her mind into distraction as much as it usually did. That is, until Stephen came in. Gregory wagged his eyebrows at her, and she threw a forgotten cap from an oat milk carton at him.

"Americano for..." Her voice trailed off when he reached for his cup.

"How are you today?" He looked at her name tag. "Brooklyn. That's a nice name. Suits you."

"Uh, um, th-thank you." Brooklyn stared at him, wondering why he had said anything to her at all. He barely paid attention to anyone. "Oh! I'm fine, thanks. How are you? Busy, I bet. So busy." She laughed nervously.

Stephen smirked. "You could say that. See you later."

Brooklyn sagged against the counter when he left.

"Ummm, what was that?! Did Stephen just talk to you?!"

"Yes. But why?"

The corners of Gregory's lips turned up in a faint smile and he pulled her off to the side. "Can I be honest with you? Friend to friend, even though we're new friends?"

"Of course."

"You were kind of a mess. Like, you had it written all over your face."

"Can you, like, stop talking, and start working?" complained one of the other baristas.

"Shut it, Becky." Gregory held up his hand and rolled his eyes. "We're having a moment." He turned back to Brooklyn. "That said, something's changed with you. Look at you." He held up a stainless-steel cup before realizing it didn't offer a clear enough reflection. "Never mind. What I'm trying to say is you look great. Healthy. Happy. I don't get that 'leave me alone' vibe from you anymore. Don't get me wrong, you still have your moody days, but it's normal moody, not like grrr moody."

Brooklyn laughed. "I get it. And thank you. That means a lot to me. I've been trying really hard to turn things around."

"Well, it's working. *Now* we need to get working before the civil servants throw their government-issued phones at us."

With a nod, Brooklyn returned to the lunch rush with a smile on her face. Change was hard, but it was easier when people noticed. It was difficult to see for herself, but she hoped one day, she could look in the mirror and like what she saw.

Brooklyn showed up early for the meeting with her Priest and sat on the steps, eagerly watching the clock. When it was 8:59, she entered the church and hesitantly headed for the rectory.

The small table by the window beckoned her and she went to light the candle and pray. She prayed that he would finally take her tonight. Realizing the irony of praying for sex, Brooklyn amended her plea to having the strength needed to endure whatever he asked of her.

She heard him enter and instinct told her to remain as she was. His footsteps drew closer and stopped right behind her. He showered her hair with feather-light touches, and her body's visceral response to such an innocent touch made her feel ridiculous.

"Good evening, my child."

"Good evening, Father."

"Are you done praying?"

"I am, Father."

"Very good. Go to my room, bend over the bed, and pull down your pants and panties."

She did as he said and proudly displayed her marked bum. The bruises were starting to fade, but they still boasted the punishment she had endured. They had been much more garish than the first marks he had left, but they didn't shock her like before and instead she immediately appreciated them.

"Beautiful," he sighed. "Stand up and turn around." He waited for her to do so. "Have you abstained from touching yourself?" he asked once she faced him. Father Mathias watched her eyes for signs of deceit.

"Yes, Father." She returned his gaze, proud that she had listened and proud that she wasn't lying, especially because she had considered it.

"Did you manage to make it into the soup kitchen?"

"I did, Father," she said with an eager nod.

"How did you like it?"

"It was great. There was a moment or two that caught me by surprise, but I was happy to volunteer. Elizabeth and Caroline are very nice."

He smiled. "They are. I had the pleasure of meeting them just last week. I'm glad you made it out and were able to volunteer." He peered at her intently. Brooklyn fidgeted, uncomfortable with his inquisitive stare.

"What is it, Father?"

He sighed with a smile. "You're radiant." He cupped her cheek adoringly. "Remember how I told you you would be stunning in your glory?"

Brooklyn shifted her gaze to the floor and nodded.

"You're stunning, but something tells me there is much more light in you. I'm already blinded, my child."

Brooklyn's cheeks flashed hot with shyness. His praise made her proud and uncomfortable all at once and she didn't know what to do with the sudden rush of emotions. She closed her eyes and did her best to accept the compliment with grace. "Thank you, Father."

"No, thank *you*, my child. It is so profoundly rewarding seeing how well you respond to my guidance and care." He paused, and Brooklyn knew he was continuing to take her in, which only deepened the red that stained her cheeks. "Get undressed and lie on your back on the bed," he said softly.

Brooklyn did as she was told and waited, still feeling self-conscious of her nudity in front of him.

"Again, you have found the strength to pray, yet you still haven't told me why you had such difficulties in the first place. I wanted to check in and see if you're ready to speak of it?"

Her trust in her Priest had grown more than she could have ever imagined possible. She felt she could trust him with her past and have faith that if she fell while remembering, he would catch her and carry her back from the edge.

Brooklyn closed her eyes. Her ears roared with the quiet panic that thoughts of her past always provoked. Instead of giving in to the panic, she took a deep breath and waited for it to subside, reminding herself that she was safe. "My mother is... an extremely, devout believer," she started slowly. "Growing up, she would always make me pray. I had to pray all the time, especially when she believed I was being sinful. Nothing was ever right.

Sometimes, even the way I would walk would be considered wrong and she'd force me to pray for hours on end, kneeling on rice on the floor. She believed the discomfort would help to 'rid me of my demons because demons don't like discomfort.'"

Father Mathias grabbed her hand. "I am sorry, my child."

Now that she had started, Brooklyn couldn't stop. She wanted to tell him her story. Part of her hoped that maybe his love for the church would wane once he heard what it had done to her. Maybe he could see that there was nothing good about the Catholic faith. "We went to church almost every day. Our priest would put me through all these cleansing rituals. My mother convinced him that I was infested with evil and that he had to do everything he could to purify me. Sometimes, the entire parish would be involved. We lived in a very small town and everyone there is just like my mother." Brooklyn opened her eyes and they glistened with unshed tears. "I truly started to believe that they were right."

"Oh, my child." Father Mathias sat on the bed and pulled her into his arms, cradling her as if she was an infant. He rocked her back and forth until her breaths stopped hitching.

"Our church had a basement, and Father David would keep me there, sometimes for days, in the dark, with nothing but bread and water. He told me that no matter how much I repented, I couldn't be saved, but that I should still do everything in my power to earn salvation anyway."

Father Mathias squeezed her more tightly and Brooklyn was grateful for it; she was coming apart. The dam had broken and the memories she kept locked away flooded towards her, one after the other. And with them came the emotions. She felt them all as if she was back there again.

Brooklyn pulled away enough to look up at him. "And I believed it even after I ran away. The priest had made sure of it." She sat up and turned so that her back faced him and lifted her hair to expose the nape of her neck. Starting just below the hairline, then disappearing into it, was block script that had been branded into her skin. "It's Hebrew for..."

"Condemned," said Father Mathias, cutting her off. He traced the scars.

"Yes. They branded me the first time I tried to run away."

"It is a wonder you ever overcame your fear of the church. What they did to you was wrong and no bishop would tolerate such treatment of a child."

He pulled her back into his arms and buried his face in her hair. "I'm so sorry, my child."

She wanted to argue with him, tell him that his church was irredeemable and the entire organization should be marked with the same symbols that had been burned into her.

"Father?"

"Yes?"

"How can you... still love the church knowing everything it's done? And I'm not talking about me. I mean, in general."

Father Mathias was quiet. "I know the church is guilty of many atrocities. But it has also done a lot of good. The word of God, in the right hands, can be a beautiful and powerful thing, and I choose to focus on that and be part of the good."

Brooklyn found it hard to accept that the ugly could be erased by questionable good, but she didn't have the energy to challenge Father Mathias's faith. She burrowed deeper into his arms and ran her fingers across the soft material of his shirt.

"Everyone was so certain about my nature, I guess I was determined to prove them right," she said, choosing to go back to the original topic.

The priest looked into her eyes. "You are more than good. You are divine. A perfect image of Eden embodied in human form."

"I still don't understand how you see that in me." Her voice cracked as the deep-rooted need for approval resurfaced—not approval from her Priest, but from *a* priest. She didn't like the feeling.

"Child?" His voice was strained now. "Have our activities..." He stopped, trying to find a way to put his question into words.

"It's not the same," Brooklyn answered without him needing to finish his sentence. "I asked for it."

"Yes, but, what if you feel that it's deserved, and you've just sought out a replacement? I don't want to reinforce any damaging ideas they tried to instill in you."

"It's not the same. I promise. When they would hurt me, it felt horrible in here." Brooklyn pointed to her chest where her heart rested. "But with you, I feel free. I don't know why, but I do."

Father Mathias squeezed her tightly. "I will not rest until you see yourself the way I do."

"I know." She truly did believe in him with so much conviction there was no room for a shred of doubt.

He pulled away, held her face between his hands, and looked deep into her eyes. "I vow that no matter what happens, I will leave you better than I found you."

Brooklyn hugged him and pressed her cheek against his chest, snuggling into his embrace as much as she could. Everything was going to be alright. Her Priest was her salvation. They sat like that for a while, neither of them saying a word. Father Mathias had no idea that as he held her in her most vulnerable state and fretted over his impact on her, he was mending her wounds, putting back the pieces that had been pried loose by her mother and the small-town priest.

He eventually laid Brooklyn down and got off the bed, stepping back to admire her naked form. He gently touched her left cheek, moved down to trace her shoulder and collarbone, then over a breast, down her belly... he lingered at her pelvis, then continued down to her thigh, shin, and to her foot.

She sighed so deeply from his attention, her body already singing from his touch. He continued with his tantalizing torture until her hands were clammy and her cheeks glowed, imitating the increasing heat between her legs.

"How was it for you? Not being able to touch yourself?"

Brooklyn blushed. "It was hard, Father."

"Sometimes, abstaining is the best thing we can do to experience real pleasure. May I show you?"

"Yes, Father," sighed Brooklyn as he continued to trace invisible lines on her skin.

"Close your eyes, my child. And whatever you do, do not open them. If you do, the consequence will not be favorable for either of us. Is that understood?"

She nodded and closed her eyes. "Yes, Father," she said breathlessly.

His fingers brushed against her clit, and she moaned a moan that came from deep within. Her legs spread involuntarily. He teased her with light strokes of his fingers then brought them to her mouth. Brooklyn parted her lips slightly and Father Mathias pushed his fingers in so that she could taste herself on them. She licked them clean before he continued, tracing light, quick circles that forced her hips off the bed. She wanted to ask him to do so much more but she was afraid to speak.

He leaned down. "You are so beautiful like this," he whispered in her ear. As he spoke, he applied more pressure, and her moans grew desperate as she neared climax. "You must ask for permission to come, child."

"P-please, Father! May I come? Oh God! Please!" she gasped as he rubbed her harder and faster.

"I want you to hold it."

Brooklyn's face scrunched with her effort to hold back an orgasm that was building up at blinding rate. She felt she would implode if she didn't release it.

"Please, Father..." she begged, choking on her words with bated breath. The electric tingling reached a crescendo in her clit, and little bursts of pleasure seeped past the imaginary door she was desperately trying to keep closed.

"Now, come now, and look at me."

She did, and his incinerating gaze bore into hers just before she was shattered by an intense orgasm. Her entire body shook, and her hips raised up high off the bed. She screamed from its intensity and from each wave that followed. It wouldn't end and her cries of pleasure were muted by her gasps. Never had she ever felt anything like it.

Suffering, indeed, exposed true pleasure.

Father Mathias was relentless, and he pressed harder still, continuing to rub quick circles until she was close to coming again.

"Please, Father!" she cried.

"Please, what?"

"Please, may I come?"

"You may."

Relief over not needing to hold it off accompanied her orgasm. It rang through her, a little less intense than the first one, but still strong enough where the sound of her pounding heart was so deafening that she couldn't hear her own cries of pleasure anymore. Through all of this, she made sure to maintain eye contact with her Priest.

After the last wave of her orgasm finished rippling through her, Father Mathias withdrew his hand and held it up to the dim light. His fingers glistened with evidence of her pleasure. His moment of hesitation was so brief that Brooklyn almost missed it before he brought his fingers to his lips and tasted her. As she watched him, Brooklyn got aroused all over again.

"You are magnificent, my child."

"Thank you, Father." He had finally given her what she'd wanted, and she was horrified to find it only managed to make her desire for him stronger than ever. She needed to feel him inside her, filling every hole so completely that he'd imprint himself in her so she could feel him always.

"It was my pleasure, child." He smiled. "Yet the flame of lust has not been quelled from your eyes. You're a ravenous little one," he mused.

"Father, I want to give you pleasure as well," she said shyly.

"I am more than satisfied with watching your face as you climaxed. We are done for tonight, my child." He lay down next to her and pulled her into his arms, holding her until her racing heart slowed to a steady pace.

Eventually, Brooklyn could sense that it was time for her to leave. "Should I get dressed, Father?" He nodded and she got up.

"When will I see you next?" she asked.

"I cannot say because I don't know at the moment." He looked at her and she could see the pained look in his expression. "This church is proving to be much more demanding than the last. Though, I wasn't on my own there. But I had assumed a smaller church would be less demanding."

A thought crossed her mind. "Have there been others? Are there others?"

"Of course, there have been others. I trained them and set them free to live as they should."

"Is that what you'll do with me?" she asked, panicked. His promise to leave her better than he found her now seemed less theoretical.

He chuckled. "Oh, my sweet child. Do you not listen when I speak? Feel when I touch? See when I look at you?" He paused. "It's wrong of me to want it, but I want to own you. To make you mine." The admission had him tense up and Brooklyn knew he had probably just crossed a line he had drawn for himself.

Brooklyn bit her lip and nodded shyly. "Why me, Father?"

Father Mathias took the time to think before replying, "I don't know."

"What would making me yours look like?"

"We shouldn't speak of such things, as they're an impossibility."

Brooklyn frowned, not liking his answer. It suggested that although he wanted her in a way he hadn't wanted the others, their path still led to a predestined dead end. "What if I want it too?"

He chuckled sadly. "Such a quick turnaround."

"Well, it all made sense to me the day we washed each other's feet. I hated the fact that I had this need to submit. It made me feel... small and... I don't know, low. I know it hasn't been long, but I feel like we're exactly where we're supposed to be."

"Your admission warms my heart so profoundly, my child." He sighed. "But being mine is not as ideal as you may think it to be."

"How could you say that, Father?"

"We'll discuss this another time. You may pleasure yourself once tomorrow morning if you'd like." His tone was final, and Brooklyn knew better than to push the subject.

"Thank you, Father." Brooklyn extracted herself from his embrace and got dressed. "How will I know when to come next?"

"I'm trusting that you'll be attending Mass?"

She nodded.

"I'll tell you then."

"Okay, Father."

"Good night, child."

"Good night, Father."

15

Work had been calling in Brooklyn in more and more often, and she wondered if it was because of the changes Gregory had noticed in her. The following day, she was still floating from her night with Father Mathias and a permanent blush had settled on her cheeks from the frequent flashbacks. Brooklyn had a hard time processing the level of ecstasy she had felt. Her life experiences thus far had admittedly been limited, but never had she encountered a lover so tuned in to her pleasure.

"Okay, spill," said Gregory at some point.

His demand roused Brooklyn from a flashback that had her grinning. "What?"

"Listen, I can tell that you've got something going on in that pretty little head of yours, and as your new BFF, I have rights to whatever that 'something' is."

Brooklyn smiled and desperately wanted to tell him about all the things she was excited about, but she shrugged instead. "You're on probation," she joked, hoping it would be enough to successfully avoid answering him without saying no.

Gregory squinted with mock suspicion, then sighed dramatically. "Fine, but just know, if I have any juicy news, I'm giving you the same lame answer."

Brooklyn shrugged again. "I think I can deal."

Gregory pouted and returned to refilling the whipped cream as Brooklyn filled out the next order.

"Medium cappuccino!" she nearly sang out.

"Well, that's new," said Stephen as he reached for his drink.

Brooklyn ducked behind the machines. "What's new?" she shouted over the whistling hiss of the steamer.

"That smile. It's beautiful."

"Thank you. Um. Your order is new."

"I like to switch things up occasionally. I was wondering... are you free tonight? I'd love to take you out for dinner."

Brooklyn looked down and swiped a rag across the counter. "Um…" Her brain was firing off at random and she couldn't string together two syllables. *Yes. Say yes. Yes is one syllable, you idiot.*

"Great! I'll pick you up from here at six. Tonight," he said, not waiting for her answer and making Brooklyn wonder if she had in fact spoken the one-word syllable out loud.

"Why?" Why was also one syllable. Not a good one, but it was a word. A full sentence, even.

"Why… what?"

Brooklyn didn't know exactly what her why was referring to.

"She'll be here," said Gregory from behind Brooklyn.

"Well, I'll see you later, then." And he was gone, leaving nothing behind but a whiff of his most-likely-expensive cologne.

"Oh. My. Fucking. God! What the fuck just happened?" Gregory shook Brooklyn by the shoulders.

"I have no idea. Did Stephen just ask me out?"

"He did. And I said yes for you. You're welcome."

The Business District was eerie after office hours. It seemed odd that a place in the city's center could be so quiet. Brooklyn waited in front of the cafe, but off to the side so none of her coworkers could see her. The last thing she needed was a bunch of people prying into her personal life. It was two minutes to six, and Brooklyn started doubting Stephen's interest, but at six on the dot, Stephen turned the corner.

"You're here," he said with a smile. "I was a little worried you wouldn't be."

As if that's actually something he'd worry about. She couldn't imagine anyone ever turning him down. "Why wouldn't I be?"

"Well, your friend had to say yes for you."

Brooklyn laughed quietly and tucked a strand of hair behind her ear. An unexpected flash of guilt halted her laugh. She wasn't even sure if she was allowed to date. Or if she even wanted to. Brooklyn looked at his face, which she realized was surprisingly kind. With his looks and money, she always imagined him as cold and aloof.

"And I'm grateful he did." He smiled again and held out his hand. "We can walk to where we're going."

Brooklyn looked at it.

"Is everything alright?"

She took a deep breath and closed her eyes. "Sorry. I'm... nervous."

"There's nothing to be nervous about. I promise. You'll see once we get to where we're going." He held out his hand again and this time Brooklyn took it.

They walked in silence and Brooklyn was grateful for it, although she hoped he couldn't hear her quick, panicked breaths. Her mind failed to comprehend the fact that she was walking hand in hand with Stephen. The act itself was too normal and contrary to what Brooklyn was used to. The men she had encountered had always wanted things to be quick and uncomplicated. Didn't holding hands complicate things? Wasn't Stephen worried she'd read too much into the gesture? Even if she was to do such a normal, wholesome thing such as walking hand in hand with a man, she never would have dreamed it would be with someone like Stephen.

"So, tell me about yourself."

"Um, I don't know what to say." Brooklyn wanted to hit herself.

"Do you have any pets?"

She shook her head. "I'm not really a pet person."

"That's excellent, neither am I. When I was about ten, my parents finally agreed to get me a puppy. After about a week, the novelty of it wore off and I realized I actually had to take care of it. He ended up being more my parents' pet than mine."

"My mother never allowed pets. She used to say..." Brooklyn shook her head. "It doesn't matter. So, do you have any siblings?"

"No, I'm an only child."

Brooklyn looked up at him. "Me too," she said with a smile. They exchanged little details about themselves during the walk. He was a foodie, loved fast cars, and loved making money. He was very close to his parents and had been engaged once but had decided he wasn't ready.

Brooklyn's tidbits of information were a lot more restrained. Her life was one huge sob story, and even now, the only good thing in it was something she couldn't even talk about. For the first time since her relationship with the priest began, that irked her. She did mention that most of her childhood had been in the country, that her neighbor had secretly given her horse riding lessons, and that she was still searching for her "thing."

The restaurant was a little twinkling hole in the wall, and as soon as they stepped in, Brooklyn was hit with an aromatic wall of cumin, turmeric, and saffron.

"I hope you like Persian food."

"I've never tried it, but I love trying new foods," Brooklyn said with a big smile. The place was empty, and Stephen must have noted her observation.

"I wish I could say I rented it out, but most of their business is take-out. The food is great, so don't let the lack of diners fool you."

Brooklyn wanted to say that it didn't matter; that sitting at a table with him while sharing a meal was enough. But she kept it to herself. She wasn't extraordinarily sentimental, and she wasn't about to start now just because she was about to have dinner with *the* Stephen.

He proved to be beyond charming, and Brooklyn found herself, chin resting in the palm of her hand, staring at him dreamily. She loved the way he spoke with confidence and with his hands. He even managed to walk that fine line between chivalry and condescension with ease. Stephen ordered their meals, but only after asking if it was alright for him to do so. He didn't pull out her chair, but he waited for her to sit before sitting himself.

Brooklyn was sad when their dinner came to an end, but grateful that it had happened. Stephen proved to be so much more than a suit and a nice haircut, and Brooklyn felt privileged to have found that out. When he dropped her off, she appreciated that he didn't look for a kiss and asked if she was okay with a hug. He was truly the perfect modern gentleman.

"Are you sure I can't walk you to your door?" he asked.

Even though her rooming house looked like any old Glebe home, the poorly maintained windows and steps gave it away, as did the littered front yard. But that wasn't why she had asked him to drop her off a couple blocks down. Just like when she would go out with Page, she was worried about the wealth her company presented and didn't want the other boarders to get the wrong idea about her financial situation. After all, having a bottle or two of vodka had been enough a display of "wealth" to catch Barb's attention.

"No, it's okay. But thank you."

Stephen clearly wasn't appeased, but he didn't pressure her. "I had a great time."

"Me too," Brooklyn said with a smile. They exchanged numbers and he promised to text her soon to set up another date.

Brooklyn walked slowly up the path to the house that wasn't her home and turned when she didn't hear him pull away. It made for an awkward goodbye, but she waved and stayed there until he got the point and drove off. She could not quell her smile as she walked back to the rooming house and up to her room. It wasn't until she closed her door that the smile faded. It was as if closing it cut a cord that released a tapestry with Father Mathias's image on it, reminding her that her availability wasn't very straightforward. She shoved the mental image away and went to sit on the sofa with a huff.

Her conscience wasn't going to let her off that easy. Brooklyn wondered if she should tell Father Mathias about Stephen. She knew she'd have to bring it up if sex came up between her and Stephen, but she decided she was getting ahead of herself and chose to daydream about her evening instead. She could still taste the spices on her tongue and remembered how Stephen didn't ridicule her for her ignorance when it came to the foreign cuisine. Instead, he delighted in her excitement as she tried their dill and barley soup, eggplant-based spreads, and lamb. It had been such a treat—to be offered not just dinner, but an experience.

In the morning, Brooklyn's phone reminded her that she had a volunteering shift at the soup kitchen. She got ready and bussed to the community center. On the way, she remembered Joe and his unsettling, accurate perception of her. It made her reluctant to go back, but she reminded herself how good she had felt afterwards.

Elizabeth greeted her and gave her a volunteer badge. "I'm so glad to see you! How was your week?"

"It was good," Brooklyn said with a smile.

"I know Caroline will be happy to see you. We're still waiting on the police check. Did you manage to get that done?"

"No, I'm so sorry I forgot. I'll be sure to get it done today."

"Hmm, we made an exception the other day because we truly needed the help, but I'm afraid we will need that police check before you can volunteer."

"Please let me help today and I promise to get it done today."

Elizabeth thinned her lips in deliberation, then broke out into a big smile. "Oh, alright, but you keep it between us. And just this time."

"Thank you!"

Caroline seemed happy to see Brooklyn. It made Brooklyn feel good to be wanted and appreciated, and throughout the day she found herself smiling more than ever. This time around, however, she decided to avoid mingling with the diners. Maybe in the future she'd be ready enough to face those who mirrored her past. Until then, she'd pass on that challenge. For now, she busied herself with grating cheese.

Sunday came and Brooklyn went to Mass, happy to be able to see her Priest. She stayed behind and prayed, and eventually, he went to her and told her to return later that evening. Her cheeks flushed with anticipation.

That evening, there was a slight hesitation when Brooklyn reached for the church doors. She hadn't thought before that her being there so late could be seen as suspicious. She looked up and down the street.

It was mostly empty, and the main floors of the houses were dark with dimly-lit second floors. Brooklyn ducked inside and went straight to the rectory and to that little table she had to kneel and pray at.

Father Mathias arrived shortly after.

"You are so precious, my child. Stand up."

Brooklyn stood but didn't turn. Father Mathias pulled her hair over her shoulder to expose her neck. He kissed it lightly as he reached around to unzip her sweater, trailing a finger along the way. He slowly pulled it down her shoulders and let it fall to the floor. Brooklyn sank into the indulgent speed at which the priest was moving. Everything felt sensual, right down to the material of her sweater rubbing on her shoulders. Her tank top and jeans joined it, and he instructed her to slowly take off her panties and bra.

There was more confidence this time as Brooklyn stripped out of her undergarments. She savored the familiarity she now felt with him. It was a special kind of intimacy, to know how someone moves and how you can move with or around them.

"Do not move. Do not look back," he said when she was done. She felt him move away from her briefly before returning. He reached to wrap his hand around her throat and buried his face in her hair. He sighed, then quickly pulled a hood over her head.

Brooklyn felt rope being rubbed against her arms.

"Hold your hands behind your back."

She obliged and her wrists were bound with the rope.

"Come with me," ordered Father Mathias. He turned her and pushed her from behind.

Brooklyn took cautious, small steps. She was certain they had passed the bedroom and felt confused.

"On your knees." His command was sharp.

She awkwardly fell to her knees. The hood allowed minuscule amounts of light through, but not enough to make out the vague shapes of objects.

Father Mathias grabbed her face and squeezed hard. "I want to destroy you, my child. I want to destroy you then put you back together. Over and over again." His voice was low and almost menacing as he spoke through clenched teeth.

Brooklyn moaned and pressed into his painful grasp, showing she did not fear him. If only she could see how this drove the priest mad with want. He grunted and let her go with a small shove and toed her thighs apart, forcing her to bare her sex.

"You are so beautiful."

"Thank you, Father."

Father Mathias reached down and pinched her nipple without warning. Brooklyn cried out from the pain.

"Hmm, so much noise and we've barely begun. Close your eyes." He pulled the hood off and replaced it with a blindfold. "Open your mouth," he ordered before shoving a large, spherical object that tasted of rubber in her mouth. Brooklyn guessed that it must be a ball-gag when she felt a strap securing the object in place so that she couldn't spit it out. Father Mathias placed a small bell in her hand. "Now that you cannot speak, you'll need to use that if it becomes too much to bear. Understood?"

Brooklyn nodded. He felt different tonight. More... beastly. His demeanor finally elicited a bit of fear. It sent delicious shivers through her body, starting at the base of her spine and traveling up to the nape of her neck. The feeling was so palpable she could swear it tangled with her hair. She began to pant heavily, and it wasn't long before she was drooling from the gag and sweating profusely from anticipation. She couldn't help but feel embarrassed when she felt sweat droplets running down the insides of her arms.

Brooklyn flinched. Something pricked at her skin that felt like tiny needles.

"I'm going to be gentle with you first, my child. Do not worry."

The prickling sensation continued as he drew the instrument across her skin. Brooklyn focused on its feeling, trying to picture what it was, but before she could zero in on it, it was replaced with something soft and ticklish. He ran it across her shoulders and down to the small of her back. "You're aroused already?" he said with a chuckle.

Brooklyn felt his breath on her face, and she turned towards it in an attempt to face him.

"I'm not sure I have the patience to go slow, my child." He pulled her up and bent her over something cushioned but firm and covered in leather. She was able to rest the entire length of her torso on it before the priest guided her knees up and onto another leather-covered cushion, so that she was in an all-fours position.

Brooklyn moaned in fear when she felt heavy straps being pulled and secured across her back.

"Only because you like to squirm," he whispered in her ear. Father Mathias started with an implement that felt new to her. She could tell it was made of multiple strips of suede. The air whooshed with the soft impact, carrying the smell of leather with it, and the suede gently pulled at her skin as Father Mathias dragged it down her back and bottom after each hit. He alternated between soft and heavy hits until her skin was warm to the touch.

She expected something that hurt a bit—or a lot—more, but instead she felt his fingers probe her sex. She tried to push back against his hand.

"Do not move." He pressed down on her lower back with one hand and slowly rubbed her clit with the other, finding the rhythm that sent electric shock waves through her body.

Brooklyn let out a muffled cry of pleasure and did her best to stay still, but her legs trembled involuntarily. She panicked when she was close to coming because she couldn't ask for permission. Still, she tried to speak.

"I'm sorry child, I can't understand you."

Brooklyn tried to speak around the gag again.

"Do you need to come?"

Brooklyn nodded vigorously.

"You may," he said with amusement.

He barely finished speaking when the orgasm ripped through Brooklyn. The restraints cut into her skin as she arched from the intensity of her climax.

"Breathe, child. Breathe." He rubbed that spot again.

Brooklyn moaned and she bucked as much as the restraints allowed as she neared another orgasm.

"What do you want, my child?"

Again, she tried desperately to speak.

"Come for me," he ordered, and again, she came before he could even finish speaking.

Brooklyn sagged and gasped for air. There was little time for her to recover before he landed a painful blow with a paddle. The blindfold was pulled off and Brooklyn saw her reflection in a wall-to-wall mirror. They were in that oddly sized room that was now painted a deep plum. The faint smell of fresh paint still hung in the air, suggesting it was something he must have done shortly after moving in. On the wall behind her was an astounding collection of implements hanging on wooden hooks, explaining the smell of wood, leather, lemon, and beeswax that mingled with the fresh paint.

"I want you to watch yourself." His eyes were alight with feral hunger. He rubbed the paddle on Brooklyn's bottom in slow circles, then landed a sharp smack without warning. And then another. And another. He switched out the wooden paddle for a rubber one. It earned him a satisfying cry from her.

Brooklyn's skin prickled from the sudden hot flash and her palms grew sweaty. She squeezed the bell tighter; afraid she would drop it. Father Mathias spaced each impact far enough apart to give her time to just barely recover from the previous one, but not enough to find a moment of relief. The onslaught of sensations that demanded her attention overwhelmed her and she couldn't figure out when she was still feeling the echoes of a previous hit or the pain of a new one.

He moved on to another implement, raining down a steady stream of pain. He brought Brooklyn to tears and only stopped when she was sobbing. She looked at him through the mirror and moaned with want. He looked so handsome. His eyes were bright with joy, his mouth slack with satisfaction and newly brewing hunger. Brooklyn never wanted to leave that room; didn't want the moment to end. She implored him with nothing but her eyes.

"Are you asking for more, child?"

Brooklyn nodded and sobbed at her helplessness in the face of her compulsions. She was enslaved to them. No matter how tired or reluctant she felt, deep down, a part of her spoke much louder and it was crying for *more*. There was a need, an itch, that even when scratched still needed to be relentlessly attended to.

Father Mathias smiled and closed his eyes to take a calming breath. His excitement was unmistakable. He turned to face his wall of pain and reached for an implement with little deliberation, pulling it off its hook. With a brandish, he lifted it for her to see.

"This one is called Rapture. I almost used it on you the other day." It was the long and narrow paddle that looked like a wooden sword.

Brooklyn whimpered around the gag and struggled against the restraints. Her change of heart didn't deter the priest. He landed a lightning-fast blow on her bottom, pulling back quickly which magnified the wood's bite. Brooklyn's muffled scream seemed to be absorbed by the walls. Either that or her ears were ringing too loudly for her to know just how loud she had been. He hit her again and she begged him with unintelligible words as she saw flashes of white. Unbearable heat washed across her face, robbing her of her breath.

"Five more strikes, my child. Will you take them for me?"

Brooklyn nodded and was sobbing uncontrollably now.

One.

Two.

She couldn't understand the building pressure between her legs. It felt similar to a building orgasm, but that didn't make sense.

Three.

The feeling coiled tightly in her belly and her legs began to tremble.

Four...

And she came, her cries of pleasure mixing with cries of pain and sobs of confusion. When she looked up at the priest, the look on his face was indescribable. It was a mixture of awe and wonderment, enlightenment, praise, adoration, arousal, carnal hunger. His expression was everything and more.

"Five," he counted before landing the last strike without breaking eye contact. He hung up Rapture and returned to Brooklyn's side, grabbing her hair and pulling her head back. "You didn't ask for permission to come, my child. And for that, there will be consequences."

Brooklyn shook her head and pleaded with her eyes. Father Mathias removed the gag.

"You may speak," he said, when she didn't say anything.

"Please, Father, I didn't know. I didn't expect it. How..." Her voice trailed off. How could she come from pain? It made no sense to her.

"How?" He ran his fingers through her disheveled hair. "You are perfect. That's how." It was almost as if he was speaking more to himself than to her. He was lost in his mind, looking at her and her welts and bruises. Brooklyn couldn't understand what was happening inside him. Father Mathias took a fumbling step backwards.

"Father?" whispered Brooklyn.

"You're my holy grail." Again, he spoke more to himself than to her, so Brooklyn remained silent.

Without a word, the priest undid her restraints, untied the rope, and carried her to his bed. He laid her down and got undressed while Brooklyn stared at him in a daze. Everything seemed to be moving in slow motion, and her body felt heavy and light at the same time. Father Mathias urged her to roll over and lie on her stomach, then rubbed a cool balm on her bottom before lying down next to her and pulling her into his arms.

"You did so well," he murmured into her hair. "I will forgive your transgression."

"Thank you, Father." Brooklyn slurred her words, caught in an unbelievable high that surpassed any drug she had ever taken.

"I'm afraid I went a little too hard on you to allow you to go home," he said, troubled.

"I'll be okay in a bit."

"It would be irresponsible of me to let you leave in this state. Never mind, enjoy this moment, child." He spoke so quietly, as if still caught up in his head. "And thank you. Tonight you gave me a gift I could only dream of."

Brooklyn nodded and burrowed into his embrace. Nothing else mattered. Nothing could harm her. She felt as if she was wrapped in a cocoon of cashmere and bliss. Everything felt amazing against her skin, especially his faint, warm breath on her forehead and the vibration of his heartbeat against her cheek. She ran her fingers across his graying chest hair and tried to commit the feeling to memory. Brooklyn never wanted to forget these details about him.

16

"Wake up, my child," whispered Father Mathias.

Brooklyn's eyes fluttered open and she sat up in a panic. "Oh my God! What time is it?"

Father Mathias chuckled. "Do not worry. It's still early morning. And need I remind you about using the Father's name in vain?"

"I'm sorry, Father."

He pulled Brooklyn into his arms and sighed. "How I wish we didn't have to rush."

"Me too."

They lay back down and savored the too few minutes they had left. Brooklyn needed to leave well before Janice's arrival.

"Father?"

"Yes, my child?"

"What were the others like?" She held her breath, afraid she may have asked a question she shouldn't have when he didn't answer right away.

"They were all different," he eventually said. "But all unaware submissives."

"Do you miss any of them?"

"No. There was never any emotional attachment."

"I couldn't imagine doing what we do without any emotions coming out of it."

Father Mathias had been stroking her bare shoulder with his thumb, but he stopped. "I never played with any of the others. I only taught them about the lifestyle. I did give them tasks, at the most, to put into practice my teachings and training. But nothing more."

Brooklyn got up to look at him. "Really?" There was the desperate hope again, and she hated it.

"Really."

"Oh," she said with a shy smile.

"Well, we better get dressed," he said before she could ask *why her*.

Suddenly, Brooklyn thought of her date with Stephen. "I was wondering..." Her voice trailed off. She didn't want to ask Father Mathias about Stephen, because she knew if he said no, she would listen, and she wasn't ready to close that door.

"Yes, child?"

She smiled. "Nothing."

They reluctantly got up and got dressed. Brooklyn moved carefully. Never had she felt as much soreness as she did then. Every muscle that had tasted the priest's wrath screamed with movement. Strangely, the rest of her body hurt as well, the way it would after an intense day at the gym. It took her a little longer than usual to pull up her pants and she felt shy when she noticed the pleasure Father Mathias took in her struggle.

He left and returned with a glass of orange juice. "Here," he said, holding it out to her. She drank and he watched her intently. Brooklyn took it as a suggestion that she finish it all.

"Go sit in the confessional when you're finished getting dressed," he said when she finished the juice. "I will open the church doors soon and we can talk for a bit, then you can leave. I doubt anyone is watching to see if you ever came in in the first place," he said with a conspiratorial smile.

"Yes, Father." He took the empty glass and left Brooklyn to finish with the struggle of pulling on her clothes. She went to wait for him, and as she sat in the booth, she considered again taking the opportunity to tell him about Stephen. Voices interrupted her contemplation. Curious, she peeked past the curtain and found Father Mathias speaking with Janice.

"Really, Father, you shouldn't be bothering yourself with opening the church. That's what I'm here for," said Janice.

Father Mathias shook his head at himself. "I keep forgetting. There was no such luxury where I'm coming from. The administrator made it very clear she wasn't there to wait on us."

"Yes, and I heard you were running a church alone in a small town in the mountains before that?"

"I was," confirmed Father Mathias.

Janice touched his arm, and a fit of jealousy overcame Brooklyn.

"That must have been very lonely."

Is she seriously flirting with him? If only she could confront the woman, but Brooklyn stayed put.

The priest cleared his throat and took a step back. "One isn't lonely when doing God's work," he said.

Janice's obvious embarrassment was enough to soothe Brooklyn's anger.

"Oh, of course, Father. Well, I'll let you get on with your day."

Father Mathias nodded and headed towards the confessional and Brooklyn sat back and rested her head against the box's wall. She took a deep breath when Father Mathias entered his side of the confessional. "Father?" she started, once again considering telling him about Stephen.

"Yes, child?"

Brooklyn was silent while she tried to find her words. Would her Priest feel the same jealousy she had felt just then? Seeing how another woman flirting with him made her feel made Brooklyn's guilt multiply, as well as her fear. She decided that maybe she needed to sort her feelings out before risking her relationship with Father Mathias. "Thank you. For last night. It was... amazing," she said instead.

"And thank you." Father Mathias touched the grate with his fingertips and Brooklyn did the same.

Redness stained her cheeks when she thought of the previous night. Something special had been touched within her, and she had a suspicion that whatever it was now belonged to her Priest, indefinitely. Brooklyn couldn't imagine anyone else reaching that thing that resided in the depths of her soul. She wondered if she could ever find the ecstasy she had experienced with anyone else. With Stephen?

"Father?" she whispered.

"Yes?"

"If you and I decide to... make things... official, what will that mean for us? Will we be like boyfriend and girlfriend?" Brooklyn felt silly asking such a question.

"That is not an easy question to answer," Father Mathias said sadly.

"Why not?"

"Because none of this should even be happening. Entertaining the idea of a fully involved dynamic and relationship just wouldn't be fair to you, child."

Brooklyn wanted to ask if he would ever consider leaving the church, but she knew that was a cruel question to ask. Had he been the one to push for their current situation, Brooklyn felt she may have had a right to ask it. But she had wielded his need to help her against him to get what she had wanted, and now she wanted more—more than what, she knew, would be possible for him to give without endangering his priesthood.

"Or fair to you," Brooklyn said. "Maybe it's time for me to go now. I heard someone come in."

He nodded. "Until next time, my child."

Gathering her things, Brooklyn left with her head hanging low. All of her clarity and direction had been shattered by her date with Stephen. Of course, something good could only be short lived.

"Oh! I didn't see you come in," said Janice from her office door.

Brooklyn looked up. "Um, yeah, I can be pretty quiet."

"I guess you finally managed to unburden yourself," she said, nodding towards the confessional, but her voice dripped with suspicion.

Hypocritical bitch. The thought came with such quick venom that it caught Brooklyn by surprise, and she didn't have a chance to hide the scowl. There was little tolerance in Brooklyn's threshold for people like Janice—the type who was quick to judge others for shared sins.

"I did. Have a good day," said Brooklyn, doing her best hide her distaste. She bolted through the doors, wanting to put as much distance as she could between herself and the church. As she walked away, she swore she saw the curtains move from a small window she could only guess belonged to Janice's office.

Once home, Brooklyn sat on her sofa with a wince. The soreness reminded her of the magical night she had shared with Father Mathias. She got up and pulled her pants down just enough to check her bottom in the mirror. He had never marked her so beautifully before. If she looked closely enough, she could make out the spots where Rapture had left a print of its detailed pattern on her skin. She traced it with her fingertips and shuddered from the feeling of her light touch on her ravaged skin.

Biting her lip, Brooklyn opened the camera on her phone and pulled down her pants all the way. She wanted these marks to last forever and pictures would ensure that. It took a few tries before she was satisfied with a couple good photos. She stared at her phone, wanting to observe every detail, and then tried to take more pictures from a different angle. Finally, she was happy with the documentation of Father Mathias's handiwork and ended up with more than ten photos of welted skin. Not long ago, the sight would have disturbed her, but now they were trophies; proof of her strength. And proof of Father Mathias's appetite and what it meant. The idea of being capable of satisfying such a hard-met need within the priest had Brooklyn flushed with sudden arousal.

Closing her eyes, she conjured up the image of Father Mathias's awe when she came from his savage attentions. She sighed and reached down to touch her welts again, wanting to sink back into that moment. A small squeeze took her there, back to the room with the lingering scent of fresh paint intermingled with leather, wood, and balsam. She wanted to stay there forever, in that plane of ecstasy where all that mattered was pain and pleasure and serving her Priest.

The sofa beckoned her and she went to lie down under her duvet, only to get back up to strip off her clothes, wanting nothing between her and the little bit of luxury her former friend had gifted her. She felt caught between reality and an intoxicating place in her mind that had been unlocked. There was a quiet buzz in her ears, her breath echoed in her head, and every movement made the world sway as if it was trying to lull her to sleep.

Her phone rang, pulling her reluctant mind back to the present. It was Stephen.

"Hello?"

"Hey there, how are you?"

"Good, you?"

"I'm well, thanks. Would be better if we could have lunch today."

Brooklyn closed her eyes tightly. The headspace she needed to be in to consider spending time with Stephen felt miles away, as she was still riding on the coattails of the previous night's high.

"Hello?"

"Um, yeah, sure. What time?"

"Twelve on the dot sound good to you?"

"Mhm."

"Alright. I'll pick you up then."

Brooklyn didn't rush to get ready. Instead, she sat with her arms crossed, her conscience forcing her to deliberate whether she should call Stephen and cancel. *Or move ahead with Stephen and stop seeing Father Mathias.* As life-altering as things had been with Father Mathias, one thought plagued her: What future could she have with a priest? Brooklyn shook away the thought. Ending things with him wasn't an option.

Placating her conscience with the reassurance that it was just lunch and well within the realm of appropriate, Brooklyn got ready. Choosing what to wear proved to be difficult. An evening date was easy, outside of the fact that she had limited options. But a lunch date? What did one wear to a casual, last-minute date with someone like Stephen? Brooklyn eyed the bins that held the designer clothes Page had gotten her.

"No," Brooklyn whispered. Those clothes didn't represent her, and even though Page wasn't around to see it, it would mean taking part in the forced gifts for appearances. So instead, she pulled out the skirt she had worn for Father Mathias the other day and paired it with one of her many plain black t-shirts.

Brooklyn left and walked to the street where he had dropped her off the last time. She panicked when she couldn't remember exactly which house she had pretended was hers and berated herself for not taking note of it. *Maybe he won't remember,* she hoped. She settled on one house, waiting at the end of the footpath that led up to it, but doubt set in and she decided to go to the street corner.

Stephen arrived on time—not a minute earlier and not a minute later than twelve. He pulled up to the house she had guessed was the one she had chosen the other night, then rolled up to the corner when she waved to catch his attention.

"Sorry, I thought you'd be coming from this side. Wanted to save you extra maneuvers." Maybe the lie was unnecessary, but Brooklyn's self-consciousness created a possible inner dialogue for Stephen that fed into her worry.

"Is everything alright?" he asked when she carefully got into the car.

"Everything is fine," she said, pushing her guilt away and forcing a smile.

"You sure? You look like you're in pain."

"I took up running and my body is mad at me for it." *Another lie.* Brooklyn doubted whether she should be there now more than ever. Nothing good could be built on lies, even small ones.

"Good for you. I love running, although I don't do it as often as I used to. Maybe we could go running together sometime."

"Mhm, that would be nice." Committing to future plans probably wasn't the best idea when Brooklyn still didn't know how she wanted to move forward, but the image of the two of them running along the canal together was a hard one to reject.

"So, what made you take up running?" asked Stephen when they were seated at a table. Stephen had opted to stay in the Glebe since it was the middle of the workday and time was limited.

Brooklyn choked on her water. Why could none of her answers be the truth? It dawned on her then that this would be her life if she continued with the priest. Secrecy, lies, discretion. She wasn't built for this. She wasn't quick enough with her answers and her nerves proved to be too fragile. She took the time to think while she recovered and cleared her throat.

"I work for the cafe casually, so I have a lot of free time on my hands." There, that was *technically* the truth. At least, that's how her running had started.

"Impressive. Of all the things to do to pass the time, you chose that," he said with a chuckle.

"Why don't you get to do it as often as you'd like?" Brooklyn wanted to turn the conversation back to Stephen.

"I have the opposite problem: not enough time. My company is growing and with that comes more demands on my time and energy. So, I'm stuck with the gym in my building and I refuse to run on a treadmill."

Brooklyn couldn't imagine being so important that one's time wasn't their own. "Yet, you make time to eat with the barista," she said shyly.

"I make time to eat with a woman of immense interest," he amended.

This made Brooklyn blush. She looked down at the menu and felt pressured to make a choice, given the current topic of limited time.

"See anything you like?"

Brooklyn froze. She wasn't used to being able to order freely. Usually, the price dictated what she chose, but she wasn't paying today. That also made her worried about her choice as she didn't want to take advantage of him. "I'll get what you're getting."

Stephen laughed. "But you don't know what I'm getting."

"I trust you," she said with a smile. Brooklyn closed the menu and pushed it off to the side.

"If you say so."

Stephen ordered quinoa bowls with grilled chicken and Brooklyn was embarrassed to admit that she had never had the South American grain before. But when the food came, she was glad she had let him order, forcing her to try something new. Between mouthfuls, Stephen shared anecdotes from his workday and Brooklyn asked questions. Originally she had merely wanted to make sure the conversation stayed on him always, but she found she was genuinely interested in what he did.

"Have you considered going to college or university?" asked Stephen.

The question caught Brooklyn by surprise "Um, no. Why?"

"It's just you're asking very good questions and you seem to be interested in the world of investing."

"Oh! Um, I don't know."

"You should think about it."

Brooklyn pushed a piece of avocado around the bowl. "I'm not really a school person."

"We all think that, until we find the one thing we gladly want to learn about." Stephen's phone buzzed and he apologized before taking the call. Brooklyn sighed with relief when he got up and went outside. She watched him through the window, wondering again what she was doing there.

"I'm sorry, I'm going to have to cut lunch short," said Stephen when her returned.

"Oh no, it's okay!" Brooklyn said a little too enthusiastically.

Stephen was clearly in a rush; he went to the front to pay the bill, then ushered Brooklyn out of the restaurant.

"What do you have planned for the rest of the day?" he asked.

"I'm not on the schedule but I'm thinking of popping in at the soup kitchen."

"Oh? You volunteer? Which one?"

Brooklyn nodded. "St. Anthony's Hope Initiative. It's one of my weekly tasks," she said absentmindedly.

"Cool. Maybe I can come with you on the weekend."

"No!" This was hers and Father Mathias's. Sharing it with another man seemed wrong. "I mean, um, it's something I like to do on my own. And besides, there's this whole process you'd have to go through." Brooklyn wanted to bury her face in her hands and all of her guilt came rushing back.

"What about Saturday night? There's an amazing rooftop bar..."

"I don't really do bars or clubs. Anymore. I used to. But I stopped."

"Alright then, how about you just agree to let me pick you up Saturday and I'll surprise you?" He checked his watch.

Brooklyn bit her lip. "Surprise me?"

"Yes."

"Okay..." She didn't like surprises, but she could tell he needed to get out of there as soon as possible and didn't want to hold him up any longer. "And don't worry about driving me back, it's a short walk."

"I have time to..."

"No, you don't, I can tell," she said with a warm smile. "Thank you for lunch."

Stephen threw her a thankful look. "Until Saturday."

Brooklyn's smile faltered. Her Priest had told her the same thing just that morning. Only they had no set time.

"Are you sure you're okay? I really don't mind driving you home."

Brooklyn fixed her smile. "I promise. Until Saturday."

"And Brooklyn?"

"Hmm?"

"Thanks for making my workday a little brighter. And not just today. Every time I go to the cafe, I'm hoping to see you."

Confusion aside, Stephen had a talent for making Brooklyn smile, and she smiled through dinner prep at the soup kitchen and all the way home. When she got home, it took her a moment to realize Page was sitting on the front doorstep of the rooming house with mascara running down her face.

"Hey, Brookie," said Page with a weak smile.

"What are you doing here?"

"I know you don't wanna see me but... I need you. I need my friend."

Brooklyn had always admired Page's ability to look photo-ready no matter what, so she was taken aback by just how haggard her former friend looked. Had Page's hair been well coiffed like it usually was and her lips touched with gloss, the running mascara could have evoked a sense of tragic beauty rather than tragic mess.

Even though Page seemed as close to human as ever, Brooklyn still couldn't muster any empathy. "Your friend? Or your doormat?"

Page's eyes widened in surprise. "I guess I deserved that," she said after a moment.

"If you need help, go to Sam. He seems to have a pill for everything." She whispered the last part so that her neighbors couldn't hear.

"Brooklyn, please!" Page got up and dusted off her designer jeans. "Can we please talk?"

"You need to go." Brooklyn looked around and up at the windows of the house, worried someone would see Page. Although she looked rough, no amount of dishevelment could hide the money she came from. Page wouldn't move.

"You have five minutes." Brooklyn decided it was at least better having Page in her room where no one could see her or hear their conversation. She unlocked the door and motioned for Page to go in. They went up to her room and Brooklyn unlocked the door reluctantly. Brooklyn hated letting Page into such an intimate space such as her room. She was the perfect contrast to Brooklyn's level of poverty and made the room appear that much sadder. They sat on opposite ends of the sofa—Page with hands clasped in front of her, and Brooklyn with crossed arms as if they could keep her safe from Page's potential venom.

"After you ghosted, I spiraled..."

"Oh, so that's what you're here for, to blame me for your problems?"

"I know I wasn't in a good place before. I'm just saying... things got bad after. Why do you always have to twist my words?"

Brooklyn held her hands up. "I don't need this right now. If you came here..."

"Wait! I'm sorry. I spiraled. I just spiraled. It wasn't your fault. 'Kay? And my parents found out and they cut me off. Sam left me. I can't afford to go out with my friends and all they want to do is to party."

Poor you. "What do you want, Page?"

"I just want my friend back. I miss you."

"Well, I'm done. We weren't good for each other."

"Brookie, I need you."

"Page..."

"You're literally the only person who wasn't around me for my money. Everyone is gone! My parents won't even talk to me."

"And what am I supposed to do about it, Page?"

"Just be my friend." Her bottom lip quivered. Brooklyn felt extremely uncomfortable seeing her so vulnerable. It seemed the lack of vulnerability was a gift they shared. Brooklyn didn't know what to do with Page's emotions and desperately wanted to shove them back into her friend and seal them off.

"I don't know how. At least not without losing myself. And I'm doing really well now."

The tears stopped just long enough for Page to give Brooklyn a look over. "Yeah, you look... different. So..." Page paused. "You're giving me shit for blaming you for my downfall but now you're saying that it was my fault you weren't doing well?"

"I'm sorry, what?"

"You're doing great, right? So great you don't want to be dragged down by your junkie ex-friend."

"I never..."

Page held up a hand. "Or maybe you're just like everyone else, just hanging around me so some of my shine could rub off on you. Well, congrats, you took it and left me with nothing."

"How could you think that?" Brooklyn's mind raced to make sense of what was being thrown at her. Logically, she knew it wasn't true, but Page spoke with such conviction that it made Brooklyn doubt herself. Had she been just as bad for Page as Page had been for her? Had Page been that terrible, or had Brooklyn shoved misplaced blame on her?

"Brooklyn, think of everything I've done for you! You hung around for that. Now, you barely let me in past the front door."

"I didn't even know about your situation! And what you've done for me? What is that, exactly? Buy me clothes that are worth more than my rent so I don't embarrass you? Here!" Brooklyn went to the stack of bins that held her party clothes and pulled out anything Page had bought her, which was almost everything. She dumped them at Page's feet. "You're having money troubles, right? Take these and sell them. Now get out!"

"When did you turn into such a bitch?" Page wouldn't even glance at the pile of clothes that had to be worth more than a few thousand dollars, even used.

Suddenly Brooklyn noticed the subtle eye twitch and lip chewing. Page was hurting for a hit of anything, and badly.

"Did you come here for friendship or something else?"

"Ha! What else do you have to give, paper bag princess?" As she spewed the insult, Page's eyes scanned the coffee table that used to also serve as a medicine cabinet, confirming Brooklyn's suspicion: Page was in search of a high, not a friend.

Brooklyn softened her face. "I don't do that stuff anymore, Page. Maybe this is a sign to get some help. What we were doing wasn't good."

"Fuck you! You're clean for what? A minute? And now you think you're better than me? You know what, I *will* take these back!" Page snatched up the clothes with as much dignity as she could muster, but she still looked more pathetic than Brooklyn had the morning she had stooped to pick up the hundred-dollar bill.

"I'm truly sorry you're hurting, Page, but please don't ever come back." Brooklyn pushed her out the door and went to close it.

"Wait! Wait! Wait! I'm sorry. Brooklyn please, I didn't mean it! I didn't mean it!" Page shouldered the door to keep it open. "And I didn't come here for this." She lifted the pile of clothes. A sob ripped through her. "I know why you kept them, and you should sell them and keep the money for yourself."

Page was referring to a time early on in their friendship, where she had instructed Brooklyn to wear something she had purchased, but Brooklyn had sold it, along with everything else Page had given her, for rent money. Page had made sure that Brooklyn would never think of doing anything like that again, even if it meant forgoing a meal better than instant noodles. Just mentioning it brought up the shame Page had made her feel, equating what she had done to stealing.

"Why? To support your idea of me? No thank you," Brooklyn said.

"I'm sorry for everything I said. I'm a mess, okay? And... I'm sorry for the way I was with you. I mean it. I threw money around like it meant nothing and you were struggling. Now I understand how shitty that must have been for you."

"No. No, you don't. You think a few days without mommy and daddy's money is perspective? Did they take away your condo? Your car? Do you have to work for your next meal?" Brooklyn tried to close the door again.

"I used your situation against you. I know what I did."

This made Brooklyn stop and she stepped back from the door. "Why?"

Page sniffled. "Do you remember when we first met?"

Brooklyn nodded.

"The way you looked at me was... nice. Everything I showed you was new for you, and it made me feel like what I had was special. Everyone else had money and I always felt like I'd never be good enough, never in the right circles. You looked at me like I was a princess."

"I remember."

"Then something changed. You weren't impressed anymore. And it made me angry."

"Yes! Page! Because after you allowed me a tour of the high life, I had to come back to this!" Brooklyn motioned at her room. "You forced all these luxuries on me that, in the end, only made me realize how miserable my life is! Do you know what it feels like to look at the crap you bought me and see them as meals that were out of reach? Because God forbid I sell a dress so I can eat."

"And I'm so sorry," she said with a hiccup. "I deserve everything that's happening to me. I'm a horrible friend and a horrible person."

"Don't try to pretend that you're sorry. All you've told me is how you miss me fawning all over you. After a while, the parties and pretty dresses are just that. They excited me for a minute because *I* live in the real world, Page. But when the club lights die out and you wake up in a bed not knowing what happened, you realize how empty it all is. How *disgusting* it all is." Finally,

Brooklyn had the courage to bring up what had hurt her more than anything else Page had ever done.

"You wanted it," whispered Page. "I swear you did."

"Fuck. You."

"Is that why you blocked me everywhere?"

"God, you are so stupid." Tears streamed down Brooklyn's cheeks, and she dashed them away angrily. "Please, just leave me alone. I don't ever want to see you or talk to you again."

Page didn't move. She paused, then finally she stepped out of the door's way. "I'm truly sorry."

"Apology not accepted. Goodbye, Page. And take your clothes." Brooklyn closed the door and leaned against it. She had lied. She *did* miss her friend. Before Page had become so cruel, she had been like a fairy godmother and afforded Brooklyn the chance to escape. More than that, after a lifetime of being told she was the embodiment of evil, Page was the first person to make her feel good about herself. That is... until things changed.

Brooklyn looked at herself in the mirror. A reminder was needed to help her keep her resolve. She looked much healthier, and only after a short amount of time away from her friend. She couldn't let Page ruin that. She hugged herself tightly and squeezed her eyes shut as guilt about turning away Page warred with her resolution.

"Fuck," she muttered as she ran outside, hoping to catch Page. But Page was gone. And she had left the clothes behind in front of Brooklyn's door.

Brooklyn sighed and picked them up quickly, tossing them back into their bins. When she was done, she unblocked Page's number and tried to call. Of course, Page's phone, with its obscene data plan, had been disconnected. Most likely due to non-payment. It was probably for the best. Brooklyn didn't need to get off track, not now when she had come so far.

17

Work called Brooklyn in the following day, and she was anything but eager to go in. She rolled onto her side and pulled the duvet up to her ears with a groan. Her newfound zest was gone. The world felt like it was ending. The other night, she had tasted heaven, and her current state felt like everything but. Closing her eyes, she replayed the moment where Father Mathias had made her come with Rapture. It still somewhat unsettled her, but at the same time, she couldn't compare it to anything but magic. She ran her fingers over her still tender bottom and let out a small sigh of happiness. Holding on to the feeling proved to be impossible, as it was quickly replaced with emptiness once again.

She checked the clock and groaned. There was no time left for hiding away in bed, and she got up with a grunt. Everything seemed more difficult than usual. Brushing her teeth. Brushing her hair. Pulling her clothes on. All Brooklyn wanted to do was sleep and hit pause until she could feel that feeling from the other night again.

Brooklyn dragged her feet on her way into work.

"Hey, you. What's going on?" asked Gregory.

Brooklyn looked at him and the concern in his eyes almost made her cry. Everything had been going so perfectly, and in one day, she managed to feel worse than before she had met Father Mathias. An overwhelming sense of uncertainty plagued her. A knot settled itself at the base of her throat and she panicked because she wasn't sure she could hold back her tears. Gregory's evident, growing concern made it worse and a small sob slipped past her lips. Brooklyn's eyes widened with panic when the feelings grew in her chest like a rolling wave about to break.

"Hey, hey, hey, it's okay. Let's go to the back." Gregory gently pushed her towards the break room and closed the door just in time before Brooklyn sobbed again, followed by a panicked breath.

"I'm here in whatever capacity you need me to be."

Brooklyn wanted to scream, cry, be held, and left alone. Which one would keep her from completely unraveling? Gregory seemed to know and pulled her into his arms.

"Shhh, it's alright."

It was hard for her, but Brooklyn accepted the hug and wrapped her arms around his waist and hid her face against his chest.

"Things have been a little rough lately," she eventually said.

"Do you want to talk about it? Is it Stephen?"

Brooklyn shook her head. How does one explain their post-bliss morose, when it was caused by unorthodox means involving a priest and his room of pain? "I'll shake it off," she said.

"Are you sure? You literally look like you're holding yourself together with discount tape."

Brooklyn took a deep breath and extracted herself from the embrace. "I'm sure." She dashed away her tears and took a few more calming breaths with the plan to hold herself together until she got home. Then she could cry and continue to hide away under her blanket.

"So it's not Stephen?"

Brooklyn half laughed, half cried. "Oh my God, no."

"Okay, thank goodness." His exaggerated relief pulled another small smile from Brooklyn. "Hey, you know what might be good for you? My boyfriend and I host a dinner once a month. You have to be queer, but whatever. Maybe you'd might like to come? It's tomorrow. Kevin is an amazing cook. I'm telling you now that you'll be missing out if you say no," said Gregory.

"I don't know," said Brooklyn with a sigh.

"Oh, come on, you're starting to give off that failed emo vibe again."

Brooklyn smiled sadly. "Okay," she said, rolling her eyes.

"Great!"

"Gregory?"

"Yeah?"

"Thank you." Tears threatened to start again at the thought of Gregory's gentleness, but Brooklyn successfully stifled them.

"Oh, please, anytime. And a word of advice"—there was a twinkle in his eye—"friends go on more than just one friend date."

"Noted," chuckled Brooklyn.

"So, it's tomorrow at five sharp. There's like a little social with hors d'oeuvres and cocktails. Then we sit for dinner at six. Oh, and it's formal."

"Five and formal. Got it."

Gregory's eyebrows shot up. "Do you even know what formal is?"

Brooklyn gave him a warning look.

"Oh, shift is done. Buh-bye!" Gregory gave her a once-over as if to confirm that she'd actually be okay, then grabbed his things and left.

Brooklyn took a few more moments until she felt pressured to return to the front. The orders eventually numbed her mind and heavy heart and she fell into a rhythm that offered some sort of relief.

Stephen came in shortly after. "How's my favorite barista?"

The comment startled Brooklyn out of auto-pilot. "Hi," she said, a bit dazed, then looked around to make sure no one else had heard.

"I'm excited for Saturday."

Brooklyn tried to summon a facial expression that conveyed some level of mutual excitement, but she was certain she failed. "So, are you going to tell me what you have planned?" Brooklyn asked quietly.

"If I did, it wouldn't be a surprise." he said, leaving with his cup of coffee.

Since Page never took the clothes, Brooklyn dug through the bins to see if there was something she could work with. Brooklyn sat back on her heels when she pulled out the little black dress Page had insisted she get. It was probably the only thing she had ever purchased *for* Brooklyn, saying that every woman needed one. It hadn't been for an event or a party, it had just been for Brooklyn to have. A true gift, one that she had refused to sell when she was still selling the things Page had bought for her.

Brooklyn slipped it on and admired her reflection in the mirror. It looked much better now that she could fill it out properly. She wore a pair of black flats and didn't bother with accessories—that was Page's thing. She did put on a touch of makeup, though. Just some tinted gloss, mascara, and blush. Then she pinned her hair up on the sides and smiled at her reflection. For the first time, she noticed the physical changes and felt good, inside *and* out. *I almost look like a proper lady*, she mused with a soft laugh.

"Well how about that, Mama?" she said to her reflection. But it wasn't a time to lament her past. Brooklyn wanted to recapture some of that enthusiasm for life and she was certain she could find some at Gregory's.

Brooklyn took a picture, something she rarely did. If only Father Mathias could see her. There was never any reason to dress up like that since they always met at the church. Going out on a real date and holding hands was something she wished she could experience with him but knew she never could. *Unless...* She shook her head, unwilling to finish the thought, which was quickly replaced by wishing she could at least send her Priest the photo. That was something that could be remedied by asking for his number... Possibly... Something about Father Mathias made her think that he didn't even own a smartphone.

Enough of that. I'm going to have fun tonight. She took a deep breath and tried to shake off the bout of negativity before leaving to make her way to Gregory's.

"Hey! You look great!" greeted Gregory with surprise. "And she owns a dress! Kevin! Come meet Brooklyn."

Kevin was beyond handsome in a pair of perfectly tailored gray pants and a well fitted seafoam green shirt. His dirty blonde hair looked as if it naturally fell into its style, but Brooklyn was certain it probably took a good amount of effort and skill to get it to look like that.

Gregory took Brooklyn around the living room and introduced her to his and Kevin's friends, who all greeted her warmly.

Gregory hadn't exaggerated when he said Kevin was a great cook. She couldn't understand why, but she savored everything much more than usual, and this dinner was a treat.

They started with a burrata and arugula salad, followed by chicken scallopini with sauteed vegetables. Every bite was enjoyed with closed eyes and a quiet, appreciative murmur.

"Always showing off," joked one of the friends when Kevin brought out dessert: the most delicate mixed berry custard tart flanked with tiny meringue cookies. "Tell us Kevin, when are you going to stop wasting your talents on us and open a restaurant?"

Brooklyn looked to Kevin, curious about her new friend's partner's aspirations.

"I'm happy cooking for you undeserving folk."

Looks were exchanged across the dining table and Brooklyn figured there must be some insider subtext that she was too new to pick up on. But Kevin cleared his throat and Gregory changed the topic.

At the end of the night, Brooklyn sat with Gregory, a little too giddy off wine and cocktails.

"I shouldn't be drinking," she unwittingly said out loud.

"Why not?" asked Gregory.

"It's a rule." *But this is different... nothing like the times with Page...*

"A rule?"

Brooklyn caught on to her mistake. She looked at Gregory and wondered if she should tell him about the priest. "Yes," she eventually answered. "Enforced by... a priest."

Gregory looked at her, confused.

How good it would feel to unburden herself. Brooklyn closed her eyes and pictured herself telling Gregory everything. Telling him about Father Mathias and how his hands did wonderful things to her, and how his commands had been shaping her into a better version of herself. And then expressing how even then, she was still sad because it was a complicated situation.

"I'm getting help at a church for a drinking and drug problem." Though part of her wanted to share, Brooklyn wasn't drunk enough to tell her secret.

"I'm sorry. I didn't realize you had one."

"Neither did I!" Brooklyn laughed nervously. "But you know, I don't think I really had an addiction. Because when I stopped, it was easy. And this"—she held up her glass of wine—"wasn't a big deal."

"Well, I'm glad to hear that. Still..." He took the glass away from her. An awkward silence followed.

"Thanks for a great night and for the great food," said Brooklyn, desperate to get back to more lighthearted conversation.

"It was a pleasure." Gregory put her glass down on the coffee table. "So, I've been dying to ask you about Stephen... What's happening there? Give me all the insider info!"

"Insider info? You're the only one who knows, period."

"Oh, honey..." Gregory looked at her with feigned pity. "So naive."

Brooklyn's eyes widened with surprise. "People know?"

"Uh... yeah! Every coffee shop within three blocks of ours knows!"

Brooklyn threw her head back against the couch cushions and closed her eyes. "We're in a trade of gossips."

"Duh! We serve tea, do we not? Now come on! Don't leave me hanging! Where'd you go? Did you do the awkward 'deer in headlights' thing?" Gregory leaned forward, waiting for all the juicy details. "Come on! You owe me! The only reason that date happened is because of me."

Brooklyn blew air through pursed lips. "Well... he took me to this Thai restaurant and was super charming and sweet."

"Did you do the dirty?"

Brooklyn jokingly punched him in the arm. "Of course not."

Gregory rolled his eyes. "With a man like that, you gotta!"

"We didn't even kiss. And then I saw him again for lunch on Monday."

"Wow, okay! Look at you go. So, when do you see him again?"

Brooklyn sighed and paused for dramatic effect while trying to suppress her coy smile. "Saturday. And before you ask, he's surprising me. I don't know what we're doing."

Gregory clutched his chest and sighed. "*GQ* hot, thoughtful, *and* romantic? I wouldn't believe he was real if I didn't know him myself."

"You and me both!"

Gregory gave her a one-armed hug. "I'm really happy for you. Also, you're welcome. For saying yes for you when he asked you out. When you get married, I want credits. And you must name your firstborn after me."

Brooklyn laughed. "Yeah, sure, okay." Brooklyn saw Kevin cleaning up and everyone else had gone. "Can I help with the cleanup?"

"No, no, we got it."

"I guess I should get going. Thanks for inviting me."

"Thanks for coming."

Gregory walked her to the door and took her coat out from the closet. "Make sure you kiss him on Saturday. Or I'll do it for you!"

The next morning, Brooklyn went straight to church and waited for the doors to open. Six o'clock came and she watched Janice unlock the front doors. She waited a few minutes before going in and aimed to go straight to the confessional, but Janice stopped her on her way in.

"Hi, there! Aren't you turning into a little regular. That much to confess? I'm starting to wonder if they changed the schedule just for you," she said, referring to the fact that early morning confessions were taken only on the weekend.

"Is that appropriate for you say?"

Janice shrugged. "I don't mean to intrude. I just find it odd that you come to St. Anthony's to confess so often, but not for Sunday Mass."

"Do you keep track of everyone who goes to Mass? Because I do come. Not that it's any of your business."

"No, but not everyone comes in for confession as often as you seem to do."

It took all of Brooklyn's will to not roll her eyes. "Maybe you should give it a try sometime." She walked away before Janice could answer and went to the confessional.

"Hello, Father," she said, her voice barely above a whisper.

"My child," replied Father Mathias with affection.

"Is it okay that I came, Father?" she asked, thinking of her encounter with Janice.

"Of course. You are always welcome in the house of God."

"Janice doesn't seem to think so."

"Has she said something to you?"

Brooklyn shook her head, choosing to keep her exchange with the prying woman to herself.

"What brings you in today, my child?"

Brooklyn bit her lip. "I came because I missed you. I was also wondering if we could exchange phone numbers," she added, remembering how she had wanted to send him a photo of her outfit. "And," she said with a sigh, "I made a mistake."

"Let's start with that."

"Last night I went to a dinner Gregory hosted. And I drank. I didn't even think. But it wasn't because I felt I needed to or anything. I don't think I really ever had a problem." Brooklyn stopped, instinctively knowing that making excuses was not becoming. "The point is I drank. And I shouldn't have. I'm sorry, Father."

He was quiet for a moment. "My child, I am so proud of you. You have made positive changes and in such a steadfast manner that no one could have expected of you. Do you truly believe you do not have an addiction?"

"I do, Father! It was something I did with Page. Last night I got a little tipsy, but I didn't drink excessively or actively seek it out."

"I trust you, child. You may drink for social occasions, but in moderation. The 'no drugs' rule stands."

"Of course, Father. Oh! Something else happened. Page came by my place."

"And?"

"I turned her away. She's not doing very well."

"How do you feel about it?"

"Guilty."

Father Mathias nodded. "I'm not surprised. I hope you realized that there is absolutely nothing to feel guilty about."

"Yes, Father."

"I'm amazed by your strength and conviction. I hope you realize the difficult strides you've taken."

Brooklyn sat back and took inventory of the recent changes in her life and had a hard time seeing them as difficult strides. Her progress just barely brought her up to speed. She thought of other people her age and what they were accomplishing. All she had managed to do was cut off a toxic friend, toxic habits, and take up healthier activities.

"I can tell you're not giving yourself enough credit."

"I'm sorry, Father. I just feel like I can't be proud of things I should have been doing anyways."

"Should have? Based off what standards?"

Brooklyn shrugged.

"I have a task for you, my child. Journal about your progress and try to be kind to yourself. Write about what you have done, how those things have impacted your life, and the positive changes you've noticed in yourself. Do not be frugal with the self-kindness."

The thought of writing about herself positively made her uncomfortable, but she nodded without complaint. "Yes, Father."

"As for keeping in touch, we can email." He gave her an email, which ended in seventy-one.

Brooklyn pulled out her phone to save the information. "Is that your birth year?" she asked shyly. She felt silly that after everything she had experienced with him, she didn't even know how old he was. She quickly tried to do the math in her head. Forty-eight. He was older than her mother. This made her blush.

"Yes, it is."

"I see." She really looked at him then, trying to find the years of his age in his face, but all she could see was a sinfully sexy priest who had done delicious things to her.

"Does it bother you?"

Brooklyn shook her head. "No, Father. I don't think it was ever even a factor." She was sure she imagined his sigh of relief because she couldn't imagine him ever being insecure or unsure. Everything seemed just so... absolute with him.

"Do you know how old I am?" Now it was her turn to feel insecure. Of course, if it ever mattered, she figured he wouldn't have approached her in the first place. But there was a chance that her rough lifestyle had aged her beyond her years.

"No. I never offer or ask for details out of habit, child. As I've said, I kept distance with the others."

"I'm twenty-two. And since I know your full name, mine is St. Jerome."

Faint sunlight lit up the edges of the confessional's curtain, signaling that someone must have entered the church. The light faded and footsteps followed.

"I should probably go." Brooklyn was reluctant to leave, but Janice was suspicious enough, and now someone else was probably waiting for their turn.

"Before you go, let me see you, my child. Undress for me," he added when she looked at him confused.

"Here? What about Janice?" she whispered.

"I beg your pardon?"

"Yes, Father." Brooklyn's breaths quickly grew shallow with excitement. Slowly, she pulled off her top and undid her bra, exposing her breasts to him.

The priest breathed in sharply. "I've missed you, my child."

Sliding off her shoes first, she undid the button and zipper on her skinny jeans and shimmied out of them until she was wearing nothing but her thong.

"Leave that on," said Father Mathias. "It looks lovely on you. Turn around for me."

Brooklyn stood up and turned slowly. He grunted when he saw her marked bottom. Brooklyn imagined that like her, the sight of her marks must take him back to the moment they were made. She paused so that he could enjoy the magenta and purple blooms before continuing her slow turn. When she faced the grate again, she bent over a bit so that her breasts were level with it, and she pressed them into the cool metal. She was rewarded with his touch, or at least however much of it she could feel through the diamond-shaped holes.

"I miss you so much," whispered Brooklyn.

"Show me."

"What?"

"Show me how much you've missed me. I want you to touch yourself."

"Yes, Father," said Brooklyn, already panting with arousal. She moved the chair so that it faced him and spread her legs. The grate's shadow made a fishnet stocking pattern on her legs. Sitting away from it, Father Mathias's face was shrouded by more shadows, but Brooklyn could still hear his labored breath.

"Go on, touch yourself, child."

Brooklyn rubbed herself through her thong that was already drenched with her wetness. It wasn't long before the pressure built up and begged to be released. "May I come, Father?"

"Not yet, child. Make yourself suffer for me."

It took all of Brooklyn's will to withdraw her hand. She waited until the buildup subsided and then started to rub herself again.

"Move your panties to the side. I want to see you."

Brooklyn did as he said and displayed herself to him. Her sex was red and the lips swollen, ripe for the taking.

"Oh, my child."

"Please let me come, Father," begged Brooklyn, making sure to keep her voice to a whisper.

"Not, yet," he ground out. "Taste yourself."

She brought her fingers to her lips and licked her juices off them. Taking a calming breath, she continued touching herself slowly, but even that managed to bring her to the edge. There was no hope. Father Mathias ruled her mind, and it didn't take much for her willing body to respond to him, even if it was through a confessional's grate.

"Please, Father. I can't." She stopped again.

"Do not stop, child."

Brooklyn whimpered and continued rubbing and trying to do a bad job at it. It made no difference. The smallest touch had her so painfully close to climaxing she feared she couldn't hold on. She gasped with her efforts and used her other hand to cover her mouth to stifle the subsequent gasps. Time suspended and came to a complete standstill, her sex screaming for release.

"Now you may come for me."

Brooklyn clamped her hand more tightly on her mouth and she did her best to come quietly. Her legs shuddered and the air hissed around her hand from the force of her breaths. Sitting up, she tentatively took her hand from her mouth, not trusting her ability to keep quiet, and took a deep breath.

She looked at her Priest through glassy eyes. "Thank you, Father."

"You are so divine, my child," he breathed. "Come to me on Monday at ten. At night."

"Yes, Father."

He instructed her to get dressed and she left, hating how unsatisfied she felt with the brief, limited contact they'd had. She needed to feel his hands on her skin and his breath on her neck as he whispered his commands. As she left, she noticed the door to Janice's office quickly close. She was definitely being watched. The thought unsettled Brooklyn and she pressed her hands to her flushed cheeks, hoping Janice hadn't noticed them.

18

Brooklyn kept herself busy with tasks until Saturday came around. Many of the soup kitchen's volunteers knew her name now and running had become a source of peace. The unexpected down spell was gone, but she still faced the stress of how she should move forward with Stephen. She flopped onto her sofa and stared at the milk crates. She hated surprises. How was she supposed to dress? What if she hated it? As if Stephen could hear her thoughts, her phone buzzed with a text from him, instructing her to dress casually. That made her relax a little. Casual meant the chances of her feeling comfortable with wherever they were going were a bit higher.

Brooklyn walked to the block where her decoy home was, this time remembering which one it had been. "Her home" had two red Muskoka chairs on the porch. She stood at the end of the path and waited. Stephen pulled up and greeted her with a smile.

"So, where are we going?" she asked when she got in the car.

"To the movies." Stephen looked amazing in a simple white t-shirt under a dark autumn jacket.

"Seriously?" The question slipped from Brooklyn's mouth before she could stop it.

He laughed. "Yes, seriously. I *was* thinking of taking you to my place and having my personal chef cook us a five-star meal. Candles, music, view of the river... But I figured a movie would be better."

"Yeah, a movie is great."

"You sound disappointed."

"No! I'm relieved." Brooklyn was uncertain how she felt. She loved the idea of being wined and dined, but that kind of luxury still left a bad taste in her mouth.

He turned to look at her at a red light. "You confuse me."

Brooklyn laughed nervously. "What do you mean?"

"I don't know, I just had this feeling that an extravagant night out wasn't your thing, so I second guessed my original plans. And you can say you're not disappointed all you want, but I can tell you are. I just don't know how to do something in between," he said, laughing at himself.

She shifted in her seat to face him. "Look, I want to know you, so do what *you* would do, not what you think I'd want."

Stephen pressed his lips together in thought. Brooklyn could see him making a choice and he did a U-turn. He drove to the business precinct and passed the cafe Brooklyn worked at.

"This is where I work," he said, pulling up to the curb in front of one of the newer buildings. "Come." He got out and led the way to a side door.

Brooklyn was confused.

"Trust me," he said with a smile, holding out his hand. Brooklyn took it and followed him.

He swiped a pass and there was a barely audible click from the door unlocking. The lobby was eerily quiet and almost reminded her of the church at night, only this church served a different kind of God: money. You could see the wealth everywhere. You could see it in the chrome finishes, the perfectly crystal-clear glass, and the shiny floors. It was hard to believe that a place so pristine housed hundreds of working people.

They took the elevator up to the twentieth floor and Brooklyn's stomach flip-flopped from the speed of the elevator. Or maybe it was her nerves. An unmanned reception area greeted them with only the lights behind the company name and logo lit. Stephen led her past cubicles and then through a few hallways.

"This is my office," he said absentmindedly while clicking through his phone. He put it away and motioned for her to look. The view was beautiful. "This is where I come to work, but it's also where I come to unwind. Nothing beats this view." Buildings blocked the view to the right, but the west end of the city twinkled with modesty. The city straddled the line between a big city and a small town, with the majority resembling more of a suburb than anything else.

"It's beautiful," she whispered. She had never been able to admire the city from this vantage point before and its restrained beauty surprised her.

Stephen's office had a seating area that faced the floor-to-ceiling windows, and they went to sit at opposite ends of the sofa, but facing each other, their bodies leaning in closer as if drawn to one another like magnets.

"I really want to know who *you* are," he said, gazing at her intently.

For almost anyone, the question would have been flattering; to have such an attractive, accomplished man care enough about them to want to know more. For Brooklyn, it was intrusive. But had she not asked him to show her who he was? She licked her lips.

"Well, I was born here but raised in the country. My mother was super religious, so as soon as I was old enough, I came back to the city."

He shook his head. "I'm not asking for your biography. *Who* are you?"

The question was unexpected, and Brooklyn sat back heavily. She clasped her hands tightly in her lap as she thought of how to answer. "A recovering train wreck, I guess." She looked down at her hands and shrugged.

"Poor choice of words, don't you think?"

She looked up at him, mostly to see the irony she expected to be there. There was none. "What do you mean?"

"How about strong? Resilient?"

"Hmph," she said with a laugh. "I guess that's one way to put it."

Stephen reached over and took her hand in his. "You're way too hard on yourself."

"If only you knew."

"I think I have an idea. Maybe not the specifics, but I remember walking into the cafe and being floored. It was like overnight you had gone from someone with no hope in their eyes to someone with a whole lot to live for."

"Really?" Gregory had already commented on her transformation, but she would have never thought that someone who didn't know her well would have noticed. It seemed a small feat when she thought of the changes she had made. Stephen's comments made her reassess herself and reconsider just how incredible her turnaround had been. Father Mathias's task seemed less daunting with Stephen's affirmations. *Father Mathias.* Thinking of the priest had her pulling her hand back and burying it in her lap.

"Really," he said with a firm nod. He looked her in the eyes so that Brooklyn could see a hint of the shadows that lurked just beneath his charming, well composed surface. She felt as if he was recognizing a kindred spirit, and she wondered what could have ever made someone like him suffer.

His phone buzzed, jarring them out of the moment. "I'll be right back."

He left and Brooklyn felt awkward, sitting in his place of work and refuge. Alone. The windows beckoned her and she went to them, resisting the urge to reach out and press her hands against the smudge-free glass. It was as if the city's west end was at her fingertips, and she could touch it and claim it. No wonder Stephen loved it. Brooklyn imagined someone like him would enjoy such a grand illusion.

Stephen returned with a takeout bag. "Hope you like General Tso's chicken."

Brooklyn turned away from the view with a smile. "There's very little that I don't like."

"I like that," he said, taking out the containers and setting them on the coffee table. They ate, enjoying the modest cityscape and each other's silence. Brooklyn liked not talking. It meant she didn't have to expose herself too much.

Stephen fed her the last piece of chicken and set the container on the table before moving closer to her. Whereas the priest smelled like the church he lived in, Stephen smelled like champagne and realized dreams. He leaned in and Brooklyn's brain went into overload trying to figure out what to do.

She wanted him to kiss her yet felt guilty for it. What about her Priest?

He stopped, sensing her hesitation. "May I?" he asked, reaching up to touch his fingertips to her chin.

Brooklyn's breaths were quick and short, and she licked her suddenly dry lips. One could have interpreted it as an invitation to move forward, but Stephen did not.

"I just don't get what you're doing with me. You could have anyone." Brooklyn wanted to hide her face in her hands. Of course, her knee-jerk self-preservation tactic was self-deprecation.

Stephen sat back. "Yes, you're right, I suppose. But here I am. With you." He went to take her hand, but Brooklyn drew back and trained her eyes on the lights in the far distance.

"I'm seeing someone," she blurted. "At least, I think I am. I don't know, but I just don't want to cross any lines that I can't come back from."

Stephen inhaled sharply. "Whoa. I see."

She turned back to him then, a pleading look her in eyes. "Are you mad? Please don't be mad. I just don't know where things stand with him, and you... well, you're not the easiest person to turn down."

"I'm not mad," he said with a chuckle. "I'm just shaking my head at myself for assuming you were available."

"I really like you," Brooklyn said quietly.

"Tell me about this person you may or may not be seeing."

Again, she wanted to tell the truth, at least for the sake of someone else knowing. The weight of her secret pressed down on her heavily. He didn't need to know which church and which priest. "He's older and..."

"Let me guess. He's married."

Brooklyn's head shot up, wide eyed and ready to deny it, but confirming his assumption was easier than admitting she was involved with a priest. And technically, he *was* married—married to the church. "Yes?"

"Well, that makes a lot of sense." Stephen's eyebrows furrowed and Brooklyn imagined it was a similar expression to the one he would make when deliberating a business choice or problem.

"What do you mean?" Was he insinuating she looked like some kind of homewrecker?

"Why you were open to going out with me in the first place. I can sense you're not the cheating type."

"I'm not! Like I said, I don't really know where I stand with him." Brooklyn looked down at her hands and pressed her thumbnail into her palm to calm her racing heart. "It's just... super complicated. And I know it's selfish, but I didn't want to pass up a chance at getting to know you for something that may not even go anywhere." Speaking the words out loud broke her heart. They were thoughts that had been lurking in the corners of her mind, and now that she had admitted them, it made her uncertain situation with the priest that much more uncertain.

"Can I give you some advice? And please let me know if I'm overstepping."

Brooklyn nodded.

"If he's seeing you behind his wife's back, he will never leave her for you. If unhappiness isn't enough of a motivator or reason to end things, happiness won't be either."

Maybe the priest didn't have a wife, but Stephen's words still struck a chord. Brooklyn had no future with the priest. He would never leave the church and she couldn't imagine a lifetime of hiding and sneaking around. *Where is the value in that? In me?*

"You're right. I guess I need to think things through."

"And while you think, I'd still like to see you. We don't have to do anything. Just hang out and enjoy each other's company."

"Really?"

"Really. Contrary to popular belief, not all men are all about just getting laid," he joked. Stephen got up and cleared the table, dumping the empty containers back into the takeout bag. "It's still early, how about we still go see that movie?"

Brooklyn nodded with a shy smile and stood up. Stephen led her back through the office and she wondered how anyone could ever remember their way around the endless hallways and maze of cubicles. They were silent on the way down in the elevator, which wasn't any less nauseating than when they had gone up.

At the movies, they compromised quite easily on an action comedy. Brooklyn didn't pay much attention to it and was too busy stealing glances at Stephen's profile instead. He was so sweet, kind, and understanding. It was still hard for her to believe that he was interested in her and, not only that, willing to wait until she sorted out her mess. She chewed on her bottom lip. Was Father Mathias worth the missed opportunity to date someone like Stephen?

A heated scene between the hero and his charge came up. Stephen absentmindedly reached for Brooklyn's hand, and she let him take it. His hand warmed her own, but only an echo of the electricity she felt with Father Mathias was present.

That can be enough. Less intense, but sustainable. It felt so normal and so good to her. His touch came with visions of a comfortable home, routine, love, and even a couple of children—things she could never have with her Priest. That's what she had moved away from her mother for: normalcy. Her relationship with Father Mathias was anything but.

"What's got you frowning?" whispered Stephen.

Brooklyn leaned in closer so she could keep her voice as low as possible. She considered making some glib comment about the movie's script or visual effects, but she opted for honesty. "Before you, I thought I had figured out what the near future would hold for me. I was okay with it. And now..."

"Now?"

"Now, I'm not so sure."

Someone shushed them from the row in front of them. Stephen raised his hand in apology, but it didn't deter him from continuing the conversation.

"Were you ever really okay with being the other woman, or had you just never considered another option?"

Brooklyn didn't give an answer and he didn't pressure her for one. Instead, they watched the rest of the movie in silence. He didn't even bring up the topic while he drove her home and Brooklyn appreciated and liked him more for it.

"Stephen?" she said when he stopped in front of her "home."

"Yes?"

"Would you think I'm a horrible person for wanting you to kiss me?"

He shook his head. "But I may be biased." He was already leaning in closer to her.

Brooklyn closed the rest of the distance and brushed her lips against his. What she had hoped for, she couldn't be sure. Maybe she wanted to find that there was no spark and then she'd have no regrets continuing her relationship with the priest. Or maybe she hoped Stephen would give her reason to leave a path she knew could only lead to heartbreak. All she got was more confusion. The kiss left her wanting more of Stephen, but it wasn't enough to help her make any sort of final decision.

"Will I see you again?" asked Stephen.

Brooklyn nodded. "Yes. I guess." She smiled and looked away, feeling more shy than ever.

"Good," he said in a quiet, deep voice that stirred something inside of her.

It was then that she knew she had just crossed over that line she couldn't come back from.

The sounds of the soup kitchen soothed Brooklyn's conflicted heart. Once a place that offered a means to keep busy, the kitchen was now therapy. The simple tasks of peeling, chopping, stirring, and serving were like their own form of meditation. But all the peeling and chopping in the world couldn't completely quiet her mind.

It was Sunday, and she had skipped going to church to avoid Father Mathias. How could she look him in the eye after her date with Stephen? Maybe if he had been the one to initiate the kiss, she could reason with her conscience, but she had not only initiated it, but done so with eagerness. She took a deep breath, both to calm her erratic heart and to express her disappointment with herself.

"Are you okay, dear?" asked one of volunteers.

Brooklyn looked up from the cutting board and tried to focus her eyes. "I'm fine," she answered.

The woman didn't seem convinced, but she didn't say anything and moved on. Much like her fellow baristas, the volunteer staff at the kitchen had learned Brooklyn's moods quickly. Brooklyn looked around the kitchen and felt like an impostor, standing there shoulder to shoulder with people who would undoubtedly judge her if they knew about her life outside of her volunteering hours. She was a cheat. A liar. A full-blown sinner, in their words. She sighed again. That wasn't being very kind to the volunteers who had welcomed her with open arms. She realized then that those were her own words. After all, she had learned them well from her mother and her kiss with Stephen proved that maybe she really *was* nothing but a sinner. It didn't matter that her relationship with the priest was undefined; it was still a relationship. An intimate one. Her heart ached when she decided the only way to ease her guilt would be to tell Father Mathias everything. But was he not considerate, forgiving, and just?

I will tell him everything tomorrow, she promised.

19

Brooklyn hesitated as she reached for the church's door, but it wasn't because of her fear of the building. Whatever fear she had had of the church was gone, at least this specific one. But as she entered the building and went towards the back, a different kind of unease came over her.

Stephen.

Father Mathias's living room was dimly lit like it was last time and the small table beckoned her. She lit the candle then knelt to pray. He still hadn't come, and she was done praying, so she prayed that she would make the right decisions. She heard Father Mathias enter the room. Brooklyn didn't move and continued to pray. He was silent for a moment before approaching her. She twitched, her body responding to his nearness, but she kept her betraying limbs in place.

He sighed heavily before falling to his knees behind her and pulling her into his arms. Whatever reservations and resolutions she'd had on her way in melted away in an instant. She was putty in his arms.

"I am overtaken by your divinity, my child. Every day I'm surprised again and again over how much you affect me."

So he felt it to. The magnetism and the cellular response when in each other's presence. Brooklyn was convinced that even blindfolded and in a room full of people, she could zero in on his essence. She twisted in his arms to look up at him and grasped his cassock desperately. "I feel like I'm drowning, Father." It was true—drowning in him and drowning in indecision... and fear.

They sat there for a while in a primal embrace that spoke words of forbidden ownership and devotion. Despite her dilemma, there was no question of her devotion to her Priest and her willingness to serve him. At least, not in her heart.

"Please kiss me, Father," she pleaded quietly. Certain he would deny her, Brooklyn was surprised when he showered her face with kisses before claiming her lips. She moaned into his mouth, barely lucid enough to marvel at how just a kiss could elicit such erotic sounds from her. She turned some more so that she could straddle and wrap her legs around him, pressing her breasts against his chest, earning her a groan.

Father Mathias stopped the kiss abruptly. "That is enough, child."

"Why?"

"Stand up," he ordered.

"No."

Her refusal clearly caught him off guard. "Do not make me repeat myself."

"I won't get up until you tell me why you keep pushing me way." Her petulance set a fire ablaze in his eyes, one of anger, and she knew she was treading dangerous waters, but she was emboldened by Stephen's words. She wanted the priest to show her just how much he wanted her, and that if push ever came to shove, he'd choose her. How else could she find the courage to choose him?

"Get up."

"I can't go on like this. I need you so much it hurts."

"Did I not give you pleasure the last time you were here? You're being ungrateful and that is something I will not tolerate."

Brooklyn stood up and crossed her arms. "I want more. I want to see you more. I want you to touch me more. I *want* you to fuck me!" Brooklyn's cheeks flamed red with her candor, but she chose to stick to her words and punctuated them with balled fists of frustration at her sides.

He stood up too, his jaw clenched and eyes wide with surprise over her forwardness and vulgar words. "How *dare* you curse in the house of God?"

"Are you kidding me?! Of all the things, you're going to get hung up on the fact that I said *fuck*?" She was angry at him now. Angry at him and herself and it was a like snowball rolling down a hill, getting bigger and bigger. But instead of snow, it was made of fire. "Fuck! Fuck! Fuck! Fuck!" she said over and over again, goading him to do something about it.

Father Mathias grabbed her hair and tugged it so that she was forced back down to her knees. She winced and gasped. "You've been so obedient. So surprisingly adept. But now... now you have crossed a line," he said, unknowingly echoing her fears after her date with Stephen. There was more than one line that she had crossed than he was aware of. "And have earned yourself correctional punishment." He shoved her so that she was on all fours. "If you know what's good for you, I suggest you do not move."

Brooklyn flinched from his tone and panted with fear. Never had the priest spoken to her that way. He went towards the back of the rectory then returned to her side. He tore down her pants and panties, and without warning, blinding pain shot through her body. It hurt so much she couldn't even cry out from her throat tightening up. Only a strangled gasp managed to escape her lips.

"You will receive sixteen hits, just like that one. Two for each time you said that dreadful word, and two for each refusal to obey my command. Do you understand?"

"Yes, Father," she whispered. Brooklyn barely finished speaking before she was hit again. She extended her fingers then curled them up into a tight fist. Her ears prickled with heat, and she quickly broke out into an uncomfortable sweat. He hit her again, and this time, her toes curled. After the third hit, she looked back to see what he was punishing her with and saw it was Rapture.

"One more will be added for looking back." He hit her again. And again. And again. She was certain he was trying to break the thing on her backside. Sweat trickled down the insides of her arms and the sensation felt odd as the rest of her body tensed and shuddered from the excruciating pain.

Mercy floated through her faltering consciousness. It dangled in front of her, offering reprieve and promising a quick end to this punishment. But she had been disobedient, and it pained her to think that she had displeased her Priest. So now she had to appease him. Brooklyn ignored the lure of *Mercy* and took the rest of the punishment with as much composure as one could under such duress.

After the seventeenth hit, she turned and collapsed, pressing her cheek to his shoe with a sob. "I'm sorry, Father. I'm so sorry."

He pulled away from her and went to put the implement away. When he returned to her side, he rubbed a cool balm on her bottom.

"'For the mind set on the flesh is death, but the mind set on the Spirit is life and peace.' Romans chapter eight verse six," he quoted with less enthusiasm than he had previously.

Brooklyn wondered if it was due to fatigue from constant devotion to the words or waning faith. She noted he hadn't quoted the Bible in a while until just then.

"There is more to this than just the desires of the flesh, my child," he continued. "You must practice self-control."

"I'm sorry," cried Brooklyn. "I can't help it. All I can think about..."

"Sit up, child," he said, cutting her off.

It hurt, but she got up and sat in front of him with her legs crossed. She kept her eyes downcast, hands clasped in her lap.

"Your desires are normal and I'm not condemning them. Look at me," he said, waiting for her to look up.

Brooklyn lifted her chin but kept her eyes down. When Father Mathias still said nothing, she finally dragged her gaze up to his. It was like looking at him for the first time. How many times had she actually looked at him? Not many times at all. She couldn't bear to look upon someone who ruled her the way he did for too long. It wasn't fear, but instead a strange kind of innate response triggered by her respect for him. Brooklyn's breath caught in her chest when they locked gazes.

"I'm condemning how you let your desires rule you. With another, this wouldn't be an issue. In fact, they would be greatly pleased. But with me, you must practice more self-control. With my tastes and my requirements, your lust must be kept in check."

"But why, Father? Please tell me, why?"

"Once I feel you have been sufficiently trained, I will ask for your complete submission. I will ask to collar and own you. When I propose this to you, I will explain all the conditions. Then, you can make a choice: to accept my ownership, or to move on."

Brooklyn wanted to complain and urge him to tell her then and there what it was that might affect her decision. But she had suffered enough punishment for one night and kept quiet.

"We are done for tonight. I will see you next Monday."

Next week?! she screamed inside her head. "Yes, Father." She left with her head hanging low and wondered what she had missed out on thanks to her lack of self-control, knowing that him ending the night without any sort of play was part of her punishment. She felt she deserved it. Not because of her actions that night, but because of what she was allowing to happen with Stephen. Spoken commitment or not, her heart was committed to her Priest, and looking at anyone but him with any romantic notion was a betrayal. Brooklyn realized then that her apology wasn't for her words and disobedience; it was for the kiss.

She stopped in the nave and stared at the altar. The crucifix taunted Brooklyn, reminding her that she would always fall short and never be enough. Her mother had told her many times that she could see the greed in Brooklyn's soul, along with other unfavorable traits. Brooklyn felt maybe her mother had simply seen the truth all along, because Brooklyn did want it all: the intensity of her dominant Priest and the promised steadiness of the charming entrepreneur. With a sniffle and swipe at her nose, Brooklyn left.

She checked her backside when she got home and couldn't believe her eyes. The welts were already turning purple, and it almost looked like he had broken skin. Walking hurt and getting into bed was excruciating. All night, every time she would move, the pain would wake her and she'd be filled with shame all over again. These marks were different. They brought her no joy as they were a reminder of his displeasure and her failure.

The cafe called Brooklyn into work the following morning and she dreaded having to go in when she was still in so much pain. It took a lot of effort to not wince with each movement and to shove away the chronic shame, which beat her down further with each wave. Brooklyn moved at a grinding pace and couldn't summon more energy or will to pretend that she was alright.

Brooklyn gazed into a tumbler, partially filled with milk and syrup, and contemplated the importance of her presence there in that moment. None of it mattered. At the end of the day, her pain, her effort, her struggle to survive another day all meant nothing.

Her manager came and took the tumbler from her. "Take a break."

"I'm sorry," whispered Brooklyn, grateful to see nothing but empathy in her manager's eyes.

"Don't worry about it. Take a breather and come back when you're ready."

Brooklyn nodded and whipped off her apron as quickly as she could. She needed to be out of the cafe before the tears started. Outside, the tears flowed freely. People were too preoccupied in their day to notice a young barista in distress, so Brooklyn felt safe enough to unravel. Just a tiny bit. She walked to the end of the block and turned the corner, going until she found a little nook with a planter. Brooklyn sat on the lip of the planter and took slow, measured breaths, wishing she could scream instead.

Her phone buzzed. Wiping her nose, she pulled it out, worried her boss wanted her to go back right away. Instead, she saw a message from Stephen.

Stephen: I want to see you tonight.

"Why!" she wanted to shout, but she whispered instead.

Brooklyn: I'm sorry, I can't.

Stephen: Tomorrow?

She bit her lip while eyeing the message. She should say no.

Brooklyn: Okay.

Stephen: Are you free during the day?

Brooklyn: Don't important ppl like you have to work?

Stephen: Important people like me can arrange days off.

Brooklyn: Okay, what time?

Her fingers shook as she typed. Planning another date with Stephen was a bad idea, but Brooklyn couldn't stop herself.

Stephen: 10AM

Brooklyn replied that she would see him then and hugged her phone pensively. Outside the church's walls and away from Father Mathias's intoxicating gaze, Brooklyn wanted to move forward with Stephen. But again, Father Mathias was intoxicating. Giving him up would be more difficult than the drugs and alcohol had been. She shook her head. Maybe she *had* had an addiction problem and had just traded one habit for another. That's all Father Mathias was: a drug.

Deep down, she knew it was more than that. "I love him," she said quietly to herself. The words felt strange on her lips. Brooklyn doubted she even knew what love meant when her life was such a dismal void of examples. Even if it was love, she was no romantic and she knew that loving someone meant nothing. It could never be enough, especially in their situation.

As always, Stephen was right on time. He had told her to dress comfortably, so Brooklyn wore her best yoga pants, a t-shirt, and her one and only fall jacket that was worn at the cuffs.

"I missed you," said Stephen.

The sentiment surprised Brooklyn. She was equally surprised to find that she missed him too, but expressing any feeling was starting to feel like more and more of a betrayal. And with her aching bottom, there was no possibility of forgetting her Priest during moments of abandon.

"What's going on?" he asked as he pulled away from the curb.

He's perceptive. That's nice. Also, not good. "Nothing worth mentioning."

"Is it the married man?"

"He's not a bad person," she blurted. Of course, Stephen hadn't insinuated anything by his tone, she just hated the connotation "married man" carried.

"I'm sorry, I didn't mean to sound so glib about it."

Brooklyn shook her head. "You don't need to apologize. I just know how bad it all sounds." She sighed, then forced a smile. "Never mind. I'm here now. So, what are we doing today?"

"It's a surprise."

Brooklyn groaned. "Another one?"

"One that you'll like. Trust me," he said with a borderline cocky smile.

Brooklyn sank into the plush leather seat and tried to relax. Soon, the city was replaced by the suburbs and the suburbs by long stretches of greenery.

"Seriously, where are you taking me?" she asked, curiosity getting the best of her, and it was just enough to let her guilt fade into the not-so-distant background.

Stephen only answered her with a smile and continued driving until finally, he turned onto a gravel driveway that wound up and through manicured fields spotted with clusters of trees. They arrived at what looked like a swanky stable ground. He parked and turned in his seat to face her.

"Remember how you said a neighbor had secretly taught you how to ride? The way you said it gave me the impression that you haven't had the chance to go horseback riding since you moved here."

Stephen's thoughtfulness stunned Brooklyn; it moved her. So much that she felt strangled by the onslaught of emotion that had suddenly worked its way up to her throat. Her eyes burned and she desperately tried to blink away the tears. There was something extra special about how he had taken a small detail she had shared casually and ran with it.

Brooklyn felt seen.

"You're upset."

She shook her head quickly. "No. I'm happy." She cursed her trembling lips and voice.

Stephen smiled. "I'm glad."

Brooklyn took a deep breath and laughed.

"Ready?"

She nodded with a smile, still unable to trust her voice. When she stepped out of the car, she was met with the smell of horses and manure. With the sound of horses nearby, it all reminded her of home—the good parts of home. She took Stephen's hand in excitement. He laced his fingers through hers and pulled her towards the stables.

"This is Bailey," he said, as he approached a beautiful, golden-brown mare.

"How come you didn't tell me you ride?"

He shrugged. "We had enough things in common. I felt I could save this for a surprise. I have three horses here." He moved to another stable. "This is Penelope. And here is Charlie. They're all pretty even-tempered."

Brooklyn was admiring Penelope. Her dark brown coat gleamed, and she had the kindest eyes. She reached up to stroke her neck, making sure to avoid the face. "She's perfect," murmured Brooklyn.

Stephen returned to her side. "She is. You can ride her today if you'd like. She seems to like you too." As if to prove his point, Penelope nuzzled Brooklyn's shoulder and let out a soft snort.

Penelope's instant liking to Brooklyn gave her a sense of validation. As a child, she had believed horses were not only pure of heart but could sense a person's character, too. It was the one thing she held onto when she rode: The fact that a majestic creature would allow her the privilege of sitting on its back and sharing the joy of rushing through the countryside meant that maybe she wasn't as bad as her mother had claimed she was.

"It's good to see you, Mr. Vera." A young woman approached them. "Going for a ride today?"

"We are. Can you have someone saddle up Penelope and Bailey?"

"Of course," said the woman with a smile. She spared a glance towards Brooklyn before turning away. Stephen gave Brooklyn a quick tour of the property while a stable hand got the horses ready for their ride.

Brooklyn hadn't considered her still painfully sore bottom until she was sitting on Penelope. Just like that, Father Mathias ruled her thoughts. Instead of guilt, however, she felt resentment. Here she was, about to enjoy a beautiful moment, and he was robbing her of it. Penelope must have felt the negative feelings because she sidestepped a few times.

"I'm sorry, girl," said Brooklyn, leaning forward to give Penelope a few soothing pats. "I promise it'll be just you and me." That seemed to appease the horse because she settled.

"There's a great trail that borders the stable grounds then goes off into the forest, if you're up for it," said Stephen.

Brooklyn smiled eagerly. She decided with determination that she would enjoy her time. They set off. At first, the jarring movement caused by Penelope's canter was painful, but eventually, she got used to the discomfort and was able to relax and sit more deeply in the saddle and enjoy herself. The property was beautiful. Most of the leaves had fallen, but the bare trees against the steel blue sky boasted a different kind of beauty—one that promised death and rebirth.

They rode in silence. Again, Brooklyn loved that he was comfortable with not talking and just sharing each other's company. The fall air nipped at her cheeks so that by the time they stopped for a break, her cheeks and nose were rosy red.

Stephen continued to surprise her when he pulled a small picnic blanket and a lunchbox from his bag. "It's a little chilly but I figured a quick lunch would be nice out here."

"Seriously, who are you?" she said jokingly.

He shrugged and unexpectedly let her see the shadows that lurked beneath his bright surface again, as if to remind her that they were on the same level. Brooklyn wanted to ask, but something told her his secrets would come at a cost—the price being her own. She opted to live with the mystery, deciding she wasn't willing to pay up, and helped him spread out the blanket. They sat and Brooklyn watched him take out sandwiches and lemonade from the lunchbox.

"I would have never been able to tell that it's been years since you last rode," he said, handing her a sandwich. He sat next to Brooklyn and unwrapped his own sandwich.

"My neighbor told me I was a natural." It was one of the few good things she believed about herself.

"I wouldn't argue with that."

Silence.

"Why were the lessons secret?" he asked.

Brooklyn stiffened and her brain raced for a half truth. She stalled by taking a bite of her sandwich and chewed slowly. "My mom didn't want me riding because she thought it was dangerous and unnecessary." *And an activity of leisure she felt I had no right to.*

"I'm glad you didn't let it stop you."

"Me too," she said with a smile. "What got you into riding?"

"I had always wanted to try it as a kid but never had the chance to. So, when I finally could, I learned. I've been doing it for a few years now and, unlike you, am not a natural."

"You seemed pretty good to me," Brooklyn said with a laugh.

"Tell that to my instructor." He chuckled.

Brooklyn had a few bites of her sandwich left and she nibbled at it, not wanting to leave too soon. It was quite chilly, but she didn't care. Stephen's warmth wrapped itself around her and it was enough to chase away the goosebumps. However, there were only so many times she could pick at the sandwich before it was gone and Stephen took the plastic wrap from her to pack it away. To her relief, he didn't move to pack away the blanket and instead lay down next to her, pulling her into his arms. The comfort of settling into his embrace almost brought her to tears.

They looked up at the sky, a stonewall of clouds that hid any hint of blue beyond. It wasn't anything pretty to look at, but Brooklyn didn't care. She burrowed closer to his side and tried to find where one cloud ended and another began.

"I'd love to do this again with you."

"Me too," she whispered. But that meant going even deeper into murky territory. She swallowed the ironic laughter that bubbled up. Of course, she couldn't be truly happy with this perfect afternoon. Hadn't her mother told her she didn't deserve it and would never find it? *Good one, God, this is extra cruel. Give her happiness but make sure she can't have it,* Brooklyn thought.

Stephen rubbed her arm. "We should head back before we get too cold."

Brooklyn nodded reluctantly. She wished she could stay there forever but her fingertips felt numb, and as warm as Stephen's arms were, they were no match for the approaching evening chill. They headed back and, once again, it took Brooklyn a second to adjust to the pain of her tender bottom colliding with the saddle.

"Thank you, Penelope," she said to the horse before the stable hand took her away.

"That was amazing," she sighed, feeling high off the clean country air. "Thank you so much for this." Her eyes stung with threatening tears.

"We will come back soon," he promised.

They made their way back towards the city, but instead of going back into the city, he headed east.

"Where are we going?" asked Brooklyn.

"I have one more thing planned for today." He drove to an outlying borough that followed the river and was comprised of mostly high-end properties, and pulled into the driveway of a large waterfront home. It was new, made of sand-colored stone punctuated heavily with dark framed windows.

Brooklyn was silent as he pulled into the garage. The opposite wall was all window and overlooked the river. It gave the illusion that if you drove through it, you'd end up in the water.

"Is this your place?"

"What's wrong?" he asked, noticing her grimace.

Brooklyn shook her head. "Nothing."

"Come on, you can tell me."

She fidgeted with her coat's cuff. "Wealth scares me."

"How so?"

Brooklyn looked into Stephen's eyes and hated that despite the sincerity and kindness she saw in them, she still feared his potential for entitlement. "I had a friend who was well off. Well, she came from a rich family. And at the beginning, everything was great until I became just another accessory. Almost like a dog that she'd carry around in her purse."

"And you're worried that I might end up treating you the same way?"

Brooklyn bit her lip and nodded, which seemed silly after the thoughtful day he had planned out.

Stephen took her hand and looked her in the eye. "I have a lot, that's true. But I didn't always. I worked hard for all of this. And I value people and their time. I also value the little things. Would your friend be able to enjoy a movie, or takeout Chinese food in an empty office building?"

Brooklyn knew he was right. "I'm sorry, you've been nothing but great and I'm here doubting your motives."

"Hey, there's nothing to apologize for," he said, rubbing the back of her hand with his thumb.

Brooklyn forced a smile. "How about a tour of the house then?"

He cleared his throat. "Um, it's a *mansion*," he said with mock haughtiness, earning a giggle from her. Stephen showed Brooklyn everything, not in a "look what I have" manner but rather a "look what I've earned" one. There were five bedrooms, three and a half bathrooms, a movie room, gym, sauna, workshop, and a backyard pool that seemed to disappear into the river if you looked at it at the right angle. The dining room appeared big enough to host a party of twenty, and the basement had been outfitted for hosting parties with a fully stocked bar and state of the art sound system. Everything was designed with a minimalist approach, the walls mostly bare and accents limited to conservative plants and a couple throw pillows.

They ended in the kitchen that had to be as big as her childhood home. Everything was so white she couldn't imagine any real cooking ever happening in it despite the industrial appliances and high-end cookware that hung over the kitchen island.

"I was thinking... we could cook dinner together?" said Stephen, unknowingly challenging her impression of the space.

"I'd love that," beamed Brooklyn. "Much, much more than some stuffy chef doing it for us." The small change from his previously scrapped plan of the other night warmed Brooklyn's heart. He was nothing like Page or the people Page surrounded herself with.

Stephen chuckled. "I figured."

They cooked side by side, mostly in comfortable silence, and she reveled in the normalcy of it. She was draining the pasta when she put the pot down and turned to face him.

"Kiss me," she said quietly.

Stephen stopped what he was doing and looked at her. She could tell he wanted to ask her if she was sure, but he didn't, and instead pulled her into his arms and kissed her so softly, silently asking for permission with each kiss. She pressed herself against him and parted her lips, inviting him to kiss her more deeply, and he eagerly accepted the invitation.

Even though their kiss was more fervent than the first one, it didn't rob her senses the way the priest's kisses did. But it was pretty damn fantastic.

Stephen pulled away. "We should eat," he said, clearing his throat.

"Yeah," said Brooklyn, tucking a strand of hair behind her ear. She took the pasta and tossed it with the Bolognese sauce they had made together. They finished cooking without saying anything else and ate in silence. It wasn't comfortable like the one earlier. Now, sexual tension buzzed between the two of them and at an unbearably high frequency. Brooklyn stared at her food until Stephen finally spoke.

"I want you, Brooklyn."

"I want you too," she replied without hesitation. "But I can't." Again, she felt silly. She had spent an entire, blissful day with him. It seemed like a long time, but not enough time.

"I know."

Another impermeable silence followed.

"May I ask what it is about him that has you so hooked when you know it's not a permanent situation?"

Brooklyn took a deep breath. "I don't feel comfortable talking about it."

He clenched his jaw and nodded.

"What is it about me that you're willing to see me when I'm... when I'm..."

"When you're in love with another man?" he finished the sentence for her, his tone so soft it couldn't be taken as accusatory.

"I'm not in love with him," she said, a little too forcefully.

He thought for a moment. "There's something special about you. A quiet grace."

"Aren't you poetic?" It was a poorly timed joke, so it came off harsher than she had intended it to, but it was all Brooklyn could say to keep from jumping out of her skin.

Stephen shook his head.

"I'm sorry," whispered Brooklyn.

"I get you. Like I said, I came from a rough background and for the longest time, I hid behind snark and disinterest."

"I'm not hiding."

"Yeah, you keep telling yourself that. You don't think I notice your carefully offered bits of information, or how you get quiet whenever the conversation is about you?"

Brooklyn's eyes widened. She thought she had done a good job at masking her need to keep her past and other vulnerable bits under wraps. "You don't know anything about me." Brooklyn clenched her fists, drawing Stephen's attention to them.

"And whose fault is that?" He got up and went to her, offering his hand. Brooklyn stared at it before taking it and he pulled her to stand with him.

"You think you understand, but you don't." Trusting Father Mathias with her demons had been difficult. How could anyone, other than a priest, not look at her differently after learning that her upbringing more closely resembled a classic horror novel than the traditional unpleasant childhood Stephen was probably imagining?

"Again, whose fault is that?"

Brooklyn looked away. "Maybe all of this was a bad idea." And just like that, the beautiful dream Stephen had so thoughtfully spun just to make her smile dangled dangerously over a precipice.

"Brooklyn?" Stephen's tone made her look up at him and into his eyes. "I'm going to kiss you. I promise I won't do anything more than that."

Wanting to salvage the moment, she nodded, and his lips crashed with hers. She eagerly reached up to wrap her arms around him. He pulled away to kiss her neck and elicited a small moan from her. There they were, the sparks that had been missing before, and Brooklyn realized the lack had been from both of them holding back. She pressed herself against him, desperately wanting more, but he pulled his lips away from her and held her in a desperate hug, pressing her face against his chest. His heart pounded fiercely against her cheek and his breaths were ragged.

"Please don't stop," she whispered.

He didn't oblige Brooklyn's plea and she was relieved. "I don't want to be the cause of any regret," said Stephen. "I should take you home." The strain from the self-control he had to employ was obvious. It wouldn't take much to break down his resolve and Brooklyn knew it. She didn't move, her mind racing to figure out if the consequences were worth a chance to be with him.

"Brooklyn?"

She nodded, mirroring his struggle to remain chaste. "Thank you," she said, not sure what she was thanking him for. Maybe for his integrity.

When he pulled up in front of "her house," she gently touched his hand. "Thank you for being so amazing and understanding. And thoughtful."

He smiled sadly. "Call me an optimist, but I think you're smart and will realize what you're doing with that person isn't going to amount to anything. That being said, I'm not stupid, or overly patient. I just know what I want. And I want to get to know you."

Brooklyn shook her head sadly. "I still don't understand why."

Stephen regarded her with furrowed eyebrows, his lips slightly turned down at the corners. "You should really give yourself more credit. But I did ask myself the same question while driving, and I know what it is about you that got me."

She looked up at him expectantly.

"I get your fear of money. Everyone is fake. Plastic. I'm always told what people think I want to hear and never the truth. You"—he paused to smile—"you were honest about your situation. Maybe to someone else it doesn't mean much. But to me, it means the world. You're so real I can't look away."

Brooklyn sat back heavily in her seat, her breath caught in her chest. "Wow." It had to be the nicest thing anyone had said about her, and it wasn't even true. "But I'm not. I didn't tell him about you. I wanted to, but I was too scared to."

"The point is I know you will. I don't think you can lie, or even keep a secret for too long."

"But I have been." Again, she considered telling him about her relationship with the priest.

"What do you mean?"

Brooklyn implored him with her eyes. "It's not my secret to tell, even if I'm a part of it."

"I don't understand what you're saying."

Brooklyn smiled sadly and leaned over to kiss him on the cheek. "I know. And I'm sorry. Good night, Stephen."

20

By the time Monday came, Brooklyn was nearly mad with guilt and longing for her Priest. Throughout the week she had rationalized that if only he would take her, in the traditional sense of the word, she wouldn't be pining for someone else.

She arrived at St. Anthony's early and waited before going in and taking her position at the small table. Brooklyn prayed that he had forgiven her. She prayed that she would understand his intentions for the evening. She prayed for the ability to be grateful for whatever he was going to give her tonight and that she may give him what he expected of her. Brooklyn opened her eyes and stared at the candle's flame. *I don't know if I can handle this.* The emotions were too intense for someone who had never experienced any connection deeper than sex in an alcoholic haze; someone who had needed to turn off her emotions to survive her mother and the church.

It was like the water tap had been turned on for the first time at full pressure and the unused fixtures couldn't handle it. She wished she could slow it down, just a tiny bit. Acknowledging the new, intense emotions triggered the beginning of a panic attack. But before it could unfold and take hold of her overworked heart and quivering lungs, the air shifted, and she felt Father Mathias enter the room.

"After tonight, when you arrive, I want you to strip off your clothes and fold them neatly before assuming your position to pray." His voice made her jump. Even though she had felt him enter, she hadn't expected him to be that close.

"Yes. Father."

"Get undressed, child. But face the wall. Do not look back."

Brooklyn stood on unsteady legs and took off her clothes, folding them and stacking them in a neat pile by her feet.

"Kneel."

She returned to her position.

"How is your bottom?"

"I'm sorry, Father," she mumbled. Brooklyn felt his fingers on her shoulder.

"Do not apologize, child. You have been punished, you apologized then, and you prayed for forgiveness. There is no need to hold on to it."

"Yes, Father."

He reached down and ran his fingers over a breast, circling the nipple and areola in small, deliberate circles. Brooklyn pressed into his touch the slightest bit. Father Mathias cupped her breast, and the full-on contact shocked her.

"Turn around."

Brooklyn turned, remaining on her knees and keeping her eyes downcast.

"How was your week?"

"It was difficult, Father. I missed you." Her day and evening with Stephen stained her cheeks red with guilt. That would have been the ideal moment to tell him.

But she didn't.

He cupped her cheek in the palm of his hand. "I missed you too, child. On Mondays, it seems the evenings are consistently free, so this will be our time together, as we are now."

"Yes, Father."

"Look at me, my child."

Brooklyn looked up tentatively, afraid her eyes would betray her.

"Always be available for me, for if I have a moment to spare, I will expect you here within the hour."

"Yes, Father."

"But, my child, always know there is still life outside of us. I expect you to socialize, see friends, and have fun. Make plans. You are entitled to one uninterrupted evening a week. You must plan it in advance and ask for permission to do so. You still have my email address?"

Again, she immediately thought of Stephen. "Yes, Father."

Father Mathias didn't say anything else and urged her to her feet then led her to his bed. Brooklyn sat on the edge, and he pushed her to lie back, then brought her feet up so that her knees were bent and her legs spread wide open. Brooklyn felt vulnerable and blushed, resisting the urge to close her legs.

"So beautiful," sighed the priest. He cupped her sex and pressed down with the palm of his hand. "Do not move," he ordered before she could rub herself against him.

Her breaths quickened, and her body was quickly overtaken by that all too familiar heat.

"As much as I demand your self-control, I cannot deny how much I love your desire for me, child."

"Please, Father, let me give you pleasure."

He shook his head, the movement so forlorn it broke her heart. She saw then that his need for her was as strong as hers for him. She wanted to ask him why he denied himself the pleasure he offered her, but she knew better and closed her eyes instead, waiting for his command.

But Father Mathias didn't move or say anything. He stood there, his hand cupping her. Brooklyn opened her eyes to look at him and saw his were closed too, his forehead creased in thought.

"Father?" she whispered.

"Close your eyes, child, and do not speak."

Brooklyn obeyed, and moments later she felt his fingers slide into her for the first time. She was already wet, and she moaned. Having him inside of her, even if it was just his fingers, was enough to bring her close to the edge. He moved them in and out in a slow rhythm, using his thumb to rub her clit. It was near impossible for Brooklyn to stay still and her moans grew desperate. She wanted to call out his name, to grind against his gentle, slow, and tantalizing touch, but she stayed as still as the air in the nave after the last candle had been blown out. The only thing that moved was her heaving chest.

Father Mathias withdrew his fingers for a moment and Brooklyn moaned again when he reinserted them. She felt the weight of his body next to her before his lips captured hers. She whimpered when she tasted herself on his lips as he kissed her deeply. His erection pressed against her hip, and again it took all of her will to not rub up against him.

"Come for me, child. I want to feel you clench around my fingers." Brooklyn couldn't be sure about how many he had inside of her but it had to be at least three. He was stroking hard now, to the point where Brooklyn's body had begun moving on its own. The more she bucked and squirmed, the harder he pressed and rubbed, until she came with an ear-shattering scream. Her legs quivered and her voice trembled as her scream turned to a moan. Then she held her breath, savoring the feeling of released tension rippling through her core and spreading to her arms and legs. When the orgasm subsided, she began to cry. Father Mathias didn't question it. He pulled her into his arms and held her tightly as she sobbed.

After some time, he smiled and brushed her hair off her face.

"Thank you, Father," she whispered.

"How are you feeling, child?"

Happy, she wanted to say. *Relieved*. Him affording her that level of pleasure meant that he truly had forgiven her for their last visit.

"Child?"

Brooklyn panicked because she wasn't just happy and relieved; she was also feeling guilty. Brooklyn looked away and failed at stifling a sob. This was why she could never have anything good; she ruined everything with her poor choices. Regret settled heavily in her chest, shoving out the happiness and guilt. Had she been honest or resisted the temptation that was Stephen, she could have truly enjoyed this moment that Father Mathias had gifted her. Even with Stephen, the good couldn't be fully embraced with her situation lingering in the background. So many beautiful things were happening to her, and she could only acknowledge their beauty, rather than experience them.

"What's wrong, child?" The alarm and concern in his voice was Brooklyn's undoing and she cried even harder.

"I don't know," she said.

"Are you alright with the way I touched you?"

It pained Brooklyn that he even considered it was his touch that distressed her. She nodded vigorously through her tears. "I'm more than okay."

"Then what is it?"

Tell him now! If you don't tell him now, you never will. Brooklyn opened her mouth to speak but couldn't form any words. "I... I can't say."

"It's alright." Father Mathias held her quietly. "I checked in with the soup kitchen. I hear you're doing phenomenal work there. I'm very proud of you," he said after some time.

Brooklyn appreciated his attempt to change the topic. "I go in as often as I can, Father," she said quietly.

"And you're still running?"

"Yes, Father."

"How often?"

Brooklyn took a trembling breath. "Um, at least a few times a week."

Father Mathias murmured his approval and pulled Brooklyn in closer.

"And how is your new friend?"

"Good."

"Have you heard anything else from Page?"

"No. Probably better that way."

"Why is that?"

"Well, because she's not good for me." Brooklyn paused. "And when she apologized, it didn't feel like one."

"What made you feel that way?"

Another deep breath and Brooklyn's heart had slowed to a normal pace. Her breath still hitched on looming sobs, but she was able to keep them at bay. "She blamed me while apologizing. And she was also hoping I had something on me." Brooklyn was vague about what that something was, but she trusted Father Mathias knew what she was alluding to.

"Child, to forgive is to be divine."

Brooklyn expected some quote from the Bible, but none came.

"There's nothing wrong with giving someone a second chance if you feel like giving them one, but you already know the negative impact Page can have on your life. You now know what leading a productive, healthy life feels like. If you feel strong enough to let her back in, and if it's something you truly want, then you should. In the end, no one is responsible for your decisions but you. Page cannot take away everything you've gained unless you decide to let her."

The insightful advice silenced Brooklyn. She hadn't voiced her worries, yet Father Mathias had addressed every single fear and thought regarding Page. *How?* she wondered.

"Yes, Father," she said after a bit of silence. "Father?"

"Yes, my child?"

"What am I to you?"

"What do you mean? I've told you many times..."

"The church is obviously your priority. Where would I fall into all of that? And I know you said at some point, when my training is done, you'll want to own me. But for how long?"

"Where is this coming from?"

"I've just been doing a lot of thinking." She sighed. "I never thought much about the future, but now I am. Because I feel like I actually have one. And I want to know what it might look like."

"You have no idea how much joy it brings me to hear you say that you see a future for yourself." His lips thinned as he deliberated his next words. "If I'm honest, this is all new territory for me. I've always trained and released, so... I don't know."

"I understand." But just because she understood didn't mean she was satisfied with his answer. Who knew how long Stephen would be willing to wait while she sorted things out?

While *Father Mathias* sorted things out.

"Gregory?" said Brooklyn from the door to the staff room.

"Yeah?"

"Can I talk to you?"

"Sure..."

Brooklyn had been thinking about her situation all night and she knew she needed some sort of sound advice. She went to sit across from him and took a deep breath. "I went on another date with Stephen."

Gregory sat up straight. "Oh? Why don't you sound excited about it? He fucked up, didn't he? I mean, no one can be *that* perfect."

"He *is* that perfect," she said sadly.

"So... what's the problem then? Why do you look like someone just told you the truth about your fashion choices?"

"Seriously?"

"What?" he said with a giggle and a shrug.

"I'm being serious."

"Okay, sorry. What's up?"

Brooklyn second-guessed her decision to tell Gregory everything, but she couldn't white-knuckle through it all on her own anymore. "I was already seeing someone, and before you freak out, Stephen knows this," she said quickly before her friend could get in a reprimanding comment. "But the person I'm seeing isn't really available."

"Please don't tell me you're seeing a married man? I mean, it would explain a lot. But please. No. That's so basic."

"No," she said slowly, forgoing the lie she told Stephen. "He's very much single and is supposed to stay that way." She took a deep breath as if trying to inhale any courage the air may hold. "He's... a priest."

"Holy fucking shit, no fucking way!"

"Shhh!" Brooklyn looked over her shoulder to make sure they were still alone.

"How? Why? Wait... do you have sex?"

"That doesn't matter. The point is I don't know what to do. I'm... really into the priest, but I don't want to be stuck sneaking around forever. You know? And I *really* like Stephen. He's amazing." Brooklyn sighed. "But I can't move forward with him while I'm still seeing the priest."

"Okay, can we stop blowing over the fact that you're..."

"Shhh!"

Gregory leaned in and whispered, "...fucking a priest?"

"What else do you want me to say?"

"Nothing! Just give me a minute to digest this very aromatic, loose-leaf tea you just spilled."

Brooklyn sat back with a sigh and crossed her arms.

Gregory stared off into space, his eyebrows moving with his dramatic deliberation. "Okay, digested," he said with a serious nod. "So, you're telling me Stephen knows you're doing a priest?"

Brooklyn rolled her eyes and looked over her shoulder again. Maybe having this conversation at work wasn't the smartest idea. "No, he guessed the same thing as you, that the guy is married, and I kind of... didn't... correct him."

"Wow."

"It's not really a lie. I mean, he's married. To the church. Or God, or whatever." This earned her a snort from her friend. "Anyway, basically, things are still super new with Stephen, and I don't know whether to end things with the priest for a possibility of what could be something good." She took a deep breath after her long-winded sentence.

Gregory looked at Brooklyn with sympathy. "Honey, don't you think you should end things with the priest regardless?'"

Brooklyn shook her head. "I can't."

"Hypothetically speaking, if the priest were to give up everything to pursue a life with you, would that be something you wanted?"

Brooklyn went to say yes but hesitated. Could she handle that level of intensity twenty-four-seven? Even if she could ride off into the sunset with her Priest, what level of normalcy could they achieve? Up until that moment, she had never considered whether she wanted a lifetime of domination and submission.

"In my few dates with Stephen, things have been amazing. And simple. So simple in the best of ways. Minus my weird situation. But with the priest, things are far from simple, beyond the obvious."

"What do you mean by that?"

Brooklyn considered telling him *everything,* but only for a split second. She wasn't that brave. "They just are... he and I have an extraordinary situation. Can we leave it at that?"

"Sure, but that still doesn't answer my question."

"I guess I'm saying I don't know," she reluctantly admitted.

"Well, I may be biased, but I totally think you should give Stephen an honest try."

Brooklyn scratched at her palm with her thumbnail and bit her lower lip. "I think you're right."

"What the hell are you two doing? Gregory your break is way over, and Brooklyn, you're not on break till four-thirty and we're getting slammed," said one of their coworkers.

"We're coming," said Gregory. "Listen, what you're doing with this priest is pretty much as bad as dating a married guy. You need to ask yourself about the integrity of his morals. I don't care for religion, but it's the intention—his intention and however he justifies what he's doing. Is that someone you can trust?"

Brooklyn's knee-jerk reaction was to defend Father Mathias, but she nodded, deep in thought over what he said. It was a valid point. "Thanks, Gregory."

They stood up and he gave her a hug. "Good luck with figuring things out. We can talk about it some more if you need to."

They went out and inserted themselves into the afternoon rush. At some point, Brooklyn was told to take over one of the cash registers because she had made too many mistakes with the flurry of orders. She was too preoccupied with trying to figure out what she should do. Gregory's advice was good, perfect even, but it didn't mean she liked it. Or was able to take it.

"Not used to seeing you at this end."

Brooklyn looked up and saw Stephen. He smiled, truly happy to see her despite the awkward ending to their perfect date. Why couldn't she just be smart and go for the obvious choice?

"Yeah, I'm not sharp enough today to handle the rush over there," she said, nodding her head towards the coffee machines, steamers, and tornado of cups.

"So... they put you in charge of money instead?" he joked.

"Good point."

"I can't imagine anyone ever being sharp enough to handle it," he said, nodding towards the baristas.

"So, what can I get for you? Actually, let me surprise you today." Brooklyn picked up a to-go cup and marked down the special barista codes for an espresso-based drink. "I hope you like it. It's on the house."

Stephen smiled. "Already getting free coffee? I feel special," he whispered so the other customers wouldn't hear. He left and Gregory gave her that smug look of someone who's in on a secret.

When Brooklyn got home, Barb popped her head out from behind her door as Brooklyn reached the landing for their floor.

"Hey," said Barb.

Brooklyn swallowed her annoyed sigh. "Hi."

"Um, I wanted to say thank you for the bottles the other day." She stepped all the way out of her room. Her movements were jerky, as if they were trying to catch up with her brain's instructions. She shot out her hand. Brooklyn reluctantly held out her own and Barb dropped a bracelet into her palm.

"What's this?"

"It was a gift from my babies. I stayed clean for a month a while back, and they gave it to me. You've been doin' good. I saw." She jerked a shoulder to her ear in an attempted shrug. "Anyway, I don't deserve it," she said with a sad laugh. "But you do." She smiled and ducked back into her room.

Brooklyn looked down at the braided bracelet with a thin strip of tarnished metal that had "One Month!" engraved in it. The braided part was frayed and its color had faded, and she wondered how long ago that one month had been. She ran her thumb across the engraving. Barb's unexpected kindness had Brooklyn erupting into silent tears. "Thank you," she whispered between sobs.

She went to her room and buried her face in her duvet to muffle the sound. Her phone buzzed with a text, but she ignored it. She wanted to block out the world and sink into her sofa's old cushions. Anything other than facing her predicament.

For the first time since cleaning her life up, she craved the bottle or one of Page's ambiguous pills.

"Fuck it," she muttered. She left without looking at Barb's door and walked to the liquor store to buy a small bottle of vodka. She didn't even wait until she got home and rounded the building's corner to open it there. The liquid burned her throat and it felt good. It took a few chugs before she gagged and pulled the bottle away. Her gags ended in a fresh set of sobs that she desperately tried to stifle.

The fall air had grown cooler in the last week and her nose ran from the chill and the crying. She swiped at it with her sleeve, then made her way back home. The vodka's effects hit her quickly and she was stumbling by the time she reached the stairs of her apartment building. It was like déjà vu after a night out with Page. She didn't like it, but it was better than facing her inner turmoil.

She knocked on Barb's door and gave the bracelet back. "I don't deserve it. See?" She held up the telling paper bag. Ignoring Barb's sad expression, Brooklyn went to her room to finish her vodka in solitude. Regret didn't hit her until the following morning when she woke up with a headache and dry mouth. She rolled over, still in her jacket and jeans, and looked at the empty bottle. Shame joined her regret and she cried again, as if she hadn't cried enough.

The little LED light that signaled an unseen notification flashed. Brooklyn checked and found a message from Stephen, asking if she wanted to go out on Saturday. *Yes, yes, yes.* But she couldn't continue living with the guilt that she wasn't even sure she should be feeling.

She replied with a no and an apology, and almost offered up an explanation but ended up leaving it at that. With a heavy head and an equally heavy heart, she got up and threw the evidence of last night's weakness in the small garbage can that sat next to her room's door. She stared at the bottle.

"You're garbage. You're everything your mother said you were." She looked up and studied her reflection in the mirror. "You're a worthless sinner—evil that only has the chance to neutralize itself in life, but never delivered." She repeated the words her mother had yelled at her daily. "Worthless."

21

Her decline was swift and discouraging, proving how fragile her hard work had been. As the week went on, she became increasingly anxious. She knew her troubles would be evident to her Priest again. Back were the dark circles and that sickly pallor to her skin from poor eating and hydration. Monday arrived much more quickly than before, and she made her way to St. Anthony's without a hint of the enthusiasm she usually felt.

Something in Brooklyn's chest fluttered when she arrived. Her issues aside, this would be the first time she would wait for Father Mathias naked—poor timing considering she wanted to shroud herself in every way possible, as if her naked form might reveal her secrets. She took a deep breath and went to the rectory. With trembling hands, she removed her clothes and folded them, stacking them on the sofa, then went to light the candle and kneel at the table. The past week had been lonely. Aside from a couple shifts at work and volunteering at the soup kitchen, she stayed at home. She avoided Stephen. Avoided people in general.

She couldn't concentrate on praying. All she could think of was how Father Mathias would see her when he came into the room. Naked and guilty. Brooklyn felt ashamed for not praying, but it couldn't be helped. When the priest entered, he took a sharp intake of breath.

"Oh, my child," he groaned.

"Good evening, Father," greeted Brooklyn, keeping her eyes closed.

The priest went to her and placed a hand on her shoulder. "Forgive me. You may not understand why I'm asking for your forgiveness, but my goodness, I can't help but to see you as mine already." He paused, clearly needing to say more but unsure how, or whether he should even say it. "One thing I haven't spoken to you about is having... relations... with others, and... I cannot bear the idea of you being with another."

Brooklyn froze. Did he know about Stephen?

"Look at me."

Brooklyn looked up at him, her eyes wide with fear. She couldn't bear the thought of losing him, not without knowing where things could go.

There wasn't a single trace of anger, just... dare she believe it? Pure love?

215

"You are mine." She felt him searching her eyes, vigilant not to make any cues that would reveal thoughts she may not want to express. "I will not collar you now, not until I feel you have been sufficiently trained and I am certain you have a full understanding of the commitment. But my God, child, you are mine."

Brooklyn wanted to turn and hug his leg and declare her devotion, but she couldn't, not when everything was still so uncertain. "Yes, Father" was all she could muster in the moment.

Father Mathias urged her up to her feet. "Is something wrong, child?"

Brooklyn shook her head.

He didn't seem convinced. "Brooklyn?"

Her head snapped up. She couldn't remember the last time he had called her by her given name. There was a time when she loved how he said her name; now, it just caused her worry. "Yes, Father?" she whispered.

"You know I do not tolerate lies."

Her breaths became short and irregular with fear. How could she explain to him what bothered her? "There is something," she eventually said. "But I'm not ready to talk about it." She closed her eyes and hoped he wouldn't push the subject.

He nodded. "Of course. All I ask is for absolute honesty. Even if it means asking to put it off until later."

Brooklyn nodded. "Yes, Father. I'm sorry."

"Think nothing of it." He waved his hand to dismiss the mistake. "Now," he said, making her look back at him, "I believe you are without marks," he said, his voice low and eyes alight with hunger.

Yes. Pain.

He led her to the bed and bent her over it so that her sex was exposed to him. "Child, what I crave tonight will be very new and different from what I have done with you so far. Let me know if you want me to stop."

"Yes, Father." Brooklyn tried desperately to bring herself into the moment. She wanted to be there, present emotionally and mentally for her Priest, but all she could hear was him admitting that he couldn't bear the thought of her being with someone else. *Worthless.* That word echoed in her head on an endless loop.

"Get up," he commanded.

Brooklyn stood. Right away, she knew: He had noticed. She was stupid to think he wouldn't.

"Turn around."

Brooklyn's heart pounded so violently in her chest she was sure he could hear it. She turned.

"I respect the fact that you don't want to talk about whatever it is that's occupying your mind, but I cannot continue while you're in this state."

Brooklyn kept her eyes on the ground. "I failed, Father," she whispered. She couldn't bear to bring up Stephen, so she took hold of her shame from turning to the bottle and ran with it. "I drank. Not socially, but because I wasn't feeling well."

Father Mathias didn't say anything.

"I'm what my mother says I am. I don't see how you think I'm special. I'm everything they said I was. Everything." Now she wasn't thinking about her mistake with the alcohol, and she didn't underestimate the priest enough to think he couldn't tell the change in tone.

"My child," he started when it was clear Brooklyn was done. "You are special and divine. I'm afraid you took those words and turned it into pressure on yourself. You will still make mistakes, and that's human. I would never expect steps without falter."

Brooklyn shook her head. "You don't understand." Her gut twisted at his look of worry.

For the first time, Father Mathias averted his gaze. "I promise you, my child, I will always forgive you for any misstep, as I hope you would forgive mine."

He knows! Oh my God he knows. Brooklyn tried to quell the panic and looked him in the eyes. "Please, Father, I want to continue."

Father Mathias measured her gaze and nodded before pulling her into his arms. Soon, Brooklyn's breaths slowed, and his scent lulled her into that place of safety she could always be sure to find with him.

"Bend over the bed," he whispered into her ear.

Wordlessly, she did as she was told. Father Mathias rubbed her back slowly and they stayed like that for a while, until Brooklyn let go of everything. Until the word *worthless* left her mind. Then she was his again—his prized possession, not her mother's disappointment. Not a woman who kept secrets and lied through omission.

He moved away then came back, and she felt something cold being spread on her anus.

"Father?"

"Are you uncomfortable, child? Be honest."

"It's okay."

"Are you certain?"

She nodded and he continued. She felt him insert something slowly.

"These are anal beads," he explained. "Stay relaxed."

"I've seen them but never tried them before," she said shyly. She concentrated on not fighting the intrusion until she felt the bead slip all the way in. She let out a small half moan, half whimper.

He pushed another bead into her. Another quiet moan escaped her lips as she tried to make sense of the sensations. Father Mathias rubbed her bottom, smacking it lightly before inserting another bead.

"How do you feel?"

"I feel... full, Father."

"Do you enjoy the feeling?"

"I do," Brooklyn answered shyly.

"Now we can begin." He spanked her with full force and Brooklyn cried out in surprise, not expecting the hard impact so soon. He hit her again and this time her cry was muffled by the bed covers.

The impacts with the beads inside of her made her dizzy. The intense pleasure coupled with pain confused her and her brain struggled to decide what to concentrate on. Father Mathias continued until her bum glowed a bright pink. Her cries turned to moans once she was warmed up and she wiggled her bum in anticipation.

Father Mathias laid Rapture next to her face so that she could see it. "My child," he said, then hit her with as much force as when he had punished her.

Brooklyn cried out, but as the pain dissipated, her cry turned to a moan. She could already feel the approach of her climax and identified it as the type that only appeared with pain.

The priest chuckled. "You are finding this a lot more pleasurable than I had expected."

He had clearly wanted her to suffer, and the thought alone set every inch of her skin ablaze. Father Mathias rubbed her warm bottom and applied pressure with the palm of his hand, enhancing the sensation of the beads. Brooklyn moaned and pressed back against his him.

She gasped when she felt the oncoming orgasm rushing at her faster than expected. "Father, may I please come?" she asked frantically.

"No."

She made a frustrated sound and sat forward but his hand followed her, continuously applying pressure.

"You're going to make me come, Father," she tried to say, but the words came out garbled between her gasps and moans.

"You are not permitted to, so hold it," he snarled. Brooklyn brought a leg up on the bed, climbing up onto it and away from his hand, but he followed her, climbing up as well and pressing down on her lower back with his other hand. He pushed two fingers into her sex.

"Please!" she begged. Brooklyn felt full, her belly tight and winding tighter by the second. "Please! I don't know how." She was desperate. This was a whole new kind of torture she had never considered, and her legs quivered as her climax neared.

"I said, do not come." As he spoke, he moved his fingers in and out while still maintaining the pressure on the beads.

"Please stop! Please, I won't be able to..." But it was too late. Brooklyn climaxed and while in the throes of her orgasm, Father Mathias withdrew his hand and began to hit her again with Rapture.

Brooklyn cried, her body torn between pleasure and pain. Her orgasm already had full control of her body and the rain of pain couldn't stop it. If anything, it intensified it. She shook her head violently, overwhelmed by the onslaught of sensations, and began to choke on air and saliva as her body forgot how to do the most basic of functions. When her orgasm subsided, so did Father Mathias's punishment. By the time it was over, she was on all fours and her juices were trickling down the insides of her quivering thighs, coaxing another shiver from her.

"I'm sorry, I couldn't stop it," gasped Brooklyn.

The priest leaned over her. "Shh," he hushed. "You did well, my sweet, sweet, child." He buried his face in her hair and she could feel his smile. "In time, you will learn how to control it. It would be unfair of me to expect you to do so with such little training."

He reached down, still hungry for her lust, and touched her sensitive clit. Brooklyn shuddered and moaned, her desire instantly renewed. She regarded her hunger with reluctance, too tired to even think of having it sated.

"Please, let me touch you, Father."

After a bit of deliberation, he nodded. "But only with your hands, do you understand?"

"Yes, Father," she said with excitement, her fatigue quickly forgotten.

He lay down next to her and she awkwardly undid his pants. Brooklyn murmured with appreciation when she finally had his cock in her hand. She had wondered if his reluctance to allow her to touch him was because of insecurity, but he had no reason to be. He was large, her fingers just meeting while her hand was wrapped around him.

Father Mathias was throbbing, the tip glistening and an angry red, and she could only imagine the pent-up need. Brooklyn stroked him slowly, slightly hindered by his boxers, but he quickly removed his pants and boxers completely, kicking them off onto the floor. Now she was free to stroke him faster. Looking up at him, she licked her lips, craving his taste and the feel of him in her mouth. His pre-come was so inviting and she found it unfair that she couldn't lick it up.

Brooklyn moaned loudly when he fingered her, finding that sweet spot that made her legs tremble.

"Come again for me, my child." He rubbed her g-spot harder, quickly pulling out another orgasm from her. She cried out and he groaned from her involuntary squeeze on his shaft. She stroked him harder and faster, and he came with her, covering her hand and arm with his come. Before he could protest, Brooklyn brought her hand to her mouth and licked up whatever she could. She was ecstatic, finally being able to taste him. Even though he hadn't explicitly said it, Brooklyn knew he hadn't wanted her to. But she had only touched him with her hand, so it wasn't straying from his instructions. Instead of reprimanding her, he watched as she greedily cleaned her hand with her tongue.

When she was done, he closed his eyes and took a deep breath, then looked up to the ceiling. "You consume me, child. I fear my ability to maintain control," he said, clearly troubled.

Brooklyn sat up. "I can't imagine you ever losing control, Father." Feeling emboldened, she straddled him, high up enough to avoid his waning erection, and let her hair hang around them like a curtain.

Father Mathias reached up to touch her cheek. The contact was so gentle, as if he was worried he might break her, and was such a stark contrast to his treatment of her just moments ago. "You are precious."

"Thank you, Father," whispered Brooklyn. She believed him.

He sat up and guided her to the floor as he stood and lead her to the bathroom. After removing the beads, they showered together and he washed her, using the soap she always smelled on him.

"Father?" she said as he fondled her soapy breasts.

"Yes, my child?"

"Do you love me?" Brooklyn had never felt as vulnerable as she did in that moment, looking up at her Priest with hope and longing. Although it was one of the questions she had been burning to ask, it wasn't the most important one. Love wasn't enough if he wasn't willing to put her before the church.

He stopped and was silent. "I care for you very deeply," he eventually said.

"Do you love me?" The question wasn't any easier to ask the second time.

He looked at her, his eyebrows furrowed. "I do." His chest heaved with his admission. "I do, very much, my child."

Brooklyn wanted to press for more answers, but right now she wanted to revel in the fact that he loved her. Whether or not it was enough to put her before the church was something she wasn't prepared to find out yet.

"I love you too," she said, finally admitting it out loud. Now that their feelings were out in the open, they stood in awkward silence. At some point, Father Mathias moved out of the way so she could rinse herself. She avoided his gaze, afraid he would see that there was still more she wanted to say and ask. The last thing she wanted was for him to see that his declaration of love still wasn't enough; that in a way, because of their situation, it fell flat.

A deep sorrow filled her. This should have been a happy moment, but instead all it did was make things that much more uncertain.

22

Now that Father Mathias had confirmed his love for her, Brooklyn couldn't justify seeing Stephen, but the depth of her pain surprised her when she considered ending things with him. Up until then, she had assumed that her interest in Stephen was just surface-level, but it seemed he had found his way into her heart. Brooklyn felt terrible, because each time she asked herself what she wanted, the answer was: everything. She wanted it all.

Brooklyn sat in her room, cross-legged on the sofa, and stared at the bare coffee table. Seeing either of them felt wrong.

"What do I do?" she asked herself. Brooklyn felt bad about it, but she called Gregory to see if he was free so that they could talk more comfortably.

"Sure, I can come to you. How does noon sound? And we can walk along the canal?" he suggested.

"Yes, that's perfect. See you soon. And! Um... thank you."

Brooklyn put on warm joggers and her heaviest sweater, then went to meet Gregory at the agreed-upon intersection. The bite in the air saddened Brooklyn. She was always reluctant to accept the going of warm weather and the coming of colder, bitter days.

One look and Gregory enveloped her in a long hug. The prolonged contact made her uncomfortable, but the part of her that was scared and confused welcomed it. Gregory led them down steps that took them from the street to the path that ran along the canal and waited for her to start.

"So, the priest told me he loved me." Brooklyn paused for Gregory to react. He didn't, so she continued, "And now I feel like I shouldn't be seeing Stephen anymore and I thought I'd be okay with that, but I'm not."

"Oh wow." Gregory's eyebrows shot up in surprise. "When did this happen?"

"Last night."

"And why does the priest loving you mean that you have to stay with him and not Stephen?"

Brooklyn went to answer, but she wasn't sure why she had defaulted to the priest.

"What do *you* want?" Gregory asked.

Her chest constricted with shame as she thought, *Everything.* "I don't know."

"Well, that's a lie."

"If I say it out loud, it'll confirm that I'm horrible person."

"You want both of them."

Brooklyn looked away and didn't respond.

"Hey." Gregory touched her arm so that she would stop walking. "Wanting things doesn't make you a horrible person. Lying and keeping secrets from people you care about? That's pretty shitty."

"That's why I need to decide as soon as possible what I'm going to do."

"Or... and bear with me now... you tell the priest the truth about what's going on."

Brooklyn's eyes widened. "I couldn't."

Gregory shrugged. "It's a shitty situation, so I'm not sure there is an easy answer to all of it."

They walked in silence while Brooklyn digested Gregory's practical advice.

"What's the worst-case scenario if you tell him about Stephen?"

Brooklyn immediately imagined Father Mathias's face overcome with betrayal, anger, and disappointment. Maybe in any other situation, it would be manageable, but theirs was unique, and not just because he was a priest.

"I can't tell you exactly why, but the worst-case scenario can't even be an option." Hurting Father Mathias would mean she had failed him when he had literally plucked her out of purgatory. She owed him more than what she was doing.

"No matter what you decide, just try to be sure you honor yourself and your feelings. You deserve to be happy too. Whatever this priest guy has over you, it can't be worth sacrificing your wants and needs."

"Thanks, Gregory."

Gregory put his arm around Brooklyn's shoulders, then they walked until they reached a bridge and used it to cross to the other side of the canal, working their way back towards where they had started. Brooklyn thanked him again before they parted ways.

Brooklyn took her time as she walked back, not wanting to be alone with her thoughts in her sad little room. In fact, she didn't want to go home at all. She walked past her place and continued down the street, walking with no destination in mind. The trees were mostly bare now, the beautiful part of fall officially over. The chill worked its way through her jacket and sweater. Winter was around the corner and Brooklyn wasn't looking forward to it. For some reason, this just deepened her sadness. Everything was dying or preparing for a long sleep, and a part of her wished she could do the same.

Brooklyn's phone buzzed.

Stephen: Let's do something tonight.

The text message was like a prod, urging her to make a choice.

Brooklyn: I can't.

Stephen: Why not?

She bit her lip as she weighed her response.

Brooklyn: Things got more complicated between me and him.

Stephen: I see...

Brooklyn: I need space. And time.

She stopped walking as she waited for his reply. It didn't come.

Brooklyn: I'm sorry.

Stephen: Sounds like you've made a choice.

I haven't, she thought, but she couldn't blame him for taking it that way. She just needed time.

Brooklyn: I haven't. I'm just confused.

Stephen: I understand.

Brooklyn hugged her phone. How could he be so understanding?

Brooklyn: Well... what did you have in mind?

Stephen: Do you enjoy live music?

Brooklyn: I do.

Stephen: Be ready for six?

Stephen: No pressure.

Brooklyn typed out "yes" slowly. It wasn't a good idea, and she should tell Stephen that she couldn't see him anymore. The priest had not only told her he loved her, but also that he didn't want her to be with anyone else. At this point, she couldn't pretend that she didn't know exactly where the line was. She stared at the unsent message, her finger hovering over the send button. Before she could change her mind, she sent her reply. The expected guilt didn't come. Perhaps her excitement over seeing Stephen overshadowed her conscience.

She walked the rest of the way home and considered going through the bins for something decent to wear. A small part of her believed it would be prudent to make the most of the night in case it was the last time she saw Stephen. Brooklyn opened one of the bins and dug through the clothes until she found a pair of true-black jeans and a midnight blue knit top. She pulled them on and inspected her reflection in the mirror. No wonder Page looked impeccable even in simple clothing. Sure, the wearer had to be a worthy model, but well-made clothes that had been made to fit the body properly certainly helped.

Brooklyn finished her outfit with a pair of pristine boots and a jacket that was much warmer than hers. She closed the bins and checked the time. Stephen would be at the house any minute. Making sure the hallway was clear first, she left and went to wait for him. He pulled up, on time, like always. Brooklyn got in and didn't know what to do, so she gave him an awkward side hug.

"You look great," he said.

"Thanks. So do you," she said, noting his fitted peacoat and perfectly coiffed hair. A silver watch peeked out from under the sleeve. Though understated, it made the impact that its price tag, Brooklyn imagined, must have promised.

"What made you change your mind?" asked Stephen as he drove.

"What do you mean?"

"About seeing me?"

"Oh... um... I just..." *wanted to see you at least one last time.* But she couldn't say that. As the thought formed in her mind, she felt terrible. This wasn't fair to Stephen. "He told me he loved me." Brooklyn paused, waiting for him to say something. When he didn't, she said, "So, this gray area just became a lot grayer."

"Why is that?"

"Because"—Brooklyn paused again, trying her best to find her words—"he also said he doesn't want me to be with anyone else."

Stephen chuckled. "So, he gets to have his wife *and* you, and you can't be with anyone else?"

"No, it's not like that," Brooklyn said with a shake of her head.

"So, what are you doing here if you're willing to accept that?"

"I haven't! I haven't." She repeated her denial quietly. "Are you upset with me?"

Stephen stole a glance at her, and Brooklyn was relieved to find his eyes were soft. Empathetic, even. "No, I'm only trying to understand the situation."

Brooklyn took a deep breath to muster up the courage to be completely honest with him. "I changed my mind about tonight because I'm not sure if I'll be able to see you again and justify it. I'm sorry, I know it's shitty of me. I just really like you and I was sad at the idea of not seeing you again."

"Well, I'm glad you told me."

Brooklyn looked at him, eyes wide and silently pleading for his unwavering understanding. "Really?"

"Yes. I can't say I'm happy, but I'll be sure we make the most of tonight. Not just for you, but for me too. I really like you, Brooklyn."

Tears welled in her eyes and she looked out the window so he couldn't see them. *You're being so stupid.* Stephen had proved, repeatedly, that he would make the ideal partner. Father Mathias couldn't offer her transparency, freedom, or a relationship. How could he? Unless he left the church.

"Thank you. You're truly amazing."

"Thanks, can you tell that to this girl I'm trying to win over?"

Despite her heart hurting, Brooklyn smiled. "Oh, believe me, she knows."

Stephen took her to a small restaurant that offered live music on the weekends. The band played Latin jazz originals with a sultry front-woman that boasted powerful vocals. The atmosphere and music instantly captured Brooklyn's attention and she leaned forward in her seat as she listened and sipped on a glass of wine.

"This is amazing," she said when the band stopped to take a break.

"I'm glad you like it."

They sat side by side so that they could both see the stage with ease, and Stephen put his arm on the back of Brooklyn's chair. She leaned back so that his fingers would brush against her arm, and she looked at him, hoping he would get the hint that it was okay. He must have because he put his arm around her shoulders, pulling her closer to him. Brooklyn leaned into him and savored the moment that was so beautifully normal. She almost wished that the night would never end as she found herself feeling peace in his arms, and the feeling shocked her.

Up until that moment, she had believed peace could only be found with the priest and at the other end of one of his implements. Could it be that Stephen was in fact a solid option? A choice worth considering and a risk worth taking? Choosing to not overthink it, Brooklyn leaned in and kissed him. Stephen pulled back in surprise, but only for a moment before he returned the kiss. Fireworks lit up in Brooklyn's mind. The elusive spark she had been looking for with Stephen ignited, brighter than the last time, and took hold.

They pulled away to look at each other, their breaths shallow. Stephen searched her eyes, but Brooklyn knew all he would see was more confusion. And she *was* confused, but Brooklyn decided that tonight it didn't matter. Stephen pulled her to him and kissed her forehead with a sigh.

"What are you thinking?" whispered Brooklyn.

"What an unfortunate situation this is."

Brooklyn tried to pull back, but Stephen stopped her. "I'm sorry," she said.

"So am I."

They turned their attention back to the band and Brooklyn was grateful that Stephen continued to hold her even with the growing tension that couldn't be assigned a definitive cause. Whether it was sexual or frustration, Brooklyn couldn't decide. Maybe it was both.

"What if we go back to your place?" whispered Brooklyn when they left.

Stephen stopped to look at her.

"I don't want the night to end just yet."

He nodded and they drove to his place, the one he had in the city. It was a newer condominium that overlooked the river. His unit was one of the penthouses and the view was spectacular. The river twinkled with the reflection of lights, and the parkway that ran alongside it pulsed intermittently with modest traffic.

"You like your views," commented Brooklyn.

Stephen came up behind her and put his arms around her. "I do."

Brooklyn let her head rest against his chest and closed her eyes. She could do this. Do normal. Do the sweetness. She turned so she could wrap her arms around him and pressed her cheek to his chest. His heart beat against it. His scent soothed her, and she inhaled deeply, exhaling with a sigh.

Stephen moved and made her look up at him. "I want you, Brooklyn."

Mouth dry, all she could manage was a nod before going up onto her toes so that she could kiss him. His lips were so soft and moved so slowly against hers. She knew he intended to savor the moment, but it wasn't long before Brooklyn's hunger grew, and she couldn't hold back. She pressed herself against him and kissed him with fervor.

"Are you sure?" Stephen barely managed to get the question out before Brooklyn recaptured his lips with hers. With fumbling fingers, she worked on the buttons of his shirt, but Stephen grasped her hands and waited for her to look back up at him. "Are you sure?" he asked again.

Brooklyn nodded.

"If we do this, I don't want to rush."

Taking a deep breath, Brooklyn nodded and did her best to slow her heart rate. "Okay," she whispered.

Stephen took her hand and led her to his bedroom. The sparse walls and monochromatic color scheme lacked personality, but it somehow seemed very right and said so much about the man that had captivated her interest. His affinity for minimalism was in everything that he did, but it was controlled; everything he owned was owned with intention. The room's window was floor to ceiling and wall to wall, allowing the moonlight to flood the unlit room.

Touching her face with subtle reverence, Stephen leaned down to capture her lips with his. He was so slow. Slow, and intentional. Always intentional. Brooklyn held back, not wanting to push the pace he had set, but she wanted to kiss him harder and faster and for him to hold her tightly. He pulled her closer with his other hand and Brooklyn pressed herself against him as she wrapped her arms around his waist.

Stephen moved her towards the bed without breaking contact. The backs of her thighs touched the bed and she sat down. She looked up at him through her lashes before closing her eyes when he ran his hands up and down her arms. His touch was so unbelievably tender, Brooklyn couldn't help but to shed a few silent tears.

"Hey, what's going on?"

Brooklyn shook her head. "Please don't stop, I'm okay."

Stephen didn't seem convinced.

"They're good tears." Brooklyn tried her best to swallow a sob. "I promise."

Semi-convinced, Stephen pulled her into his arms and Brooklyn buried her face in his shirt and took a deep breath. Looking back up at him, she touched his forearms hesitantly with her fingertips. Initiating touch felt wrong after all her time with Father Mathias, and she searched Stephen's face for signs of displeasure. She found the opposite. This emboldened Brooklyn and she moved to his waist, poking her fingers under his shirt and touching the skin just above his belt. Soft hairs tickled her fingertips as she ran them along his waist.

Stephen's hands found their way into her hair, and he coaxed her gaze upwards with the gentlest of tugs. He looked into her eyes—ever searching and ever admiring.

"I don't think you're aware of how beautiful you are," he whispered.

Brooklyn wanted to look away, but his hands kept her in place.

"I know compliments make you uncomfortable, but I want you to know how amazing I think you are." He punctuated his sentiment by leaning down and kissing her deeply. This time, he didn't try to temper the pace and he received Brooklyn's eagerness with his own. He pushed her back so that she was lying down and then stood to take off his shirt. Brooklyn let out an involuntary gasp of appreciation.

Stephen was perfection. Soft cuts and edges outlined his modest build, a dusting of hair covered his chest and abdomen, and his waist tapered off past his belt line. Brooklyn watched as he undid his pants and let them drop to the floor, then moved to pull off hers more easily. Sitting up, she pulled off her top and Stephen stopped her when she went to undo her bra. He got into bed and pulled her towards him so that they could lie comfortably, face to face, and he held her, continuing his light touches and soft kisses. Brooklyn followed his lead and returned his touch, running her fingers lightly up and down his back.

Time slowed, and Brooklyn felt as if they had been lying that way for an eternity. Stephen pulled her closer and she felt his erection against her belly. Brooklyn wanted to reach down to touch him, but again, her training stopped her. She pressed herself against him instead and wiggled. Stephen grew harder still, and he let out a quiet grunt.

"I want you," whispered Brooklyn, wanting to eliminate any doubt he may have of her willingness to go all the way.

Heart pounding, she reached down and took hold of him through his briefs. The anticipated reprimand never came. He twitched in her hand and pressed into her touch. Stephen grabbed her bottom and somehow managed to pull her even closer even though it seemed there was no more space left to breach. He squeezed and massaged her, all the while pushing his hardness against her. Brooklyn panted and matched his rhythm, her need growing to a point where she wasn't sure she could respect the pace he had set.

He must have sensed her need, because he pushed her to lie on her back and reached down to where her arousal had coiled so tightly. Stephen groaned when he found her panties soaked through. He rubbed and Brooklyn raised her hips, desperate for his touch.

"Please! I don't want to go slow."

Stephen ignored her plea and continued his tantalizing touch. Brooklyn reached for his lips with hers and kissed him desperately. He pressed against her sex a little harder, then slipped his fingers underneath her panties. Brooklyn was more than ready for him and his fingertips glided with ease over her clitoris. The unhindered contact made her legs tremble.

"Please," she begged again. She pulled at his underwear and tried to drag them down past his hips, then gave up and reached under them. Feeling the soft skin of his cock sent her over the edge.

Stephen pressed his fingers into her and teased out the cresting orgasm. Brooklyn came and gasped against his mouth, breathing in his air and giving him hers.

Stephen pulled away and Brooklyn heard the sound of a wrapper. *Finally,* she thought. Stephen positioned himself on top of her, ready to finally give her what she wanted. Pulling her panties to the side, he slowly slid inside of her with a slow, low groan.

"Fuck, you feel so good," he grunted. Brooklyn's muscles were still spasming from her subsiding orgasm and grasped at his considerable size. Stephen's eyes were closed, which allowed Brooklyn to look at his face as he thrust into her. Thinned lips and furrowed eyebrows gave away his intense focus and she knew he was fighting off his own orgasm. His barely controlled pleasure gave her an unfamiliar feeling of power. The priest's ability to resist her had had her doubting her desirability, but in that moment, Brooklyn couldn't even try to deny Stephen's desire for her.

She clenched around him and rejoiced in his response, a subtle twitch in his lips and a stutter in his rhythm. When he paused, Brooklyn lifted her hips to him and he growled from his efforts to hold on, but there was no will left. Stephen let loose and thrust into her harder and faster until he came. The sensation of his pulsing cock was enough to make Brooklyn come again, and she squeezed around him without mercy, wrapping her legs around his waist to draw him deeper into her.

Stephen collapsed on top of her, and they lay there, panting and spent, coming down quietly from the heights of their passion. He buried his face in the crook of her neck and played with her hair while Brooklyn held him tightly.

"I don't want this to be the only and last time," he eventually said. "We're meant for so much more than just one night."

Reality hit Brooklyn and she braced herself for the expected guilt. But still, none came. What they had just shared was too beautiful to regret or to paint in a negative light. She wanted to tell him that she wanted more than just one night with him too.

"What if we have a few nights?"

Stephen propped himself up on an elbow so he could look at her. "It won't be enough."

"It has to be."

"So, you have made a decision."

Brooklyn tried to move out from under him and pulled away. She sat up and hugged herself. "You don't understand, it's not as straightforward as you'd think."

"You keep telling me I don't understand but you refuse to explain anything to me."

"I'm ugly on the inside," she whispered. "I know you see me as this strong, resilient person who is honest, and I don't know what else you see in me, but I'm not good."

"I don't get why you're so intent on painting yourself so horribly. Give me some credit, Brooklyn. I'm a smart man with good judgment... maybe you should listen to what others have to say about you instead of whatever stories you tell yourself to justify blocking other people out." He paused. "Is this what he tells you? That you're not a good person?"

Brooklyn jolted from the accusation against her Priest. "No! No. It's the opposite. He's seen all of me and still accepts me."

"Why don't you give me the chance to see all of you?"

"Because... I just can't."

Stephen shook his head and got out of bed. "I'll take you home."

His dismissal crushed Brooklyn. "Stephen..."

"No, I'm not doing this anymore. How can you look at me the way you do, share what we just shared, and not offer me some level of preliminary trust to let me in? It makes no sense."

He was right; it didn't make sense and Brooklyn knew it. Stephen hadn't given her any reason to think he would judge her. As she acknowledged that, the root of her reluctance hit her: She wasn't afraid of his judgment, she was afraid of his pity. She sighed deeply as the realization sat heavily in her gut. There was no chance for them because she refused to go there with him. She got up and wordlessly got dressed, avoiding eye contact with Stephen but still very much feeling his disappointment. It hung heavy in the air.

When she was dressed, she waited awkwardly for Stephen to finish as well and followed him out. The drive was silent, and although she had previously found the quiet with him comfortable, this one was anything but. She wanted the drive to end and to get out of the car and away from the awkwardness as soon as possible, but part of her wanted to sit in it if it meant staying with him a little bit longer.

Stephen said nothing when he pulled up in front of "her house." Brooklyn considered telling him that this wasn't her home and showing him just how sad her life was. But she didn't.

"I'm sorry," she said instead.

"Me too." This time, there was no softness, only bitterness.

She paused before reaching for the door handle and got out without another word. Brooklyn couldn't bring herself to say goodbye, and there was nothing else to say. When Stephen drove off, it felt final, and she knew she wouldn't hear from him again. After all, as he had said, he was a smart man. And smart men didn't hang around disasters like herself.

23

Monday came and Brooklyn went to her Priest, lacking her usual enthusiasm. The guilt she had been waiting for still hadn't come and she was surprised to feel resentment instead. This hurt her. Father Mathias had admitted his love for her the last time she had seen him, but their situation cast an opaque shadow over the beauty that should have ensued. Although resentful, she still waited for him as he had asked: naked and praying.

"I have a gift for you. Stand up and turn," he said when he came in.

Brooklyn got up and her eyes were drawn to a little box wrapped in shiny, silver gift paper. He handed it to her.

"You may open it," he said, clearly pleased that she had waited for his permission.

Brooklyn carefully unwrapped the box and opened it. "Rosary beads?"

"Not just any. These were custom made. Look at the cross."

She looked at it closely and noticed something engraved on the back.

"It's the triskelion, the symbol for BDSM. The beads are silicone and they're also reinforced so that I can do something like... this..." He took the beads out of the box, quickly wrapped them around her neck, and squeezed and pulled, forcing her up to her tiptoes so that she was eye level with his lips.

Brooklyn took a tentative breath, and he loosened his grip.

"Or this..." He turned her around and hit her backside once, earning himself a sweet yelp from Brooklyn. "Stings, doesn't it?" he said, rubbing the spot he had hit.

He handed the rosary back to her and she took it with renewed interest. The pale gray silicone beads were spaced with cylinder, disk-shaped stainless steel ones. The cross and "Glory Be" beads were also stainless steel. It looked uninteresting but striking all at once. They were beautiful.

"Thank you, Father."

"I suspect your skin will grow to love them very much," he said with subtle promise.

Brooklyn smiled, but it didn't reach her eyes.

Father Mathias searched her face. "You don't seem like yourself tonight, child."

"I have a lot on my mind, Father."

He pressed his lips together and took the beads from her to put them around her neck. "I want you to always wear them."

"I will, Father." Brooklyn's voice was flat.

"Shall we talk about what's weighing so heavily on you, child?"

"I'd rather not. If that's alright, Father."

Father Mathias frowned, then pulled Brooklyn into his arms and held her, holding her head against his chest. "What do you need in this moment?" he eventually asked.

Answers. "I don't know." It was a lie—one that had slipped out so effortlessly, but only because it was necessary.

Without any verbal command, he took her hand in his and led her to his room, then motioned for her to lie down. The usual bloodlust in his eyes was absent as he lay next to her and pulled her back into his arms. Brooklyn's sensitive nipples rubbed against the material of his black button-up shirt, striking up her hunger for him. But she knew nothing would happen tonight because he wouldn't give her what she needed, and she didn't have the fuel to try and feed the hunger. It was an empty feeling, an echo of what she usually felt.

Despite her reservations, his scent still managed to slowly coax her into a state of contentment, pulling her into the now. It may have been the most peace she had felt since that first date with Stephen. The feeling was short lived, because with this peace came safety, and with safety came the small internal suggestion to ask the hard questions.

She moved her lips, prepared to call his self-given title, but no sound came out. This peace also came with weakness and the willingness to give in to her subdued state. It was easier to occupy that head space, where all she had to focus on was his word and command. She let go and sank deeper into his arms. Instead of voicing her concerns, asking for answers, or confessing her recent actions, she said, "I love you."

Father Mathias didn't say it back. He did tighten his arms around her, ever so gently, but nothing more.

With Stephen out of the picture, Brooklyn existed only in the instances she was with Father Mathias. When she wasn't with him, she drifted, and her days would only be productive with something short of a miracle. When she was with him, she was alive. Every nerve ending that went dormant in his absence would come back to life in his presence with the full intention of making up for lost time.

Week after week they saw each other, and the more time that passed, the harder it was for her to push for an answer to the ultimate question: Where did she stand in his life? She needed to find out before it was too late.

It was probably already too late, Brooklyn figured. Their time together without the uncertainty Stephen's presence had brought proved that she could fall more deeply than she thought possible. There was no end to the levels of her want for him and it had gotten to a point where she was willing to accept any sort of situation if it meant she could keep seeing her Priest, which was why she couldn't bring herself to ask. Not even during her confessions, which she began doing every Sunday after Mass, was she able to bring up the topic.

Until finally, she decided she would. One Sunday when Mass ended, she left with everyone, only to return to the confessional shortly after. Brooklyn sat and waited, anxious to get it over with. As she waited, she quickly started to lose her nerve. Father Mathias was always on time. She peeked out into the nave and found it empty. A few more minutes passed, and Brooklyn went to look for him in his office.

"I don't understand where anyone got these ideas from," she heard her Priest say through his office door.

"There is no proof, but there has been a lot of concern about your conduct with one of the parishioners."

"This is absurd!"

"Father Mathias, you have an upstanding reputation and have bettered many churches during your service. We'd hate for that to be tarnished by rumors and we believe it may be best to relocate."

Brooklyn covered her mouth to hide her gasp.

"But I have *just* settled in here."

"I know this is unfavorable, but it is for your own good."

"I'll think about it."

The man cleared his throat. "Father Mathias, if I may, many of us have made... mistakes. We may be men of the cloth, but we are not impervious to the lure of a beautiful woman. I recommend you end your affair before proof of it arises, or leave. But I strongly suggest you leave if there is love involved." The man lowered his voice. "Between you and me, I have fallen victim to the devil's temptations myself. But God forgives. And before you can receive his forgiveness, you *must* correct your failure."

Brooklyn sagged against the wall next to the door. *If there's love?* She almost wished she hadn't implored Father Mathias to admit his feelings. What if he took this man's advice?

"Is that all?" said Father Mathias.

"Yes. I'll wait for your answer."

Brooklyn stepped back from the door when it opened. The man that had spoken to Father Mathias saw her and seemed to know exactly who she was, because he shook his head before passing her.

He stopped. "Young lady?"

"Yes?" she said meekly.

"If you love him, you will let him be. He has a bright future ahead of him. Do not ruin him any further with your advances." He left, not giving her a chance to lie, and she was grateful for it.

Brooklyn wondered who had blown the whistle and the first name that came to mind was Janice. "Father?" Brooklyn knocked on the door that had been left ajar and stepped inside the office. She found her Priest with his face buried in his hands.

"Good afternoon, child," he said without looking up.

"What are you going to do?" she asked, not hiding the fact that she had listened in on his conversation.

He shook his head. "I don't know."

This was her chance to find out how important she was to him. She hadn't been brave enough to ask, so now fate, with its twisted sense of irony, had forced them into it. Brooklyn's face grew hot with fear and the room felt like it was ready to close in on her. "Please don't leave me." She wanted to kick herself for her relentless weakness.

He looked up at her then and stared as if it was the first time seeing her. His eyes were red. "I love you." He choked over the words. "My God, I love you, and I don't know what to do about it."

He loved her. He had said it for the first time since that night she had pressured him to tell her how he felt about her. *He loves me!* Brooklyn said to herself before shaking her head. *No. No, weakness.* "And what does that mean?" She paused to swallow, but her mouth was too dry. "With all of this?" She gestured towards the walls.

He took a deep breath. "We must be more careful." He nodded to himself, reasserting his role of composed leader. "We can't change much because that would confirm their suspicions. You will continue to come to Sunday Mass and confess afterwards. But when you come to me at night, we must find a way to make sure no one sees. That's the only time I could imagine someone would have seen anything suspicious," he said, murmuring the last sentence more to himself than to her.

Brooklyn closed her eyes. An intense rush of frustration came over her. Instead of basking in the knowledge that he still loved her, she had to put her guard up and ask questions she didn't care to ask. "That doesn't answer my question." When she felt she could, she opened her eyes again to look at him.

"Come to me." He held out his hand.

"No. Not until you answer my question. What does loving me mean?"

He pleaded with his eyes. "It means I will do everything I can to make this work."

"But you won't put me first. I'll always be second to the church. Right?"

"Child, please. Now is not the time to discuss this. Have faith." His voice faltered on the last word.

"How can I? When clearly, you're losing yours, Father."

Her words struck a chord, and for the first time, she saw Father Mathias's resolve crack and she knew it was no ordinary crack. It was one in a dam with unbelievable amounts of pressure behind it. What would spill out when the dam gave way? Would it be his faith in the church? Or his faith in his call to dominate a "divine" creature such as herself?

"I'll see you tomorrow night," he eventually said, ignoring her comment.

Brooklyn bit her tongue. "Yes, Father."

Deep down, Brooklyn already knew the church would always come first. The hope she had been holding on to for weeks had been misplaced and regret took its place as she walked home. She thought of Stephen and what she had walked away from. A knot grew in the pit of her stomach, growing tighter with each step and making it hard to breathe. She panicked, worried she would give in to the wailing sob that promised relief right there on the sidewalk. Pressing her lips together, she did her best to hold it in and rushed the rest of the way home. Not that she could let it out there either. With her many roommates, there was never enough privacy to do something like scream-cry into a pillow.

When she got home, she sat on her sofa, legs crossed, and pressed her nails into the backs of her hands. The sobs escaped in breathy gasps, but they were quiet enough. Brooklyn went over the last few months, searching for that point of no return, and was embarrassed. There had been many points, too many to count. No situation or reasoning could justify such stupid decisions.

She hugged herself and rocked back and forth to manage the nausea caused by her immense self-pity. And the grief? The grief waited in the peripherals of her heart, because the small part of her that was still able to reason knew that she needed to end things with Father Mathias. Not just for her, but for him as well. Her sanity and his identity were on the line. Brooklyn had been to enough services to know how much the priesthood made Father Mathias who he was: Father Mathias. She wasn't certain there would be much left of the man if the cloth was taken away from him.

24

Even with the new speculations, Father Mathias expected her to still show for their weekly Monday visits and instructed her to go through the back service door. Maybe it was her mild dramatic air, but Brooklyn thought it would be best to dress in black too. The space between the church and its neighboring house was dark and a little disconcerting, but she managed to find the door. It opened to the back hallway on the opposite end of the door that led to the rectory. She walked to it, went in, and waited for him on the sofa.

Father Mathias frowned when he found her clothed and not in position.

"Child?" he said, confused.

"I-I—I think it's better if we stop this." Brooklyn spoke before she could change her mind.

Father Mathias was silent.

"I..." she started.

"No. Stand up."

Brooklyn ground her teeth and obeyed.

"No," he said again. He pulled her into his arms, hugging her with obvious desperation. He buried his face in the crook of her neck and squeezed her harder. "No," he repeated.

Brooklyn wasn't sure she had heard right, but the last "no" sounded more like a sob than a word. She tentatively reached up to touch his forearms and stroked them with her thumb.

"We can't go on like this, Father."

He pulled away and bore his eyes into hers. "You're mine," he ground out.

Those words acted like a switch to an uncontrollable inner furnace. One moment, Brooklyn was afraid and grieving, and the next, she was on fire and overtaken in her own flames. One more time. She would enjoy one more night with him and then end things. She nodded, not trusting her voice.

He led her to the middle of the room and made her stand under a beam. She looked up and saw a chain hanging from it with silver loops at the end.

"Get undressed."

Maintaining eye contact with the priest was hard for Brooklyn, but she boldly held his gaze as she took off her clothes. She folded them and placed them neatly on the sofa. When she turned back to him, she found him holding black leather cuffs and instinctively held out her hands. He secured them onto her wrists then attached them to the clips above her and stepped back. He groaned when he saw her like that, in all her naked glory, bound and defenseless. Brooklyn pressed her thighs together, aroused by his open appraisal.

He left and returned with various implements and laid them out on the sofa. He picked up a leather strap first and ran it across her breasts. She shivered from the cold leather against her nipples, and they instantly hardened. He circled her like a predator stalking its prey, his hunger for her flesh evident in his blue eyes.

"You have experienced a lot of pain at my hand, child. Tonight, I crave for much more. Are you prepared?"

"Yes, Father," whispered Brooklyn. She was already wet with anticipation.

The priest groaned with approval. "With all that has gone on, I had forgotten what a beautiful masochist you've become," he said.

Brooklyn whimpered when she saw his hunger come to life and grow alongside his obvious need to claim her. They fed into each other so well. Her willingness and his appetite—a never-ending vortex of pain and pleasure. He stood behind her and tapped the strap lightly on her bottom, gradually increasing the strength until he elicited a soft whimper. Brooklyn knew this was their warm-up and she looked forward to the blinding pain that was to come. She hadn't noticed just how much she needed it, but he continued with the gentle hits and that's when she realized the longer warm-up promised much greater pain.

On and on he went until finally, he hit her with incredible force and her knees buckled. She cried out, but the cry was quickly followed by a moan. He moved to stand in front of her and hit the fleshiest part of her thigh, stopping only to adjust the cuffs of his shirt before landing another strike. The impact on the thigh was new for Brooklyn and she yelped. Her thigh tensed up and the sting of the leather's bite didn't dissipate as quickly as she would have liked.

He was quick as he changed out the implements, the new one hurting more than the last. He continued, marking her backside, her thighs, calves, and back, until he worked his way to his prized toy, Rapture. But he stopped, picking up a flogger instead. Moving to stand in front of her, he looked at her breasts, deep in thought.

He traced their curve with his finger. "I've yet to leave marks on these."

Brooklyn looked at him with fear. She couldn't imagine her breasts receiving punishment; they were so fragile and sensitive. He hit her left breast with the flogger.

It felt nice. Not painful at all.

Then he hit the right one. Like he did with her bottom, he gradually increased the intensity, reveling in her facial expressions. Brooklyn closed her eyes to focus on the sensation and how it made her feel. Father Mathias replaced the flogger with his hand and slapped her chest. It hurt much more. The hit turned her chest into a drum only she could hear and feel, and its vibrations echoed inside her, tickling the base of her throat. He hit her again and she let out a gasp that was insufficiently fueled with air. The pain wasn't unbearable, but it felt uncomfortable.

Brooklyn shook her head, wanting to ask him to stop but wanting it to continue at the same time. She pressed her lips tightly together to keep them from betraying her as he hit her again. And then again. Her breaths grew shallow as he repeatedly slapped her breasts before going back to the flogger. This time, he made it hurt, and she cried out but it didn't deter him. The impacts came so quickly, they were like a waterfall of torturous leather. A strange sense of panic filled her and that's when he stopped. The chains tinkled from her trembling.

"Mmm, yes, they are beautiful like this," said the priest.

Brooklyn looked down and her breasts were a beautiful deep shade of pink that promised magenta in the morning. She could already picture the purple that would bloom by tomorrow evening.

Father Mathias picked up Rapture and returned to her bottom. The first hit made her scream like she had never screamed before with him. Having been ignored, her bottom had cooled down enough to become less tolerant of his attention.

"Yes, my child," he growled. "Show me how you suffer at my will." He hit her again.

She was crying now, but she didn't flinch or move away as she stoically waited for the next hit. She heard another groan of approval from the priest. "Tell me what you want."

"I want you to hurt me, Father... please."

"More than I have now?"

"As much as you want."

He removed the rosary beads from around her neck and wrapped them around his fist. He kept his eyes trained on her, then circled around to her back. Nothing happened and Brooklyn braced herself for the hit that never seemed to come. It wasn't until she had begun to relax that he landed a hard punch in the fleshiest part of her bottom. She gasped with surprise, then he landed another. He punched her until Brooklyn grew comfortable with the different type of pain that delivered less sting. Instead, it was like a deep massage. But then he whipped her with the beads, making her regret her comfort.

The beads licked at her skin like fire, and she shrieked and cried with each hit. The priest stopped and moved to her front to return the rosary to her neck. Brooklyn couldn't look at him as she sagged in her restraints. She was drenched in sweat, her body a quivering mass.

"I'm not done yet, my child."

Brooklyn let out a deep, pitiful groan when she saw him pick up Rapture once more. He rubbed it across her face and stomach and circled her again so that he was behind her. He picked up from where he had left off with it. The onslaught of impacts he rained down on her left Brooklyn dizzy. What made this more painful than any other time was the pace. He gave her no time to recover. It was one hit after the other for what seemed like forever so that nothing else existed outside of him, her, and the pain.

The world seemed to stop; the moment suspended in an infinite manner that robbed her of the ability to perceive the passage of time. Brooklyn saw flashes of white and wished she had been bent over because she couldn't come from the pain while standing. Her legs trembled violently until they eventually gave out, proving that her body would break before her spirit. It was then that Father Mathias stopped and took her down from her restraints. She collapsed in his arms, and they sank to the floor together.

He brushed her hair away from her eyes. "I will always crave this sight—your face stained with tears; your lips swollen from crying. You are so undeniably divine, my child."

"Thank you, Father." Brooklyn reached up to touch her cheek. She hadn't even realized she had cried, but her fingertips came away wet.

Father Mathias took her hand to lick the tears from them. "I own your tears." He licked another fingertip. "These are mine. You are mine," he growled.

"Yes, Father," breathed Brooklyn. Her eyes fluttered and she floated further into the abyss, letting herself go completely with a sigh and giving in to the euphoria. Her breaths grew shallow and it felt as if the bottom of her stomach had dropped out. She trembled violently and nausea quickly replaced the sweetness she had sunk into.

"Shhh, it's alright, child." He stood up and carried her to his bed. He left and returned with orange juice and held the cup up to her lips. Brooklyn moved away, her stomach turning from the thought of consuming anything.

"Please drink, my child. It'll make you feel better. I promise."

Brooklyn accepted the beverage and sipped slowly. As soon as the juice touched her tongue, the nausea began to subside, and she drank more with less hesitation.

"Better?"

Brooklyn nodded sluggishly.

He left and returned with fruit and fed her grapes and pieces of pineapple.

"Thank you, Father," murmured Brooklyn with a raspy voice.

Once Father Mathias was certain she felt better, he motioned for her to roll onto her stomach and groaned when her saw her backside and ran his fingers across her welts. The light touch tickled her, causing her to shiver.

"I will tend to your bruises."

"No thank you, Father. If it's okay, I'd rather not do anything that would speed up the healing." She looked over her shoulder and up at him through her lashes.

He nodded and lay next to her instead, pulling her into his arms. He held her close, playing with her hair while whispering sweet nothings into her ear until she fell asleep.

25

"So, you do this twice a week?" asked Gregory, tossing a peeled potato into a bucket of water.

"Mhm," replied Brooklyn absentmindedly.

"And it's because the priest told you to."

Brooklyn nodded. "Volunteering keeps me busy."

He sighed and shook his head. "I still can't believe you didn't end things with him. What are you thinking, Brook?"

Brooklyn shrugged. "I told you..."

"Yeah, yeah, yeah," he said, rolling his eyes, "he 'saved you.' But still."

There was no way Brooklyn could tell him exactly what had her hopelessly drawn to Father Mathias, but her sore body answered for her silently. She pretended to stretch with her arms out front so that she could feel the tenderness in her breasts from the previous night. A blush stained her cheeks.

"Jesus Christ, aren't you smitten," commented Gregory. "Oh, I'm sorry. Am I allowed to say that in front of a priest's *girlfriend*?"

"Shhh!" Brooklyn giggled.

"Oh... my... fucking... God," he gasped. "This soup kitchen is run by St. Anthony's Catholic Church. Is that the church your priest is at?"

The blood drained from Brooklyn's face. "Gregory, please be quiet." She looked around to see if anyone heard.

"Sorry, sorry. Jeez, Brook, that makes it so much more real." Gregory looked at the potato in his hand as if it could answer the million questions that were most definitely running through his mind.

Brooklyn looked down at her own half-peeled potato.

"Have you heard from Stephen?" he asked, trying to change the subject, not that it was a much better one.

"No." Brooklyn bit her lip. She missed him more than she had expected. Stephen had added something to her life that the priest couldn't. Sure, she found peace with both men, but Stephen offered a level of tenderness Father Mathias was incapable of. Brooklyn couldn't imagine the priest planning picnics or engaging in simple small talk or living without rigid structure.

The rules and the protocols had saved her, but now she had a hard time not feeling burdened by them. Stephen didn't come with any of that. He just wanted *her*.

"You should message him."

"I can't."

"He won't wait forever."

Brooklyn could feel Gregory's empathetic, searching gaze but she couldn't meet it. "I know and he's not waiting anymore," she finally said. "I feel so dumb. I know it's obvious. Things would be so much simpler with Stephen and he's more than I ever hoped for. But..."

"Wait, what do you mean he's not anymore?"

The thought of her last night with Stephen made Brooklyn's eyes burn. How could intimacy feel so right with two different people and in such different ways?

"What happened?"

Brooklyn pleaded with her eyes, preemptively asking for his understanding before she told him what happened. "I told him about the position I was in and wanted to have one last date with him. We had sex and then..."

"What!?"

"Shhh!"

"And then?"

"Well... it was beautiful. And he thought so too and said it didn't make sense why I was choosing Father—the priest."

"I'd have to agree with him."

Brooklyn threw Gregory a look, but it wasn't as cutting as she had hoped it to be. Instead, her eyes burned more, and she bore the look of someone who knew they were drowning and without hope.

Gregory reached out and put a hand over Brooklyn's. "Hey, hey, it's okay."

Air caught somewhere in her chest, causing her to hiccup. "What if I'm making the biggest mistake of my life?"

"The only mistake is not preparing yourself for what could happen. I know you're looking for comfort, but in this kind of situation, a disaster is unavoidable, and you know I can't lie and tell you everything will be okay."

He sighed. "But I can tell you that when the holy shit hits the fan, I'll be here."

Brooklyn's bottom lip quivered. "I'm afraid it already might have." She put the potato and peeler down and leaned forward with her elbows on the table. She took a deep, trembling breath. "People at church are suspicious. Some guy was at the church the other day trying to convince him to leave before there was proof of our relationship."

"Holy fuck, that's insane. And what did the priest say?"

"Mathias."

Gregory gave her a questioning look.

"That's his name. Father Mathias."

"Oh. Well, what *did* he say?"

"Nothing really. Just that he would do whatever he could to make it work. Whatever that means," she said, muttering the last part bitterly. Brooklyn finished peeling the abandoned potato and plunked it in the bucket, then wiped her hands on a rag.

Gregory looked around them. "Are we done? Oh, thank God, I don't think I could look at another potato again."

Shaking her head, Brooklyn pushed him. "You're such a baby." Her attempt at humor fell flat, but Gregory was always one to pull comedy through.

"These babies are used to stainless steel and coffee beans, not starch monsters," he said, holding up his hands to boast his pruned fingers. "Hey, I have an idea. Instead of the movies, what if we go to a day spa? I have one of those online coupon things."

"Um, I don't know," she said, uncertain. The last time she had gone to a day spa was with Page and she didn't have fond memories of that day.

"Come on. Who would turn down the spa?"

"I'm just not the self-pampering type." Brooklyn shrugged.

Gregory gave her a look.

"Fine!" she conceded.

"One condition: You message Stephen. At least let him know you're thinking of him. I'm positive he'll appreciate it."

Brooklyn bit her lip, then raised her eyebrows after brief deliberation. "Wait a second, what is this? You twist my arm to go and now you're putting conditions? And no. I told you, we ended things."

"You know you want to." He shrugged with a cheeky smile.

Wordlessly, she took out her phone and let her thumbs hover above the screen.

Brooklyn: Hey, just wanted to say hi. And sorry.

She showed Gregory what she wrote, and he nodded tepid approval.

"Well, don't sit there and stare at your phone. Let's get cleaned up and go pamper ourselves."

Not staring at the phone proved to be more difficult than expected, for both Brooklyn *and* Gregory. Brooklyn's poor phone suffered the wrath of steam, oils, and water due to her checking it every few minutes.

"Hey, don't worry. Maybe he's just having a busy day at work."

"Or he doesn't want anything to do with me. And, I mean, I don't blame him."

Her phone finally pinged, announcing a new message.

"Oh my God, is it him?"

Brooklyn nodded. "He said, 'It's fine, I understand.'" They both stared at the message in silence. "What does that even mean?"

"Ugh, he couldn't give us something more? We can't even dissect and obsess over that." Gregory pouted.

"What should I say?"

"You can't really reply to that."

Brooklyn shook her head. "It doesn't matter. I can't string him along, so it's better to just let him go." She pressed her lips together to keep them from quivering.

The following Sunday, a man cornered Brooklyn after Mass. "Can I help you?" she asked when he didn't say anything.

"I'm the new deacon, Thomas," he said, holding out his hand.

"Hi?" said Brooklyn, confused as to why he made a point of introducing himself.

"I'm going to be frank. I was placed here to keep an eye on the"—he looked over his shoulder at Father Mathias, then back at Brooklyn—"charismatic priest."

"Why are you telling me this?" Brooklyn tried to act unaffected, but even she heard the hitch in her voice.

"Come now, I'm positive you know why. I already spoke to Father Mathias and asked him what your frequent visits were for. Would you care to verify that for me?"

"I don't even know you, so I don't need to verify anything." Brooklyn went to step around him, but he blocked her way. Only then did she notice Janice off to the side, watching with interest and an undeniably smug look on her face.

"If you care about Father Mathias, I suggest you answer my question."

"Look, I just started coming to church, I don't know anyone here well enough to care about them." She tried to walk away but the deacon blocked her path again. Brooklyn's breath got caught in her chest and prickling heat encompassed her face. Her breathing quickly grew shallow, and the room began to spin. "Let me go," she whispered, not trusting herself to use her full voice. But the deacon didn't move. "Please stop."

"Answer my question first."

"I said let me go!"

Her shrill voice and wide eyes had Deacon Thomas stepping back in surprise at her sudden panic.

"Deacon Thomas!" shouted Father Mathias. He rushed towards them. "Why are you pestering this girl?"

"I just asked her a simple question. Then she became flummoxed for no apparent reason." Brooklyn could almost hear him silently say, "*Other than guilt.*"

"He... he... wouldn't let me go," Brooklyn barely managed to say. The deacon reminded her so much of the churchgoers in the small town she had grown up in. Trapping her. Judging her. Flashbacks of late nights in the church's cellar assaulted her. Every time she blinked, her vision alternated between the present and the past.

"Let us all go to my office, away from curious eyes," suggested Father Mathias.

Brooklyn's panic grew at the thought of going into an even more closed space with the deacon. All she could think of was bolting out of the church as quickly as possible. Of course, then she would give a show to the parishioners, similar to the one she had given Page all those months ago. A small part of her mind didn't want to disappoint her Priest in that way, so she tried to regain control over herself. It culminated in a mostly failed attempt. There was no flailing, screaming, and crying, but she couldn't speak or move, and Father Mathias had to guide her to his office.

"What is this nonsense? I simply asked her a question..."

"You blocked my way. You wouldn't let me go." Brooklyn had to dig her nails deep into her palms to ground herself enough to speak, but her voice still sounded strangled.

Father Mathias sighed. "Deacon, when you asked me about Brooklyn, I had told you she was a troubled girl. It took a lot of effort for her to feel comfortable in the house of God due to a traumatic upbringing in a fanatical church. What you did, simply blocking her path of exit, most likely triggered her anxiety."

With Father Mathias there to speak up for her, Brooklyn felt safe to retreat into her mind. She stepped back to lean against the wall and slid to the floor so she could hug her knees and hide her face.

"I... had no idea. I apologize. But in my defense, I was only trying to help you, Father Mathias. These rumors are rampant, and I simply wanted to make sure that you spoke the truth. Isn't that so, Janice?"

Janice is here too? thought Brooklyn angrily. From the corner of her eye, she could see the woman standing at the door.

"Yes, Father. People are talking," she said, whispering the last part.

"The 'people' most likely being you?" ground out Father Mathias. "Don't think I don't know who's been spreading the rumors, Janice."

Janice harrumphed with indignation. "Father! That was rude and uncalled for."

The priest sighed. "Janice, I would appreciate it greatly if you left."

She did, with a huff.

"Deacon Thomas, you have known me for but a day, and you dare question my character because of some petty rumors? And, in the process, upset a poor soul whom I have been desperately trying to show that there is nothing to fear in the house of God?"

"I am truly sorry, Father."

Brooklyn wanted to scream at the deacon. She knew he didn't mean the apology sincerely. The look of envy on his face when he had first referred to her Priest said it all. Deacon Thomas was a frumpy man whose hooked nose whistled when he breathed. She could only imagine the jealousy he must harbor for someone like Father Mathias.

"Brooklyn, do you feel well enough to leave?"

Brooklyn looked up and realized her face was drenched with tears. "I can't come back," she said more to herself than to Father Mathias.

To the deacon, it probably sounded like she was talking about returning to church. But she hoped Father Mathias knew she was referring to him and her; that she wanted to end things. Her resolve had yet to be tested, but the idea of living a life in which she was being watched by men like Deacon Thomas and bitter church women like Janice was enough to convince her to turn her back on Father Mathias. He had pushed her to see what life could offer, and in that moment, that was what gave her the strength to turn her back on something that, although she loved dearly, was too closely tied to a past that needed to be left in the past.

"My child, do not let this small hiccup deter you from your path to finding God."

Brooklyn heard what he truly meant.

The weight of her grief over her silent decision coupled with her resurfaced anxiety was too much to bear. When Deacon Thomas approached her to help her up, she snapped.

"Get away from me," she hissed. "You're all the same."

Deacon Thomas stepped back and held up his hands.

"I'm never coming back," she repeated. Brooklyn dug her nails further into her palms, desperately trying to keep herself from going into that dark place. It scared her, because back home, her breakdowns that manifested as tantrums had only convinced the church that she was truly possessed. She would act out like a wild animal, unable to make eye contact, perpetually caught between fight or flight.

She could feel Father Mathias imploring her to look at him. That could have grounded her, but her already festering shame kept her from looking up.

"Brooklyn," he implored.

Finally, she looked up, blinded by the ceiling light. But her Priest's eyes were able to capture hers. After a few minutes, Brooklyn relaxed her fists. Her palms had grown numb, but with the release of tension, they burned where her nails had dug into the skin.

She didn't say anything. She just got up and left. Walking aimlessly, she recited her mantra until her anxiety subsided and she could think clearly again. Even with a somewhat clear mind, she didn't know how to feel about what had happened. One thing for sure was she couldn't go to Sunday Mass anymore, not after everyone had seen her break down.

Pulling out her phone, she scanned her sadly short contact list. Two people jumped out at her: Gregory and Stephen. Shaking her head, she pushed away the temptation to reach out to Stephen. There was no way she could ask him for help after what she had done. Gregory was her best bet and her thumb hovered above his name in hesitation. She didn't want to be alone but was too afraid and ashamed to reach out when she was still so vulnerable.

Just as she was about to hit dial, a car horn blared, making her jump. Brooklyn looked up and saw she was crossing on red and had walked out in front of a car.

The driver rolled down his window. "Look where you're fucking going!" His tires screeched as he drove around her.

Shaken, Brooklyn stepped back onto the sidewalk and pocketed her phone. The world seemed so big and so angry. There was nowhere to go and she felt alone. And she was. Because no matter what Father Mathias said or did for her, she could never go to him in times like these. Too many people were watching, and he seemed to think that his priesthood was worth living under that kind of scrutiny.

"Things wouldn't be like this with Stephen," she whispered to herself.

26

Two Years Ago

The room echoed back the years of torture. The time had come for Brooklyn to leave. She was free. But no matter how hard she tried, she couldn't turn her back on the room where she had spent countless hours kneeling at her bed, praying for forgiveness and the ability to be good. So, she stood there, staring at the empty white walls and clutching the straps of her backpack that held her few possessions.

The front door slammed shut downstairs, making her jump. Brooklyn grimaced. This meant now she would have to face her mother as she tried to leave. She considered hiding her bag and trying again tomorrow, but she balked at the thought of spending one more night under her mother's religious wrath. She had waited too long for this day.

"Mary!" her mother, Beth, called out.

Brooklyn went downstairs, shoulders back and chin up, desperately trying to put on the face of strength.

"Mary, what are you doing?" asked her mother, eyeing the backpack.

"I'm leaving, Mama. And my name is Brooklyn. That's what my birth certificate says."

Without fail, her mother's face turned red in a matter of seconds. "How dare you say the name given to you by that man?" she said, referring to Brooklyn's birth father.

"Yes, Mama. Because no matter what name you pull from the Bible and put on me, I'll still be me. So, I'm leaving. And I'm starting over."

Beth crossed her arms and smiled cruelly. "And how do you plan to leave, *Mary*?"

"That's not your problem anymore." Brooklyn went to leave but her mother blocked her path.

"Don't make me call Father David," she threatened.

"Go ahead, I'll be long gone." Brooklyn shoved past her and left, vowing not to look back this time.

The walk to the bus stop took her thirty minutes, undercutting her certainty that she would be long gone before her mother, armed with Father

David, could reach her. Brooklyn kept looking over her shoulder. Even once she reached the stop, she felt she couldn't relax; not until she was on the bus, on her way to the city of her birth, could she do that.

A large cloud of dust appeared in the distance, and soon the roar of pickup trucks followed. It was too late. Panic filled her chest and she hugged her backpack. If they caught her, they'd find the money she had been saving up for years and take it away, leaving her stranded for longer than she could bear.

Another cloud appeared from the opposite direction, and she could make out the bus through the heat's haze. Brooklyn looked back at the trucks, then back towards the bus. And then she ran. She ran faster than her legs could take her, and every step promised a stumble, but she refused to slow down, and instead pushed herself to run faster. The roar of the pickup trucks became deafening, and she couldn't be sure if it was because they were getting closer or because of her fear.

Don't look back. The story of Sodom and Gomorrah came to mind and Brooklyn thought of Lot's wife who was turned into a pillar of salt. Brooklyn wished for that fate instead of the one that waited for her if she was caught and taken back.

The bus was close enough for her to make out some of the letters that announced its destination. She waved her arms frantically and tears streamed down her face. She was *so* close.

The trucks were upon her and one drove up ahead to block her path. Father David got out from the passenger side. He shook his head as he approached her.

"No!" she cried.

"Mary, why do you insist on defying your mother? The church? The will of our merciful God?" He looked up and raised a hand towards the sky.

"Please, just let me go. You won't have to deal with me ever again. I'll go and I'll never come back," she said, the words mangled by desperate sobs.

Father David shook his head. "But, Mary, that's not what your mother wants for you. And as a God-fearing woman, she deserves to see the day her daughter is saved. God wants that for her. Now, that can't happen if you're gone. Can it?"

"I'm eighteen now. She can't force me to stay."

The bus honked at the truck blocking the road. Father David turned and held up his hand in acknowledgment. "Come now, Mary, let us go so that the good bus driver can continue on his way."

Brooklyn looked at the waiting bus. It was right there, filled with people and close enough to smell its fumes. She couldn't imagine Father David and his goons taking her against her will in front of all of them. Her mind raced, trying to find a way out of this. Freedom was too close to give up.

"Father David," she said, walking towards him. "I don't want any more trouble," she continued. She held her hands up in front of her, as if trying to calm down a rabid dog.

"That's the spirit," he said with his usual confident smile.

"But my name... is Brooklyn!" She ran past him and waved her hands at the bus. "Help!" she screamed. The tinted windshield hid the driver's face, but she was relieved when the door swung opened. She only let herself look back once she had a foot on the first step.

Father David looked on helplessly, confirming his loss of power in front of so many witnesses. Even with tears still fresh on her cheeks, Brooklyn smiled victoriously and saluted him before boarding the bus. She was free.

"You okay, miss?" asked the driver. He looked nervously at the small brigade of pickup trucks.

"I am now. Thank you."

Present

Brooklyn's phone buzzed with a notification. It was an email from Father Mathias.

Come to me, now.

Her heart stopped. It had been a little over a week and a half since she had last seen him. And it had been brutal. Brooklyn had turned down multiple shifts and was on thin ice with management, forgone her tasks, and spent her days hiding and crying under her duvet.

I can't. Not after what happened.

She waited. He replied right away.

Is it the church, or me, that you're avoiding?

Brooklyn stared at her phone. "Both." She spoke to the screen, not sure if she could send him the answer at all. Her phone buzzed with a new email.

I miss you.

Brooklyn took a deep breath, looking up at the ceiling and searching for the much-needed strength to say no. There was no denying her suffering in Father Mathias's absence. It was like the color had been seeped from the world. Everything was muted. After that day, she'd had a rude awakening about the emotional risks she took being around all of it. She had barely escaped her mother's church; how could she walk through the doors of another so willingly? It didn't matter that Father Mathias was different when those around him weren't. Another email came through, as if her silence was response enough.

Child, I demand that you come to me.

With tears in her eyes, she responded and hit send before she could change her mind.

Mercy.

She let her cell phone slip from her hand, and it tumbled to the floor. The room suddenly felt cold, and she burrowed deeper under the covers. This was a waking death and she felt every bit of its pain.

But she couldn't go back.

The following days were darker than the previous ones. Brooklyn only got up to go to the bathroom. She couldn't even feel her hunger pangs anymore. Her nights were filled with nightmares where Father David and her mother came after her; ones she hadn't had since she had first moved to the city.

About five days went by when someone banged on her door, waking her up from her restless sleep.

"Who is it?"

"It's Gregory."

Confused, she stumbled to her door and unlocked it.

Gregory stood there with a wide-eyed Barb peeking out from her own room.

"What the fuck is going on?" Barb asked, confused.

"Shit, you look terrible," said Gregory.

Brooklyn looked at him numbly.

"When was the last time you ate?" he asked, concerned.

"They're going to find me," Brooklyn muttered.

"Who?"

"My mom. And Father David. They're gonna find me and take me back," she said, the last word getting caught on a sob.

Gregory looked at Brooklyn with worry. "You're not making any sense. Let's get you in the shower because, well, you smell like ass. Then we're going to get you something to eat. I promise you'll feel better afterwards." He pushed her towards the bathroom and turned on the shower before closing the door.

Brooklyn stared at her reflection but didn't see herself. The mirror became opaque with fog, and she turned to the shower. The idea of hot water running over her skin called to her and she stepped in with her clothes still on, turning the shower to its hottest setting. She sat in the tub and stayed there until Gregory came in.

"Are you kidding me?" he grumbled, shutting off the water. He made her stand up and undressed her, then turned the water back on. "Shower yourself," he ordered. "This is already getting too weird."

"I don't have soap."

"Oh, right." Gregory left and returned with her shower caddy.

Brooklyn took the bar of soap and weakly ran it across her body, but it reminded her of the time her mother would force her to wash herself until her skin was raw from the harsh soap in an attempt to "wash away the evil." She dropped the bar and collapsed, hugging her knees and crying.

Gregory came bursting in. "Brooklyn, what's going on? Please, just talk to me." He shut off the water again and wrapped a towel around her, coaxing her to get up. She let him lead her back to her room and to her sofa. They sat in silence.

"I'm afraid of churches," she finally said. "I didn't have the best experience growing up and..."

"You don't have to say anything else. I know what small town churches can be like," said Gregory as he rubbed her back. "And you're seeing a priest? How did that happen?"

"Father Mathias is different." She stopped talking but Gregory didn't pressure her to explain. "The last time I was at church," she continued, "I was cornered by the deacon and..." Her voice trailed off.

Gregory hugged her. "You were triggered. You poor thing."

Brooklyn nodded and cried silent tears.

"Trust me Brooklyn, let me help you get ready. Then we can go grab something to eat. You'll feel a lot better."

She nodded and slowly got dressed. They walked to Bank Street and went to a bagel shop where Gregory ordered her a ham and cheese sandwich.

"Don't eat too quickly, you might get sick," Gregory warned once they were seated at one of the metal, picnic style tables.

There was no danger of that. As inviting as the bagel looked with fresh lettuce and cheese peeking out, she couldn't bring herself to eat.

"Please, Brook. One bite," coaxed Gregory.

She looked up at his pleading face and nodded. One bite. She picked up a half and took a small bite, chewing slowly with Gregory's gentle encouragement. Then she took another, and as promised, she felt a little more human and a little more put together. Really, Gregory's support and company were what brought her partway out of the malevolent mist.

"Thank you," she whispered as she continued to pick at her food.

"You're welcome. And not that you're even thinking of it, but don't worry about work, I covered for you and told them a family member died."

"If only," she said. Her only known living family member was her mother. And although it was a horrible thing to wish on someone, she wished death on her mother for everything she had done. "How did you know where I live?" Shame stained Brooklyn's cheeks as it dawned on her that Gregory saw the squalor she lived in.

"I snuck into your employee file," he admitted with a nervous laugh. "And before you say anything, don't be embarrassed or ashamed."

Brooklyn nodded and didn't really care in the end. Gregory knowing the truth about her living and financial situation were the least of her worries.

It was slow, but every day, Gregory checked in on Brooklyn either before or after work, helping to pull her from the dark place she had fought to stay out of since escaping her home. She was grateful to him, and grateful to Father Mathias for honoring their safe word.

27

When she was ready, Brooklyn sent an email to Father Mathias with her phone number, saying that she refused to see him before talking and she didn't want to do it over email. That same day, he called her in the evening. She answered but couldn't bring herself to say anything.

"Hello?" said Father Mathias. "Child?"

His voice warmed Brooklyn from the inside out after having gone so long without hearing it. "Hi," she said meekly.

"Are you alright? I was so worried. I hope you know that I was only trying to respect your wishes."

"I know, Father. And thank you. I needed the space."

"Are you upset with me?" he asked.

It was strange for Brooklyn to hear him sound so vulnerable. She shook her head. "No," she said, realizing he couldn't see her nonverbal answer. "After what happened... it just hit me a lot harder than expected. It brought up a lot of old memories. But I'm okay now."

"Are you willing to come see me?"

"What about the deacon?"

"He's not here in the evening. The rectory wasn't built for two people. He's a safe distance, a few blocks down the road. I promise he will never bother you again, child. Please, come to me."

"Yes, Father." As she spoke those words, all the color she had lost in the previous weeks came rushing back, and her senses woke up, hungry for whatever the priest had to offer. She quickly got ready and went to him. On the way, Gregory texted, asking where she was. She felt guilty about it, but she ignored the message and made her way to St. Anthony's.

Father Mathias was waiting for her at the back door.

"I was worried you might have difficulty reentering the church," he explained. He had guessed right because even walking down the short alley had wreaked havoc on her gut with anxiety. She took his hand and let him lead her to the rectory.

Once in the living room, Brooklyn was unsure what to do, so she defaulted to his prior instruction to wait for him by the table. He watched as she slowly took off her clothes and folded them.

"Come," he said when she went to kneel.

She went to him and stood in front of him with her eyes downcast. When he didn't speak or move, she fell to her knees and waited. He buried his fingers in her hair and pulled her against him, pressing her face into his inner thigh.

"Talk to me," he commanded.

"I—I don't know what to say."

"I wish I could have been there for you. How did you manage it?"

"Gregory helped." She sobbed, touched by Gregory's relentless care.

"I am grateful for him. It pains me that you found that kind of pain within these walls. I had so wanted you to see St. Anthony's as a place of safety."

But could she? Yes, St. Anthony's was under Father Mathias's leadership, but it was still under the same belief system that her mother operated by. That would never change. Suddenly something new roiled within her chest towards her Priest. Anger. Betrayal. He too should hate the church for what it had done to her. She pulled away from him.

"What is the matter, my child?"

"St. Anthony's will never feel safe. Do you understand what happened to me? They didn't hurt me just with words. I was beaten, starved, tortured mentally and physically by them. And they all did it in the name of *your* God. How could you love me and the church at the same time knowing what damage it's caused?"

"Child, you cannot condemn an entire religion for the actions of misguided believers. They chose to twist the word of God for their agenda."

Brooklyn nodded, but it wasn't good enough for her. "I shouldn't have come." She stood to leave but he grabbed her wrist.

"You will not go home tonight." He spoke with a strong command, but still left space for a response; she always had the option to call *Mercy* as she had done over email.

She considered it, but ultimately she whispered, "Yes, Father," her tone void of willing obedience and instead filled with bitter fatigue.

"You may never trust the church again, but I will show you that as long as I'm living, you will never live those horrors again. This is my house, and you are mine, and no one will take that away. Do you understand?"

Brooklyn looked up at him in surprise. *Has he lost his mind?*

"Tonight will be arduous for you," he promised.

She couldn't imagine him still wanting to play after everything. But she still obediently held out her hands when he commanded her to.

He cuffed them, then pulled her up to her feet and to the bedroom, guiding her to the foot of his bed. He restrained her to a bedpost that had already been outfitted with chains for this purpose. Then he stripped off his own clothes and climbed into bed after turning off all the lights besides the one on his nightstand. The lamp cast a soft glow, lighting up the warm olive tones in her skin, highlighting each dip and curve of her body.

He silently watched her, and Brooklyn stared down at the floor. "You will stay there all night."

"Yes, Father."

She kept her eyes downcast and peeked up from time to time, reminding her of one of their first meetings where he made her kneel until she challenged him what the point of it was. Now, she understood it was yet another demonstration, showing her that no matter what happened, he would always be sure to claim her. Time passed slowly and Brooklyn rested her cheek against the bedpost with a sigh. She checked the digital clock next to the lamp; it had only been an hour.

"I cannot stop marveling over your beauty; your beauty of body and spirit," said Father Mathias. He had startled her, and she looked at him with wide eyes. He got out of bed and went to her to run his fingers across a cheekbone. Light kisses followed his touch, and the simple yet unexpectedly erotic contact had her moaning. He chuckled, but there was no humor in the sound. "So responsive."

Despite it all, Brooklyn's need roared to life, the numbness replaced and completely taken over by passion in one fell swoop. "Father, I need you, please." After weeks of solitude and depression, Brooklyn desperately needed to feel alive again, in the way only Father Mathias could make her feel.

"You are here to serve me, child."

Brooklyn knew what that meant. "For how long?" *How long do I have to go without coming?*

"That is not a question for you to ask," said Father Mathias. He fingered her rosary beads. "Have you worn these, even during your attempt to leave me?"

Brooklyn nodded somberly. "Yes, Father."

He released her from the bedpost and bent her over the bed. He leaned down and pressed his lips against her ear. "Do not come." The priest inserted his thumb into her sex and pressed down on her g-spot. He maintained the pressure for a few moments then rubbed slow circles.

Brooklyn's moan came out with a quiver.

Father Mathias continued, applying pressure and releasing it. "I said... do not come," he warned, recognizing her pre-climactic moans.

"Please! I won't be able to stop it. It's been too long, Father!" gasped Brooklyn. Not only had she worn the gifted beads, but she had also adhered to the rule of not coming without his permission, not that it had been difficult considering the state she had been in.

He stopped and waited for the oncoming orgasm to subside, then started again, earning a bereaved moan from Brooklyn. It wasn't long until she was close to coming again, and he stopped, only to start again. His ministrations were so slow and so deliberate, as if pressing out the secret code to her pleasure.

"Please don't do this to me," cried Brooklyn. She couldn't bear the tease.

"I beg your pardon?"

"I'm sorry, Father." Her title for him came out with a gasp when he pressed harder on that spot. And again, she was close to climax.

Withdrawing his hand from her sex, he made her stand and reattached the restraints. She was soaking wet and had to stand with her feet apart to ease the discomfort of her wet thighs rubbing against one another. She looked at her Priest, silently imploring for release with her eyes. He ignored the look as he got back into bed and watched her until he fell asleep.

Brooklyn fell in and out of sleep, waking up whenever her fingers went numb from leaning on the restraints. The discomfort and her compromising position only fueled her desire because she enjoyed being like this for him.

She enjoyed suffering for him and felt foolish for ever thinking she could leave.

The priest woke her up by bringing a cup of orange juice to her lips. She received his offering while still half asleep. Brooklyn was beyond exhausted. He released her from the restraints, carrying her lovingly to the side of his bed, and tucked her in.

"If only waking up to you could be an everyday occurrence," he whispered before kissing her tenderly on the forehead.

"It could be," said Brooklyn, still half asleep.

When she woke up next, Brooklyn was disoriented. She could hear the church was awake and busy, or as busy as it could get, and knew that leaving the rectory was not an option. She wanted to check the time, but she felt so weak and drained that the idea of crawling out of the bed seemed impossible. So, she stayed there and fell back asleep. When she woke again, she got up and found food on the coffee table in the living room. She checked the time when she was done eating and found that it was past noon. The church was still bustling, so she was stuck.

Trapped.

Her breaths quickened as the feelings from her last disaster of a visit came creeping back. She paced back and forth, wishing she was anywhere but in the rectory. Brooklyn tried to keep herself distracted with the books on the priest's shelf, which thankfully held more than just religious texts. It turned out Father Mathias was interested in non-fiction and the topics varied from history to biographies to self-help. Oddly enough, it still didn't say much about him, other than the fact he didn't seem to find any pleasure in the works of fiction.

Occasionally, she would carefully peek out the tiny windows through the curtains whenever she heard someone pass by the front door that opened out to the small lawn. She wondered if it was an actual working door or if it was just ornamental. Still, she'd seize up with fear, worried the person walking across the gravel path would come in and find her. Brooklyn put on her clothes when she realized that, if she was discovered, her being naked wouldn't help the situation. She got dressed and curled up on the sofa with a book on the monasteries of Bulgaria.

She had just finished the introductory chapter, which proved to be difficult considering how dry the topic was, when she heard a creak coming from the footbridge. Brooklyn's heart pounded and she gripped the edges of the book as she deliberated whether she should try to hide or stay where she was. Before she could consider getting up, the lock clicked and the door swung open.

Brooklyn gasped.

Father Mathias stood in the doorway and smiled. "Relax, my child."

"I was so worried," she said, her tone accusatory. "Why did you do that?"

He came to sit next to her. "You spending the night and then the day here was to show you that no matter what the deacon, or anyone, has to say, *I* am still in control. And as long as I am in control, you are safe. Tell me, child, who made you feel unsafe back at home?"

Brooklyn shook her head. "I don't want to talk about it."

"Answer me."

"Why?" she said, throwing her hands up in exasperation. "You already know who."

"Humor me," he said, overlooking her disobedience.

Brooklyn sighed. "My mother, as you know. But especially Father David."

"And why do you think that is?"

"Because he had power over..." She stopped when realization dawned on her. "He had power over everyone."

"Does he have power here?"

"Of course not, Father."

"You must separate what your fear is associated with. It's not the church, it was him. It was your mother."

"But the deacon..."

"Is a harmless fool. A fool with no power." He opened the curtains, making Brooklyn gasp. Anyone could see inside if they looked. "Out there is a quiet neighborhood. We are not isolated. There are no hidden rooms. This church is small. Too small to carry out the twisted acts that sorry excuse of a priest did." He returned to Brooklyn and tenderly held her face between his hands. "Don't you see, my child? Deacon Thomas can judge and corner you all he wants, but he can never hurt you. He can never touch you. Words cannot harm you if you don't let them."

Brooklyn nodded. "Yes, Father."

He kissed her, his lips mirroring her need. Would this hunger ever be quelled?

"Come back to me tomorrow night. Wear something pretty."

"Yes, Father."

Brooklyn did her best to walk with confidence as she emerged from the back end of the church and into the nave. Although it was empty, she couldn't help but feel she hadn't gone unnoticed. The stretch from the hallway to the front doors seemed far away and she wished she didn't have to walk it without Father Mathias's reassuring presence. Brooklyn recalled the facts he had pointed out to reaffirm her safety. *I'm safe. This church is safe.* Squaring her shoulders, she walked the rest of the way to the doors and stepped through them with relief.

The sun glared brightly through the thinning canopy of trees that lined the street, causing her to shield her eyes with her hands. Once she rounded the corner of the block, she checked her phone and found a half dozen missed calls from Gregory. She couldn't call him back because she felt she'd have to lie about where she had been, and she couldn't bear to lie to him after all he had done. She went home, thinking up the best way to explain herself and feeling very much like a rebellious teenager.

"What the hell, Brook?! I was so fucking worried!" Gregory shot up from the front step of the rooming house's door.

"I'm still alive, relax," she tried to joke, but he wasn't having it.

He sat back down, deflated. "You're gonna hate me."

Brooklyn froze. She hadn't expected that. "Why?"

"Stephen is on his way here."

"What?! How? Why?!" She looked up the street towards her decoy house.

"He came into the cafe about a week ago and I told him you were having a rough time. He asked me to keep in touch and, well, you fucking disappeared, and I panicked."

"For, like, one night! Call him quickly and tell him not to come!"

"Okay! Okay," he said, pulling out his phone and fumbling with it.

"He is already here," said a voice from behind her. She turned and saw Stephen standing on the sidewalk. He looked up at the rooming house in confusion. Brooklyn turned back to Gregory, who shrugged with a nervous laugh.

"You live here?" Stephen asked.

Taking a deep breath, Brooklyn turned back to face her almost-love-story.

"Can we talk? Privately?" he asked.

With a resigned sigh, Brooklyn led him to her bedroom and watched him nervously as he looked over the small space.

"Great, so now that you've confirmed how poor I am..."

He stopped her with a shake of his head. "Resourceful," he said, nodding towards the milk crates.

"Right, I forgot. You're the king of positive perspective," she snapped. She was met with that knowing smile and it infuriated her. Why couldn't he have a fatal flaw? "What do you want to talk about?"

"I can clearly see you don't want to see me, I just wanted to let you know that whatever it is you're going through, I'm here."

"Why? Why do you have to be so nice and perfect? Why can't you be normal and be mad and hate me?" Brooklyn needed his anger; it was the only thing that would make everything—her regret and guilt—better.

"Because I'm in love with you, Brooklyn. In case that wasn't obvious." He held up his hands. "I know we barely know each other, and the situation is messed up, but I do. And when Gregory messaged me today, worried because he couldn't get a hold of you, I regretted the fact that I never told you how I felt."

Brooklyn was dumbfounded. So much that she couldn't speak, or even react.

"I'll go now." He left and Gregory came in shortly after.

"I know you're fragile and shit, but I'm just gonna say it: You're stupid," said Gregory.

Brooklyn choked on a laugh, or maybe it was a sob. She couldn't be sure. "Yeah. I am."

"You were with him, weren't you?"

"It's none of your business," Brooklyn whispered, because she knew it was wrong for her to even think her thoughts after everything Gregory had done for her. Especially when he didn't have to.

"Forgive me for caring, but I do. And I think we've reached a point where it *is* my business."

"Fine! Yes! I was with him. Happy?"

Gregory shook his head. "This relationship is going to kill you."

Brooklyn was too tired in every way imaginable to deal with her friend's well-intentioned meddling. "I know."

Candles lit a path to the nave from the back door and she followed them. The nave was dark, the only light coming from more lit candles behind the alter. Father Mathias waited for her at the alter like the day he had first spanked her. The green dress Brooklyn had chosen to wear had a flared skirt and betrayed the church's eerie silence as it made soft swishing sounds when she walked. Her hair cascaded past her shoulders and down her back, beautifully framing her face that was lightly touched with makeup.

Brooklyn walked to the front of the alter, falling to her knees and pressing her nose to the floor, worshiping the closest thing she could recognize as a God: her Priest. Father Mathias was dressed in his cassock and looked so regal, so worthy of her submission, that she couldn't help but display it to him.

"Today, my child, is a day I have been anxiously waiting for." He sighed. "I am eager to make you mine but am filled with trepidation, for I fear you'll decide to move on. You've already come close to that decision."

Brooklyn looked up. "I'm already yours, Father. I made that decision the day I came back." Fighting it was hopeless. As long as the priest wanted her, there was no chance of her moving on and finding happiness with another. Stephen's declaration of love came to mind, as if to test her resolution.

"Stand up, my child. For now, we will speak as equals."

"If I'm your equal right now, then I choose to stay right here, Father." Brooklyn did sit up so she could look at him.

His eyes glinted with hunger, but it was quickly quelled by the topic at hand. "I have the intention of collaring you. We have spoken about your limits, and I am fine with them, but we haven't spoken about mine."

Brooklyn tilted her head to the side. Since he was the one in control, she had never considered that his limits would be of any consequence.

"I have one in particular that may not be favorable to you." He gripped the sides of the lectern and looked down. His eyes were shut tight, paired with a wince that suggested he may be in actual, physical pain. "I have made a vow to the priesthood and have already broken it to some extent when I penetrated you with my fingers and allowed you to touch me with your hands. But I refuse to transgress against it any further."

Brooklyn's heart raced. "What are you saying?"

"I am celibate, my child. And I don't intend on changing that."

Brooklyn sat back heavily on her heels. *Celibate.* That explained so much. "So, what? You pick and choose which rules you follow?"

His lips thinned. "I have a calling..."

"No!"

"I have a calling and that will always be my first priority. It's why I have only trained submissives with the intent of releasing them."

"Yeah, well this is different. You said so yourself. The church can't be your first priority. I won't play second to anyone. Or anything." As much as she wanted to stand, Brooklyn remained on her knees. "I may not know much about all of this, but I know that this is wrong. I'm supposed to be your priority if you collar me, not some book of myths and a bunch of men that screw around whenever they want, only to then point their fingers at others."

"Child!"

"What? What do you want me to say? That I'm okay with it? All in the name of... Jesus?"

"Then you have made your decision."

Brooklyn didn't know what to say. That feeling of being cornered came back. The church always took from her, and she was upset at herself for thinking it could be any other way. "Please don't do this," she finally said. "I thought you loved me."

Her words seemed to hit him as he leaned forward against the lectern. His shoulders shook with silent sobs. "I knew you'd be my undoing."

Brooklyn crawled up the steps and stopped at his feet. "This isn't a bad thing, Father. Maybe your true calling is this. Us. Me. You can leave the church..."

"No."

"Why not?"

He crouched down and took her chin in his hand. "As much as I had tried to deny it, there is no doubt of my love for you, my child. But I love the church as well. I love the priesthood."

"More than you love me?"

"*Do not* ask me those kinds of questions."

"Why? Because it's true?" She searched his eyes, but they gave nothing away. "Let me ask you something. You say you have love for me, but you're willing to let me walk out of here and never come back?"

Father Mathias was silent.

Brooklyn took a deep breath and nodded. She had wanted to learn of her importance to him and now was her chance. Even then, she wasn't sure if she truly wanted to find out. "Well then." She smiled with tears in her eyes. "I don't know if you hoped I would be okay with all of this, or if you're truly willing to lose me over your precious church, but I'm calling your bluff." She stood up and squared her shoulders. "Goodbye, Father," she said and kissed him on the cheek before turning to leave.

Doubt settled in the pit of her stomach when he allowed her to take a few hesitant steps. Maybe she was being selfish. What they had was amazing, as is. But Brooklyn needed more. Stephen came to mind again, and she thought of how there was no doubt that, if she chose him and things went well, there was a prime spot in his life waiting for her. The thought wasn't enough to console her, though. Each step hurt as much as if she was stepping on spikes that drove up through her heels.

"Brooklyn."

The sound of her name made her falter a bit, but she chose to ignore Father Mathias and continued walking, even though she was afraid and somewhat certain that he really would give her up. She kept her eyes trained on the front doors, deciding that if she was going to leave St. Anthony's for the last time, it wouldn't be through the back. But for the first time, she wasn't eager to reach them.

"Brooklyn."

I have to call his bluff.

"Brooklyn!" His voice reverberated with a boom in the nave, filled with desperation and surrender. The rustle of his cassock was furious as he strode down the aisle and grabbed her by the wrist to spin her around. He kissed her violently and she returned it with as much intensity.

"I knew you wouldn't let me leave," she cried through tears of relief.

He pulled her head back by her hair and gazed deep into her eyes. She could see his fear and confusion, and seeing him so vulnerable only made her want him more.

"I knew you'd ruin me."

Brooklyn shook her head. "No, Father. You're seeing it all wrong."

He didn't reply and pulled her by the hair towards the altar. She stumbled along next to him. Father Mathias led her up the steps then bent her over the lectern. He pulled up her dress and spanked her sharply a few times. He dug his fingers into her flesh and squeezed so that his short nails could be felt. Father Mathias leaned over her, pressing her chest into the lectern's wood, and kissed her neck in a frenzy. He grunted with frustration as he pulled away and spanked her again, harder this time. She could feel the desperation in the hits, as if grasping for something that surely couldn't satiate his sudden hunger.

He grunted again and pulled Brooklyn up by the hair, forcing her to look at him. She breathed in sharply when she saw the darkness in his eyes. Her Priest wasn't there, but neither was the beast she had become lovingly acquainted with. No this, was someone—*something* else entirely. She'd barely managed to say, "Father?" before being shoved down to her knees.

Father Mathias pulled on her hair, forcing her chin up, and Brooklyn knew to stay that way when he released his grip.

"My child, tonight, you rule me." He pulled up his cassock in a flurry and, without warning, shoved his cock into her mouth.

Brooklyn choked from the sudden invasion but she did not push him away. Instead, she grabbed his legs and opened her mouth wider so that he could thrust freely. Her gagging didn't deter either of them; Father Mathias used her mouth mercilessly and Brooklyn stayed put. Her eyes watered and saliva dripped down her chin every time he pulled out so that she could take another breath.

With hazy vision, Brooklyn could still see the unrecognizable creature in the priest's snarl. As if sensing her scrutiny, Father Mathias stopped and looked down at her.

"It's not enough," he growled, but he wasn't speaking to her. "Stand up."

Brooklyn scrambled to stand and he quickly bent her over the lectern once more. He pulled up her dress, tore down her panties, and plunged into her.

Brooklyn cried out with joy as they, for the first time, became one. He thrust into her with abandon and the sweetest sounds of pleasure came from his lips.

"Thank you, Father. Thank you, Father," Brooklyn repeated with each thrust. The priest pulled out and shoved her to her knees so he could bury himself in her mouth once more and came. Thick, hot spurts of come filled her mouth and Brooklyn greedily swallowed every drop as he groaned and shuddered from his orgasm.

"Thank you, Father," she said again, looking up at him as she licked her lips.

But there was nothing good in Father Mathias's expression, and he fell to his knees and cried. His grief was so overwhelming she immediately felt guilty for pushing him.

"What have I done?" he cried. He looked down at his hands and his come-stained cassock.

"Father?" Brooklyn reached out to touch him.

He grabbed her hand and pushed her onto her back and mounted her. He stared into her eyes, but his gaze went right through her; she felt he wasn't seeing her at all. He was hard again, and he took her once more, caught up in a frenzy of lust that had nothing to do with her.

Nothing to do with them.

Or with their love.

Maybe this is okay, she thought, and she moaned and cried and grabbed at his clothes so that she could hold onto something. "Father, tell me you love me."

He didn't reply, and that was when she accepted it—that this was wrong. She looked up at his face and recognized what had taken the place of her tender Priest: war. It waged inside of him and, as a consequence, parts of him were dying. She wanted to push him off. It wasn't supposed to be like this.

Where's the love? The affection? The disappointment was palpable, and she was certain he could feel it too, because he finally withdrew from her and sat back on his heels.

"Go home," he said without looking at her.

"But... Father."

"I said go home."

Brooklyn hugged herself, unwilling to listen to his request.

He looked up at her, eyes pleading. "Mercy."

The word hung in the air before hitting Brooklyn in the chest. She had subconsciously believed Mercy was hers alone. She was so stunned, all she could do was stare at his contrite face.

"I said GO!"

Never had he yelled at her in that way. Brooklyn's eyes widened like a deer caught in headlights, then she moved quickly to rearrange her dress and leave, not understanding at all what had just happened.

28

The cafe's manager called the next day and offered her condolences for Brooklyn's "loss." If Brooklyn had had an official part-time position, she was certain they would have fired her by now. No reasonable amount of bereavement days could have covered the many times she had turned down shifts.

"I'm ready to come in," Brooklyn said numbly.

"Great!" Her manager cleared her throat. "And, um, again, I'm sorry for your loss."

Agreeing to go in proved to be a bad idea because Brooklyn messed up order after order. Nothing could take her mind off what had happened the previous night and she couldn't shake the feeling that maybe things were over between her and Father Mathias. But that wasn't what hurt her the most; her lack of desire to see him again was the most painful. Things had shifted and for the worst. Brooklyn couldn't help but see her Priest in a different light. As hard as she tried, she couldn't keep him up on the pedestal she had put him on, not after she had seen something truly ugly inside of him. Had she not experienced the sweet moments with Stephen, Brooklyn may have been alright with the previous night's events, but that wasn't her reality.

Gregory came in and Brooklyn wanted to talk to him. He was the only one who kind of knew what was happening and she needed someone to confide in to make sense of things. He was in for a short shift so they finished at the same time, but she couldn't bring herself to broach the subject with him. After all, she already knew his opinion.

"What's going on?" he asked when they left work.

Brooklyn chewed on her bottom lip. "I had sex with him," she blurted.

"With Stephen?"

Brooklyn shook her head.

"With the priest? Wait, you hadn't had sex with him before?"

"No, and I found out last night that he was planning on staying celibate. So, I pushed him and threatened to leave. We had sex and then he got all weird... I think I messed up."

Gregory face-palmed. "Are you serious? What were you planning? To date him forever with no intimacy?"

"We *have* been intimate, just not in that way."

Gregory snorted. "Gotta love the religious folk and their convenient loopholes."

"Please don't talk about him like that."

Gregory stopped walking. "What do you want me to say, Brook? I've already told you I can't pat your back and tell you everything is gonna work out. Because it won't. He's a fucking priest that you now know isn't willing to leave the church for you."

"I know," she whispered.

Gregory sighed and ran his hand through his hair. "How about we go catch a movie? Keep you distracted for a bit. I didn't mean to be so harsh."

"No, no, I appreciate it. You're right." Brooklyn's bottom lip quivered.

"Still doesn't help you at the moment. Look, I can't give you false consolation, but I can keep you occupied until I have to go home." Gregory put his arm around Brooklyn's shoulder and she melted into him, welcoming his warmth. She was grateful Father Mathias had made her seek out a new friend. Page would have never been so supportive.

When Gregory needed to go home, Brooklyn went back to the church. She stood across the street and stared it down. The doors had been propped open and she could make out Deacon Thomas's silhouette against the church's soft lighting. Father Mathias was probably in the confessional and Brooklyn wondered if it would be safe to go in with the deacon around. She decided to just go and act like nothing was wrong. Surely that would prove there was nothing going on.

Her heart raced as she walked up the stone steps and into the church. The deacon's back was to her, and she contemplated running to the confessional, but instead opted to take the "act normal and casual" route. Brooklyn still walked quietly in case the deacon didn't end up turning around. When she got to the booth, she ducked inside and let out a sigh of relief.

"Child," said Father Mathias. "What are you doing here?"

"I always come to confession," said Brooklyn. The tone of his voice was hard to place, but it wasn't good, and Brooklyn's fear that she had ruined things took hold of her.

"I... I can't see you. Not now."

"Why not?"

"What we did... what *I* did... last night... was horrendous. Yet all I can think about is the smell of your skin and the sound of your voice as I took you," he said, his voice cracking.

"It wasn't 'horrendous,'" whispered Brooklyn. But that was a lie. He was right; it was horrendous.

"I feel as if my mind has been poisoned. I am being consumed by hell fire," he continued.

"No. This is good. This... is human, Father." Brooklyn couldn't believe her own words. She had been there, and it had been anything but good. It had been ugly. Disgusting, even.

"It's disgraceful."

Or that.

She wanted to shake him by the shoulders and tell him that they could overcome this, but all she could feel was immense grief over the distance he seemed so desperate to put between them. The church truly was robbing her all over again. In the face of potential loss, her hesitation over seeing Father Mathias again was gone. Yes, it had been a huge let down, but she was certain they could move forward and fix everything. It wasn't his fault. Brooklyn knew better than anyone how damaging the church could be, and for the first time, she saw her Priest as a kindred spirit. Even as a priest, she couldn't imagine him being at peace with who he was, no matter how hard he tried to reconcile it with words from the Bible.

"Father, I don't think the church was meant for you. What if you became this"—she gestured towards him—"as a way to be okay with who you really are? The entire world tries to tell us that we're wrong."

"I can't see you anymore," said Father Mathias, ignoring what she had said.

So, he is choosing the church. She sat back heavily against the wall of the confessional. "I see. So, I guess you answered my question. About who you'd choose when it came down to it." She stood up. "Father, I know it's wrong, but I hope you never 'train' another submissive again. Because this"—she motioned between him and herself—"isn't fair."

Fighting the urge to storm out of the church, she left slowly, walking as casually as she had walked in. But once she had turned the corner of the block, she had to duck her face to hide her tears. And that's all she felt, the warm droplets rolling down her cheeks, because everything else shut off. Her ears rang and her heart was suspiciously steady, as were her breaths. Brooklyn knew she was being consumed by grief but she couldn't feel it. And that was probably a good thing. Otherwise, she would have found herself thinking of all the things that were now lost to her: the pain, the pleasure, his scent, his voice, the gleam in his eyes when he hurt her.

Her peace.

Acknowledging her loss wasn't an option. Brooklyn had to just keep putting one foot in front of the other until she got home, and even then, she had to keep from thinking. Once she got home, however, the thoughts came and the grief ripped through her numbness and squeezed tightly around her heart. She stifled a sob with her hand and stumbled towards her sofa.

How can I go on? Brooklyn couldn't believe she had ever considered a future without her Priest in any capacity. Not when she felt as she did then. She cried. Then her cries turned to gut-wrenching sobs. Obviously, none of it had been real, otherwise Father Mathias wouldn't have discarded her the way he had.

Brooklyn sat up and thought of Stephen and felt horrible. She had chosen unsustainable passion over someone real. The idea of going to him filled her with shame. How would he ever believe that she was truly interested in him and that he wasn't just her second choice? How could *she* believe it? She shook her head. Now wasn't the time to be running from one person to another. If there was one thing she could be thankful for, it was the growth Father Mathias had inspired, and she wasn't prepared to go into another month-long self-pity party.

Looking around her room, she felt she needed to do something big. For her. On her own. As much as she wanted to wallow in the grief that threatened to swallow her whole, she got up and pulled out the expensive clothes that Page had gotten her. She did quick math and figured that with the shoes and accessories, she could get anywhere from three to five thousand dollars on them if she wanted to sell them quickly. She swiped at her tears with determination. It was time for change. She would sell everything and move, or maybe travel—anything but stay stagnant.

It took a couple of months, but Brooklyn managed to find some level of equilibrium after Father Mathias's rejection. The nightmares, in which he would knock on her door and tell her he was wrong and that he wanted to be with her, only to be swept away by some unseen force, eventually stopped.

Mostly.

Brooklyn managed to sell off everything. She was a few thousand dollars richer and with a few more options in her pocket. What they even were, she wasn't sure, but she knew they were there.

Before figuring that out, there was one thing she knew she had to do: see Stephen. Most of her clothes were gone, so her options were limited as to what to wear. Nothing would make her look like she should be escorted out by security, so she settled on a pair of her darkest jeans and a sweater. Brooklyn couldn't remember exactly where Stephen's office building was, so she made her way to the business district and wandered the streets, looking for a familiar building. They all looked the same, but she knew when she was standing in front of the right one. The building was newer and stood out from the rest with its preference for glass and a modern entrance.

Brooklyn cursed herself for not paying more attention to the floor he had taken her to or even his company's name. So, she went to the security desk and asked for Stephen's floor.

The security guard looked at her, annoyed. "Do I look like the directory?"

"Sorry to bother you." Brooklyn found the directory on the wall to the right but there were only companies listed. Undeterred, she went through the ones on the higher floors to see if anything rang a bell. Vera Global Investments seemed familiar, so she searched it on the internet to look up the founder and there was Stephen's photo, subtitled with his name and "CEO and Founder." It was on the twenty-fourth floor.

Brooklyn went to the elevator bank and took one up, disliking the way it made her stomach turn over when she was already queasy with nausea. The elevator doors opened to the large reception area and a redhead in a sharp suit stood behind a desk. She greeted Brooklyn with an icy, disinterested stare.

"U-um, I'm here to see Mr. Vera. Please."

The receptionist's eyes widened in surprise. "Oh? Do you have an appointment?"

"Yes," lied Brooklyn. She knew a no would mean a prompt dismissal, but a yes meant a phone call and Stephen would at least know that she was there.

The woman checked her computer. "I don't see anything here."

"It must be a mistake. It's Brooklyn. Brooklyn St. Jerome."

The woman took another glance at the computer and shook her head. "Nothing."

"You can call him and check. Please."

"I'm sorry, I know for a *fact* that Genny is thorough with Mr. Vera's calendar. The only mistake that's here is probably you." She raised a perfectly plucked, skeptical eyebrow.

"It's fine, I'll just call him myself." Brooklyn reluctantly pulled out her phone, knowing very well she had deleted all his contact information and there was no way to actually make the call.

The woman thought for a moment and looked at her computer again. "Wait. I'll confirm with him, but only because he isn't in any meetings." She picked up the phone and dialed his extension.

"Thank you."

The receptionist turned away from Brooklyn and spoke quietly into the phone. When she was done, she hung up, clearly not happy. "Turns out there was an error. Follow me." Her nose went up a few notches higher and she walked quickly towards Stephen's corner office.

"Mr. Vera?" she said, opening the door. "Miss St. Jerome."

"Thank you, Mylène." Stephen turned from the city view he loved so much.

"My pleasure, Mr. Vera." She closed the door behind her, and Brooklyn was alone with him.

"I'm surprised to see you," he said when Brooklyn said nothing.

"I wanted to apologize."

"For?"

"The way I treated you when I last saw you and... for going AWOL."

"And the married guy?"

Brooklyn looked down at the floor, the shame still as strong as the day Father Mathias had turned her away. "You were right. I was just so caught up and I couldn't see what I was passing over for a bit of..."

"You know, I thought I'd be okay to wait until you realized that nothing would come of your affair. But you didn't come to that conclusion on your own, did you?"

Brooklyn clasped her hands in front of her. She shook her head, unable to take away her eyes from the floor.

"So, things fell through and now you've come to your second choice."

She looked up with pleading eyes. "No, it's not like that. I really just came to apologize. And to tell you the truth. You saw me as an honest person, and I wanted to live up to that. I figured that was the least I could do."

Stephen raised an eyebrow, then, after a bit of contemplation, gestured towards the sofa on which they had had their second date. They sat like they did that night: opposite ends and facing each other.

"So?" he prompted when Brooklyn said nothing. His cold tone hurt, but she knew she couldn't expect softness from him after what she'd done.

Brooklyn took a deep breath before starting. "He wasn't married." That got his interest. "He's..." She paused and closed her eyes to summon the courage to tell him the thing she had hid so well. "He's a priest."

Stephen's eyebrows shot up.

"I was too ashamed to tell you, so when you assumed that he was married I went with it. Because, well, technically he is... and I wasn't up against a wife, but the church. And he did choose the church. So, you were right. And I realized it was all an illusion I had gotten really caught up in." Brooklyn stopped to swallow what felt like a ball in her throat. "Like, where would that have gone?" Brooklyn cursed when she felt her eyes burn with unshed tears. She had been so sure that she was done crying over Father Mathias.

"I don't know what to say."

"Stephen, you're not second choice. I was already caught up with him and then you came along and made me question everything. I was just too afraid to ask the questions because he had given me so much. I was in a really bad situation, and he guided me out of that. I think maybe I mistook gratitude for love."

"And now what?"

Brooklyn took a deep breath and looked down at her hands, scratching her palm with her thumbnail and contemplating whether to press harder. "After he made it clear that... that I wouldn't have a primary role in his life, I was tempted to come running to you. And I'm glad I didn't, because that wouldn't have been fair. To you, or even to me. I needed time to think, and to heal. And the more I thought, the more I questioned whether I should come asking you for a second chance at all."

Stephen's eyebrows furrowed. "What are you trying to say?"

A tear finally escaped, but Brooklyn was okay with it, because it was for Stephen and, for once, not for the priest. "You deserve someone who knows that you're meant for them. I don't deserve you."

Stephen's conflict was apparent, and it warmed Brooklyn's heart. The warmth didn't come without a sting, though, because it further proved her foolishness.

"Fuck, Brooklyn, you have me all sorts of fucked up. I know I should nod and agree with you, but..."

He was so forgiving that it hurt Brooklyn. It made her second guess her choice to forgo trying things with Stephen. Instead of accepting the fact that she didn't deserve him, she could fight to earn his affection. The idea was short-lived as the fundamental question she had been asking herself repeatedly came back.

If Father Mathias ever decided to choose me, would I leave Stephen for him? The answer had always been, and was still, yes. She hated the answer and wished it was anything but. Brooklyn felt cursed.

She moved closer to Stephen and took his hand. "I want to try this, more than anything, but I can't."

He squeezed her hand. "I understand. And I respect you, and sadly, I want you all the more for it."

"You know, I spent a lot of time imagining things differently. A world where I never went into that church, and we had a first date without the shadow of my... strange situation. But then I remember the change in me that caught your attention was brought on by him," Brooklyn said, laughing sadly. "There would be no you without him, but I can't be with you because of him."

"Brooklyn?"

"Yes?"

"What if I told you I was alright?" said Stephen.

"What do you mean?"

He took a deep breath. "Here goes my male ego." He laughed nervously. "What if I'm okay with still trying things? Maybe it'll turn out that you can't move on, at least not with me. Or maybe it'll turn out that you can. How would we ever know without trying?"

Stephen's sincerity hit Brooklyn in the chest. She couldn't imagine anyone being so gracious and she let out an unexpected sob of disbelief. "Why would you even consider that?"

"Because you lived up to my opinion of you. You're honest. Thoughtful. And you don't put your agenda before others. It would have been easy for you to come in here with the thought of trying to salvage things. But you didn't. I admire you, Brooklyn. And I'm more than positive I could fall in love with you all over again."

She sobbed again and her tears flowed freely. "I really don't deserve you."

Stephen pulled her into his arms. "You have no idea how wrong you are."

Leaning into his embrace, Brooklyn wrapped her arms around his waist.

"So? What do you say?"

Brooklyn nodded. "I'd love to give us a try. More than you could imagine."

"There's just one thing..." said Stephen, his voice all businesslike.

She pulled away to look up at him.

"Will I be allowed to touch you?" he said with smirk.

Brooklyn nodded. "Please do."

Stephen touched her cheek lightly before leaning in to give her a kiss—one that promised so much more.

END

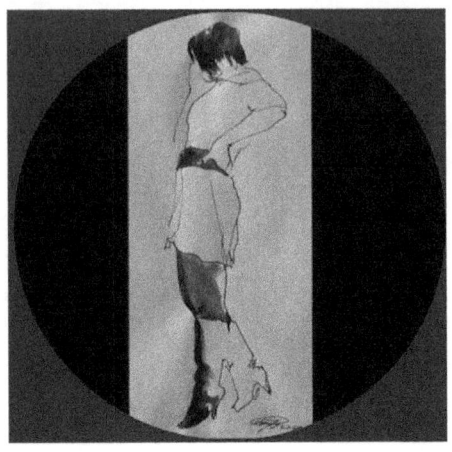

About the Author

When Ashley isn't writing or editing, she spends her days exercising and coaching. She considers the gym as her second home and family. As a sufferer of various chronic conditions, she has grown passionate about managing her health through lifestyle changes and helping others do the same. She enjoys anything involving nature, although she detests bugs with as much fervor as her love for the outdoors.

BDSM & THE LIFESTYLE

A burning question for Ashley's readers is: Does Ashley write from personal experience?

Everything in her books are works of pure fiction (all the priests she's come across when she dares to step inside of a church have sadly made no advances), but she does write from a place of knowledge founded on experience. She participates in the lifestyle and since her emancipation from the 'nilla world, as some kinksters like to refer to anything that exists outside the realm of BDSM, has been lucky enough to experience a majority of the broad spectrum of the human experience.

If there is an acorn of truth in her work, it would be the potential for healing and growth that can be found in healthy dynamics and experiences. She believes people tend to label everything in black and white, good and bad... but sometimes pain can be cathartic and pleasure can be found in places one would have never thought to look. It's this sentiment that she brings to her stories and that breathes life into the characters she creates.

Read more at https://www.ashley-matthews.com/.